Frienda

Maureen Martella was [...] sisters and a brother. Sh[...] with an Italian and retur[...] her children. Travelling again she spent time in Bel Air where she worked as an assistant to a mortician. She is also the author of *Maddy Goes to Hollywood, Annie's New Life* and *A Perfect Partnership*. She now lives and writes in rural Ireland.

Also by Maureen Martella

Maddy Goes to Hollywood
Annie's New Life
A Perfect Partnership

Friends & Lovers

Maureen Martella

arrow books

Published by Arrow Books in 2007

4 6 8 10 9 7 5 3

First published in Great Britain in 2007 by
Arrow Books
Random House, 20 Vauxhall Bridge Road,
London SW1V 2SA

www.randomhouse.co.uk

Addresses for companies within The Random House Group Limited can be found at:
www.randomhouse.co.uk/offices.htm

The Random House Group Limited Reg. No. 954009

A CIP catalogue record for this book
is available from the British Library

ISBN 9780099469407

The Random House Group Limited makes every effort to ensure that the papers
used in its books are made from trees that have been legally sourced from
well-managed and credibly certified forests. Our paper procurement policy
can be found at: www.randomhouse.co.uk/paper.htm

Typeset in Plantin by Palimpsest Book Production Limited,
Grangemouth, Stirlingshire
Printed and bound in Great Britain by
Bookmarque Ltd, Croyden, Surrey

For my daughter Marie-Elena
My sisters Bernadette, Noreen
Joan, Patricia and Denise

Friends & Lovers

1

I sat on the rumpled bed, watching in disbelief as Gerry ran around the room tearing open wardrobes and drawers, grabbing shirts and jeans, and throwing them into his holdall, as if his life depended on it.

I had tried pleading with him. Begged him to stop and think, or at least to calm down and listen. I had even (fleetingly) considered threatening him with his own gun, a fair indication of how high my emotions were running.

He turned. 'Do I have any shorts?'

'Shorts?' My mind went blank.

'It's ninety degrees in Arizona. I thought maybe you . . . Sometimes you surprise me with . . . things!' It sounded like an accusation.

'Not shorts. I'd never surprise you with shorts.'

He was running again. 'My razor. I'll need my razor.' He disappeared into the bathroom.

I slid off the bed to follow. 'You can't take a razor on a plane.'

'What?'

'Not when you're only travelling with hand luggage.' I indicated the holdall. 'But you know that.' *Well, when your head isn't up your arse you do.*

'Jesus. I won't be able to shave.' He clutched his chin as if this was cataclysmic news, as if chin stubble wasn't practically his trademark.

'No razors to be found in Arizona then?' It was such a pathetic attempt at a joke that even as I was saying it I was squirming. But we used to laugh so much together, I thought it was worth a try, although flogging a dead horse did spring to mind.

'What?' His frown deepened.

OK forget the jokes. Try something else, Annie, quickly now.

'Look, if you'll just take a calming breath, and wait a while, I'll bet Sally will be back on any minute now, to say everything is hunky-dory, and—'

'Wait?' He looked at me in disbelief. 'My ten-year-old is wandering somewhere in a desert, and you think I should sit down and wait?'

'Sally didn't say he was wandering. She said he's not in the house.'

'She said he's missing!' He pulled his favourite shirt from the overflowing wash basket. A faded blue denim, it looked like it had been used to beat out bush fires. He sniffed it cautiously, before squashing it into the now bulging holdall.

'She didn't necessarily mean—'

'She can't find him, Annie!' he yelled as if this was my fault.

I wanted to say Sally couldn't find her arse without an AA roadmap, instead I heard myself saying meekly, 'I'll help you pack'.

I found two neatly ironed business shirts at the

back of the wardrobe and exchanged them speedily for the grubby blue denim. I didn't want his ex thinking we lived like slobs, although compared to her domestic perfection, we probably did. But I knew her game. This morning's call was just another one of her attention-seeking ploys. Since her second marriage disintegrated, she had taken to ringing Gerry at the weirdest times. And always about the weirdest things. This week alone she had woken him twice, in the small hours. The first time to tell him of her growing concern about their elder son's troublesome overbite, and then, twenty minutes later, she was back on again, this time in tears, to say she was worried about a serious outbreak of verrucas in the boys' school. After eavesdropping for a boring five minutes, I had turned over and gone back to sleep.

Then came this morning's call. The one guaranteed to scare the bejaysus out of Gerry.

'Gerry! David is missing!'

I always suspected that under Sally's saintly exterior, there lurked a repressed drama queen. This morning's call was proof positive, and yet Gerry couldn't see it. All he heard was the word *missing*. And the galling thing was that our morning had started on such a high note.

I had woken first, to find myself pinned to the mattress by Gerry's fit body. Reason enough, I felt, to dismiss any lingering resentment over last night's Class A row. Everyone rows, I told myself, and there can't be a woman alive who hasn't stormed off to bed, after a real barney, and given her man the cold shoulder when he followed. OK my shoulder was so cold it possibly appeared cryogenically frozen, but still. This was a brand new day. And his body felt so good against mine.

I ran a finger along his flat stomach.

No response.

I checked the bedside clock. Seven twenty-eight. Thirty-two minutes to go before the alarm would have us tearing about like lunatics. Throwing on jeans. Grabbing toast on the run. Abandoning half-finished coffees as we raced to make it to the detective agency before the phones began their daily chorus, and Naomi Lawlor-Billings flounced down from her middle-floor showrooms, spitting vitriol in all directions.

Still. Thirty-two minutes is thirty-two minutes. You can pack a surprising amount of pleasure into thirty-two short minutes, if the will is there, and the right man is pinning you to the mattress. And Gerry was looking über-right this morning. But then he never actually *looked* wrong. He never woke to find his hair had turned into a giant haystack overnight, or his eyelashes had glued solid with supposedly waterproof mascara.

This time I reached lower down to grab his attention.

'Eeeeem.' His eyes flew open.

'Morning,' I dimpled.

He smiled sleepily, his eyes crinkling up at the corners, in a way that was guaranteed to make me hot. Four years into our admittedly stormy relationship, yet one sleepy glance from those

4

clear blue-green eyes could still set my hormones racing.

'Morning.' Strong fingers laced through my haystack, pulling my head down until our mouths met, and meshed. His tasted hot, and hungry and . . . bliss.

I melted into him, and his whole body went hard.

I was climbing on top when the phone shrilled. His mouth still working against mine, he reached for the receiver.

Sitting astride him I tried to wrestle it from his hand.

'Let the machine take it.'

'Jesus!' He sprang into a sitting position, almost catapulting me from the bed.

'Gerry!'

'What do you mean missing?' He was yelling. 'Have you looked . . . ? I am *not* yelling! No! You calm down. Have you tried . . . ? OK. OK. Let's both calm down. I'm . . . yeah . . . yeah.' He leaned back, the blood draining from his face, and another even more vital place.

'Gerry?'

He threw aside the sheet. 'Of course I will!' He was bellowing now. 'What do you take me for? Yes. No. Yes. I'll do that.' A pause. 'Sometime tonight. I'll fax you the details.'

'Gerry?' I reached for him, but he was already halfway across the room, and pulling on a pair of jeans.

Watching him close the zip I squealed, 'What are you doing?'

He threw on a cotton shirt. Started scrabbling around for his shoes. 'It's David . . . Sally can't find him . . . he's gone missing.'

'Missing?' I gaped.

'Yeah. She can't find him.'

'That doesn't mean he's *missing*.'

'She's been searching for hours.'

'He's obviously hiding,' I chuckled. 'Remember the last time? All that mad panic, and he was only up in the attic, fast asleep. He's probably just . . . hiding up a tree?'

'They live in a desert. Where's he going to find a tree in a desert?'

'You know what I mean. Boys love playing hide-and-seek and all that . . .'

'Get real, Annie. He's not playing hide-and-seek in some leafy Dublin suburb. He's in the middle of feckin' Arizona, where even schoolkids carry guns.' He swallowed hard, then vented his fury on his shoelaces. 'Stupid feckin' laces . . . feckin' stupid idea . . . expecting me to wear laced-up . . .'

Three weeks earlier I had surprised him with these Italian leather brogues, waiting until he was asleep to chuck his worn old loafers in a skip. Despite his reputation for never holding a grudge, he had yet to forgive me for that little surprise.

I racked my brain for the right thing to say.

'Maybe . . . maybe you should just . . . wait a bit. Sit tight. Dashing off the second Sally rings is a bit stu— I mean you'll look like a right eejit, if you tear off to Arizona and he turns out to be hiding in the pool-house!'

That was when he shot me a filthy look, and started packing.

'I'll drive you to the airport,' I offered now. 'Give me two minutes to shower and dress.'

'I'll drive myself. You concentrate on the agency. Try keeping it solvent 'til I get back.'

Our eyes locked, last night's row threatening to rear its ugly head again.

'Hey.' He forced a tight smile. 'You said you could run the agency without me. Here's your chance to prove it.'

'I never said . . .' Actually, I did . . . but that was after too many double vodkas in The Randy Goat. After the kind of drinking session that has Barney, our youngest PI, spouting off about becoming a rock star, and Declan, our senior detective, swearing he's going to join Alcoholics Anonymous.

Nobody took them seriously.

Gerry closed the holdall. 'Keep an eye out for Mutual Irish. They want us to look into an insurance fraud. Keep them sweet. It could turn out to be a very lucrative case. And lead to a lot more.'

'*I'm* to keep them sweet?'

'Don't look so worried. I'll be back before anything can go wrong. Bluff them if you have to. Anyway, they haven't sent us the case file yet.'

'The case file?' I squeaked in terror.

But he was busy on the phone again, sorting his flight. Snapping at the unfortunate ticket clerk. 'That's no good. What if I went via Heathrow? OK. I'll take business class.'

He rattled off his credit card number. *Our* credit

card number, since he decided to cut down on extra expenses last month. This meant I would be helping to pay for this visit to his increasingly neurotic ex. I didn't really mind sharing his expenses. Not totally. Once that was all I was sharing. Sally's persistent late-night calls were making me mega anxious. But then the thought of dealing with the all-powerful Mutual Irish without Gerry's backup had me frozen with fear. Mutual Irish were the Goliath of insurance companies. Plus this was a trial run they were giving us. And only because Gerry had successfully investigated several insurance fraud cases for Ansans, a small private company Mutual had gobbled up without trace. It was Gerry's expertise they wanted.

My only experience of insurance fraud had been watching my friend Fiona fill in a claim form for a broken picture window. A form that clearly stated *sign here for accidental damage*. Fiona signed with a flourish. Ignoring the fact that she had deliberately fired a stainless-steel pasta maker at the window, when her husband's Italian relatives were less than complimentary about her fettuccini carbonara.

Gerry pulled on his jacket, and we exchanged a brief kiss. A sure sign that his mind was elsewhere?

He reached for his holdall.

'Don't go,' I pleaded with his chest.

'No choice, Annie. I can't leave Sally to cope alone. She's not like you. You're . . .'

'Scared shitless of Mutual Irish?'

'See. Always the joker! That's your strength.' He smoothed my hair away from my eyes, and before

8

the disobedient curls could spring back into place he was gone.

I went to the window to watch him getting into the jeep, and he waved. I was waving back when I realised he was saluting our next-door neighbour. The bulky blond Dane was obviously coming in off an early flight. He was a real eyeful in his fancy pilot's uniform, his stylish Aviator glasses glinting in the sun. They exchanged a couple of words, and Gerry drove off like a bat out of hell.

I flopped down on the bed, choking back tears. He hadn't even glanced back. There was a time when he would miss a train, a ferry, or even a plane rather than miss out on a hot session with me.

Bloody Sally, anyway. She couldn't cope with a kid hiding up a tree? She had coped well enough with running off to a life in the sun, with her new man, while stinging Gerry for exorbitant child maintenance. I hadn't believed then that an Olympic-sized swimming pool was utterly essential for any child emigrating to Arizona. And I didn't believe now that David was genuinely missing.

The alarm suddenly pealed. I reached out to smack it into silence, but hit the phone by mistake.

'You have awone amessage,' a metallic voice announced.

This time I *was* aiming at the phone.

'This message was recorded at athree aforty-afive a.m.,' it continued.

Sally's saccharin-sweet tones slid into the room. 'It's eight p.m. here Gerry, so I guess it's three in the

9

morning your time.' Pause. 'David is acting up again. He wants to spend the fourth of July weekend at that dude ranch he's so crazy about. He says all his friends are going. His whole class. It is a special family weekend, so maybe we should go? Would you like to join us? It would please the boys no end. Think about it and get back to me ASAP.'

Hands trembling, I tried Gerry's mobile. Busy.

I legged it into the shower. The cold water hit my skin like iced needles.

2

Ignoring the freshly painted double-yellow lines, I parked the Honda Civic in my usual spot in Diggs Lane, and tore around the corner to the Café Naturalle to pick up my morning muffins.

'What a heavenly day, Annie.' Mary, the petite, dreadlocked waitress, was in love. She even had her boyfriend's name tattooed (badly) on her upper arm.

'Heavenly!' I smiled. 'And how is . . .' I glanced at her arm, '. . . Hairy?'

'Harry is perfect.' She held out a wrist-full of beads for inspection. 'Guess what he gave me last night?'

'Nothing contagious, I hope?' I pretended to shrink back.

'Oh give over, you,' she giggled. 'Look closer!'

I did. On the third finger of her extended hand there was a twinkling little diamond. 'You got engaged? Congratulations.'

The word engaged was enough to trigger a female stampede to the counter. You could practically smell the oestrogen in the air as a dozen girls leaned over the glass to admire Mary's engagement ring, and enquire about her upcoming nuptials. Even the hard-core fund accountants, from the nearby Financial Services Centre, abandoned their lattes and corporate speak for long enough to twitter like tweenies over the neat little diamond.

I paid for the muffins and left.

'You'll never guess who just got engaged,' I called out to our receptionist as I elbowed open the agency door. Sandra, a genuine romantic, likes to keep up with all the local news – engagements, births, marriages, deaths, and, most important of all, horoscopes.

But not this morning. This morning she was deeply immersed in conversation, with a pink-cheeked young cop.

'What's up?' I glanced at her worried face.

'I've told Brian about your calls.'

'What calls?' I feigned innocence.

'You know very well!' She waved a purple-painted talon in reprimand. 'And Brian says I did the right thing, telling him. *He* says you *have* to take those calls seriously.'

Brian nodded, his pink cheeks gleaming with excitement, or maybe it was sweat, as even his light summer uniform couldn't handle the Mediterranean heatwave that was startling Dublin right now. Then again, he may simply have been over-excited because Sandra was presenting him with a mug of coffee, and an already melting Hobnob.

'We're not going over that old ground again Sandra.' I shot her a warning look.

'Old ground? There was one this morning. A really sick one this time.' Her big eyes widened in dread.

'He always sounds like he's talking through a sock. Pervert.'

My heart gave a lurch. 'I hope you hung up on him.'

'Yes. But he said filthy things, Annie. You can't keep shrugging them off.'

Again I tried to send her a silent signal – *please shut up*! Too late. Brian was already taking notes. 'He may be using a muffler.'

Shit. This morning was stressful enough without the hassle of having to regurgitate the sort of filth my weirdo liked whispering into a telephone.

'He's just a pathetic perv.' I took Brian's pen, and shoved it back in his pocket. 'And I am a PI, remember?' I stood tall. 'I can handle it.'

'You should have heard the things he said, Brian,' Sandra persisted. 'Dirty animal.'

'I said I can handle it,' I snapped. 'He's just some low life, who gets his kicks whispering dirty words into a phone. Sick? Yes. But hardly Jack the Ripper.'

'He said he's going to tick you! Or maybe it was stick!' Sandra's lip quivered.

'This person is committing a serious offence under the harassment section of the Non-Fatal Offences Against the Person Act 1997. This makes it an offence to "by any means, including by use of the telephone, harass another person by persistently . . ."'

Brian was still rambling on when I held out my hand for my post.

'Very interesting, Brian. Is this the lot, Sandra?'

I knew she was upset by my refusal to take these calls seriously. But they were just nuisance calls. And

I could handle them. Besides, the last thing I wanted was for the other PIs to get wind of them, and start treating me like a girl again. It had been a massive uphill struggle to get them to treat me like an equal, and I wasn't going back to the starting line again. Back to getting the *girlygirl* treatment. Especially with Gerry away.

'Giving attention to a perv just feeds his ego.' I checked to see if the lift was there. 'Right, Brian?'

Once again Brian took refuge in Garda-speak. 'This person is breaking several laws. Under section . . .'

'My God. Is that the time?' I checked my watch. 'I'll take Gerry's post, Sandra. He'll be away for a few days. When the other PIs come in, send them up to my office immediately, will you? I'll have to assign cases,' I said importantly, and ran.

I was at my desk, hammering away at my computer, when I realised I had forgotten to give Sandra her morning muffin, breaking a tradition that was nearly as old as the agency.

I swallowed hard, and tried to think only happy thoughts. But apart from the good news about Mary and Hairy, I couldn't think of a single one, just knew in my bones that this whole day was on a downhill trajectory.

Declan and Barney arrived within seconds of each other. Barney whistling happily, in no way embarrassed, or inhibited, to be wearing a badly-fitting school uniform. The one Gerry insisted he wear in order to infiltrate a student shoplifting gang. Beside him, Declan moved like the undead, his eyes flat and lifeless, the collar of his long black coat turned up against the cold. In late June? In a heatwave? Did he really think a turned-up collar could disguise a hangover?

It was now four weeks since Gerry gave him his final ultimatum – *Sign up for AA, or risk finding your P45 on your desk.*

'You . . . OK, Declan?' I asked.

His lips moved a fraction. Then a nod. 'I could do with a coffee, though.' An understatement to the power of ten.

'Help yourself.' I indicated the tray. 'And eat something. Try a muffin. That'll raise your blood sugar.' I encouraged hopefully.

Barney didn't need encouraging. He was already halfway through a raisin muffin.

But then Barney is Declan's polar opposite. He starts every day as if he's been woken by fifty volts, and continues to radiate endless energy for the next twelve hours. Hardly surprising, given the amount of calories he consumes. And yet he never gains a single surplus ounce on his boyish body. As lean now as the day he joined the agency nine years ago, he could pass for seventeen (and frequently does) instead of his openly declared twenty-seven. Or twenty-eight, depending on who he is dating at the time.

'So Gerry's kid is lost in the desert?' he mumbled through a mouthful of muffin.

'How did you . . . ?'

He waved his mobile, and continued eating.

I turned to Declan. 'Did he ring you?'

An affirmative nod.

Great. Gerry expected me to deal with a terrifying conglomerate like Mutual Irish, but he hadn't trusted me to explain his sudden departure to his two investigators? Before I could comment, Barney was sniffing the air like a bloodhound.

'Naomi is coming,' he intoned like Count Dracula.

He was spot on. Naomi swanned in, her trademark Chanel No. 5 preceding her as usual. But, just back from a trade trip to Milan, she had clearly had a total fashion makeover. Gone was her familiar sleek, honey-blonde bob, and in its place was a pure Nancy Dell'Olio hairdo, complete with long curly extensions. Even more startling was the heavy black mascara, coal-black eyeliner, and lips outlined for business.

'Jaysus,' Barney muttered, dropping crumbs on the floor.

I hoped Sandra hadn't seen Naomi's new look. Always ready to push the boat out fashion-wise, Sandra wasn't above copying any or all of Naomi's more startling fashions, which usually proved to be harmless, but two Nancy Dell'Olios might be more than our building could take.

'I want something done about that filthy window cleaner.' With her spindly heels adding further inches to her already five ten, Naomi towered over me. 'He's vile.'

'What do you want Annie to do?' Barney snapped. 'Give him a . . .' He grinned cheekily, '. . . wedgie?'

Naomi cut him with a look. 'I'm expecting a visit from a group of Japenese VIPs. Two yen billionaires *and* a diplomat. They adored my drawings of Shoji doors but asked to see samples in situ. An order from these people could bring Dreamland Interiors international recognition, on a grand scale.' She threw her arms wide, then paused. 'But cleanliness being an integral part of Japanese culture, I have a problem.'

Naomi always had a problem.

'The window cleaner. That dreadful little man. He persists in wiping the grime from one side of my showroom windows to the other!'

'Dick!' Barney said.

'What?' Naomi swivelled angrily.

'That *dreadful little man*. His name is Dick.' Barney hates Naomi. But then he thinks anyone who doesn't say *Howya*, is a poser.

'I have no interest in the man's name,' Naomi shuddered. 'I'm here to warn you that if that filthy creature loses me a single Japanese order, I'll have my accountant deduct the monetary equivalent from our rental agreement. Or . . .' She eyed me threateningly, 'I may begin looking for alternative showrooms.'

'I'll see that he does a proper job, Naomi.'

Satisfied, she marched out, the click, click, of her stilettos echoing along the empty corridor.

'Rotten auld mare!' Barney slammed the door behind her. 'Why do you let her talk to you like that, Annie? You should have smacked her across the kisser.'

17

'I find that tends to antagonise some business people, Barney,' I grinned.

He gave a snort of laughter.

Even Declan almost smiled.

They weren't to know, of course, but I was so pleased to be asked to do something I could easily handle, I'd have let Naomi smack *me* across the kisser.

It was the thought of the impending Mutual Irish file that was giving me serious stomach cramps. Well either that or my notorious PMS.

Trying not to think about Mutual Irish, I collected a pile of enquiries from Gerry's in-tray and took them to my office. At the very least sorting the dross would keep my mind occupied. But I might even find a case begging for my attention. Something so pressing I would just have to take it, and put Mutual Irish on the long finger. OK, I'd then have to face Gerry's wrath when he got back. But anything would be better than taking on the Mutual Irish case and making a botch of it. Given that MI regularly swallowed up smaller insurance companies without compunction, imagine what they could do to a struggling detective agency that failed them.

The in-tray was a bit short of pressing cases. But then Monday morning habitually brought out the timewasters and head-bangers. Nutters who read our small ad over the weekend, and thought we could put their whole world to rights. Then there were the wannabe wits, the bored desk jockeys who spent the morning sending what they thought were funny emails – *Could you please find my runaway wife. She's a real bitch.* Signed, A. Terrier.

Funny? Not.

Most of our actual cases came from word-of-mouth recommendations. Satisfied clients who passed on the name McHugh Dunning, and never questioned the VAT figures which were clearly printed on their bill, below our hourly rates.

And of course every Monday there was the call from West Cork. A man asking if we could arrange to have his wife killed. Painlessly.

I picked out one interesting enquiry. The Emerald Hearts introductory agency was having trouble with a hacker, who was getting into their files and sending their registered clients porn through the post. Porn with their clients' faces superimposed on the energetic participants. As Emerald Hearts was used by high fliers, they didn't want any Garda involvement. They asked politely if we could guarantee them absolute confidentiality.

No problemo, I smiled to myself. Maybe this day was about to look up.

I was checking out their ad in a glossy mag when my phone rang, an outside line, which meant the caller had my desk number.

'Hello?' I answered brightly.

Soft breathing.

'Hello?' I repeated.

'Annie?' A muffled voice.

I froze.

'Are your nipples hard, Annie? They can't be as hard as my dick—'

19

I put him on hold.

It was a tactical plan. Bound to be successful. Surely even the most hard-core pervert will grow weary of spewing out filth with 'Greensleeves' playing in his ear.

But this time he had used my desk number.

I rang reception. 'Sandra, I'm moving into Gerry's office until he gets back. It's a bit of a nuisance, but will you redirect my calls to his desk. And . . . don't put anyone through until you double-check their credentials.'

'It's him, isn't it?' She was on it in a flash. 'I can hear it in your voice. The dirty fecker got your desk number. I'm ringing the cops.'

'Calm down. This is my problem, and you're not ringing the cops because they'll want to tap our phones. How do we guarantee confidentiality then?'

'We have to do something, Annie. Remember the woman in Kilcock? The one killed in her bath? Her son said she'd been getting filthy calls.'

'I only have showers, Sandra,' I lied. 'And no one is going to murder me. For God's sake, if I can't handle a few pervy calls, I'm in the wrong business. And don't you dare tell Brian about this call! Or anyone else for that matter.'

I could practically hear the wheels turning in her head as she mentally ticked off a whole slew of people she was bursting to tell.

I knew how to distract her. 'Sandra?'

'What?'

'Could you do something for me?'

'Yes.' She became eager.

'Get me some chocolate.'

'Chocolate? Are you . . . ?'

'Depressed? Frustrated? Suffering from PMS? All of the above.'

She broke into a giggle. 'Fruit and Nut OK?'

'Perfect.'

'And I'll bring you fresh coffee, as well. Will I?'

'What would I do without you Sandra? I'll be in Gerry's office.'

She giggled again. 'Depressed, frustrated, *and* suffering from PMS? There's no one cure for all that, is there?'

'Yes there is. Unfortunately Gerry took it with him to Arizona.'

'Annie!' Her hoot of laughter nearly burst my eardrum.

I collected all my bits, including the bar of chocolate I'd already been eating, and threw them into my Tardis bag. Gerry always said that if you want to keep Sandra happy, you ask her to do you a favour. And he knew Sandra better than anyone. He even gave her away at her wedding, when her father was too drunk to show up.

3

Sandra jigged about so much she was making me dizzy. It wouldn't have taken a genius to figure that she was aching to share something with me. And not just her giant bar of Fruit and Nut. We were already halfway through that.

'You not having coffee?' I asked. As if she wasn't already wired enough.

'No.' She stopped jigging for a nanosecond, her eyes searching my face.

'Thanks for bringing mine up, then.' I drained my cup. 'Better get back to work now,' I hinted.

She nodded, but didn't move. Hadn't I thanked her enough for the Fruit and Nut? Sandra liked to be thanked. A lot.

'I'm totally grateful for this Sandra.' I forced myself to finish the last square.

She fiddled with the discarded list of enquiries that were about to be shredded. 'Nothing much here, then?'

'No.' I didn't try to disguise my disappointment.

'I typed up a real gem for Gerry last week.'

'Good for you.' I turned to check my emails.

'He locked it in his desk.'

I lost interest in the emails. 'He locked it away?'

22

Gerry hadn't mentioned any particularly sensitive case to me. All he talked about was the incoming Mutual Irish one, and we hadn't yet received that file.

Sandra flushed bright red. 'The key is under the little Buddha.'

I eyed the little Buddha. I had given him to Gerry as a joke. A fun birthday gift because he was feeling particularly down that year, because he hadn't yet received any birthday cards from his sons.

You just rub its belly for luck.

When he raised a sceptical eyebrow, I had added, '*You can always use it to stamp out your cigarette, when you hear me coming*'.

Seeing my hesitation Sandra said, 'If Gerry was here, I bet he'd be giving you that case right now.'

The key turned easily, and there were no dark secrets in the drawer anyway. Just a half-empty pack of Benson & Hedges, and a slim case folder.

'Perfect case for you.' Sandra cracked her knuckles, a trick Barney had taught her much to Gerry's disgust.

Sandra never lost hope that one day she'd awake to find she was working for CSI Miami. Or at the very least that overnight the whole McHugh Dunning staff had been transformed into Hollywood-style PIs, complete with holstered guns and too-tight T-shirts. She never quite accepted that our work mostly consisted of tracking sleazy shoplifters and collecting evidence against adulterous spouses, or sometimes even against environmental polluters. Those sub-normal citizens who thought it OK to pollute rivers and beauty spots with their discarded cookers, fridges and washing machines. Somewhere in Sandra's romantic head we were up there with the James Bonds of the world. Tirelessly fighting (in Armani suits) against power-crazed megalomaniacs, who were intent on annihilating the universe. Her young gardener husband once confessed to Gerry that he frequently pleaded with her to take a safer job. Maybe in their local supermarket. He possibly thought she wouldn't have to face too many power-crazed megalomaniacs at the checkout in Tesco's.

Eyes shining with triumph, Sandra winked at me, and left.

I opened the file.

It said a busy Dublin garage was looking for a smart PI to work undercover in their accounts office. The garage owner suspected two of his staff of smuggling in cheap motor parts, selling them off the books to his customers, and pocketing the cash. He could have sacked the mechanic involved, but decided that one of his accounts staff was involved in the scam, otherwise discrepancies would have appeared on the customer's account. He had no proof of wrongdoing, just a gut instinct that he was being ripped off. Garda involvement was a no-no. Tod McGill was a self-made man who prided himself on taking care of his own problems. He heard that McHugh Dunning were trustworthy. Even more important, discreet, so he was prepared to *give them a go*. McGill claimed he frequently turned a blind eye to *low-level fiddling*, but things were getting out of hand, and he wanted heads to roll. First he needed to know which heads. Gerry had obviously spoken with him at length, because there were scribbled question marks all over the notes, all of which Sandra had faithfully typed in.

The phone rang.

'Well?' Sandra sounded breathless.

'It's . . . interesting.'

'Interesting? It's mega. McGill was on TV twice! His girlfriend is always in the *Sun*. She's a model, and her brother is in that new boy band, Hunks. They're all famous. Even her mother had a kitchen makeover on TV, and Mary in the Café has a friend who is a researcher in RTE and she said that Maeve, that's McGill's girlfriend, is going to be presenting that Fashion Can Be Fun programme, while Jilly Aherne, the usual presenter, is away having her twins. By caesarean of course. Famous people always have their babies by caesarean, don't they? Too posh to push, ha, ha, ha.'

I was more excited than I let on. I had no interest in McGill or any of his crowd, I'd never even heard of them. But the case was perfect for me. Gerry obviously saw that. He was always saying I could find discrepancies in the Pope's accounts, which was clearly why he put the case aside, before either of the lads saw it. Then Sally rang about David and the case slipped his mind.

'You still there, Annie?' Sandra's voice was shrill with excitement. 'Want to hear your horoscope? *A surprise development is about to lead into one of the most successful, and exciting phases of your whole life.*'

I laughed. 'And there I was thinking horoscopes were rubbish.'

25

'Wait, there's more – *The fabled tall dark stranger will sweep you off your feet in—*'

'Don't push it Sandra.' I hung up.

Gerry rang at midday.

'How are . . . at . . . agency?' The line faded at two-second intervals.

'Perfect,' I yelled. 'Where exactly are you? The dark side of Mars?'

'I'm still . . . Heathrow . . . security checks . . . havoc . . . with schedules . . . boarding soon.'

'Anything from Sally?' I yelled.

'Yeah . . . David with . . . kid . . . safety in numbers.'

I frowned. 'Did you get Sally's earlier message?'

The line suddenly cleared. 'Yeah. I told her to check the dude ranch. No joy. But Arizona is so vast the chances are that David and his pal are still making for the ranch. Anyway, David is a smart kid. He'll . . . got to go, Annie, my flight . . .' He was gone.

Mildly disappointed that I didn't get to mention the McGill case, I hung up.

The phone rang again instantly.

'Gerry?' I chuckled. 'I found the McGill file.'

'It's me, Annie.' Sandra sounded nervous. 'Mags is here. She won't leave.'

'Offer her money,' I teased.

'I'm not kidding. Naomi's Japanese VIPs are up in her showrooms.'

'Shite. I forgot to speak to Dick.'

'Too late. These guys look mega important. You should see their car. It's longer than the 19A.'

'I thought they were due tomorrow?'

'Well, they're here now. And they'll be coming back through reception any minute. Naomi just rang down and ordered me to clear the decks, but I can't shift Mags. And you know how she normally stinks? Wait til you get a whiff of her today. It's unmerciful.'

I raced to the lift, and hit the call button. Nothing. Naomi liked to wedge the lift doors open on her middle floor, so her clients would assume the lift was for her private use. I legged it down the stairs.

Racing past Dreamland Interiors I could hear Naomi's cut-glass voice singing the praises of white recess lighting for minimalist interiors. She could probably be heard in her VIPs' home base, in Japan. Naomi subscribes to the belief that if a non-English speaker doesn't understand you, you just shout louder.

The first whiff of Mags hit me as I rounded the stairs. A hideous mix of smelly clothes and runaway BO, it made me retch. I had shared Gerry's sympathy for the homeless Mags, but since she got a roof over her head, I refused to share his tolerance for her ongoing avoidance of soap and water. I'll happily give her as much free coffee as she wants. I'll even share my morning muffins with her. But when she hangs around stinking out our reception, my tolerance evaporates.

She saw me coming. 'I haven't finished me coffee yet.'

'Take it with you, Mags. Sandra, give her a lid for that Styrofoam cup.'

'Huh!' Mags shook her filthy, matted head. 'You're not the boss. You're just in charge while Gerry's in America.'

27

Jesus, was Gerry texting *everyone* in Dublin?

'Out!' I pointed to the door.

'Gerry lets me stay until I finish me coffee.' She came towards me aggressively.

I staggered back, trying not to inhale.

'He lets me stay for *hours*. Sometimes even for . . .' She became confused, 'twenty minutes.'

'That's in winter, Mags,' I softened. 'It's nearly thirty degrees Celsius today.'

'Cel . . . si . . . us?' She considered this for a second, then, 'I don't know what that means. But I know what time they're going to tow all the cars away from Diggs Lane!' She challenged.

'Of course you do, Mags. Now off you go and watch them,' I said.

Sandra ran out of patience. 'Just get out, Mags! Find somewhere else to drink your coffee.'

'They won't let me in the café!' Mags' toothless mouth pouted.

Sandra held her nose. 'Oh Jesus, I wonder why?'

'Don't you be taking our Lord's name in vain! Blasphemers will burn in hell for all eternity.'

'Annie! The lift is coming.' Sandra was in a serious panic now.

The lift *was* descending. And for once it was moving smoothly, not stopping and starting every few seconds.

I pushed Mags into the street. 'Out with you.'

Sandra ducked behind the desk and came up with a can of air freshener. She was spraying it in all directions when it suddenly went silent. 'Oh Jesus! It's empty.' She hammered it against the desk, forcing a final weak squirt from it.

Mags yelled back from the street. 'Blasphemers!' Then disappeared from view.

The lift doors slid open, and Naomi stepped out with three Japanese men, all three of them immaculately groomed, but tiny. All three of them walking ramrod straight, with dignified heads held high. Well, as high as they could, given that even the tallest man didn't reach beyond Naomi's armpit.

He suddenly paused, and to my absolute horror sniffed the air suspiciously.

'Oh shite,' Sandra muttered. 'We're fucked.'

She was right. Bad enough that I'd forgotten to tell Dick to do a better job on Naomi's showroom windows; now Mag's excruciating BO was blitzing her VIPs. I wasn't fond of Naomi, but she worked hard. She deserved better than to have her customers frightened off by a smell that could stun the senses, at three yards. Besides, she was a woman of her word. She would penalise us heavily for this, which would send Gerry ballistic. He might be a good detective, but he was a bit of a tightwad when it came to money.

I legged it to the door. If I held it wide open, there was always a chance that the wind which was now rising to hurricane proportions, might diffuse Mags' lingering smell. I put my all into it, bending my head to lend weight to my pathetic efforts at holding the heavily reinforced door open.

The VIPs' leave-taking seemed to take forever, all three of them going through a long formal ritual of extended handshaking, bows, and even serious mutterings about cherry blossom.

I didn't raise my eyes 'til they were gone. Then I legged it behind the safety of the reception desk. Nothing for it now, but to wait for Naomi to come back in and give us a bollocking.

She was still out in the street, grovelling shamelessly. Waving both arms in farewell, until the shining car was out of sight.

'Think they noticed the smell?' I turned to Sandra.

'Definitely.'

'Then we're doomed.'

'Not necessarily.'

'What do you mean, not necessarily?' I snapped.

Her smile becoming mischievous, she tried to squirt the empty air freshener at me. 'Didn't you hear what the little man said?'

'What little man? They were *all* little.'

'Well, the last little man out then.'

'I could only make out two words – cherry and blossom.'

'Exactly.' She stuck the aerosol can under my nose.

On it was a picture of a long sweeping cascade of cherry blossom.

4

Barney finished his third jam doughnut, wiped the sugar off his fingers and switched on his laptop to show me photos of the shoplifting gang. He had burst into my office demanding that I drop whatever I was doing and check out the pictures.

When I hesitated, he tried to bribe me.

'Please, Annie, I need a fresh pair of eyes to view them. I'll give you a doughnut?'

When I stopped laughing, he repeated his offer.

'Please, Annie. OK, I'll give you *two* jam dough-nuts? *And* a tube of Pringles. How's that?'

'What are you like?' I sat back. 'It must be that school uniform. You not only look like an adolescent, you're beginning to talk like one. And eat like one.' I pointed to the bag of doughnuts.

Affronted, he walked away, then sidled back, his forehead rucked with frown lines. 'How do you know that I haven't been medically prescribed all this stuff, to . . . to counteract low blood sugar?'

'Because any doctor who prescribed cans of coke, jammy doughnuts, and sour cream Pringles for a medical condition would be struck off.' I continued to input into my computer.

'Oh you think you know everything.'

'For feck's sake Barney! I'm trying to work here. Plus I've heard you use that same argument to defend your Big Macs, *and* Chinese takeaways.'

'That's because there's *some* truth in it.'

'Have you actually been diagnosed as having low blood sugar?' I swung around to face him.

'Well . . . OK, not exactly.'

'How about a tapeworm?' I turned back to my computer screen. I was trying to gen up on cars. All I knew about them so far, was how to drive them. If I was to do a good job in McGill's I'd need to be a little better informed.

Barney sat on the edge of the desk, sighing dramatically.

I gave in. 'Oh for feck's sake, show me your bloody pictures.'

'Teamwork,' he grinned. 'That's the route to success.'

'Speaking of which,' I watched him enlarging one of the digital pictures, 'Sandra played a blinder today.'

'Sandra?' He turned the picture the right way up.

'Yeah. She was brilliant with Naomi's VIP clients.'

'Huh.' Naomi's name was enough to make Barney lose interest.

'This is Jacinta Rowlans.' He pointed to the girl in the digital picture.

Jacinta was an eye-catching sixteen-year-old. Even the dull grey of her school uniform couldn't detract from her stunning looks. And didn't she know it. In the diamond-sharp picture she was tilting her head provocatively, allowing her long fair hair to tumble over one shoulder and down past a startlingly well-endowed chest. Her baby-blue eyes shining with confidence, she was a girl any parent would be proud of. If she wasn't sticking a handful of stolen goods up her school blouse.

'Her third trip, that afternoon.' Barney pointed to her mountainous chest. 'Under all that gorgeous hair her pockets are bursting with stolen goods. Top fashion earrings, bracelets, nose rings, even watches. Some haul.'

'She looks like butter wouldn't melt.'

'That's Jacinta.' He gave a tight little laugh. 'All those speech and drama classes darling Daddy shelled out for are finally paying off. But there's a hard little tart under that sweet expression. Even while I was taking that shot she was giving me the come on. 'Course she didn't know I had a camera in my pocket.'

'Is that it?' I asked as we finished viewing photo twelve.

I was impatient to get going on my new case. And besides, watching spoiled rich kids stealing for the hell of it gave me a pain. Jacinta's daddy was a wealthy horse breeder, with friends in high places. It was the hard working shopkeeper who had my sympathy. A self-made man, he was showing real balls by insisting that Jacinta and her mates be prosecuted, regardless of who their parents were.

'Reckon I have enough evidence to convince a judge?' Barney waited.

'Definitely.' I bit into a doughnut while checking the final photos again. There were enough shots of cheese-cutter thongs, silk neck scarves and top-of-the-range make-up disappearing up the private-school jumpers of Jacinta and her three friends to convince even the most sceptical judge.

'Nice work, Barney. Don't know how you do it, getting such clear shots of those spoiled brats in action,' I munched.

'It's not exactly cutting-edge stuff.' He popped open another can of Coke.

'Drop the false modesty,' I teased. 'You're the king of undercover and you know it. If I get in trouble with my new case, I'll know where to turn for help.'

'Your new case?' He feigned interest.

'It's really exciting.' I couldn't resist showing off a bit. 'Sandra found it for me. Told you she's playing a blinder these days. Starting tomorrow I'll be working undercover in McGill's Motors.'

He jerked upright, spluttering Coke down the front of the grey school shirt. '*McGill*'s Motors? You don't mean Dirty McGill's?'

'What's the problem?' I was miffed. 'If you can pass for a teenager, I can pass for an accounts clerk in McGill's Motors. Oh wait,' I covered my mouth melodramatically. 'I *am* a trained accounts clerk.'

'That's my case, Annie!'

I froze. 'What do you mean your case?'

'I mean I'm working it! It's been arranged for days. Why do you think Gerry's been hassling me to sort this shoplifting gig ASAP? McGill doesn't hang about.'

'But you . . . you don't know anything about accounts.'

'Damn right.' He threw the empty Coke can into the wastepaper basket. 'Still my case.'

'Who's in charge here?' I snapped, looking for somewhere to dump the remains of the doughnut.

'You are, Annie. But Gerry already allocated the McGill case. Anyway, McGill is filthy, you'd never . . . he's a . . . aw . . .' He stood up tugging at the crotch of the tight school trousers. 'Bloody yokes are crucifying me. And they don't half itch. It'll be a relief to put on a suit tomorrow. For McGill's office?' He answered my startled look. 'Sorry about the case, Annie, but . . . well, Gerry gave it to me, and . . . too late now to start changing stuff around.'

Before I could argue further, he grabbed the photos from the printer tray, and legged it.

I dropped my half-eaten doughnut in the wastepaper basket. The bit I'd already swallowed was now threatening to come right back up again. Not Barney's fault. He didn't allocate cases. *The boss* did that. But I couldn't recall Gerry ever doing it in such a sly, underhand way before. Hiding a case in a locked drawer? In case I'd spot it? Then buggering off to Arizona and leaving me completely in the dark. I was supposed to be a full partner here for God's sake. In every sense. It wasn't like he'd have to send me an inter-office memo to keep me informed of his plans. The most he'd have to do was turn over in bed. Was our relationship in an even worse state than I'd suspected? Or was Gerry just playing the macho card because he could?

My head completely done in, my stomach churning, I headed for the lift. I was reaching for the call button when the doors shot open, and Sandra appeared.

'Annie!' she beamed. 'Gerry just sent me the coolest text ever. Here. Read it.' She stuck her mobile in my face, her eyes shining.

I brushed past her. 'I don't want to read anything Gerry sent. And you know better than to have your mobile switched on during office hours!'

She watched open-mouthed, as the doors closed between us.

The lift stopped on the second floor and a cloud of Chanel No. 5 announced Naomi's arrival.

'Annie!' If *her* smile got any wider her head would have fallen off.

'Hidetoshi just called,' she gushed. 'He asked me to thank you for your kindness. For the gentle respect you showed to his countrymen.'

When I didn't react, she continued, 'The cherry blossom scent was perfect. But holding the door open like that? *And* keeping your head bowed? That was a masterly stroke! I couldn't have done better myself.' She tossed back a wayward hair extension.

'Not now, Naomi,' I hissed so hard, my teeth hurt.

Out in the street the earlier hint of rain had turned into a deluge. It bucketed down without mercy, sending people scurrying for cover. In less than three seconds there were mini lakes on the street; even worse, threatening rumbles of thunder in the distance. I shrank back into the doorway, trying to decide what to do, then, my mind made up I headed for the car. In the time it took me to run to Diggs Lane, the downpour had plastered my hair to my head, and was running down my cheeks as if I was crying.

I had the car door half open before I spotted the wheel clamp. Bright yellow, it was a dripping, malevolent claw. The final affront. Rain pounding against my head I kicked it, cursed it, and swore vengeance on every clamper who had ever been born. And on Gerry who, much as he promised, never did arrange a parking spot for me.

The sky suddenly lit up with sheet lightning, followed almost instantly by a loud crack of thunder.

I legged it around the corner and hailed a passing taxi.

'Where to, love?'

'Where to?' Another flash of lightning had me hugging the seat.

'Where do you want to go, love? The meter's ticking,' the cabby growled.

'Er.' My mind frozen by another ferocious crack of thunder, I tried to think. 'A . . . er . . . a pub please. Any pub. With no windows?'

The driver double-checked me in his mirror, then looked at his windscreen wipers, which were fighting a losing battle against the downpour.

'No windows,' he repeated.

A huge flash, the brightest ever, had me cowering again.

'No windows it is.' He edged the cab out into the growing traffic.

Fifteen terrifying minutes later we were outside what looked like a derelict building on the quays.

Practically windowless, and definitely joyless, it was the complete opposite of the cool and trendy pubs that were taking over the city.

'This OK, love?'

'Perfect.' I threw him the fare, and a ludicrously large tip, and darted inside, before the next flash of lightning could strike a direct hit, and sizzle me up like a piece of barbecued meat.

5

Fiona did a double take when she saw me standing, red eyed and dripping, in her front porch.

'Jesus, what happened to you?'

'Nothing.' I stumbled in out of the torrent. 'I . . . I stopped off for a couple of drinks.'

'A couple?' She guided me along the hallway as if I was incapable of finding my own way. 'You're feckin' legless! *And* you're drenched.' She touched my dripping hair. 'Where were you drinking? Out in the street?'

''Be silly,' I shivered. 'You know I hate thunderstorms.'

A sudden flash made us both jump.

'You were caught out in that?'

I waited for the roll of thunder.

'Relax.' She pried my fingers off her arm. 'It's moving off.' She led me into her enormous glass-walled kitchen, its gleaming stainless steel and recessed lighting making it look uncannily like the bridge of the Starship Enterprise, as another flash of lightning lit up the sky.

Fiona propped me against her fancy stove, and darted across the room to hit a hidden switch. A bank of roller blinds fell across the windows, shutting out the storm.

Breathing heavily with relief, I stuck my head under the massive stove hood. 'Beam me up, Scotty.'

'You're pissed! What were you drinking?'

'Lemonade?' I giggled.

'Yeah? Mixed with a quart of vodka, was it?' She disappeared for a second, to reappear holding out a large fluffy dressing gown.

'What's that?' I backed away. 'Rent a tent?'

'Stop messing, and get out of those wet clothes.'

I tried, but gave up after a long struggle with my sodden jeans. 'They're glued to my legs, Fiona,' I whimpered.

'Maybe if you removed your Nikes first?' She knelt down and began pulling off my wet trainers, slapping my hand away when I tried to help.

Finally, cocooned in the big dressing gown, I fell back into her padded rocking chair.

'Always wanted one of these,' I rocked. 'Do you have to have a baby before you can buy one?'

Fiona stood over me, her face scrunched in disapproval. 'Jesus, Annie, I know you're practically phobic about thunderstorms but . . . how did you get in this state?'

I thought hard. 'Em . . . I think I . . . I dunno.'

'Where were you drinking?'

'Dunno,' I rocked.

'You didn't drive in that state?'

'Couldn't. My car was clamm . . . clammed.'

'Clamped?' she asked.

I nodded. 'Gerry did it,' I accused.

'Gerry clamped your car?'

'No . . . but . . . all his fault . . . no denying it.' My

eyelids were now lead weights. Closing of their own accord.

Aeons later a gentle hand shook me awake. I opened my eyelids to see Fiona's worried eyes staring into mine. 'Tea?'

'Thank you. Thank you very, *very*, much, thanks.' I drained the wobbly cup.

Satisfied, Fiona began feeding me slim little soldiers of buttered toast.

'Feeling any better?' she asked.

'I love soldiers,' I giggled. 'Do you like soldiers, Fiona?'

'Oh Christ.' She pushed another butter-covered soldier into my mouth. 'Never mind what I like. You just keep eating. How much did you drink anyway? You've probably killed off half your brain cells in one go. What the hell were you doing going drinking on your own, anyway? Look at you, anything could have happened, the state you're in.'

'I found my way here, didn't I? Safe and sound. All Gerry's fault, anyway.'

'Yes, you told me he clamped your car.' She smiled.

'He left me alone,' I accused. 'To face a thunderstorm.'

'But he's had to go away before. It's his job. Why are you so upset this time?'

'Because this time it's not his job! It's bloody Arizona! This may be the end of the road for me and Gerry.'

'Sure. Sure.' She sat back on her heels. 'He's gone to see the kids, has he?'

41

'Maybe yes. Maybe no.' I nodded off, too wrecked to care that there was a half-eaten soldier hanging from the corner of my mouth.

Next time she woke me, Fiona sounded worried.

'Wake up, Annie. You've been crying out in your sleep.'

'OK. OK. I'll go now.' I tried to scramble to my feet, but the room kept tilting sideways.

'You're not going anywhere. Except upstairs to bed.'

'Is that why you woke me? To put me to sleep?'

'Come on. Link my arm.'

'Calum is so lucky to have such a great mum. I wish you were my mum, Fiona.' My lip started quivering.

She got the giggles, and I laughed with her, although I wasn't sure why.

She was putting me to bed when I remembered why I was here.

'I wanted to tell you how much I hate Gerry.'

'Why do you hate him, this time?'

'Because . . .' I tried to remember, but my eyes kept closing, making me sleepy. 'I'll have a little sleep first. Just five . . . minutes. Then I'll remember. Don't you move. I want to tell you why I hate him.' I closed my eyes.

The sun came flooding into Fiona's kitchen just as I finished my bowl of Bran Flakes.

'No more lectures, Fiona. You're wasting your time.' I reached for the sugar-free marmalade to spread on my high-fibre, brown toast. 'Any white bread?'

She shook her head. 'Why am I wasting my time?'

'Because I've made up my mind. It's all over with me and Gerry.'

Fiona wiped a blob of milky porridge from the arm of Calum's high chair.

'So you said. A dozen times.' She smiled knowingly. 'And this time next week you'll be shagging each other senseless.'

'No way. We're finished,' I grimaced as I sipped my decaf. I hate decaf. Never saw the purpose in it. But Fiona was on a health binge. Probably because someone in her Mums and Toddlers group said their life coach recommended it. Or it could have been their Yoga teacher. Even their Pilates coach. Fiona's Mums and Toddlers group are spoiled for choice. They have everything, except herpes.

She gave me another funny look, and I knew what was coming. It was always the same. I'd come here after a row with Gerry, and she'd tell me how great he was. How lucky I was to have him. How women my age – thirtysomething – had more chance of being struck by lightning than meeting a single, straight man, with no emotional baggage, and all his own teeth.

I blamed her Mums and Toddlers group. I'm convinced there is something in their secret manifesto that says all your friends must be firmly attached, or you drop them like a hot snot. Having reached their ivory towers I think they want to pull up the drawbridge to prevent unclean singles from contaminating their perfect little world. Even Fiona barely made it in, under the wire, because knowing her aptitude for making a clean breast of things I knew that she had probably (under the influence of a few dry sherries) confessed that she used to enjoy mindless shagging. Actually revelled in it. Fiona's new friends all lay claim to having been virgins when they married. Doh!

While I was meditating on this unlikely scenario, Calum was shunting his bowl of milky porridge backwards and forwards like a toy car. Suddenly bored with this game, he lifted the bowl and chucked it on the floor.

'Finished!' he shouted triumphantly at me.

'See!' I laughed. 'Calum agrees with me.'

Fiona shot me a look of disgust. 'Calum is twenty-two months old!'

'Still entitled to his opinion,' I said.

''Pinion,' Calum echoed happily, as Fiona ran to get a mop.

She was cleaning up the mess when he fired his porridge-coated spoon into the mix. And again looked to me for approval.

'Calum!' Fiona screamed, trying to mop up the blobs of porridge before they could solidify like cement. 'I had a terrible premonition this morning. I just know this is the day Mrs O'Kelly will walk out. She'll take up Heather Flanagan's offer for sure. That bitch gave her last cleaning woman a fur coat as a retirement gift. Mrs O'Kelly said it was the talk of the flats for weeks. I could have told them that bitch Flanagan only did it because she'd been threatened, twice, by the anti-fur brigade. I hope her villa in Spain does burn down.'

Fiona lived in terror of losing her cleaning woman to one of the wealthier mums in their Mums and Toddlers group. Convinced that they were all intent on poaching her gem, she sometimes gave the size sixteen Mrs O'Kelly her size ten cast-off designer suits. Then she heard that Heather Flanagan gave her woman a fur coat, and it was open warfare. Fiona was now getting up at dawn so she could have the house like a new pin before Mrs O'Kelly arrived to clean it. Only fly in that ointment was Calum. He could undo all Fiona's good work in ten minutes flat.

'She'll be here any minute.' Fiona was now sponging down the fridge door. 'I told Pino we'll have to give her more money. He suggested an early Christmas bonus, instead of her usual new wrap-around apron.'

Calum banged his retrieved spoon in approval.

'Calum!' she wailed, as lumps of porridge flew in all directions.

'I'll leave you to it, Fiona.' I got up, checked my reflection in the gleaming cooker hood, and groaned. 'Jesus, I look like shit. I can't go to work looking like this.'

She shot me a cursory look. 'Blow-dry your hair, throw on a bit of slap, a coat of mascara, and—'

'Shit,' Calum yelled happily.

'Oh God, he's starting that again! Yesterday he swore down the phone at Nonna Molino.'

'She doesn't speak English,' I consoled her. 'She wouldn't have known what he was saying.'

'He swore at her in Italian! Copied something he heard Pino say. He's like a little parrot, and Pino just laughs it off. My Dad used to wash our mouths out with soap if we even said shit.'

'Shit!' Calum echoed gleefully.

'See what I mean?'

'He'll stop. He'll get bored.' I patted Calum's angelic little head.

'Shit, shit, shit,' Calum sang, while accompanying himself on the spoon.

'Calummmmm!' Fiona's screech was interrupted by the French doors opening.

'Morning all.'

She turned, red faced. 'Oh, Mrs O'Kelly. You're early. Why don't you sit down and have a cup of coffee, and I'll . . . I'll—' Panic stricken, she began tidying the table, pushing everything to one side.

'No thanks.' Mrs O'Kelly was already shedding her anorak, rolling up her sleeves, and pulling on a flowery apron over her pink nylon housecoat. 'I'd rather get on, if you don't mind. Don't like coffee much, anyway. Gives me the acid. Did you get the lime buster I asked for?'

'Yes.' Fiona's hands shook. 'It's in the utility room. I'll get it.'

'You stay where you are,' Mrs O'Kelly ordered. 'I'll find it.'

'Isn't she great?' Fiona was in total awe of her. 'She never stops.'

Calum was silent now. Sitting in his chair like someone hypnotised, his eyes followed every move Mrs O'Kelly made. His mouth hanging open he watched her pull on a giant pair of yellow rubber gloves.

'I'll make a start upstairs.' She disappeared with her basket of cleaning fluids.

'Uptairs,' Calum muttered, and slid out of his chair.

'Get back here, you!' Fiona ran after him.

'Leave the child be,' a disembodied voice floated back down. 'He's no trouble.'

Calum scrambled eagerly up the stairs.

'Jesus.' Fiona ignored her cooling coffee and bit her thumbnail. 'He'll start pulling everything out of her cleaning basket. I can't afford to lose her, she's a gem.'

'He's not going to mess with anything while she's around. He's in awe of her.'

'You're right,' she nodded. 'It's great, isn't it? I'd pay her just to sit there and terrify him.'

'Fiona!'

'Well. I'll tell you a secret, she terrifies me.'

'You'd never guess.' I busied myself lashing on mascara. 'Anyway, that's what you get for climbing the social ladder. Your mum did all her own housework, didn't she? And brought up a gaggle of kids to boot.'

'Actually my da did the booting,' she laughed. 'If you slap a kid now you'd be arrested.'

'Drink your coffee.'

She waved the cup away. 'No more coffee for me. I've already had three cups.'

'Not afraid of the acid then?'

'Shut up,' she grinned. 'What I need is a strong tranquiliser.'

'Join the club.' I grimaced at my reflection again.

'I'd also need a gallon of eye drops. Or maybe a course of iron injections?' I pulled down my lower eyelid to check for signs of anaemia.

'Relax, Ms Hypochondriac. You're just hungover. In another hour you'll be hale and hearty again. I'll still be a nervous wreck. If Mrs O'Kelly walks out, I'm doomed. I have that big summer dinner party coming up, remember? Heather Flanagan will be checking my surfaces for dust.'

'Your house always looks magnificent.'

'Because of Mrs O'Kelly!' she said, as if I was witless. 'What if she's not here?'

'Pino can help out.'

She gave a dismissive bark. 'With the house? I'm surprised he even remembers where it is.'

'Just get another cleaner then.'

'Jesus, Annie, what planet are you living on? Nobody can get a cleaner these days. They're all working in American banks. Or over in Intel.'

'Doing what?' I was shocked.

'Cleaning! What do you think? I'll get your clothes.' She disappeared into the utility room, and came back, holding out my clothes as if they were infected. 'You'd best borrow some of mine. The rain didn't do this lot any favours.' She wrinkled her nose.

'They're fine.' I grabbed them. 'I wasn't planning on entering any fashion competitions today.'

She watched as I zipped up my jeans. 'You putting on weight?'

'No!' I sucked in my stomach, and forced the zip the rest of the way up. 'See? Perfect.' I held my breath as the zipper slid downwards again.

'Buy yourself some new clothes for God's sake.'

'These are fine. It's your bloody clothes dryer, it shrinks everything.'

'Doesn't shrink *my* clothes.'

'Oh la-de-dah.'

'No listen . . . maybe you should get your hair done, or something. Have it restyled? Try some new make-up?' She frowned at my un-made-up face.

'Are you trying to depress me?'

'No. I'm just saying. Gerry will be back soon. And . . . except if you have someone else in mind . . . it would be nice to see you two acting like lovebirds again?'

'Have you been reading Mills and Boon again?' I accused with a laugh.

She flushed. 'So what? They help me get to sleep.'

'I thought your rampant sex life did that?'

Her face clouded. 'Sex? What's that? Oh, I remember, it's what men like to do when they're *not* working twenty-four-seven. You should thank your lucky stars Gerry's not in the restaurant business.' She sighed. 'You'd be a total arse to leave someone like him.'

'Sally left him.'

'Sally *is* a total arse. But she's not stupid.' Her sudden vehemence surprised me. 'I never said it before because I didn't want to sound bitchy, but sod it, Sally is a cunning mare, and you're too straight for your own good. She may look fragile, but she's a player, Annie. Maybe you should learn to play games. Start tarting yourself up a bit and—'

'I'm not tarting myself up for any man. Certainly not for someone who runs off to Arizona at the drop of a hat.'

There was a sudden loud blare of a car horn.

'That'll be Barney,' she grimaced. 'Subtle as ever. I gave him a bell earlier on, asked him to sort the clampers, save you turning to drink again.'

The car horn blared a second time.

I hurried to the door, with Fiona at my heels, still talking like an agony aunt.

'This is my very last word on the subject, Annie,' she lied. 'I know it's your life but I think Gerry is totally yummy. If he wasn't penniless when I first met him, I'd have set my cap at him.'

'I didn't set my cap at him!' I bristled.

'Oh, give me a break, I saw you beating off the competition at my engagement party.'

'That's a filthy lie. I never—'

'Your eyes came out on stalks when you spotted him.'

'That's because I thought he was George Clooney.'

'George Clooney my arse. You couldn't wait to get your hands on Gerry when you saw him in those Calvin Klein jeans and that sexy linen shirt.'

'I didn't even know his shirt was linen,' I defended myself.

She chuckled. 'Liar, liar pants on fire! Tell the truth and shame the devil, Annie, you're really pissed because you think Sally is looking for a leg over, for old times' sake.'

I wrenched open the front door. 'I'm reviewing

our relationship because he betrayed me by giving my case away.'

'Rubbish! You're just mad jealous of Sally.'

'I am *not* jealous of Sally! Gerry and me haven't been getting along lately. Sally is almost incidental to—'

'What's all this about Sally?' Barney bounced up the pathway, jingling my car keys. 'Looking to back-date her conjugal rights, is she?'

'Don't you start!' I warned.

'Just asking about Sally,' he grinned. 'Where's the harm in that?'

'Fuck Sally,' I said.

'Fuckasally!' came an echo from behind me.

Before Fiona's hand could land on Calum's well-padded bottom, Barney picked him up and swung him high in the air, then yelped when Calum dropped a big dribble on his face.

'Yuk,' Barney cried.

''Gain,' Calum pleaded.

'Once is enough.' Fiona took Calum, as Barney wiped the dribble off his face.

'Fuckasally,' Calum shouted gleefully.

'See what you've started!' Fiona accused. 'He'll be repeating that all day now.'

'Better leg it, Annie.' Barney grabbed my arm.

'Fuckasally,' Calum shouted after us.

'That kid is a little head case!' Barney was delighted.

'He's a little dote. But Fiona is genuinely worried about his language.'

'Yeah, he has got a bit of an Italian accent all right. I wouldn't worry about that.'

I waited for him to laugh, but he was totally serious.

'It's not his accent that . . . oh forget it.' What was I thinking anyway? That Barney would be shocked by a couple of repeated fucks?

My mobile buzzed.

'Er . . . Mutual Irish were on.' Sandra sounded nervous. 'They want to know what's the best time for their man to come over.'

'Just check the work diary,' I said. 'If I'm free around twelve, tell them he can come over then, and we'll discuss the case thoroughly. For ten minutes. That's when you'll come in and interrupt us. Have you got that? You'll say I'm needed elsewhere. I'll turf him out, and hopefully never have to set eyes on him again. OK?'

A pause. 'Er . . . I think I should tell you, Annie, when the secretary asked what time he could come over, I think she meant . . . she seemed to think he'd be working here.'

'What do you mean *here*?'

'In the agen— in your office.'

'*My* office?'

'Don't blame me. I'm just telling you what she said.'

'She actually said he'll be working from my office? As what? A spy?'

'I dunno, but I think Gerry OK'd it.'

'We'll see about that.' I ended the call, and began dialling again.

'Trouble?' Barney frowned.

'Nothing I can't handle.'

6

Barney was being incredibly supportive. He sat in my car, risking a late start on his first day at McGill's, in order to give me the backup I needed to sort out Mutual Irish. Even getting through to them was proving to be a nightmare.

'That's it, you hang tough, Annie,' Barney encouraged as I dialled, and redialled their number.

A recorded voice finally answered. It rattled off a list of numbers for me to choose from. 'If you wish to enquire about an insurance policy press one. If you wish to enquire about a life assurance claim press two. If you wish to . . .'

As there was no number on offer for someone who wished to refuse to work with one of their staff, I chanced pressing two.

A snotty voice asked for my claim number.

'Actually, I'm not ringing about a claim. My name is . . .'

A click and I was back to an automated response. 'If you wish to enquire about an insurance policy press one. If you wish to enquire about a life assurance claim press two. If you wish to . . .'

I was wishing I could beat her about the head with the receiver, when Barney wrestled it from me and pressed a random number.

'I have just crashed into your claims manager's Mercedes,' he said. 'Put me through to him and I'll give him my details, otherwise I'm off . . . Ah . . . good morning, sir . . . you are the claims manager? McHugh Dunning investigations here. We are happy to be handling a case for you, Mr Duggan, but I have to inform you that we have a strict policy at McHugh Dunning. We *never* work with non-McHugh Dunning personnel.'

I squeezed his arm in gratitude.

He listened intently for another few seconds, said 'Perfectly clear.' And hung up.

'What did they say?' I tugged nervously at his sleeve.

'They said you work with their in-house investigator, or they shred our contract.' He pried my fingers off his borrowed suit.

'They can't do that.' I was horrified.

'They can. Our original contract was with Ansans. Mutual Irish don't have to honour it.'

'You told me to fight them.'

He gave me a long, thoughtful look. 'In retrospect, Annie, that would be like the Isle of Man threatening to invade the US.'

'Give me the phone, I'll ring them back.'

'You can't win this one, Annie.'

'Maybe not, but I can tell them to send their man over, right now! This very second.'

He raised an eyebrow.

'I need to exert *some* control. Can't lose face entirely,' I said, and began dialling.

He caught my face in his hands, and kissed me

full on the lips. 'Way to go, Annie,' he said, and legged it.

I was pulling my hair into a businesslike bun when Sandra buzzed to let me know the Mutual Irish investigator was waiting in reception. Although she worded it differently.

'Jaysus wait 'til you see the hunk Mutual Irish sent over,' she shrilled.

'Lower your voice, Sandra.'

'He can't hear me. He's over at the far wall admiring them black-and-white prints Naomi made Gerry buy last year. Them Picasso yokey . . . thingies . . . whatsit. God, he's luscious.'

'Has he got much stuff with him?'

'No. But he has an arse you'd want to bite. And the cut of his suit! If Jimmy looked like that in a suit I'd—'

'You're a married woman, Sandra. Behave like one.'

'Right. I'll tell him I have a headache.' She giggled.

Refusing to be drawn into her sillyness, I said, 'Give me two minutes to make myself presentable, then send him up.'

He was obviously within earshot of her now because she instantly adopted the ludicrous accent she uses when she's dealing with a wealthy client. Or trying to impress Naomi.

'Miz McHugh is turribly busy. However, she will see you in a mewmont.'

A deep male voice thanked her, making her so flustered she cut me off before giving me the man's name.

55

With a deep sigh I prepared to get back to her, but she beat me to it.

'And his name is . . . ?' I waited.

'Are your nipples hard, Annie?'

'Aaaaaaaaaah!' I lashed down the receiver.

Declan came running in, moving at a speed I hadn't known he possessed. 'Is it your pervert, Annie?'

'My . . . pervert? Who told you about—'

The phone shrilled.

'I forgot to give you his name,' Sandra giggled. 'It's Sizemore. How sexy is that?' She laughed like a drain.

'Sandra!'

'I'm just saying. He has these long sexy fingers, and he's so . . . posh. The secretary did say said something about his father being somebody, or something, but I can't remember what it was because—'

'I don't care if his father is King Billy. Now you listen to me, if you tell one more person about my psycho you'll be out of a job. And keep this Sizemore there 'til I'm ready. Bad enough to have some poncy git forced on us, like some school monitor, but if he thinks he can just walk in and—'

'But Annie—'

'Shut up, Sandra! I'll see Mr Sizemore in my own good time, and when I do I'll run the Mutual Irish arse off him. I'll make him wish he never heard of McHugh Dunning. I'll have him legging it back to their fancy offices like—'

'Annie?' Declan said.

'Don't you start, Declan. And I'll thank you to mind your own business about my psycho. If you

breathe a word about him to Barney or this Size . . .
less, I'll have *your* head on a plate! Now get back to
your pedigree dog case. Maybe you could sort that
before the end of the year?'

Stony faced, he turned to the door.

A tall thirty-something man was standing there,
looking faintly bemused, and a lot embarrassed. Given
Sandra's description of the Mutual Irish investigator,
it was pretty obvious who he was. I mean what were
the odds against *two* head-turning hunks arriving at
the agency at once, when we hadn't seen one in the
past four years? Well, not of this calibre. This one
had gleaming honey-coloured skin, thick dark hair,
and brown eyes you could drown in. And his mouth
wasn't exactly repulsive either.

I hated him on sight. And not just because I was
caught on the hop. In the unlikely event that I'd
been wearing a Vera Wang ballgown, and had my
hair styled by Jennifer Aniston's hairdresser, I still
would have hated him. I don't go for men who are
that handsome. Too much trouble. Or maybe too
much competition. Plus this guy reeked of my other
pet hate – old money. It was love of old money that
made my birth mother give me away before my
umbilical cord was dry. Sizemore reeked of it. It
was in his self-assured walk. The way he held his
head. Even his handshake, when it came, was calm,
and measured, when it should have been as sweaty
as everyone else's, given the mini heatwave we were
experiencing.

This man didn't belong in a PI agency. Except
if he was buying the building. And he was far too

57

well dressed to work with me, even on a temporary basis.

Mutual Irish were clearly using us, and not just for their case. This guy was being groomed for their top job. I had seen it all before, when I worked for Pussy Grub Inc. Somebody's son or nephew would be brought in, and moved through the company at warp speed. Thrown into every department for five minutes before being moved upwards again. In less than six months this one would be sitting in a director's chair, in Mutual Irish, drinking thirty-year-old brandy, and halfway to developing gout. We were being used. We were to teach him first-hand how we go about investigating insurance fraud. Only problem was, our fraud investigator was in Arizona.

'You're here to work a case with Annie?' Declan asked, as Sizemore treated him to a measured handshake.

Sizemore shot me a quizzical look.

'Gerry is away.' I gave him a frosty smile. ''Fraid you'll just have to make do with me.'

Give him his due, he didn't even blink. Didn't appear to balk at the prospect of working with someone who looked like she got her clothes from a skip, and styled her hair by sticking her fingers in a wall socket.

We shook hands, our eyes met, and for a zillionth of a second something in them connected. Then it was gone, and I hated everything about him again.

I turned to Declan. 'Pick up the jeep from the airport. You'll need it for those big dogs,' I said, in my best *I'm in charge* voice. 'Gerry left the keys at the customer service desk.'

'I know,' he nodded. 'Sandra told me.'

'Sandra should be working for CNN,' I said, and I thought I saw Sizemore's lips twitch. Or that may have been wishful thinking.

'I'll see you later.' Declan included him in his magnanimous wave.

Declan was behaving very strangely this morning, what with speaking to people and everything. It made me extra edgy. He swore he was on the wagon, but there he was again, smiling as he left. I hoped he hadn't met Jesus. Gerry once took on a gifted investigator to help us out over a particularly busy Christmas period, when shoplifting was up a thousand per cent. A brilliant sleuth, this guy was admired by everyone. Turned out he had a personal relationship with Jesus, which is all very well, but when this relationship developed to such an extent that he started talking to Jesus as he walked around shops, Gerry had to let him go.

I turned back to Sizemore, who was busy checking out my office. The uppity way he did this got right up my nose. He stood there as if he was reviewing his personal fiefdom.

'You can use that end of the desk.' I pointed to the bit of my desk that extends well beyond the heavy mahogany legs, but is too close to the wall for even a modicum of comfort. Let him try stretching his posh legs under that.

He was clearly thinking the same thing because his perfect brows knitted in a frown.

'It's roomier than it looks,' I lied.

59

He didn't reply, just began deftly emptying his soft leather briefcase, most likely a gift from his well-heeled, rich bitch, girlfriend. I watched covertly as he produced a tiny state-of-the-art laptop that at a guess probably cost the same as my Honda Civic. Curious to see what other rich trappings he deemed essential, I leaned over for a better view, and just for spite my intercom buzzed. He looked up and caught me watching him.

'What is it, Sandra?' I got a bit fuddled.

There was a pause, which could have meant anything. She could have been trying to gauge my reaction to Sizemore, or even trying to finish a mouthful of cheese and onion crisps, which are strictly forbidden in reception, because some people find their smell offensive.

'Sandra? Are you eating?'

She swallowed quickly. 'Gerry's on the other line. I'll put him through.'

'No! Wait a minute!'

There was a low click.

'You there, Annie?' Gerry sounded so frosty you'd swear I was the one who gave away the McGill case. *And* disappeared off to America, practically mid-coitus. 'What the hell is going on over there?'

'Nothing.'

'I've been trying to call you all night.'

'Did you find David?'

'Yeah. Well no . . . but we know where he is. He hid in the back of a camper van that had stopped for gas at a truck stop on the highway. He's with another kid. They thought they could make it to Phoenix before dark. Christ! Luckily the camper owners decided to bed down for the night. They found the kids fast asleep in their bunks. They're now spoiling both kids rotten, by the sound of it. We're meeting up in Phoenix tomorrow. Sally is . . .' He treated me to a long discourse on how Sally was feeling. Her delight when she heard David's voice on the phone, the way she hugged everyone. (Including passing strangers?) He only stopped short of telling me what she was wearing at the time.

'You still there, Annie?'

I cleared my throat. 'Why did you give the McGill case to Barney?'

'What?'

'That case was made for me, and you know it.'

There was a discreet cough from somewhere to my right. Sizemore. Jesus. He must have heard everything. I'd completely forgotten about him, he was so bloody quiet.

He pointed to the door. 'You want me to . . . ?'

I shot him a vicious look. Did I want him to leave? The question was, why was he still standing there? The second he realised I was having a private conversation he should have legged it from the office. What kind of man stands around listening to other people's calls? Well . . . I suppose investigators . . . but still. I picked up the receiver.

'The McGill case?' Gerry said in my ear. 'You think I should have given you the McGill case?'

'Well, it's pretty obvious isn't it? McGill wanted a *bookkeeper*! Rack your brain, Gerry. Know any other bookkeepers, do you? Think hard now.'

There was a long silence. Then my door handle rattled. Sizemore seemed to be having trouble getting out.

'Sorry,' he said. 'Door seems to be stuck.'

'Kick the base board!' I yelled. 'It sticks in humid weather. It's July, in case you haven't noticed.'

'Listen to me, Annie!' Gerry sounded miffed. 'Tod McGill has a gangland connection. Why do you think he's known as Dirty McGill?'

'Because he doesn't wash?' I muttered.

'I checked with the cops before I took the case. Remember those drug-related murders last year? The two eighteen-year-old kids found floating in the canal? The cops suspect Dirty McGill of . . .'

'He killed those two boys?' I was horrified.

'No. But the cops traced the suspect car back to his garage.'

'Wh— what does that prove?'

'Nothing. That's the problem. That's why the cops wanted my investigator to wear a wire – a hidden mike taped to his chest?' He explained, as if I wouldn't know what a wire meant.

I shivered. Was that why Barney was so jittery this morning?

'I thought McGill just needed someone to keep a check on his account books. Find out who was pocketing his profits.'

'He does. But the second DI Bailey heard McGill's name, he practically wet himself. Said this was the break they'd been waiting for.'

'I know that feeling,' I muttered.

'The cops have been trying to get evidence on

McGill for years, but he's always managed to stay one step ahead of them. To have an undercover working on McGill's accounts is like a wet dream for Bailey. 'Course he'd prefer to use one of his own men, but McGill can smell a cop a mile off. And he's a vicious bastard. You still think I should have sent you in there?'

I went silent.

'Wearing a wire?'

'Well . . .'

'Speak up, Annie, I can't hear you.'

'I . . . I suppose not,' I said grudgingly.

'Who told you about the case, anyway?'

'Er . . .' I didn't want to get Sandra in trouble.

'It was Barney, wasn't it? He has a big loose gob on him.'

'Is that why you'd let him put his life on the line?' I said slyly.

'It won't come to that.' He was instantly dismissive. 'The cops will keep a close eye on him. At the first hint of danger, they'll have him out of there.'

'If you believe that, why didn't you give me the job?'

'Oh for feck's sake, Annie.'

'You think I'm a crap investigator, don't you?'

'I left you in charge of the agency. Would I do that if I thought you—?'

'You obviously wish I was as perfect as Sally. All she has to do to make you come to heel is crook her little finger.'

His laugh was a mirthless bark. 'Make up your

mind, Annie! Are you angry because I didn't give you the McGill case, or because I came to Arizona?'

I gritted my teeth. 'Maybe I'm angry because I was jackknifed across the bed the second Sally phoned.'

'My son was missing!' His voice rose.

'He was in the back of a camper van being spoiled rotten!'

'I didn't know that then, did I? He could have been lying somewhere in the desert, calling my name.'

'I was calling your name. I still got jackknifed across the bed.'

'This is stupid, Annie. You know I have to be there for my kids.'

'Yeah, well I have to be there for myself.' I hung up.

I dropped my head on the desk and, despite my best efforts, the tears started. God, I hate being premenstrual. I hate it. First hint of PMS, and I'm crying like a baby. Half blinded by tears, and runny mascara, I groped about for a tissue, knuckled my coffee cup instead, and sent cold coffee flying across the desk and soaking into everything in sight including a couple of pristine papers belonging to Sizemore.

I was about to bang my head in frustration when I felt a handkerchief being pressed into my hand.

Sizemore was standing over me, his brown eyes dark with concern.

Of course he was concerned. He came here expecting to be teamed up with Gerry Dunning, a hardboiled ex-cop, and gifted PI. Instead he found himself saddled with a woman who appears to collapse in tears over spilled coffee? Sizemore obviously saw his speedy rise to the top slowing down before his very eyes.

I wiped away a blob of mascara, blew my nose on his hanky, and gave it back to him. 'Right.' I cleared my throat. 'Now where's this case all the kafuffle is about?'

Unsure. He looked at his balled up hanky.

'Sorry,' I grabbed it and threw it in the bin. 'Now come on, Sizemore. Give me the bloody file. You must have seen a woman cry before? You are a *seasoned* investigator, aren't you?'

He nodded, his razor-like cheekbones threatening to break through his well-pampered skin.

'Let's get to work, then.'

Still uncomfortable, he took a file from his briefcase, and put it in front of me.

I stared at the name on the cover. 'Bolger?'

I looked up at Sizemore, then back at the file, torn between excitement and terror. 'They want us to investigate the *Bolger* fire?'

He didn't reply. Just looked increasingly like an animal caught in a trap. As if, given the choice, he'd chew off his own foot to escape both me and the situation he found himself in.

'OK,' I said. 'You can stand there if you like. But I'll be ages getting through all this.'

I opened the file.

He sank into a chair, his brown eyes never leaving my face.

7

It was elbowroom only at the bar of The Randy Goat. After two failed attempts to find a quiet corner, Barney, Declan and I trooped out to the paved back courtyard; which had been recently extended to facilitate die-hard smokers. It was modelled on a Mediterranean garden, complete with pot-bound hydrangeas, a tinkling water fountain, and uneven cobblestones. But even out here people were squashed together like sardines.

'I can't believe you're going to investigate the Bolger fire, Annie,' Barney hissed. 'Are you out of your mind? You'll be lynched.'

'I'll have Sizemore to protect me,' I whispered.

'What'll he do? Blind the lynch mob with his gold cufflinks?'

'Tell Mutual Irish you're too busy,' Declan advised.

'Tell them to eff off.' Barney turned his back on a Garda acquaintance who kept trying to attract his attention. 'Seanie Bolger is a national hero. The tabloids love him. Inner city Dub turned footballing legend? Golden Balls Bolger?'

'He hasn't played for years.' I dismissed this.

'Only because that Spanish bollocks wrecked his ankle, with that filthy tackle. If it wasn't for that foul, we would have won the World Cup that year.'

Declan shot him a look of disbelief.

'OK, maybe not *won* it, but we could have given the Germans a run for their money.'

'Mutual Irish are convinced he started that fire,' I whispered.

'Bollocks! They just don't want to pay out on the insurance claim.'

'Sizemore says they're happy to pay out on legitimate claims, the only reason they want this one investigated is because they got a tip-off.'

'A tip-off? From who? Some jealous prick who hates Seanie, because women still throw their knickers at him?'

'Actually, the caller was a woman,' I said. Then checked that I couldn't be overheard, before adding, 'A week before the fire Seanie gave a post-dated cheque to his new business partner. It was for nine hundred thousand euros. His bank account was at zero, and his shop was mortgaged to the hilt. You do the sums.'

'You saying that shop was insured for a million?'

'Try three.'

'Jaysus! No wonder Mutual Irish don't want to pay out.'

'Seanie won't live to see a payout,' Declan's funereal tones cut in. 'Third-degree burns are the worst.'

'And how did he get burned?' Barney hissed. 'Running into that inferno to try to rescue his wife. Hardly the actions of someone who torched the place.'

'Mutual Irish think he miscalculated the speed of the fire, but they need proof. And guess who's going to get it?' I said smugly, still unable to believe that such a juicy case had landed in my lap. This case would trump ten Dirty McGill's.

'You think you're going to find proof that Seanie Bolger . . .'

'He's not a saint, Barney! I've done my research. He's had more women than hot dinners.'

'Screwing around is one thing. Burning your wife alive is—'

'I believe he miscalculated . . .'

'Huh, you and Mutual Irish? There's a turn up for the books. Anyway, Seanie's brain is mush, you're not going to get any information there.'

'Mush? Do you have to be so crude?' I turned to smile at a couple who were squeezing past us, both of them wearing startled expressions.

'For God's sake, he's been unconscious for weeks.' Barney ignored their curious looks. 'His brain has to be mush, why else would there be talk of *turning off his life support?*' He quoted the latest tabloid head-line. 'Now Mutual Irish want to wreck his good name to save themselves a few lousy euros?'

'A few lousy euros?' I waited 'til the curious couple were beyond earshot. 'A minute ago you were shocked by the amount of the—'

'Yeah . . . well . . . Three million is just loose change to Mutual Irish. Tell you what I'd do, Annie. I'd keep the file. Fluff around with the paperwork. Play for time. And if you do find anything that'll dirty Seanie's name, let it fall down the back of your desk. There's only one reason why Mutual Irish would give us this case. They're terrified the press will find out they're holding back on paying out to a national hero. If you find any evidence against Seanie, they'll say your investigation forced their hand. They're using you, Annie.'

I went cold, all my earlier excitement dwindling away.

'We're in business to be used,' Declan growled.

I wanted to hug him. Declan never said much. But what he did say usually made sense. He was a rock. When he was sober.

Barney seemed to have lost all interest in the Bolger case, anyway. He was now leaning back at a forty-five degree angle to get a better look at a girl standing a little way from us, by the fountain. She was what he'd call a fine thing. And, happily for him, wearing the thinnest muslin top, and no bra. Risking eye-strain, or a serious slap, Barney kept trying to get a better look at her, his expression no longer that of a man concerned about any insurance company. Or national hero, for that matter.

I elbowed him in the ribs. 'The Bolger case, Barney? Do you really think—'

'What? Oh, ring Gerry. He'll tell you what to do.'

That was enough to cement my resolve. First thing tomorrow I would begin investigating the Bolger fire.

I did wonder, momentarily, about the continuing tabloid interest in Seanie.

'Who was it said that all publicity is good publicity?' I mused hopefully.

'I dunno.' Barney's eyes were still on the muslin top. 'Some arsehole?'

As I couldn't remember the name of the arsehole either, I drained my glass and prepared to leave.

69

'Let's move. I have an early start in the morning.'

'OK, OK.' Barney finally tore his mind off the nipple-revealing top. 'All I'm saying is don't set yourself up for trouble, Annie.'

'Thanks. Maybe I should drop this case, and go back to finding lost moggies?'

'For fuck's sake, Annie, when did you get so prickly?' He turned.

Again, his loud voice attracted attention, making a couple of bored drinkers stare curiously at us, possibly hoping to see a prickly woman in the flesh. Someone like Vampira maybe, all sweeping lashes, inch-long nails, and blood-red lips. I wish.

'Shut it, Barney,' Declan growled.

'Better still, finish that pint so we can go.' I sighed. 'I knew it was a bad idea meeting up here. We could have talked in the *office*.'

'Should have made an executive decision, Annie.' Declan's expression gave nothing away.

'He's right.' Barney was his happy self again. Possibly because we had to squash past the nipple girl, and her three flirtatious friends. One of them was wearing a mini-skirt that wouldn't cover a three-year-old, and Barney was now torn between checking out her tanned legs, and watching her friend's nipples dance against the muslin top.

'Never mind, Annie, I'll just have to come back later, and investigate this place properly.' His voice rose against the noisy clamour. 'Find out why moonlit courtyards are so popular with . . . hot women.'

The nipple girl raised her glass invitingly.

'See that.' Barney nudged Declan as we stepped outside. 'I'm in there. God I love girl-friendly pubs.'

Declan grunted. A pub held only one attraction for him, and being on the wagon again he couldn't see any reason to linger about in one, although he never went against the popular vote when people suggested such a venue. He tagged along without complaint, sipped two mouthfuls of non-alcoholic beer, and tipped the remainder into the fountain.

'Those girls are all cop groupies,' I warned Barney as we walked to the jeep. 'If you can't produce a badge within two minutes, you don't stand a chance with any of them.'

'Two minutes? That's all the time I need.' He snapped his fingers then, realising how that sounded, he tried to backtrack. 'What I meant is I can pick—'

'Get in the jeep, Barney, before you lose all credibility.'

'Aw, you know what I meant.'

'Get in the jeep!'

'Prickly or what?' He rolled his eyes, and climbed in beside Declan, who was already gunning the engine.

I sat in the back re-reading the official reports on the Bolger fire, which seemed perfectly straightforward. The underwear shop had been jam packed with highly inflammable lingerie in preparation for the next day's big spring sale. A rack of heavy spotlights, which were carelessly wired, had slid lower and lower until they were leaning against a bunch of wax roses, which were draped with a selection of naughty thongs. It was an accident waiting to happen, according to the official fire investigator. The ensuing fire gutted all three stories. If it wasn't for the death of Seanie's young wife, who was sleeping in their flat on the top floor, the whole thing would have read like a Marx Brothers farce, because the report said two things acted as fire accelerants. One was a whole wall of posters of Seanie in his Golden Balls hey-day. The other was a dozen (under the counter) boxes of cheap, imported, rubber sex aids.

The coroner said Seanie's wife died from smoke inhalation. An elderly insomniac walking his incontinent Jack Russell on the empty street, said he saw Seanie make repeated attempts to get back inside to rescue her. On his third attempt he was overcome by smoke, and had to be resuscitated by the arriving fire brigade.

Barney turned to frown at me. 'Reading it won't change the facts, Annie. Seanie isn't exactly the Brain of Britain, but even he wouldn't have torched the place then started running back in to get his wife.'

'Fires are not as controllable as people think. Mutual Irish believe it got out of hand before he could stage-manage his wife's escape.'

'How come he was out in the street in the first place?' Declan asked.

'He smelled smoke? Went down to investigate?' Barney turned.

'Without waking his wife?'

'People do strange things.'

'When it suits them,' Declan said quietly.

'Ah Jaysus, Declan,' Barney protested. 'Now that's a bit filthy.'

'People sometimes do filthy things to get what they want.'

He drove in silence until we came to my gate. He frowned at the brightly lit hall. 'You got those lights on a timer, Annie?'

'Either that or her perv broke in and left them on.' Barney chuckled. 'Want us to check out the place, Annie?'

'Don't be silly. He's just a phone pest. He doesn't know where I live.'

'Take the phone off the hook, anyway,' Declan advised.

'I need the phone.'

'Keep your mobile charged.'

'He only rings the agency,' I protested.

'Take your phone off the hook, anyway,' Barney sided with Declan.

'God, you're all turning into Brian.'

'Brian?' Barney frowned, as I got out.

'Baby cop? The one who likes his morning Hobnob?'

'Don't we all,' he laughed. 'Why do you think I'm going back to the pub? I think I've pulled.'

'That lucky girl. How long did you say? Two whole minutes? Wow.' I slammed the door before he could retaliate.

His window shot open. 'Better clean out the Honda before tomorrow, Annie. Posh boy won't be happy if he sits on a half-eaten Mars bar and ruins his pretty suit.'

'Feck off, Barney.'

I was closing my bedroom blinds when I spotted

the Great Dane getting into his car, his flight bag tucked under his arm. Back on nights, was he? But he wasn't wearing his sexy pilot's uniform, and without it he looked almost ordinary. Borderline flabby. No longer the flaxen-haired god who caused such a stir when he first moved into the neighbourhood. Gerry had laughed at what he called the communal sigh of disappointment when the Great Dane's wife appeared. A year later she went back to Denmark, and he buried himself in his work. Didn't even date, according to the local grapevine.

Poor bugger. Lonely, *and* flabby. Somebody should have told him to keep wearing his pilot's uniform off duty. Shiny wings on a uniform had to be a guaranteed puller. Not that I was an expert on pulling. I'd only had one proper boyfriend before Gerry, and he wasn't up to much.

I took the phone off the hook. Then put it back again. Took it off, and climbed into bed, to snuggle low under the covers. I was reaching out to turn off the bedside lamp, when I changed my mind. Hell is waking up alone, and finding yourself in darkness. I wondered if Gerry was sleeping well. Would Sally sneak into his room for comfort? He once told me she was emotionally needy. Maybe that was my mistake, pretending I wasn't. Sod that. I was a survivor. I turned off the lamp, and was nearly asleep when, almost of its own volition, my hand sneaked out to flick it on again.

8

'So where is this Adonis now?' Fiona was so excited she loosened her grip on Calum, who took instant advantage of this momentary slip to hare across the room in his bandy-legged fashion, his training pants sliding lower and lower until they exposed a little baby-builder's crack.

'He's out in the car,' I said. 'I can't get rid of him. I keep telling him we're not joined at the hip, but he just looks at me with a sort of – puzzled expression. He does that a lot. It's very irritating.'

Fiona legged it to the nursery window. 'Oh my God, is that him checking the tyres?'

I joined her. 'That's him. He must have got tired admiring his own perfection in the mirror. What am I to do, Fiona?'

'That's between you and your conscience. I know what I'd be tempted to do, if I were you.' She gave me a *Carry On* nudge. 'Will you be working with him *every* day?'

'Until the case is sorted to my satisfaction.' I tried not to sound boastful.

'Ooooh. *Your* satisfaction? What about his?'

There was no talking to Fiona when she was in this silly *Carry On* mood. I think I almost preferred her *Gerry is perfect for you*, one. But Sizemore was riling me so much I had to confide in someone.

'All messing aside, Fiona, how would you like to be forcibly joined at the hip with a man you can't stand?'

'If he looked like that.' She peered out at Sizemore. 'I'd probably lie back and enjoy it.'

'Don't be disgusting! The last two days have been pure hell. I can't move without Sizemore, and nobody will say a word against Seanie Bolger. I'll become public enemy number one if I keep asking awkward questions about him. Barney thinks I should let the file fall down the back of a desk, but Gerry is now emailing the office every five minutes to see how the case is going, and I'm damned if I'll let him think I can't handle it.'

'Happy days, huh?'

'You don't know the half of it. Sally is now insisting on family counselling. Family counselling? Hello! You're divorced, Sally. Remember? She's actually made an appointment for her, Gerry and the two kids to see a renowned counsellor because she thinks the kids have been damaged by her two divorces. The guy she moved to America with legged it with a twelve-year-old aerobics instructer . . . well OK, a nineteen-year-old . . . and she thinks *Gerry* needs counselling? With her, of course. And he's *agreed*? He's afraid to say no to her, because she's emotionally needy. But I'm to brave the wrath of the whole bloody country by trying to prove that Ireland's favourite son is a homicidal pyromaniac?'

'Em. He's tall, isn't he?'

'Seanie?'

'Sizemore.' She was fascinated by the languid Sizemore.

'I suppose he is,' I grumbled. 'But there's definitely something iffy about him. Sandra can't find anyone who'll even admit to *knowing* him. And Sandra could dig up dirt on the Pope.'

'I don't think he's Irish.'

'The Pope?'

'Sizemore. He doesn't look Irish. Too sallow.' She peered out at him.

'Well, he's worked in the States for years. Probably got too much sun.'

'How do you know he worked . . . ?'

'Someone said. Besides, he slips up sometimes. This morning he told me to hold the *elevator*!'

'Definitely a hanging offence.'

'You know what I mean. Yesterday he asked me if I ever cleaned out the *trunk* of my car. Bloody cheek. If he didn't irritate me so much it might almost be funny. Brian said he asked him if he ever *carried heat*.'

'Heat?'

'Apparently it means being armed.'

'He sounds brilliant. He must be great craic to work with,' she chuckled.

'No he isn't!' I stiffened. 'And he's not that perfect. He has a big shaving cut this morning. Besides, I don't care where he worked before. He could have been in the bloody French Foreign Legion for all I care. All I want is to get this case sorted . . . show the lads that I can handle a really big case. So would you ever give us a cup of tea and a slice of that coffee cake I saw in the kitchen? I'm famished. Sizemore never snacks. Doesn't even stop for coffee. Weird.'

'Does he carry a gun?'

'What?'

'French investigators carry guns.'

'He's not French!'

'How do you know?' She turned.

'Because he . . . he has an Irish sense of humour.'

'I thought you couldn't stand him?' Convinced that she had caught me out in a lie, she gave me another *Carry On* nudge.

'I can't. I just said he has an Irish sense of humour.'

'Hmmm . . .' She was watching Sizemore again. 'He looks like he would carry a gun. He has a dangerous air about him. I wonder would he take a bribe? Would he be up for shooting Nonna Molino? For the right money, of course?'

'Fiona!' I gasped.

'I wouldn't want her killed. Just grazed. A little flesh wound? Well, maybe something a bit more substantial . . . because I need her hospitalised. I have to think of something to stop her flying over to check on her only grandson.' Her smile fading, she looked like she might cry. 'I told her Calum is fully potty trained.'

'Why did you say that?'

'Because she kept annoying me about it. And I thought by the time she saw him he would be. Now she says she wants to come here before the weather gets cold. You'd think we lived in bloody Iceland, to hear her talk. But she's bound to notice that Calum will pee anywhere but in a bloody pot. According to her, all Italian children are fully trained before they're two.'

Fiona was hissing in disbelief at this, when she realised that Calum had disappeared.

We darted out to the landing. No sign of him. We split up to search the bathrooms and we met up again on the landing. Fiona checked the safety gate at the top of the stairs.

'The bedrooms!' she said. 'Calum? Where are you Calum?'

'Caaalum?'

'You haven't told me what you think of Gerry extending his stay in Arizona?' I said as we checked behind the curtains of her fourth palatial bedroom.

'*You* said I wasn't to mention him!' She looked in the wardrobe.

'And you always do what I tell you?' I knelt to peer under a four-poster bed that could comfortably fit six, if they were close friends. 'Anyway, the news about David is excellent.'

'I know.' She checked out the en suite bathroom. 'Gerry emailed me.'

Before I could react there was a scream from across the landing. We raced out, hearts pounding. But Calum was safe and sound. And happy. And stark naked as he paddled in a steaming little pool of pee.

'Look, Fona.' He pointed jubilantly at the widening pool.

'Oh Calum!' She covered her eyes in horror.

'Ah don't be mean, Fiona. I like the way he calls you Fona. It's cute.'

'Oh bugger off, Annie!'

'Buggeroff.' Calum splashed happily.

'He is *nearly* trained.' Fiona's voice was a desperate squeak. 'Aren't you Calum?'

'Buggeroff,' he chortled.

'Nearly trained? Does that mean he stands *near* the potty and pees on the floor?'

'Ah fu—' She caught herself in time, smiled at Calum and said politely, 'Boys are notoriously hard to train; everyone knows that.'

Well, that was me fecked then. I'd been trying to train Sizemore for two whole days. Trying to get him to adapt to my investigative methods.

'This is Ireland,' I told him repeatedly. 'In Ireland you don't just appear on someone's doorstep and start firing questions at them. You inveigle your way into their house, have a cup of tea, or two, and a sit down, ask how they are faring with the new bin charges, or the rising fuel costs, and only then do you mention the actual case. That's how it works here.'

Fiona watched me as I recalled his reaction.

'You can drop that miserable look, Annie. You're not getting any sympathy from me. You want me to feel sorry for you because you're forced to spend all day with a gorgeous man. Look at me for feck's sake.' She glanced nervously at Calum, who was pulling the head off his Postman Pat doll and trying to eat it. 'I spend my days mopping up pee. What happened to my dreams?'

'Your dreams? All you ever wanted was to marry a filthy-rich man, have great sex, and lie around eating walnut whirls all day. You got two out of three!'

'Oh, right.' She tossed back her long glossy hair. 'But what you don't realise is that I practically have to make an appointment to see Pino these days. His excuse for working eighteen-hour days is that he only does it for me and Calum. So we can have everything we want. What we want is to see more of him. Yesterday in the park, Calum called a complete stranger Daddy.'

'Come on, that's funny.'

'His wife didn't think so!'

I tried to distract her. 'Count your blessings, Fiona, you have a magnificent home.'

'Yes, but mopping up pee is mopping up pee, no matter where you're doing it. I'm beginning to think I'd be better off with less money, and a simpler lifestyle.'

I pretended to reel backwards with shock.

'Oh give over, Annie! I could live in the country. In some pretty little village, maybe. Calum could go to the local school, and I'd join the Irish Countrywomen's Association, and learn to knit, and do wildflower arranging. Take up hill walking.'

'Hill walking?' I stared at her spike-heeled Jimmy Choos. The longest distance Fiona walks is from her door to her car. Well, maybe ten yards plus in the park, on an exceptionally sunny day. Watching her awkwardly wheeling Calum's pushchair I once tried to talk her into buying a pair of sensible flats. She reacted as if I was recommending a Zimmer frame.

'Oh yes.' She went all dreamy eyed now. 'I could

get a couple of dogs and walk them every day. Better for my health than driving that massive gas guzzler Pino bought me.'

'You don't even like dogs,' I said, omitting to mention that the gas guzzler was her choice.

'I could get to like them, while I was walking them!' she insisted. 'And . . . you could come and visit every weekend. Stay over in our little flower-filled guest room. Meet my ICA guild for herbal tea in the village tearooms.'

She was beginning to scare me. I hadn't been this unnerved since she told me two years ago that she was planning to give birth in her living room, with all her friends in attendance.

'Have you discussed this rural idyll with Pino?'

'Discussed it with him? I've just told you I don't even get to *see* him any more. He's just a blur these days. He runs in, changes his clothes, fires kisses in all directions and runs out again. Always running. Always busy. Work, work, work. If it's not in the restaurant, it's in that new premises he's bought. He's project-managing all the refurbishing, since his foreman went backpacking in New Guinea. And in case he'd be in danger of having any free time, he signed up for another TV food show.'

I was shocked into silence.

'I don't know who he is any more, Annie. It's like sleeping with a stranger.'

'That used to be your fantasy, remember.' I tried to lighten the mood. 'You'd see a total stranger on a plane? Your eyes would meet across the drinks trolley, and boom . . . the mile high club. Remember that time you tried to gatecrash first class?'

She looked so sad, I wanted to bite my tongue off. This was my funny, upbeat friend. The woman who tried everything, including a herbal cure for chlamydia. It frightened me to see her standing there looking sadder than Joan Evans, a friend of ours whose husband left her after ten happy years, for their child's dance teacher. A man.

'At least you . . . at least you're not Joan Evans,' I tried again.

She shot me a poisonous look.

'You have no money problems,' I persisted.

'So money is the answer to everything?' She managed a cryptic little smile.

'You always said it was.'

'Yes. When I was twelve. Or maybe thirteen.'

Actually it was always. But this wasn't the time to remind her of that, because Calum was now screaming as if he was being disembowelled.

We practically knocked each other down in our hurry to reach him. And there he was in the next room, playing happily. A miraculous recovery, or an Oscar-winning performance?

He danced around until Fiona tried to pull on his training pants, which he had abandoned in the middle of the room. She barely touched him when he started screeching again, while struggling and kicking like a little mule.

'Ah, shag it.' She threw the training pants on the floor.

'Shagit.' Calum's recovery was instantaneous. He

ran around chortling happily, only stopping to admire the little trail of drops he was leaving behind him.

'You don't know how lucky you are, Annie.' Fiona slumped against the bed in defeat. 'You and Gerry working together, having adult conversations all day. Able to exchange ideas about the job.'

'Not while he's in bloody America, we can't.'

She wasn't listening. She was mopping up pee again. This time with Calum's help. He took her hand gently, and pointed out the bits she missed.

'Dere Fona!' He pointed to a brand new pool.

'Oh Jesus, Calum.'

'Jesuscalum.' He shook his head in disgust.

'Ah for . . . sake Calum.' She made a dart at him, but he legged it out to the landing like a three-minute miler.

'The bathroom, Calum, pleeeease, there's Mummy's best boy. Your blue potty is in the bathroom, darling. If you use your blue potty Mummy will take you to the paaaark. We'll feed the ducks together. Whoooo loves feeding the duckies?'

Obviously not Calum. At least not while he was in this mood. He streaked into Fiona's bedroom, the only room in the house that was carpeted in white wool. My harlot carpet, she called it fondly.

'Jesus, Calum if you piss on that carpet I'll . . .'

'Piss!' he chuckled.

'I'm off, Fiona.' I headed downstairs. 'This probably wasn't the best time to call.'

Silence. Pleased that they had settled their differences, I opened the front door. I was closing it when I heard an outburst of swearing that would make a sailor blush.

I hoped it was Fiona. And that Calum was well out of earshot, because he has a memory like an elephant. Once he finds a word that will shock, he uses it repeatedly. If he tried that in front of his Italian Nonna she might call in an exorcist. For Fiona.

I hurried out to the car.

'Want me to drive?' Sizemore looked hopeful.

'No thanks!' I jumped in and had the car in gear before he could click on his seatbelt.

Irritated by his closeness in the little car, I took the corner on two wheels. For someone so slim he took up an inordinate amount of space. We always seemed to be brushing against each other. And his legs were endless. All over the place, no matter which way I looked. And whenever he moved I got a slight whiff of Issey Miyake cologne, possibly the most expensive, if not the sexiest, cologne on earth.

Gerry only ever smelled of cigarette smoke. That Issey Miyake was doing funny things to me. Making me light headed.

I opened the car windows, and floored the throttle, so the Honda surged forward.

Except for one quick glance at me, Sizemore didn't react. Didn't say a single word. Didn't even gasp in horror, which was the most common male response to my driving.

I sneaked a sideways look at him. With his Gucci

shades and lightweight suit he couldn't possibly have looked any cooler. Except if he was dead. He sat there, his endless legs stretching out, his expression one of complete and utter calm. Smug bastard. Speeding off at a busy roundabout, I chanced another quick look. This time I was happy to see a fine film of nervous sweat building up above his chiselled top lip.

I hit the throttle harder.

His hand curled around the edge of his seat, the knuckles showing Daz white.

Still not a word of protest, and as we were now being sucked into increasingly busy lanes of traffic, I had no choice but to drop my speed.

We were nearing the agency before he spoke.

'Have you ever consider motorsport?' he asked, his eyes still on the road.

'What exactly would that entail?' I played dumb.

'Pretty much what you seem to do on a regular basis.'

Bingo! I *had* managed to unnerve him. So he wasn't as cool as he appeared. But he wasn't going to embarrass me. I was the lead PI here. I was in charge. I could embarrass him, but not vice versa.

My phone rang. Seeing the agency number flash up, I put it on speakerphone.

'Annie McHugh here.' I even sounded like a lead PI.

'Annie?' Sandra's shrill voice filled the car. 'Where have you been? Mutual Irish have been looking for you. Hope you haven't been off dropping the hand on sexy Sizemore. Naughty, naughty. Ha, ha.' She giggled. 'Anyway keep your phone switched on and I'll—'

I cut her off mid-flow and, looking intently ahead, I drove straight through an amber — well, maybe it was on the cusp of red — light.

9

I brought the Honda to a sudden stop outside the agency, checked my watch, and told Sizemore to take a lunch break. 'It's one o'clock. I'll meet you back here in an hour.'

'Where do you lunch?' He unbuckled his seatbelt, and stretched one arm along the back of my seat.

'Me?' I edged slightly forward, so we wouldn't touch. 'Sorry. I'm . . . meeting someone.'

'I wasn't asking you to lunch.' He pocketed his fancy shades. 'But given those phone calls you've been receiving, I think I should know where you'll be for the next hour or so.'

'Phone calls?' I was about to bluff, when I saw his eyes. Feck. Why was everyone always talking about those stupid phone calls? I wasn't frightened by them. By their very nature anonymous calls only came from complete cowards. Some right wuss.

'We are working together, Annie.' Sizemore didn't sound proud of this. 'So if someone takes you out while I'm . . . I could have serious questions to answer.'

'If someone takes me out?' I gawked.

'Kills you,' he said calmly.

My chest tightened. 'Y . . . you don't seriously think . . . ?'

'I would never underestimate . . .'

'Yes, but I . . . I don't think . . .' I suddenly spotted a tiny twitch at the corner of his mouth.

The bastard was winding me up. Well, two could play at that game.

'Don't worry, Sizemore, I'll be well protected for the next hour. I'm lunching with a . . .' Would he believe an SAS troop? '. . . a . . . top undercover Garda.'

'Where?' He took out a pen.

'W . . . where?'

'Yes. I need to know where you'll be.' Pen raised, he waited.

'Er . . .' Glancing around for inspiration, I spotted the glass-roofed Irish Financial Services Centre. 'The IFSC,' I said.

'You're lunching at the Irish Financial Services Centre?'

'Yes. There's a good . . . er great pub over there. Practically a superpub. Terrific food. Nice carvery. Drink is . . . well you know the price of drink in Ireland. Ha, ha. Second mortgage time. Ha, ha.'

I waited for him to get out. I knew I was babbling, but I got so caught up in my story, I almost believed it. Could actually picture myself sharing a table with a shaven-headed undercover cop. See him leaning across to whisper in my ear, his gun bulging under his badly-cut suit.

Sizemore didn't move. Just sat there looking over at the IFSC.

'Phelim likes it there,' I said quickly.

'Phelim?'

'My undercover . . . friend . . . mate . . . Garda.'

'He likes being surrounded by bankers? Listening to talk about options and swaps and futures and—' He actually laughed.

'I didn't say he *likes* it . . . well maybe I did, but what I meant was he eats there because it's . . . handy for him. His office is . . .' I was running out of ideas.

'His office is . . . ?' Sizemore prompted.

'I'm not going to give *you* that information. Phelim's work is . . . top secret.'

'Top secret?' I could tell he was impressed.

'Yes. He calls it covert. It means deep undercover!'

'Deep undercover?'

'You wouldn't understand! You're just an insurance investigator.'

'True. Any chance I could meet this . . . Phelim? Sounds exciting . . . his work I mean.'

He waited.

Jesus Christ. What had I got myself into? I had just made up a whole non-existent person to lunch with, even gave him an exciting career, because, for some reason, Sizemore got right under my skin. Somehow managed to rattle me like no one else could.

'Can you tell me the name of the pub?'

'No!' I snapped. 'That's . . .'

'Top secret as well. I understand.' He scribbled something on a scrap of paper. 'I'll be in that café down the street. The Café Naturalle? I'm told their wholewheat pastas are world class. Pasta Ragu fit for the gods. Here, take this.' He put the slip of paper in my hand.

'What is it?' I looked at the scribbled number.

'My mobile number.'

'What am I supposed to do with it?'

'Memorise it. Then eat the paper.' He put on his posh shades, smiled and was gone.

The wind from the bay practically scalping me, I hurried along the Liffey Walk to the mini skyscraper that was the IFSC. And with every windblown step I hated Sizemore more. I hadn't eaten breakfast this morning, because I was running late. And with bloody health-conscious Sizemore sitting less than three feet away and watching my every move, I had barely touched my morning muffin. I was now utterly famished, and would have killed to be sitting in the Café Naturalle, eating the wholewheat pasta that only Mario Lauro, their young Sicilian chef, could make.

Sizemore had not only ruined my morning, he had managed to spoil my hopes of lunching like a queen in the café I'd been lunching in for years. Bastard. I wished I *were* meeting a tough undercover Garda. Someone who could sucker punch Sizemore for me.

Pasta Ragu, fit for the gods? He even pronounced it properly. Who did he think he was, anyway? Rick Stein? Why couldn't he eat burger and chips, like any normal investigator?

Sandra obviously told him about the café. She couldn't keep her mouth shut around an attractive man. Not that Sizemore was especially attractive. He was handsome, there was no denying that, but as my adoptive mother said when I began swooning over my very first boss – who turned out to be a cold-hearted tyrant and seducer of teenage girls – handsome is as handsome does.

Something else was worrying me now. After seeing the underhand way he forced me to bypass my favourite eatery, I had a feeling he wouldn't be beyond sneaking out to check out my fictitious undercover cop.

I was too hungry to care now. Besides, I could always say my fictitious cop had been called away to deal with a . . . a student uprising . . . a rebellion . . . Or he could be having an illegal smoke in the Jacks. That's what normal men did. They didn't boast that they loved Pasta Ragu, or go around smelling of Issey Miyake.

The food in the pub was OK. Nothing like the wholewheat pastas in the café, where all the staff greeted me by name. The pub barman insisted on calling me Miss, and treating me like his sixth-form gym teacher. I told myself there were worse things in life than being called Miss by a bat-eared eighteen-year-old, while being hemmed in on all sides by suits, dodgy corporate haircuts and hearing non-stop discussions about financial spreadsheets.

Forty minutes later I opened the door of my office to see Sizemore sitting at *my* computer, his hands flying over the keyboard.

'What the hell are you doing?'

He was on his feet. Apologising profusely. Waving his hands about without looking remotely silly.

Possibly because he has ridiculously perfect hands, with slim fingers, and skin tones which, if not exactly olive, were nowhere near regulation Irish blue-white.

'Just checking something.' He moved to shut it down.

'Don't do that. I want to see what you were *checking*.'

I sat down, and touched the mouse. My special database flashed on screen. The one nobody in the agency ever mentioned, except when they ran out of something to joke about.

'Sorry,' Sizemore apologised again. 'I got back early and . . . I shouldn't have . . .'

'What were you looking for?'

'I thought I might find someone who had a . . . a grudge against you?' He shifted uneasily.

My smile came unbidden. 'You mean apart from people who have been forced to work with me?'

He didn't reply, just leaned across to indicate a number on the screen. 'Your database has quite a number of disgruntled men on it.'

'Disgruntled?' I bristled.

'Men who might possibly harbour a grudge.' He shrugged. 'I don't know which of these cases you've worked on personally, this list covers the whole agency doesn't it? But . . .'

'Yes?' I folded my arms.

'I don't doubt that you've already scrutinised the files, but sometimes a fresh eye can . . .'

'Can what?' I tried to hide my growing interest.

He backed off, as if he thought I might bite, then

saw my expression. 'Want me to go on?' he asked eagerly.

'Why not?' I tried to sound bored, but the idea of someone showing more than a passing interest in my database was practically exciting. Not to mention flattering. Sizemore assumed I had been such a thorn in the side of some lawbreaker that they had begun a vendetta against me? I assumed I'd been chosen at random by a lazy-arsed perv. Someone who just started at the As. If my name was Zara, I'd probably never have heard from him. He'd have been in the clink before he got midway through the alphabet.

'I found a possible suspect.' Sizemore looked pleased. 'One Bullet Nugent?'

'Wrong,' I tried not to sound smug. 'One Bullet Nugent is in Portlaoise Prison. Still has three more years to serve.'

'Oh.' Sizemore leaned against my shoulder in disappointment. 'I . . . I see that he was picked up for wife-battering. Broke her jaw in two places?'

'Armed robbery.'

'What?'

'He isn't doing time for wife-battering. He just got a slap on the wrist for that,' I hissed.

'A slap on the wrist?' Sizemore seemed equally peeved.

'I'll show you.'

I brought up a line of horror pictures that left Sizemore gasping.

'I took these photos of her. Gave copies to the Gards. They tried their best, but the judge deemed it a *domestic*. The Gards did finally get him. For armed robbery. He shot a postmaster in the leg. One bullet.'

'Let's go through the others again.' Sizemore slid down beside me until we were practically sharing my chair. 'Start at the beginning . . .'

We were hunched together discussing the possibilities of another social misfit being angry enough to be a serious threat to me, when Barney appeared looking like one half of The Blues Brothers.

He pulled off his dark glasses. 'What's going on here?' he growled.

Sizemore stood up. 'We're going through Annie's database.'

'You don't say?' Barney's eyes were narrow slits.

'What are you doing here?' I was peeved at the interruption. My pervy calls were beginning to unnerve me a bit. I wasn't exactly scared, but I'd be happy to have them sorted, given that Gerry's stay in Arizona appeared to be open ended.

'This stupid wire hasn't been working all morning.' Barney tugged at his hidden body mike, yelping in pain when several chest hairs came away with it. 'I didn't know. And the cops couldn't contact me, so I spent the morning working my ass off. Trying my damnedest to get the office staff to talk about dirty practices, and not a word of it was getting through. Then we got a bomb threat. Whole staff had to evacuate. I legged it to a pub and rang Bailey. He tells me my feckin' wire isn't working. Says I'm to come here for a meet. Make like I'm heading for Dreamland Interiors.'

'I thought they had an undercover Garda van in the street?'

'They did. Gang of kids from the flats sussed it. Started pegging bricks at it. Jaysus.' He checked his watch.

'Your contact is coming here?' Sizemore was surprised.

'Not here. Dreamland. He'll make like a customer. We'll meet in the Jacks. He'll fix my wire, and I'll leg it back to McGill's, flashing a bundle of design catalogues, just in case.' He sighed. 'Feel like a fuckin' bender.'

'What about your contact?' Sizemore smiled. 'Will he have to buy silk wall hangings?'

Barney shot him a murderous look. 'He'll slip away later.'

'With a bundle of design catalogues under *his* arm?' Sizemore started to laugh.

Barney made a threatening gesture.

'Aw, come on, Barney.' Sizemore held up both hands in surrender. 'It does sound a bit Keystone Kops . . . ish? Doesn't it?'

Barney looked as if he wanted to kill him.

'There's nothing funny about a bomb threat,' I defended him. 'Barney could be putting his life on the line working in McGill's. You may not realise it, Sizemore, but there are still ex-paramilitaries in Ireland who wouldn't think twice about bombing a garage if the owner was obstructing their . . . what's wrong Barney?'

Barney squirmed. 'It was DI Bailey who rang in the bomb threat.'

This was too much for Sizemore. He collapsed against the desk laughing so hard I thought he'd choke.

Convinced that Barney would box him, I jumped in between them.

'Are we still on for that new steakhouse tonight, Barney?' I asked.

'Yeah,' he said, his face tight.

'Looking forward to it?' I smiled.

'Sure.' He relaxed a little. 'Declan suggested the Chinese again, but I've gone right off Chinese. Five minutes after eating Yung Chow Fried rice I'm starving again. Who in the name of Christ could live on Chinese food?'

'One and a half billion Chinese?' Sizemore said.

If Barney had a gun there would have been a killing.

'He was practically sitting on your lap when I walked in.' Barney stopped wolfing his steak long enough to give me the dirtiest look.

'He was checking my database, you idiot.'

'And to do that, he had to sit on your lap? Nice job if you can get it, huh?'

Barney had been bad-mouthing Sizemore since we got here. Apart from his fear that Sizemore was stealing his thunder, he was in rotten form anyway because the Dirty McGill case was going very badly. There didn't appear to be any snitches at McGill's. Plus Barney had to deal with account books all day.

I never once said I told you so.

Barney was an action man. He'd prefer it if McGill

kneed him in the groin twice daily rather than ask him about this week's profit and loss.

Declan kept his head down. Monosyllabic as ever, it was all he could do to order his food, before clamming up again. Then I caught him watching me.

'Oh not you too, Declan! What *is* the problem?'

'Posh boy,' Barney said through a mouthful of chips.

'What is this weird male thing you all seem to have? A strange man steps into what you guys consider to be your territory, and suddenly you all become Raging Bulls?'

'Ah ha! So you admit he's strange?' Barney pounced.

'He's an investigator, Barney! Bound to be strange.' I laughed.

'None of the investigators I know hide behind a cloak of secrecy. I spent two hours trying to get information on our Posh Boy. Not a dickey bird. It's as if he didn't exist before he walked into McHugh Dunning.'

I sat back in disgust. 'You've been checking on him?'

'I just asked a few questions. No harm in that.'

'Not if you're his employer, which we are *not*. He works for Mutual Irish, remember? The second I get a result on this case he'll be gone, and I doubt we'll ever see him again.'

'Jaysus, I hope not.'

'Why are you so set against him?'

'Just don't like him.' Barney examined his plate.

'Barney thinks he's a pouf,' Declan said.

'I never said that.'

'You did.'

'I said he dresses like a pouf.'

'What's it to you, anyway?' I tried not to laugh.

'What's it to me? Oh nothing much. I'll just have to sit in The Randy Goat and listen to Toss Nolan and his crowd of wankers slagging us off. I get enough hassle from them as it is without them thinking we're working with poufs.'

'Ah, poor Barney.' I patted his back. 'Afwaid all the udder boys in the gang will give you a wedgie?'

Declan smiled, but Barney glowered at me. 'They're a pack of wankers and you know it, Annie.'

'Well, you can tell them for me that Sizemore isn't gay.'

His head shot up. 'How do you know?'

I gave him a cheeky wink. 'Women know.'

'He's got gay hair!' Barney hated to lose.

'Eat your steak, Barney, or next time we will go for a Chinese,' I said. 'And maybe if you stopped calling gay guys poufs, Toss Nolan's gang would ease off on us.'

'Why?' He stared. 'Are some of them poufs?'

'For feck's sake, Barney!'

'What did I say?' he puzzled.

'You're flogging a dead horse there, Annie.' Declan drank his soda water.

'Hey, did you hear the one about the dead pouf?' Barney chuckled.

'No! And I don't want to.'

I left them to it. Barney would never be politically

correct anyway. And the truth was he didn't care if anyone was gay, as long as they didn't interfere with his life.

Driving home I did mull over what Barney had said about Sizemore. Was it possible? He did move beautifully. But so did every top soccer player in the world. His hands looked artistic. I ran everything about him through my head, like a movie. The way he spoke, walked, even laughed. His mouth. The way his upper lip curved and . . . Enough. It was becoming too distracting. And what did it matter to me where his inclinations lay anyway? I just worked with him. And even that was only a temporary situation. After we closed the case I'd never see him again.

10

After a restless night, I set out for the agency determined to speed things up on the Bolger case. It was ridiculously early, but I didn't care, I needed to get things moving. I was almost there when I spotted the light in reception. Nobody would be in this early? Heart pounding, I pushed open the door.

'Morning, Annie.' Sandra was standing at the desk, arranging a bunch of peony roses in a tall vase.

'God, you gave me a fright.' I slumped.

'What? Oh you didn't think your perv would . . . ?'

'No! I just . . . I didn't expect anyone else to be here this early. What's going on?'

'Jimmy gave me a lift. And a huge bouquet of these roses, so I brought some in for . . .' She paused.

'Looks like a bribe to me.'

'I'm not trying to bribe anyone.' Her face turned tomato red.

'No, I didn't mean you. I meant Jimmy . . . I . . . forget it.' I legged it to the lift.

'Hold on. I'm coming up.' She ran after me, clutching the heavy vase awkwardly.

We stood side by side in the lift, without exchanging a word. I did chance a wary little smile. *What the hell was she up to?*

She followed me into my office. 'The flowers are for you, Annie.' She plonked the vase on the desk. 'And they're not a bribe.'

Shit. I'd have to learn to be more sensitive where Sandra was concerned. For a start, she never came in early. I should have known things were a bit rocky on the home front when she got here before eight. And Jimmy was suddenly giving her bouquets of flowers? And lifts to work? Better walk on eggshells this morning, and keep the conversation light. Impersonal.

'Thanks so much, Sandra.' I gave her a quick smile. 'Any progress on Declan's Red Setter case?'

'Not so far.' She turned away.

Damn. I was sure the Red Setter case would be up for discussion. After all, it came from Naomi. And in Sandra's eyes Naomi was practically Kate Moss. Second only to the late great Princess Diana. Naomi's uncle had died suddenly, leaving his three adored dogs homeless. But only temporarily, because he willed his valuable home to which-ever one of his estranged children would move in permanently to take care of the prizewinning dogs. Only snag was the house was a trillion miles from the hubbub of Dublin where his three sons all had major careers. A doctor. A dentist. And an accountant. The old man had stipulated that the dog adopter must live full time in the big rambling house. A part-time owner was unacceptable. Plus they must allow the dogs to roam the house for the rest of their natural lives. And naturally a family feud ensued. It simmered for a while until it became open warfare, with one bitter family member threatening to kill the dogs rather than let his younger brother have them. And more importantly, the valuable house.

Naomi had asked if we could find a safe place for the dogs, until the dispute was sorted. Declan volunteered to collect the dogs and take them to the safety of a boarding kennels, tucked away in the Wicklow Mountains.

'Declan and animals.' I smiled at Sandra.

'Huh,' she grunted.

I turned to my computer. I wanted to get an early start before Sizemore arrived in and rattled me. At my door, Sandra paused.

'Er, Annie . . . would this be a bad time for me to ask for a couple of days off?'

'What?' I looked up.

'I mean I know Gerry is away and all but . . . ?'

'It's not exactly a good time.' I frowned. 'Couldn't you wait?'

She squirmed. 'I . . . er . . . I can't wait. It . . . might be too late. I need this Monday and Tuesday off.'

'What for?' I checked my watch. No sign of Sizemore yet. Maybe he'd had enough of us. Maybe he thought *we* were the Keystone Kops and had run back to the relative sanity of New York, or Iraq. Where had he worked in the States, anyway? Somebody must know.

'I'm about to ovulate,' Sandra said.

'You're . . . ?' I frowned.

'It means produce an egg.'

'I know what it means.' I turned. 'I didn't know you were trying to conceive. Anyway, you don't need two days off for that.'

'My gynaecologist says I do.' Her face was now so red it was threatening to blister, and her eyes were looking everywhere but at me. 'He said that . . . afterwards . . . I'd have a better chance if I lie in bed with my bum raised. We've been trying for three months.'

'To raise your bum?'

She gave a little giggle. 'I knew you'd laugh. But the gynaecologist says becoming pregnant is a *very* serious business. He says it will change our lives.'

'Precisely. That's why I'm surprised. I thought you and Jimmy were happy as you are.'

'We are happy. But . . . well, everyone wants a baby. Don't they?' She fiddled with the flowers that were now threatening to shed some of their huge petals. When she forced one into a more upright position all its petals fell off.

'Not everyone.' I snapped my desk diary closed. Jimmy must have got the flowers cheap.

'I think they do. Deep down,' she insisted.

'Talk to me later.' I turned back to my computer screen bringing up a list of people I wanted to speak to about the Bolgers' marriage. So far I was getting nowhere fast. My biggest fear now wasn't that Gerry might delay his return even further. It was that he might arrive home and find I hadn't got anywhere with the Bolger case.

Thirty minutes later Sandra was back. This time with a laden tray, and an ear-to-ear smile. She was clearly determined to get her two days off. My big concern was that this sudden craving for a baby was just another passing phase. She had worked for Gerry since leaving school, and I'd lost count of all the mad phases I had seen her through. From blonde Mohican rebel with studded Dr Martens, to her blue tattoo phase, and on into the three-bellybutton-ring phase, which left her with a serious infection and frightened the wits out of Gerry.

Was this just another passing phase? If so the problem here wasn't just that it might disappear as quickly as the others, but that it could leave her with serious fallout. For roughly eighteen years?

Thing was, Sandra knew how to twist me around her little finger. Her opening salvo always began with giving me piping hot coffee, and a mountain of chocolate biscuits, and sometimes a rake of funny stories about her and her cheeky girlfriends. This time only the stories were different. All about her twitchy-eyed gynaecologist. After five minutes of side-splitting laughter I could feel myself starting to weaken.

Then she took a wrong turn.

'Does Gerry's ex never sleep?' She perched on the edge of my desk, to munch one of the biscuits she had brought me. 'I mean she has two kids

105

and yet she called him so many times before he flew over there I reckon she must stay awake all night. I worked out the time difference between here and Arizona, and even when she was only calling him twice a day I wondered when she slept.'

'Twice a day?' I frowned. 'She was ringing him twice a day?'

'Sometimes three times.' She became eager. Being first with the news is a full-time hobby of Sandra's. 'It's a bit peculiar, isn't it, to be ringing your ex-husband three or four times a day.'

'I thought you said twice?'

'That's on average. I worked it out. If you add up the actual amount of calls, and divide that number by . . .'

She babbled on, explaining to the last decimal how she worked out a mean average of all Sally's calls to Gerry. Calls I knew nothing about. And each time she mentioned a specific number my chest went into spasm. 'Every day on the dot . . . come hell or high water . . . at eleven fifteen . . . well sometimes a bit later . . . but mostly—'

'Three times a day?' My chest felt like it was caught in a vice. And someone was tightening it horribly.

'Twice on average.' She held up two fingers. 'The only reason I began to keep count is because I take my temperature three times a day. Dr Feely recommends taking it once. But I like to check it three times, just to be sure. Dr Feely says taking your temperature is the best way to keep track of your cycle. He says it's the most accurate way to predict ovulation. See the way it works is, your temperature begins to rise as you round the cusp of the middle of . . .'

She meandered on into a long gynaecological road map. But I had stopped listening. Gerry had been getting three calls a day from Sally? Well, two on average. And I hadn't known a damn thing about them.

Sandra rabbited on and on. 'See, our plan is that I wait until my temperature is about to peak, then I call Jimmy, tell him to haul his arse over here and . . .'

'And?' I had completely lost track, all I could think of was Gerry and Sally sharing all those long-distance, yet intimate, calls that I knew nothing about.

'So is that OK, Annie? Jimmy will rush here to collect me. In the van.' Sandra waited.

'The . . . van?'

'Save me getting the bus. We'll dash home and—'

'Wait a minute . . . hold on . . . why would you be dashing home?' I clutched my forehead.

She giggled. 'Well, you don't expect us to do it here?'

'Do what? What are you talking about?'

She rolled her eyes heavenward. 'Conception, of course! What else have we been talking about for the last fifteen minutes?'

'For feck's sake, Sandra, I have a trillion things on my mind. I hardly slept last night, I come in early to get some work done and you barge in and start rabbiting on about you and Jimmy shagging each other in the back of a van?'

She slid off the desk as if she'd been struck.

'Sandra? I . . . I'm sorry.' I jumped up. 'I didn't mean . . .'

She was gone. Slamming the door so hard the building next door shook.

Shit. She'd sulk for the day now. Maybe for a week. Leave the phones unanswered. Ignore incoming faxes. Spend hours in the loo. Damn Sally, anyway. The woman was living half a world away and could still wreck my life.

Poor Sandra. All she wanted was to share her baby plans with me. Now I'd have to go down to reception and grovel. Do my damnedest to appease her.

The phone cut through my gloom.

Sandra's voice was icy. 'I have a Mr Philip Sorensen on the line.'

Christ. Sorensen was the big-mouth brother who was throwing his weight around with his feuding family about the orphaned dogs. Not that he had much weight to throw. Skinny as a dried-up cadaver, and just as repellent, he tried to disguise his short-comings by shouting. For days now he'd been trying to intimidate his whole family by threatening to shoot the disputed dogs.

'Did he say what he wants?'

'No.' Her tone practically iced up the phone line. 'Ask him.'

'He won't speak to anyone but you.'

'Tell him . . . tell him I'm out.'

'But I already said you were in . . .'

'I'm out!'

She hung up.

I crept down to reception. Nothing for it but to appease Sandra. Eating humble pie should do it. That was something I'd had lots of practice at. So much experience I could probably put it on my CV, as a major life skill.

Sandra was busy at her computer. Head bent, fingers flying, she was a picture of a workaholic employee.

I cleared my throat noisily.

No response.

I tried a deep cough, making it sound almost tubercular. Nothing. I leaned across the desk deliberately knocking against the selection of nail varnishes Sandra liked to display in a colourful, symmetrical curve.

Her response was immediate. Typing forgotten, she grabbed the bottles, and threw them into a drawer behind the desk, which was where they belonged anyway, according to Gerry's rules.

She returned to her typing, her fingers a dizzying blur.

'How do you do that?' I puzzled. 'It takes me ages to type a single letter.'

A warm pink tide crept up her neck.

'And without chipping those *gorgeous* nails?'

'I went to night classes.' She brushed back a non-existent wisp of hair, to give me a closer view of her perfect nails.

'Don't be mad at me, Sandra. I'm sorry if I was curt earlier. I didn't mean to be.' I leaned across the desk, and blocked her keyboard with my broken-nailed hand. 'I couldn't get through a single day here without your support. I'd kill myself if I had to deal with these bloody macho detectives without you.'

Seeing her mouth twitch, I went for the big one. 'I miss Gerry.'

'Oh, why didn't you say?' She patted my arm. 'It must be hell for you, left all alone while he's in Arizona with his wife and family.'

'His *ex*-wife.'

'Yeah, but still . . . when Jimmy goes to the Chelsea Flower Show I'm suicidal!'

'Oh I don't feel sui—'

'Some nights I think I'll just throw myself in the river. Then I remember you telling me about that girl they pulled out of the bay, and how awful she looked. I mean, you wouldn't want people gawking at you like that. Seeing you looking like a drowned rat. That's probably why women use pills when they kill themselves. Much tidier. No mess. You could put on all your make-up first, even have your hair done. A few streaks!'

'I've never felt suicidal, Sandra.'

'Me neither. I'm just saying that if someone *was* they should make sure not to be caught out looking like shite.'

The phone rang.

'No woman wants to be found—'

'Will you get that, Sandra?' I pointed to the phone.

She finally picked it up. 'McHugh Dunning Detective Agency. May I help you?' She waited, frowning in puzzlement. 'Hello? Hello? Who is this? Hello?'

I took the receiver. 'Who is this?'

Sandra wrestled it back from me. 'It's him again. I know it. Listen, you filthy prick, I have a garden hoe here, and if you ring again, I'll find you and ram it up your hole. Oh.' The colour drained from her face. 'Yes. This *is* the Dunning Agency . . . but I . . . hello? . . . hello?'

Shamefaced, she lowered the receiver. 'They hung up.'

'It wasn't my perv, then?' I stared at her bloodless face.

She shook her head.

Sizemore came in, looking anything but his usual self, with his hair standing on end, and his eyes still swollen with sleep. He dropped his briefcase at my feet.

Sandra caught a piece of her shiny hair, and began chewing it.

'Who was it, Sandra?' I asked.

She pulled a second lock of hair into her mouth, and chewed both of them simultaneously, while eying Sizemore nervously.

'Don't mind him! Tell me.'

'I think it . . . it might have been . . . a . . . a Mr Bennett from Mutual Irish?'

Sizemore practically lifted me aside. 'Bennett from Mutual Irish? He's one of our directors. What did he want?'

Sandra eyed me nervously. 'I'm not sure . . .'

Sizemore glowered threateningly at her.

'Well, you see, we thought . . . I thought it was Annie's pervert, so I said . . .' Her eyes welled up.

'It's OK, Sandra.' I tried to silence her, but nothing can stop Sandra when she starts.

'See, Brian said to be more aggressive when Annie's perv rings. To curse and swear at him. To be even nastier than he is . . .'

Sizemore's frown was now full blown. 'But that was a director of Mutual Irish on the line?'

'I didn't know that . . . at first.'

'What did you say to him, Sandra?'

'I told him I'd ram a hoe up his . . .' The rest was an inaudible mumble.

'That you'd *what*?'

'Ram a hoe up his . . . you know.' She started to cry.

'Stop bullying her,' I yelled at Sizemore. 'She made a genuine mistake.'

'Christ. You have no idea how much they dislike me in Mutual Irish.'

'I'm not surprised if this is how you treat members of staff.' I hugged the now sobbing Sandra.

'Hang on. What did I do here?'

'What did you do? Look at the state of Sandra.'

'I simply asked what she said to Bennett.'

At the mention of Bennett, Sandra cried harder. And louder.

'OK, OK.' Sizemore raised a hand to placate her. 'I'll . . . I'll speak to Bennett. I'll . . . try to sort it.'

'It's the least you can do.' I gave Sandra a tissue. 'Here, Sandie, blow.'

En route to the car Sizemore's expression was so ferocious that a couple of surly street thugs stepped aside to let us pass. Struggling to keep up with his long strides, I realised that if we were to continue to work this case together, someone would have to call a truce.

I held out the car keys. 'You'll need these.'

His frown softening, he took the keys.

'Except if you *want* me to drive?' I said.

'Hah!'

'I've never had an accident.' I sneaked a sideways look at him.

'Me neither.'

'Yes, but the traffic flow in Dublin has changed drastically in the last few years. Free flow areas are now more—'

'I'll toss you for it.' Without breaking stride he threw me his briefcase, produced a five-cent coin, and slapped it onto the back of his hand. 'Call it.'

'Hhheads.'

'You lose.' He pocketed the coin.

'I lose?' I nearly tripped over my feet. 'But I didn't see the coin.'

'Would I lie?' He didn't look at me, just grabbed the briefcase and strode ahead of me again.

'I dunno,' I shrugged. 'Maybe you would.' I tried to catch up with him.

He stopped so suddenly I crashed into him. He swung around and steadied me so our faces were only inches apart, except that my eyes were in line with his mouth. For the first time I noticed that his top lip protruded ever so slightly more than his bottom one. And one of his perfect teeth was slightly chipped.

'Could you look directly at me, Annie? Please.'

I tilted my head to look him in the eye.

'Trust is an essential part of any working relationship,' he said. 'So while we're working on this case, we need to trust each other. Agreed?'

I held his gaze. 'But *did* the coin come up tails?'

There was a glimmer of amusement in his eyes.

'Yes.'

'You swear?'

'On my life.' He dropped the briefcase at his feet, took the little coin from his pocket and slapped it onto the back of his hand again, keeping it covered.

'Want me to call it?'

I hesitated for a second. 'Yes.'

'Tails.'

We checked the coin. Tails.

'OK. You win.' I nodded.

He caught my arm. Flipped the coin over. Tails.

Despite myself I got the giggles. The idea of someone like Sizemore carrying a spivvy double-tail coin was just too ludicrous for words. Even he knew this because we both laughed our way to the car.

He held up the keys, his expression questioning.

'Oh just drive,' I said. 'But if you take a wrong turn, don't ask me for directions.'

'I won't.' He smiled at me across the roof of the little Honda. 'But it might help if you told me where we're going?'

'Tallaght.' I blushed at my forgetfulness. 'A place I'm sure you're well familiar with.'

'I know the area intimately,' he lied through his perfect teeth. Well nearly perfect, there was that one tiny little v-shaped piece missing from one of his right incisors. Or was it the left molar? I wondered if I'd ever get close enough to check that again. Purely in the interests of research.

He caught me staring at him, and smiled. I turned away quickly. Didn't want him getting the wrong idea. Judging by Sandra and even Fiona's reaction to him he was probably used to women staring lasciviously at him. Didn't want him thinking he had that sort of effect on me.

11

Sizemore handled a couple of desperately awkward roundabouts on the Tallaght bypass, with practised ease. He also drove without speaking. It wasn't until we were approaching Springfield, the area where our interviewee lived, that he found his tongue.

'You're convinced this Sadie Rowlands can give us some pertinent information about the Bolgers?'

'She'll definitely know stuff about Kathy Bolger. They worked together in A & E for the longest time. Even before Kathy married Seanie. Sadie is a staff nurse at the hospital.'

'I see,' he said.

I doubted it. What would he know about exhausting twelve-hour nursing shifts, changing bed pans, or stitching up heads that had been smashed in drunken melees on Saturday nights in Dublin? Or any night of the week, for that matter.'

'So what's the story with Sadie?' He slowed down to let a gang of footballing kids cross the road.

'She was chatty on the phone. Sounded like the type of woman people tend to confide in, and hopefully share their secrets with.'

'You think we'd be that lucky?' He threw me a sceptical look.

'I believe in making my own luck,' I lied.

'So what's your plan then?'

He drove through the sprawling housing estate without once taking a wrong turn. I would have lost my way at the first signpost-free junction. Every road, every turning, began to look exactly like the preceding one. Sizemore didn't appear to have a problem with this. But then he didn't appear to have a problem with anything, except me.

'I asked about your plan, Annie?'

'I don't have a plan,' I snapped. 'Just remember what I told you. Be polite. Friendly. Keep the questions light. If she starts to get long-winded and girly, steer the conversation back in the direction of Kathy and Seanie's relationship. That's what we need to find out the truth about.'

'I'm glad you don't have a plan.'

I checked to see if he was teasing, but it was hard to tell. He masked his emotions beautifully. Did he do everything beautifully?

'I'm just saying, we get her to stick to the point. Or we'll be here all day.' When I tried to sound professional, I sounded like Hitler. 'We need to know if the Bolgers were *genuinely* happy.'

'I thought we were trying to find out if he started the fire?'

'We are.' Again, I suspected he was laughing at me. 'Happily married men don't usually torch the building where their wife is sleeping.'

'Not even when it's heavily insured?'

I bit my lip and began counting the house numbers.

'Well?' He waited.

'That's Rowlands' house, there. Number eleven. Remember she thinks we're interested in health and safety, so just follow my lead.'

'Yes ma'am.'

'Sizemore, if you . . .'

He was staring at me, his brown eyes guileless. 'If I what?'

'Nothing.'

Number eleven had a postage-stamp lawn that was trimmed to the bone. Not one blade of grass was allowed to disturb its razor-sharp edges. It also had a laurel hedge that suffered from the same over-zealous attention.

Sadie greeted us politely, but warily. Definitely on her guard.

The house was obviously a rental. Borderline shabby inside, with worn furniture, and walls in need of a lick of paint. But it was clean, and smelled pleasantly of lavender polish. Even on her day off Sadie was no slacker. And somebody had worked hard on that garden.

She made us a pot of tea. Not the tea bag variety. Real tea. Watching her expressive face as she poured it into sparkling clean cups, I tried to think of a good opening gambit. Gerry always said the right one could make or break an interview. But he wasn't bloody here, was he? I was still trying to think of a light, girl-friendly question, when Sizemore suddenly spoke.

'Lovely garden,' he pointed admiringly. And Sadie melted.

'I love gardening.' She looked out through the shining window. 'I had hoped to have my own house by now, but prices keep rising. I'll get there. Problem is, I want a real garden. I like growing things.' She waited for Sizemore to comment.

'So how long did Kathy Bolger work with you in the hospital?' I asked.

Sadie tore her attention away from the garden. 'Two years. Almost three.'

'So you knew her well?'

'Pretty well. Not that we had much time to chat. A & E can be a nightmare.'

'Kathy loved it,' I quoted a line from a newspaper piece I'd read.

'Well, I mean . . .' she shrugged. 'Better than home, wasn't it?'

Sizemore was on this in a flash. 'She wasn't happy at home?'

'With that airhead? Would you be?'

'She married him,' Sizemore said quickly.

'That's women for you. A flash car and a pinch of facile charm will do it for most of us.'

I thought she liked Kathy? Sizemore's eyes signalled me.

'She met Seanie when he was brought in to A & E?' I asked.

She nodded. 'Even as a patient I couldn't stand him. He thought he was God's gift! Hair streaked golden blond. Golden Balls, I believe the fans called him. Shame his brown roots were showing when he was brought in. Still, the kids queued up for his autograph. 'Course he made sure his flash car was parked by the door, where no one could miss it. Our car park wasn't good enough for Golden Balls.'

'Kathy liked him from day one,' Sizemore said.

'Oh, she fell for him like a ton of bricks. Couldn't do enough for him. And of course when he saw her in her sexy little uniform. Well, you can imagine.'

'Sexy?' I said. 'It was a nursing uniform.'

She smiled 'You think they can't look sexy?'

'I . . . I'm sure they . . .'

'It didn't hurt that Kathy had a perfect figure. That's her in the photo there.'

In the photo Kathy was standing between two uniformed nurses, one of them Sadie. Kathy's hair was sun-bleached. Her skin deeply tanned. She was very pretty, but something about her was . . . distant?

'She'd been on holiday with her parents.' Sadie frowned. 'And still had that gorgeous tan when he first saw her.'

She milked our tea as if we were children, put the sugar bowl by my elbow, only stopping short of stirring it in as she continued talking.

'He was a complete airhead. Always boasting. Telling anyone who'd listen that he was going to open a massive club here in Tallaght. The coolest club in Ireland. Then another day it was going to be a big leisure centre for the whole family. With an Olympic-sized swimming pool.'

'Where would he get the money to do all that?' I asked.

She laughed. 'Don't ask me. Last time I saw Kathy

was at an underwear party she was giving. She handed out free gifts to entice other women to host parties in their homes because the shop was going down the tubes at a rate of knots. After the excitement of the first opening weeks it was doing no business. The stock was cheap rubbish. Knickers made in Taiwan? Hardly Janet Reiger. Even the young ones who fancied Seanie began giving it a miss. He was never there, anyway.'

'But Kathy liked running the shop? She told people.' I chanced my arm.

She gave me a look. 'News to me.' She sipped her tea. 'Have a scone. I make them myself, you can't beat a home-made scone. Plenty of real butter, that's the secret of a really good scone.' She sipped her tea.

I tried a scone. 'Delicious.'

Sizemore stirred his tea.

'Kathy loved my scones.' A shadow crossed Sadie's round face. 'I always bring them into work for my tea break, and once she tasted them, she wouldn't touch a shop-bought one ever again. Once she asked if she could tell Seanie that she made them.' She laughed. 'Big eejit believed her.' She held out a little glass dish. 'Here, try jam on them. They're lovely with jam.'

'Terrible about the fire. Such a tragedy.'

'Don't.' She put her hand to her face.

'It wouldn't have . . . someone wouldn't have started it . . . out of spite?'

She seemed startled. 'Spite? But the fire was an accident. Those big lamps started it, didn't they? One of them overheated?'

'You're right,' Sizemore said quickly. 'But when there's a fatality, I think all fires bear further investigating. Someone has to take responsibility.'

'Exactly!' In her excitement, Sadie grabbed his hand. 'I've been saying that from day one. Someone has to be held responsible for Kathy's death. The Garda investigation was far too perfunctory.'

'You think so?' Sizemore forgot about his tea.

'Yes, I do!'

'So what do you think should be done, Sadie?'

'I think the cowboys who put those lamps in should be charged. Along with the one who hired them.'

'You mean Seanie?' I asked.

'He killed her.' Her voice was a whisper.

Sizemore leaned forward eagerly. 'You think he—?'

'Oh, I know what you're going to say. That it wasn't deliberate. But she's still dead, isn't she?' She rummaged in her pocket, pulled out a huge hanky and blew her nose.

'You're talking manslaughter?'

'Why not? If he'd killed her with that flash car of his he'd be charged.'

'Did he ever threaten to—?'

'No! I'm just saying that people who kill someone in a road accident are charged. He killed Kathy as surely as if he set that fire. He hired those cheap cowboys to wire those big lamps. I've seen Gards in A & E waiting to arrest men for less.'

The phone rang. Sadie excused herself and hurried out into the hall.

'Hello? Ah, Nelly.' She pulled the door closed.

'What do you think?' Sizemore whispered.

I was thinking that he seemed to know exactly how to worm information out of people. Maybe he wasn't someone's favourite nephew after all. Maybe he . . . He was as skilled as Gerry at getting information.

'How long have you been doing this job?' I whispered back.

He leaned close to my ear. 'Twenty minutes.'

'Ah, Nelly!' Sadie squealed.

Hard as I fought them, the giggles erupted.

Then Sizemore started. We were both red faced and coughing, when Sadie came back.

She looked from me to Sizemore. 'Is it too hot in here?'

'A bit,' I lied.

Sadie opened the window, giving the garden a loving look as she did so.

'Heavenly scones, Sadie,' I repeated, for want of something better to say.

The garden forgotten, she sat by me. 'Real butter, remember, that's the secret. Never skimp on the butter, my mother used to say. God rest her soul. More tea? Two sugars, isn't it?'

'You're very observant,' Sizemore said.

'Hospital training. In my job a bad memory can cost lives. That's why Kathy was a pleasure to work with. So thorough. And sharp as a tack. Then she goes and marries that airhead. 'Course she was pregnant.'

'Kathy was pregnant?' There was no mention of this in any report.

'When she married. She didn't tell her parents 'til *after* the wedding, of course. Daren't. Someone said

Kathy's father was a spoiled priest, but that was just a rumour. Anyway, Kathy miscarried. Probably for the best, as it turned out.' She saw my frown. 'I'm an A & E nurse. We have to be pragmatists. Even if Seanie recovers he won't be fit to care for a child. If he ever was.'

'The newspapers are calling him a saint?' Sizemore said.

'Please.' She rolled her eyes heavenwards.

'You think their marriage was under pressure?' Sizemore asked.

'Kathy was working in that awful shop three days a week *and* doing a night shift in the hospital? Would you call that pressure?'

Sizemore was scribbling like mad.

'Now I have to listen to people calling him a hero.' She became heated. 'Some hero! Kathy got the bus to work while he drove around in that flash convertible. Or should I say the loan company's convertible. They weren't slow to reclaim it after the fire.'

Sizemore was scribbling again. 'Was the car damaged?' he asked.

'No. It was perfect. It was parked around the corner that night. In an alley. I thought airhead would always leave it on show, but apparently not.'

'Thanks, Sadie.' I got up to leave.

'If I can help you with anything let me know. I'm always here on Mondays.'

'You've already been a great help.' We shook hands.

'Good.' She was pleased.

'I bet you were a great support to Kathy.'

Her eyes welled up. 'I wish. May she rest in peace.'

'A lot of people are praying for Seanie's recovery.' Sizemore watched her closely.

'Good luck to them,' she sniffed. 'They weren't married to him. I hear there's to be a big insurance payout. Bit late for Kathy.'

She walked us out to the low gate, closing it carefully behind us. She gave a quick wave and walked back to the house, running her hand along the tightly-boxed laurel hedge, as if she was checking it for surgical precision.

12

Sizemore was lost in thought as we drove back into town.

'I think we can safely assume that Sadie doesn't like Seanie,' I said.

'Em.' His expression gave nothing away.

'You think she's right about him being a lazy airhead?'

'No law against that.'

'So we're not one step nearer to proving anything against him?'

'No.' He pulled up at an amber light.

'You still think he planned the fire?'

'He parked his car well out of harm's way. Coincidence? Or an evil plan?'

'There was nothing in the Garda report about his car.'

'That's because they were investigating a shop fire.'

'And nobody thought to question why the only survivor parked his car hundreds of yards away from his shop?'

He nodded. 'Then again, when was the last time you parked your car exactly where you wanted?' He hit the left indicator.

'True. Maybe he just grabbed the first available

space. Why are you turning here?' I frowned out at the unfamiliar little row of terraced houses, each one painted a different garish colour from its neighbour's.

'I want to have a look at the burned-out shop. I thought this way might save time.'

'Dream on,' I laughed.

I was right. The lines of traffic grew tighter and tighter until we were wedged into a rock-solid jam of cars, trucks and fume-spewing buses.

'Think we should have gone straight through Rathmines?' I asked.

Sizemore wrenched the handbrake into place.

'Sorry. One driver, OK?'

'Works for me.' He drummed the steering wheel.

I turned to face him. 'So, Seanie claimed he wanted extra insurance because of the increasing number of break-ins in that area? Right?'

'Maybe he was planning ahead. Saw his insurance as a surefire investment.'

I groaned at the awful pun.

'I swear I didn't intend it to sound like that.' Sizemore grimaced. The traffic began to move, and he released the handbrake to inch the car forward.

'Poor Kathy,' I said.

'She chose to marry him.'

'Maybe she didn't have a choice. She *was* pregnant.'

'Hang on. What century are we talking about?'

'You heard Sadie. Kathy's family are died-in-the-wool Catholics. I know families like that. Somewhere to the right of the Pope. You think today's Catholics are all liberal? All à la carte? Free to pick and choose which rules to obey?'

'OK. Let's run with your idea. You think Kathy was afraid to tell her parents she was pregnant?'

'Maybe. Which meant marriage was her only option.'

'She was a trained nurse! If she didn't want the pregnancy she had other choices.'

'Easy for you to say.'

He gave that little wry grin that was becoming almost familiar. 'We're taking the feminist line, are we? Fine with me. So explain why she hooked up with *airhead* Bolger in the first place? She was intelligent, had a good career, supportive friends, and a family that gave her financial support.'

'Once she towed the line.'

'What?'

'I don't doubt her family adored her. But sometimes adoration comes with a price.'

He turned to look at me. 'OK. I can see that. Still doesn't tell me why a woman with so much going for her would hook up with Seanie Bolger. An airhead. A penniless has-been. And then work herself so hard that she had a miscarriage?'

'Maybe she was in love with him.'

'Jesus.' He closed his eyes.

Sizemore took a whole roll of shots of the fire-blackened shop frontage. Or what remained of it. He included several shots of the surrounding area, not the most picturesque street in the world, and probably in line to be knocked down to make way for a whole rake of apartments.

'We're not going to find any clues here,' I said, as he continued to take even more pictures. 'What the fire didn't destroy, the water hoses did.'

'Em.' He looked along the street. 'Those curtained windows, above the boarded-up shops. Are they all rented flats?'

'Most of them, yes.' I knew what he was thinking. If there were people living all along this street, how come someone didn't notice the fire earlier? There must have been some smoke? Then again, it did happen on a popular bank holiday weekend, and the old flats above the shops were mostly occupied by young singles. The very people who bail out for bank holiday weekends.

'Not exactly the type of neighbourhood where you chat over the garden fence, is it?'

'It's not New York,' I snapped. 'Our damp weather doesn't encourage people to sit on their front steps.'

He glanced at the blazing sun and smiled. And there it was again, that superior attitude. That know-all look that got right up my nose. As if I was too dumb to notice that this week our temperatures overtook those in Barcelona. And probably New York.

He was frowning at the blackened building again. 'The Gardai think Seanie smelled smoke, and went downstairs to check.'

I nodded. 'Leaving Kathy in bed.'

'If he didn't plan the fire he could have thought it was something minor. If he did plan it, it would be pretty stupid of him not to realise how quickly a fire can take hold in these old buildings.'

'You think he's that stupid?'

'He's not Einstein. He did run back into a burning shop.'

'Which could prove that he loved his wife?'

'Or that he knew it would give that impression to witnesses.'

'Hard to believe he'd deliberately . . .'

'I don't think he planned for Kathy to die. I think he pictured the fire service arriving in time to get her out. There was that very early 999 call, which was suddenly cut off.'

'That was from a mobile. Some lads falling out of a pub up the road called the fire brigade. They were so drunk nobody paid any heed. Thought it was a hoax call. Plus they gave wrong names.'

'No, before that. There was another call before that. On a landline. The caller hung up in a panic and . . . uh, oh, I think we have an audience. Don't turn.'

Of course I turned. And a movement at a top-floor window across the way caught my eye. A flash of blonde hair. I waited. There it was again, long blonde hair framing a perfect oval face, as its owner stared directly across at us.

'A possible witness?' I said.

'Cross your fingers. We may have found our chatty neighbour. Or at least a curious one.'

'Seanie was adorable. Well, I'm sure he still is . . .' The leggy blonde gushed, as her tight little rear disappeared up two flights of stairs to her top-floor flat.

We followed in silence.

'His wife was a bit of a pain. Little Miss Prim, I called her. Always rushing. And always wearing that horrible nurse's uniform when she went for the bus. Seanie was always fashionably dressed. And friendly. She wouldn't even give you a wave. He was sooo different. He smiled at everyone. To be honest, I suspect that's the only reason anyone would go near that awful Lingerie Lounge. What a name!' She shuddered.

Inside her revamped flat, she directed us to two stainless-steel chairs with torturously hard seats, while arranging herself prettily on a well-padded white sofa. 'I cried non-stop after the fire. Could not believe it. Of course I was in New York, at the time. Filming.'

'You're an actress?' Sizemore asked.

'You recognised me! It's such a thrill when that happens.' She fell back into the sofa, clutching herself with delight.

Sizemore shifted uncomfortably. 'Of course you er . . . em . . . ?'

'Yes! I'm the girl in those beer commercials. The one where the big guy comes in with his three friends, sees me standing at the bar, and his eyes light up, and he falls in love. Then someone hands him a beer and he has to act as if he prefers the beer to me. As if!' She laughed again, showing two rows of blindingly white teeth.

'As if,' Sizemore echoed. 'Now, as I explained, we're writing a report on—'

'I've already had dozens of enquiries.'

'About the fire?' Sizemore frowned.

'No.' She tossed back her glossy hair, which

almost reached her hand-span waist. 'About the commercial. I sent a copy to Oliver Stone. I'm hoping he'll want me in his next movie. It's a thriller. Set in France. A lot of people say I have a certain Gallic quality, plus I'm setting up my own inter-national website. You have to have a website, don't you? It makes it lots easier for people to contact you, and my agent is . . . well, he's a busy man.' She rearranged her endless legs into a perfect Lotus position. 'I don't suppose you know any casting agents?'

'Sorry,' I said.

'How well did you know the Bolgers?' Sizemore took over.

'God, what a tragedy. I was completely devastated when I heard. I said to my friend Natasha, well, if their story isn't made into a movie, there is no justice. It would make the most perfect romcom. With a deeply tragic ending, of course.'

'Of course,' I said.

'So you knew them well?' Sizemore asked.

'Not intimately. But I did see a lot of them. From that window there. I had a perfect view of the shop from that window. A French director once said . . . or maybe it was Fellini . . . anyway, whoever . . . said it's good for an actor to some-times view life from a distance . . . so I read my scripts in that window seat, which has a distant view of the street . . . although some of the dross I'm sent you would not believe . . . it is beyond anything I could express to you . . .'

Sizemore crossed to the window. 'You do

have a perfect view from here. But you didn't see the fire?'

'No.' She sounded disappointed. 'Like I said, I was in New York, auditioning. A three-minute shampoo commercial, which you'll soon be seeing on Sky. They wanted someone with perfectly manageable hair so a friend recommended me. He told the agency I would be perfect for the shower shot and—'

'Did you see anything of the Bolgers before you left for New York?'

'Oh . . . yes . . . I saw Seanie almost every day. He was dishy. Sorry . . . is dishy. He could be an actor. He has the looks. He ran that big club in town for a while . . . what's it called? Roxy? Boxy? I think he part owned it, because he put a lot of free passes in my post box. But the film crowd don't go there, so I never used them. Anyway, my career takes up most of my time, what with acting classes, my vocal training, auditions—'

'So you never actually spoke to either of the Bolgers?' I asked.

'No. But I could tell she was completely uptight. She should have taken up yoga. It's worked wonders for me, I'm practically a new person since I—'

'Did you . . . did they have friends over at all?' I asked.

'Em . . . I don't think so. Didn't they both work at night?' She tried to frown, but her Botoxed forehead was set like cement. 'There was a mumsy type who used to drop in. I noticed her because I thought she might be Seanie's mum.'

Sizemore took a press photo of Seanie's mum from his briefcase. 'Is this her?'

'Em . . . ?' She made another brave attempt at frowning. 'No . . . not sure. Women that age all tend to look the same, don't they?'

'What age is that?' I said.

'Forty? Fifty? In my profession if you haven't made it by thirty it's curtains.'

'Thanks for your help, Leticia.' Sizemore gushed charm.

'Oh is that all you want to ask? There's so much more I could tell you. I could fill you in on—'

Every audition you've ever been to, I muttered under my breath.

Sizemore shot me a warning look. 'If we need any further information, Leticia, we'll definitely get back to you.'

'Yes,' I said. 'But don't ring us. We'll ring you.'

'Would you like to see a shot of Seanie going into the shop the day of the fire?'

Sizemore stopped dead. 'You have . . . ?'

'Just as we were about to leave for the States my friend Miles suddenly screams, "Oh my God, Leticia, look at the light. The way the sun is going down. I have to get a shot of that."'

'And out he goes into the street. Takes a whole roll of film. He's hoping to make it big in New York. He got two commissions while we were over there. Mind you, I said to him, you have a long way to go before you're Mario Testino.'

'You have a shot of Seanie going *into* the shop on the day of the fire?'

134

She pulled open a drawer. 'It's somewhere in here. Miles says it's not good enough for his portfolio, but I like it. Besides, you never know, it might eventually be worth . . . here it is.' She handed it over.

Miles was right, it wasn't a good picture. But there was no mistaking Seanie. Or his car. It was parked directly in front of the shop. In the exact spot Sadie said she'd have expected him to leave it.

'You sure this was taken the evening of the fire?' I asked.

'I was leaving for my flight, wasn't I? Hysterical with excitement because William Grimes was going to audition me. Also worried sick that I might not be looking my best after such a long flight, so I asked Miles to stop taking bloody photos of the sun and put my heated rollers in his bag. I knew the New York models would have an unfair advantage, anyway, and I wasn't prepared to be the . . .'

'Could we borrow this?' Sizemore held up the photo.

'Sure. Here, take a couple of me as well. I have lots and you never know, talent scouts can turn up in the most unexpected places. A friend of mine was spotted going into the Wax Museum and—'

We left.

13

Naomi was standing at the reception desk, waving what looked like an obscene doll at Sandra. Sandra backed away in revulsion, as the phones rang unheeded.

'It's a priceless fertility doll,' Naomi announced grandly. 'You place it over your bed and if you're not pregnant within three weeks, I'll eat my Philip Treacy hat.'

I came up behind her. 'That'll probably be the most calories she's consumed all year,' I said to Sandra.

'What do you think, Annie?' Sandra grimaced at the doll.

'Give me a look.' I took the doll. 'Er . . . modelled on one of your wilder fantasies, Naomi?' I frowned at the repulsively-endowed male doll.

'It's from the South Sea Islands,' Naomi said. 'A valuable and much sought-after fertility doll. Guaranteed to get Sandra pregnant.'

'I'd stick with Jimmy, if I were you, Sandra,' I grinned.

She giggled. 'I think I might already be . . . you know.'

'Are you serious?'

'I said maybe.'

'Why didn't you say?' Naomi was annoyed. 'There are people queuing up to borrow this doll.'

'You know some very strange people, Naomi,' I called after her as she walked off in a huff. 'And, Sandra, I don't want to appear pushy, but is there any chance you might answer the phones?'

She tossed back her newly highlighted hair and picked up the receiver.

I was heading back to the lift when I heard her say, 'Can you speak up? Hello?'

Heart thumping, I turned.

'It's Declan.' She clamped her hand over the receiver to add 'He sounds upset.'

'You mean drunk?' Fury had me scuttling back to the desk.

'No. He's upset.'

'Annie's here. Do you want to . . . ?' She held out the receiver.

I grabbed it roughly. 'Declan? What's happening?'

'He got to the dogs, Annie. He killed them.'

'Oh my God.'

'Lying bastard denied it to the Gards. Said vandals must have broken in and killed all three of them because they were barking so much. The lying . . .'

I clamped a hand to my mouth, and gave Sandra the receiver for a second. Then she was crying, and I had to take the phone again, and try to find the right words for Declan. 'You . . . you did what you could. You did your best.'

Water, I mouthed at Sandra.

'It wasn't good enough, was it?'

'You're not to blame. You couldn't stand guard over them day and night. There are just some rotten people in the world, Declan. Sometimes you have to accept that bad people do bad things . . . where are you now?' I sipped the water.

'In a bar.'

Oh Christ.

'It's the only place around here that serves real coffee. I won't come back today. I need to clear my head. Can you manage without the jeep?'

'We don't need the jeep,' I lied. 'You stay in Wicklow as long as you want.'

'He poisoned all three . . . all three . . .'

'Listen to me, Declan. You get out of that bar and do some walking. Sometimes that helps.' I paused. 'And, Declan? I'll keep my mobile on all day. If you want to talk or . . . if you want me to drive up there, I could be there in . . . thirty minutes . . . forty tops . . . do you want me to come and—?'

'I'm drinking *coffee*, Annie.'

'I . . . I know that. Kn . . . know you wouldn't lie to me.' I crossed my fingers. 'Sorry about the dogs, Declan.'

'Like you said – things happen. I'm drinking coffee, Annie. Lots and lots of coffee.' He hung up.

Sizemore came hurrying out of the lift. 'All ready to go,' he called over, then saw me and Sandra hugging each other.

'OK.' He came to a halt. 'Who died?'

Looking completely out of place, Sizemore brought our drinks down to a corner table in the grubby little pub.

'What's this?' I frowned at the amber-coloured liquor in mine.

'It's whiskey.' He handed me a little bottle of soda. 'Put some of this in it, and I guarantee you'll feel lots better.'

'I asked for a soft drink,' I protested.

'It's a single malt whiskey, Annie, not a bottle of Red Eye. Just take a few sips if that's all you feel you can take. You look terrible.'

'Thanks.'

'No more games, Annie.' He checked his watch. 'We're meeting Kathy Bolger's parents in less than an hour. Can't have you scaring them with those big sad eyes, can I? Drink your whiskey. Please.'

He made short work of his, and I knew he was right. I was feeling rotten, and it wasn't the time for game playing, or sparring. Or trying to score against each other. Sizemore wasn't ashamed to let me see how badly he felt for Declan, so why should I hide the way I was feeling? And the whiskey was a good idea. I needed something to help fuel me up if I was to talk to Kathy's parents without breaking down altogether.

'How did you find this place?' Sizemore looked around the gloomy bar.

'A cabby brought me here one night.'

'A cabby?' He frowned.

'Not on a date. There was a terrible storm and . . .' I closed my eyes to blot out the memory.

'You don't like storms, then?' He watched me.

'No.' I tried to keep my voice even. Didn't want him thinking I was a complete wuss. Bad enough that he caught me crying over three poisoned dogs. He had seen me cry before. Twice in a couple of weeks? He must take me for a right . . .

'I'm not a wimp.' I stuck out my chin defiantly. 'I just don't like storms.'

He looked me straight in the eye. 'No shame in that. I had a friend who was terrified of them. And he was a big tough cop. He'd take on a whole gang of armed punks single handed, but electrical storms terrified him. Something to do with his childhood, I think. He grew up in Kansas.' He smiled, touched my hand, and poured more soda into my drink.

If he kept behaving like this I might even get to like him. Once he didn't start telling me more stories about Kansas. Maybe about the Tin Man and the Cowardly Lion. Kansas! I ask you!

14

Kathy Bolger's mother – Mrs Angela Newman – had a mountain of candyfloss hair, two chins and weighed at least twenty stone, yet there was something almost fragile about her. Maybe it was her state of mind, courtesy of all the tranquillisers she was clearly popping. She turned another page of the leather-bound photo album she was clutching to her enormous body, and pointed to yet another picture of Kathy.

In this one Kathy was standing before a backdrop of a snow-covered mountain, wearing skis and a blue snowsuit, laughing into the camera with a bunch of girlfriends.

'Beautiful,' I said, for the umpteenth time.

Sizemore nodded in agreement.

The Newmans' whole living room was a shrine to Kathy. Everywhere you looked there were photos of her. A newborn sleeping in her mother's arms. A pudgy toddler astride a little three-wheel bike. A red-cheeked schoolgirl brandishing a hockey stick. A nursing graduate holding a ribbon-bound degree. In the biggest picture of all she was a glowing bride, wearing a big white meringue of a dress, her bride-groom conspicuous only by his absence. He was relegated to a bit part in a tiny photo, standing shoulder to shoulder with Kathy and a pious-looking priest.

'She's even more beautiful in her wedding video,' Mrs Newman said. 'But it hurts to watch that.'

'I understand,' I said softly.

The only other images in the room were two full-colour pictures of Popes. One past. One present. Both in full ceremonial. Trimmed with ermine.

Kathy's sports medals and cups fought for space with silver-framed pictures of her playing tennis, swimming, and skiing. Even the window ledges of the shuttered room were lined with pictures of her.

'Very nice.' Sizemore looked around.

'So pretty,' I said.

'Our only child,' Mrs Newman reminded me, her eyes searching mine for answers.

'We'll never have grandchildren now. Even that has been taken from us. She had a miscarriage. Did you know that? She miscarried our grandchild.'

'I'm very sorry. I . . . er . . .'

'We were hoping for a boy.' Mrs Newman sipped a colourless drink. Water? Gin?

'You wanted a boy?' I turned to the pictures of the pretty little girl again.

'A grandson!' she said. 'But it wasn't to be.'

I looked to Sizemore for help, but he avoided my eyes. 'Do you . . . have you been to see Seanie?' I tried.

'We sent flowers.' Mr Newman spoke for the first time. He had kept his distance since we arrived, but was clearly on guard. Protective of his wife. He was a slim man. Looked a lot younger than she did. Maybe their daughter's death had aged her.

'Do you know how Seanie is . . . doing?' I asked.

'Lots of flowers.' Mrs Newman turned to her husband. 'Didn't we dear?'

There was another long silence. Trying to catch Sizemore's eye was a complete waste of time.

'Kathy loved him,' Mrs Newman said suddenly.

'That was good, wasn't it? She married the man she loved.' I forced a smile.

'We sent flowers, didn't we?' she repeated like a mantra.

I waited but nobody commented. I shifted uneasily and stared at Sizemore. Where was his magic this afternoon? The Newmans possibly knew more than anyone about Kathy and Seanie's marriage. Why was Sizemore sitting there like a stuffed dummy? He was supposed to be asking pertinent questions. What the hell was going on? For the first time I pictured Gerry in this situation. He'd have somehow made a connection with Mr Newman. He was good at that. Probably what he was doing in Arizona – making connections.

'It's all we could do,' Mrs Newman said. 'Send flowers.'

'Were you pleased when they opened the shop?' I dared.

Mr Newman stood up. 'Time for your nap dear.' He helped her out of her chair. 'My wife hasn't been well,' he said, as if she wasn't even there.

Sizemore said later that she wasn't.

'We'll let ourselves out,' I offered.

When there was no reply, we did exactly that.

*   *   *

'Did you get the feeling they liked Seanie?' I asked as we drove away.

'They certainly don't dislike him. All that talk about flowers.'

I was totally confused. I had expected Kathy's parents to . . . well, rail against Seanie. Maybe blame him for her death. But there was no sense of resentment there at all.

'They seemed pleased that she had married him,' I said. 'See the big framed picture of her in her wedding finery?'

'Makes you wonder if it was the same Seanie that Sadie was talking about.'

All our previous evidence suggested that Seanie was a waste of space. Even the flaky actress/model who fancied him, considered him a lightweight.

Sizemore grew increasingly uneasy. 'Sadie tells us in no uncertain terms that Seanie was nothing but a burden on Kathy. Kathy was the practical, hardworking one. Now Kathy's parents all but tell us she was happily married. It doesn't add up.'

'The Newmans would know their daughter best.'

'Better than Sadie who worked with her, under stressful conditions? A & E night shifts? That's hard-core,' Sizemore insisted.

'I . . . I think the Newmans are in such grief they need to believe Kathy was happy with Seanie. You heard them about their lack of a grandchild. They're not young. They must have had Kathy late in life. I think they're coping with their loss by convincing themselves that at least she had a happy life. Even if it was cut short.'

Sizemore nodded. 'And what parents would want to accept that their only daughter chose a waster as a life partner? That would be a terrible indictment of their parenting.' Sizemore winced at his own conclusions. 'Pop psychology?' he grimaced.

Pop psychology it might be, but it was all we had. Well, that and Sadie's version of Seanie, which given the facts made the most sense. He *did* swan around in nightclubs. Drive a flash car. And there was the small matter of the huge promissory note he had given his prospective business partner, when he didn't have a penny to his name. All he had was a massive insurance policy, on their failing shop.

Sizemore made a decision. 'Let's focus on finding who made that anonymous call to Mutual Irish. If we find her, we're home and dry. Something she knows drove her to make that call.'

'What if she was just being malicious? Does that mean . . . ?'

'That we're up shit creek? Yes. Fancy a coffee?'

He knew I did. But instead of heading for Café Naturalle, he surprised me by going straight back to the old pub on the quays. A good choice, as it was becoming my favourite place to relax in.

'Two coffees,' Sizemore called out to the elderly barman who was set into the racing pages.

'Coffees?' He clearly didn't like being disturbed by coffee drinkers.

Ignoring his disgust, Sizemore took my jacket and draped it carefully across the back of a bar stool.

I sat down. 'I thought you'd be totally bummed

out after that meeting with the Newmans.'

'No,' he said. 'I like a challenge. Why do you think I agreed to work with McHugh Dunning?'

'I have my suspicions.' I shot him a look. 'But you tell me.'

Our eyes duelled for a second. 'I asked you first.'

'How old are you? Six?'

'I'm old enough.' Again the extended eye contact, with neither one of us prepared to look away first.

The grumpy barman shouted. 'Yis don't want cream with these coffees?'

'God forbid,' I said.

'Grand. I don't do cream.'

Sizemore stood up. 'I'll get the coffees.' He marched to the end of the bar, paid for the coffees and left the shocked barman a five-euro tip.

'He'll remember you,' I laughed as he came back.

'That's the plan,' he smiled. 'I might make this my local.'

15

If Sandra tried, she couldn't have chosen a worse day to ovulate. Sizemore and I were almost out the door, all set to re-interview the telephonist in Mutual Irish, when Sandra came running out of the toilets waving a thermometer. Yelling as if her arse was on fire, Sizemore said later. And in a sense it was. So I had no choice but to stay back and cover reception, while Sandra went home to make a baby, and Sizemore hightailed it (his words) to Mutual Irish.

Keeping my fingers crossed in the hope that he would arrive back with a hot lead, I sat in reception trying to decide between plain aspirin or Solpadeine. I knew I'd need something to ward off the tension headache that had been threatening all morning. Outside the weather was glorious; the rising temperatures delighting everyone, especially the tabloids that had been endlessly preaching about global warming.

I was wondering how Sizemore was getting on, when the first call came in.

'McHugh Dunning Detective Agency. Can I help you?'

'I want . . .' The voice was muffled, indistinct.

The little hairs on the back of my neck rose like needles.

'. . . need . . . to . . .' The line suddenly cleared.
'. . . speak to Gerry.'

Recognising the voice, I relaxed. 'Ms Stowe?'

'Yes, this is Alicia Stowe. Get me Gerry.'

'Sorry, Ms Stowe, he's—'

'You get him right now, you stupid girl! He knows me.'

We all knew her. Barney called her a professional nutter, but she wasn't really. She was just a lonely woman who insisted that she was being stalked, by a sex maniac. After her first dozen calls to us Gerry had managed to convince her that not every male who walked behind her in the street was a sexual predator.

He even met her a couple of times to tell her that in future she had to call her doctor, not us. That worked. Until the next month, or the next full moon, or whatever.

'I want Gerry to come here now,' she said. 'I can hear the stalker. He's in my attic.'

'Sorry, Ms Stowe, Gerry can't—'

'I'll pay for his time.'

'It's not about money. Gerry is in America.'

'But the stalker is in my attic,' she hissed. 'I can hear him.'

I sighed. 'Ring the Gards.'

'They won't help.' She was crying now. 'I'm frightened.'

I crumpled. 'Tell you what, Ms Stowe, one of our detectives is due back from Wicklow soon. The second he comes in I'll send him over to check out your attic. OK?'

'I'm not having *two* strange men in my attic! Send Gerry.'

'Gerry is in America,' I repeated.

'Fine! I'll wait.' She was gone.

I closed my eyes, sipped my now lukewarm coffee, and wondered what were the odds of developing renal failure if I took two more aspirin, on top of the trillions I had already swallowed earlier on. Why didn't Sizemore ring? How long does it take to discuss an anonymous call?

I took two Syndol tablets from Sandra's secret hoard behind the desk, and was on my knees rummaging through cans of hairspray, jars of cuticle cream, and a mountain of fashion magazines in a vain hope of finding a Diet Coke, when a whiff of body odour told me I had company.

'Any papers?' Mags' weather-beaten face appeared over the desk.

I gave her three newspapers and the free coffee, which was the real purpose of her visits, and waved her out. But she looked so small and frail, and so lost without Fred, the little mongrel who used to be her constant companion, before he died of distemper, that I called her back and gave her a breakfast muffin, and five euros from petty cash.

'Sandra gives me ten.' She looked me straight in the eye.

'Muffins? No wonder you're getting fat.'

Muttering to herself, she pocketed the five euros and left. Giving up on the Diet Coke, I was searching for an air freshener when the phone buzzed again.

'McHugh Dunning Detective Agency.'

'Annie?' Fiona sounded grumpy. 'What are you doing in reception?'

'Sandra has the day off.'

'And you couldn't get a temp?'

'Temps are *verboten*,' I quoted Barney.

'So you're . . . what kind of eejit are you?'

'What do you mean?'

'Well, it's a bit rich, isn't it? Your name is on the door, yet you're sitting in reception, answering the phones? Every little hairdresser in the city has at least two gofers these days, running around doing stuff for them. Taking their calls, making—'

'This isn't a hairdresser's, Fiona,' I said coldly. 'Given the confidential nature of our business we can't allow untrained people to take our calls.'

'Ah, would you ever feck off!'

'Right. Talk to you later.'

'Ah, no, wait.'

'Fiona, Declan could be trying to get through. I expected him back . . .' I frowned at the clock, 'two hours ago?'

'See . . . now that's exactly what I'm talking about. Declan does what he likes when Gerry's not there. They all do. You're the boss for God's sake. Put your foot down. You have to demand respect before you get it. Your problem is you're too soft. And where's the hunk? What's he doing while you're answering the phones?'

'It's a long story.' I massaged my aching temples.

'Jesus, Annie. Cop yourself on!'

'Cop myself . . . ? We had an unexpected emergency this morning. Sandra is ovulating.'

Her hoot of laughter made my head vibrate. 'Oh my God! Only in McHugh Dunning. The receptionist is ovulating so the boss has to sit in reception answering the feckin' phones?'

'I'm not just answering phones, I'm . . . hold on, there's another call coming in.'

'Annie!' Fiona hated being put on hold. 'You're now a professional investigator. Did you sink every penny you possessed into that agency so you could sit on your arse all day answering telephones? Would you ever assert yourself? Express yourself more.'

'Express myself more . . . is this the same woman who until two months ago only talked about expressing breast milk? Who rattled your golden cage this morning?'

Silence.

'Fiona? Fiona?'

Loud throat clearing. 'Pino is flying to Italy tomorrow. He's bringing his mum back to stay with us. He says she'll help out with Calum. He says I need the company.'

'Oh.'

'I want you to talk sense into him, Annie. Tell him it's a stupid idea.'

'No way. I'm not getting involved.'

'Please, Annie. My marriage could be in jeopardy. I could be driven to the brink of despair.' She was in full melodramatic mode.

'By a little old lady of seventy-nine? I don't think so.'

'She's no little old lady, she's . . . Mussolini in drag,' she spat. 'And the scary thing is, Pino can't see it. He worships the woman. In his eyes she can do no wrong.'

I sighed. 'She's a frail old lady, Fiona.'

She wasn't listening. 'You have to talk sense into him. He'll listen to you. Call into the restaurant in . . . in your professional capacity . . . present him with the facts . . . tell him I need my own space. If Gerry was here he'd do it for me!' she said slyly.

I rang Declan's mobile.

Fiona was still talking. 'I know you think I'm being hard about this, but I swear I'm not. I'm thinking of her well-being too. Nonna Molino would be miserable in Ireland. She adores her own little home . . . she has a view of the Adriatic that you'd kill for, and the smell of bougainvillea is only . . .'

Declan's mobile was out of range. I waited a second or two before trying again.

'. . . and, as I said to Mrs O'Kelly, she doesn't even like me. It's Pino she wants to spend time with, and when is he ever at home? Will you talk sense into him, Annie? Convince him that she . . .'

'You're asking the wrong person, Fiona. Since when have I been able to convince anyone of anything?'

'Please, Annie, Heather Flanagan will have a field day with this, sneering at me in front of everyone.'

Oh Christ, not bloody Heather Flanagan again. Heather Flanagan was the scourge of the Mums and Toddlers group. They all hated her. And every six months they all voted her back in again as hon. sec.

'Just because she's stuck with Hugo's mother.'

'Fiona—'

'Pat Redding told me in strict confidence that

Heather said that having Hugo's mother living with them is what poisoned their marriage. The mother blocked Hugo's vasectomy.'

Declan's mobile was still out of range.

'Isn't that just evil?'

Fiona now began a tirade against Hugo Flanagan's mother. The mother had apparently opened his post, found confirmation of his appointment to have the snip, hid the letter, and when she was challenged about this, she clutched her chest and collapsed.

Fortunately Hugo is a cardio-vascular consultant. He was able to diagnose his mother's medical problem in an instant. Severe acid heartburn. The mother then recovered enough to say that if Hugo went ahead with the snip she'd cut him out of her will.

'I mean, I can't stand Heather. But *five* children!' Fiona's voice rose. 'If you ask me, someone should have taken a knife to Hugo's willy years ago.'

Another call light began flashing.

'McHugh Dunning Detective Agency. May I help you?'

'This is Ballymoney Gardai station,' a gruff voice said. 'We have a Declan Storey here. One of your investigators, I believe?'

'Yes.'

'He's being charged with a serious assault, an unprovoked attack on a chartered accountant called—'

'No! There must be some mistake. Declan Storey would never . . . may I have a word with him, please?'

'Ma'am, he's not capable of speaking to anyone right now. He is so intoxicated he parked a Jeep

153

Cherokee in the middle of our award-winning summer bedding display.'

'Please talk to Pino,' Fiona was saying. 'You know I love him. I'll do anything for him . . . anything in the world . . . except let his mother come and stay with us.'

'Sorry, Fiona, got to go.' I cut her off.

Fingers trembling I tapped out a quick text, and sent it to Sizemore, Sandra, and then, as an after-thought, to Naomi.

It said – DEC IN NICK. HELP.

16

Sizemore arrived, his face tight with concern. Without asking for an explanation he instantly volunteered. 'I'll get Declan. Where are they holding him?'

'Hang on. I'm coming with you.' I grabbed my bag.

'I thought you couldn't leave.' He eyed the empty desk.

'Naomi is going to keep an eye on it 'til Sasha gets here.'

'Naomi?' Even he was shocked. 'In your reception?'

'It's her reception too! Well, sort of . . . besides, the dog owner was her uncle. She got us involved. And Sasha is already on her way.'

'Who is Sasha?'

Before I could explain, Naomi appeared, looking like she was bound for Royal Ascot. She gave Sizemore a lingering look, dismissed me with an imperious wave, and slipped behind the desk, to hit the switch with a gold-tipped pen.

'McHugh Dunning?' She held the receiver as if it had scabies.

Sizemore and I hurried out into the sun-drenched street.

Until I saw it sitting there I had forgotten that

Sizemore was using his own car. My first thought on seeing the sleek Lexus was that Mutual Irish must pay their staff way over the odds.

He caught my look. 'It's environmentally friendly.'

'Sure.' I rolled my eyes.

Once outside the city limits the Lexus ate up the road.

'What do you think finally pushed Declan off the wagon?' Sizemore looked at me as we stopped for a red light.

'I blame myself. He was so cut up over those dogs, and I knew it. When he rang to say he was in a pub I should have gone straight to him.'

'You knew where he was?'

'I didn't know which pub exactly, but . . . I should have tried to find it.'

'How?'

'I dunno. I just feel I should have done something. I definitely should have guessed he was drinking something stronger than coffee.'

'You're not a mind reader. And there's no law against getting hammered. So why was he busted?'

'An unprovoked assault, the cop said. Could he go to prison for that?'

Sizemore said something clearly meant to sound comforting, but as we were now on the move again, and overtaking every other vehicle on the road, I wasn't really listening.

Ballymoney Garda Station looked more like a well-loved country cottage than a cop shop. Built in natural grey stone, and with a low slate roof, it was surrounded by yellow climbing roses. It even had the ubiquitous water barrel by the door. And out by the gate three colourful flowerbeds only added to this picture of a rural idyll. The only jarring note was a fourth flowerbed. It looked like it had been attacked by mortar fire. The culprit stood beside it, covered in incriminating evidence. Our Jeep Cherokee, its bull bars dripping mangled marigolds and battered lobelia, its tyres coated in moss peat. I turned away.

Inside the cop shop, Sizemore knocked on a shining glass panel that ran above a Pledge-scented counter.

Nothing.

'Hello?' I called.

No reply.

'Anyone there?' Sizemore's deep tones echoed along the stone hallway.

There was a distant, muffled grunt.

We exchanged glances, before tiptoeing towards the sound. More muffled sounds, but louder now. Sizemore pushed open a creaking green door.

We looked into what was clearly an interview room. Windowless, and sparsely furnished, it looked like a torture chamber, compared with the county-cottage tweeness out front.

Or maybe it was because a battered-looking Declan was being held against the wall by a fat Garda with sweat stains under his arms. My first instinct was to take a run at the cop. Then I realised he was actually supporting Declan, trying to give him a sobering drink of tea. A difficult feat given that Declan kept sliding to the floor.

'Declan?' I said.

'He killed shree dogs!' Declan shouted at the perspiring Garda. 'Why aren't shoo charging him?'

'Relax now, son. Calm down.' The panting cop tried his best to hold him upright, but Declan slid floorwards again.

I hurried over and Declan turned.

'Annie.' His bloodshot eyes widened in surprise. 'Have they harrested shoo?'

'No. You OK?' I knelt beside him.

'I'm not shrunk.' He slumped against me, leaving a trail of blood and snot across my pale linen jacket.

I looked at the blood, and turned accusingly to the big, overweight Garda.

'You should see the other man,' he said wearily. 'Broken nose, blood everywhere.'

'I'm not shrunk,' Declan slurred again.

''Course not.' Sizemore took his weight with practised ease. 'Let's get you out to the jeep.' He shot a defiant look at the Garda.

'Is that OK?' I asked quickly.

The Garda nodded, barely able to hide his relief.

'Whaisting your time.' Declan pointed an unsteady finger at him. '*He* won't let me trive.'

Sizemore's laugh became a cough. 'Thank you Sergeant . . . Dillion,' he said, reading the cop's name tag.

'Let's go Declan,' I said gently.

Sergeant Dillion mopped his brow and didn't say a word about the ruined flowerbed, for which I was truly grateful. Stories abound in Dublin about mad rural cops, ready to die in defence of their summer bedding displays.

I helped Sizemore get Declan into the jeep. We strapped him carefully into the back seat, ignoring his demands to drive.

The big Garda stood watching, mopping his sweating forehead.

'You OK to drive, Annie?' Sizemore worried, as I took a second to catch my breath.

'I'll trive,' Declan slurred, before slumping over the locked seatbelt saving him from smashing his face on the floor.

I stayed with him, while Sizemore joined the Garda in the station.

'He killed 'em,' Declan mumbled.

I turned to console him, but he was out for the count, his mouth gaping, his smelly whiskey breath wheezing like a steam train.

Sizemore came back, pocketing his wallet, his face grim. Clearly blue lobelia and French marigolds didn't come cheap in this neck of the woods. He gunned the Lexus, taking care to avoid the three remaining flowerbeds as he headed out to the road. Before following, I checked that Declan still had a pulse.

We were halfway to Dublin when my mobile rang. Sizemore.

'Everything OK, Annie?'

'Yes. He's looking a bit rough, but he'll survive.'

'I made a few calls. I may be able to sort this. The cops don't want to summons him.'

'Thanks, Sizemore.'

'Niall.'

'Who? Oh. Thank you . . . Niall.'

'Where will you take him?'

'To his digs.'

'Need help?'

'No. I'll call his landlady; she's a good sort.'

I drove on, smiling to myself. Sizemore and I were doing pretty well. Beginning to make a real team. I was wrong about him being a snob. He was just . . . he was just Sizemore. Niall, actually. My smile broadened. You should never judge a man by the cut of his suit.

I eased off the accelerator, taking my time now, enjoying the drive. Feeling a lot happier and more content than I had in ages despite the drunken snores, grunts and farts coming from the back seat.

17

Next morning, Dublin could have twinned with Florence. The sky was a virginal blue, the city-centre temperatures hitting twenty-five degrees, and rising, and though it wasn't yet nine o'clock, the streets were milled out of it with visitors. Everywhere you looked there were flocks of tourists. The tanned, braless and beautiful packing out the pavement cafés that were springing up on every corner, like mushrooms after rain.

Determined to make the most of the beautiful weather I had asked Sizemore to meet me for a break-fast coffee, which was why we were now sitting outdoors at Café Naturelle. He hadn't taken much convincing. After our joint foray into the mountains to rescue Declan, and our growing pile of evidence against Seanie Bolger, we were finally beginning to relax with each other.

Eyes twinkling, he smiled across the table at me, holding my gaze until I buried my face in my frothy cappuccino. When I lowered my cup to smile back at him, he leaned across to dab at my upper lip with his napkin. Two days ago I would have snarled like a wildcat at such easy familiarity, this morning I willed his hand to linger on my mouth.

'Froth,' he mouthed silently.

Just then, someone standing close by moved away, allowing the sun to shine directly onto his face, illuminating his perfectly-chiselled mouth. Maybe it was the heat, or the bright sun, but I couldn't stop looking at it. It was like I was mesmerised. I couldn't stop staring at the curvature of his top lip. And he knew. I saw it in his eyes, and I wanted to run. To ring Gerry. Fiona. Anyone, to take my mind off what I was thinking.

'Continental,' he said.

'What?'

'This weather.'

Of course it was bloody continental. Wasn't that the problem? It was making everyone behave out of character. It was bloody eight fifty in the morning, and a couple at the next table were kissing. Tongues and all. Unwarranted at this hour.

OK, it was Friday, and casual dress day in a plethora of nearby offices. But did people have to lose the run of themselves? There wasn't a business suit in sight. It was all blinding colours and in-your-face casuals. Practically sensual. Even I had fallen into the hot weather trap. I was wearing a cheeky little Ghost top and skirt Sandra had persuaded me to buy a month earlier when the weather was so stormy it had the fashion shops frantically discounting their summer stock. But was it a little too cheeky? Too brief? I glanced down at it, then back at Sizemore.

'Nice top.' His eyes lingered over it. 'Run out of baggy shirts, did you?'

I smiled at him, and the tension rose again. This time we both became awkward. Ill at ease. Unsure what to say next.

My phone rang.

'Hi, Gerry,' I said. 'How's the weather in Arizona?'

Sizemore went into the café to pay for the coffees.

'The case is going well,' I assured Gerry, as I watched Sizemore's back view. What had Sandra said that first day? *You'd want to bite his . . .*

'No. Everything is fine,' I cut across Gerry's fervent apologies for his prolonged stay. 'We may get a good result. You take as long as you like. No rush. No rush at all.'

Sizemore was now walking towards the agency. I ended the call and darted after him.

'Wait up,' I said, and fell into step beside him. 'Beautiful day.'

'Beautiful.' He turned to look at me, but I couldn't see his eyes. He had put on his shades. Protection against the bright sun? 'You OK?'

'Yes.' Our hands brushed as we walked together.

'We're to interview that girl from the club, this morning?'

'Yes.'

Our hands brushed again, and for one mad moment I was tempted to grab his long fingers, and hold on. But sanity prevailed. The volume of people on the street forced us to walk close together, though, which meant more brushing against each other. He even had to rescue me once, when a brat of a kid came straight towards me, almost mowing me down

163

with a bicycle. Without breaking stride Sizemore pulled me protectively against him. And I so wanted to stay within the circle of that strong arm. Then the kid was gone, and we were at the agency, and gearing ourselves up for work.

Sizemore held open the door for me, and I leaned so far away from him I nearly overbalanced. That's when I hit the real obstacle, and tripped clumsily. Again Sizemore was my saviour, catching me before I smacked onto the floor.

'You OK?' He steadied me.

I nodded and he let go, to kick out at the heap of sprawling bin bags, and old rucksacks that were strewn dangerously close to the door.

'What the hell is all this?' He hunked down to investigate the mysterious junk. He was tearing open a cardboard box when the lift clanged, and Declan stepped out looking like a refugee from a war zone – red-eyed, unshaven, and as if three people had been sleeping rough in his clothes.

'Sorry about that.' He indicated the junk. 'All my worldly goods.'

There was an awkward silence. I raised an enquiring eyebrow at Declan. What was happening here? Yesterday I had delivered him safely to his digs. Even helped him to open the door before driving off.

'I suppose you're wondering what my things are doing here?' He watched me through bloodshot eyes that looked like they'd been ringed with soot before being pushed back in his head by an angry fist.

'Well . . .' I shifted uneasily.

'Yes.' Sizemore said in his up-front American way, although he's not American.

'Mrs Dolan threw me out.' Declan was shamefaced. 'But she gave me back my deposit.' He offered in mitigation.

'Oh that's good. Isn't it?' I asked.

'Where will you go?' Sizemore asked.

'Can't afford a hotel. I made coffee.' He turned to the bubbling machine. 'Fresh!' He announced as if this was some magical feat, instead of a five-times-a-day occurrence in the agency.

I tried not to stare at his quivering hands as he spilled what looked like pints of coffee before a single drop made it into the waiting mugs. His knuckles were horribly swollen and one of them had an ugly looking cut running along it. I stood beside him, to indicate support, busying myself with milk and sugar.

Sizemore took his coffee black. Unsweetened. Not a good sign.

The silence became so unbearable, I tried to think of something cheerful to say.

'You know what I was thinking this morning?' I smiled. 'You'll probably laugh, but I was thinking that Dublin could be twinned with Florence. It's so hot and sunny and . . . and almost continental with the Spike shining in O'Connell Street, and all those tourists packing out the cafés' and—'

The door flew open and Barney came rushing in wearing his Dirty McGill office suit. Before anyone could warn him he nearly came a cropper over the carelessly strewn bags as well. Again it was Sizemore's speedy reflexes that broke his fall.

'Who the fuck put this shaggin' lot here?' Barney ungraciously shrugged him off.

'Who owns this shit?'

'That'll be me.' Declan held up his hand.

'What's it doing here?'

'Nowhere else to put it.'

'Oh.'

'Mrs Dolan threw him out.' I tried to spare Declan the ignominy of having to explain his situation again.

'Jaysus.' Barney looked at me as if I was responsible.

'She gave him back his deposit,' I offered.

This time it would have taken a chainsaw to cut through the silence.

It was obvious that someone would have to offer Declan a place to stay, but given the present unsettled situation between Gerry and me, I didn't feel I could invite him to stay in my place.

I had once invited Fiona to stay with us. She was in desperate need, and I had only meant for the weekend. But that particular weekend stretched into months, leaving Gerry with a morbid fear of ever again offering hospitality to anyone, no matter how serious their need. To this day he remained convinced that if Pino hadn't appeared on the scene, and whisked Fiona away to his luxury pad on the coast, the three of us would still be living in enforced celibacy, due to my very real fear of being overheard having sex.

'Barney, you have a big sofa in your bed-sit,' I whispered as he geared himself up for another boring day at McGill's.

'I also have a promising sex life,' he whispered back.

'Since when?' I hissed.

'Since tonight when my new girlfriend is coming over.'

'What new girlfriend?' I was surprised.

'Tara. You remember the tall blonde stunner in The Randy Goat? The one wearing—'

'Very little? I remember her all right. But Declan is really in need,' I pleaded.

'And I'm not? You think girls like Tara come along every day of the week? She's so hot she sizzles. Her dad was a detective, so she thinks we're better than rock stars. Last night she begged me to take her to my place, and show her my Glock.'

'You don't have a gun,' I reminded him.

'I know that, and you know that. But as long as Tara doesn't, she's hot to trot.'

Sasha, Naomi's receptionist, turned out to be perfect. She was everything Naomi promised, and more. Attractive, polite, well-groomed and totally professional. And with absolutely no interest in gossip.

'This is Declan, our senior detective,' I introduced them.

They shook hands in silence. If Declan was a man of few words, Sasha was a woman of even fewer. Tall, and slender as a boy, her blonde hair cropped tight against her long pale neck, she moved with the grace of a trained ballerina. And just as silently. And she might look as if a feather could knock her over, but she didn't even blink at the sight of Declan's battered face and torn, bruised hands.

I left them to out-silence each other, and went to

fetch Sizemore. We had a hectic day ahead of us. We'd had another stroke of luck when someone called Carole Stapleton finally agreed to meet us. If she was Seanie's bit on the side, as Sadie hinted in a call, she could possibly supply us with the definitive piece of evidence against him. A sexual motive was always a winner.

Sadie had called me the day after we spoke to hint that this girl and Seanie were definitely more than friends.

'Why else would Kathy have hated her so much?' Sadie asked. Then, in a sudden confessional rush, she added, 'I know for a fact that *Airhead* phoned Kathy at least twice that last week, while she was on night shift, to say he'd be crashing at Carole's flat near the club, because he'd been drinking.'

'That might be seen as commendable.'

'Commendable! As if he cared about driving with drink on him!' Sadie's fury sizzled down the line. 'And anyway, guess who poured his drinks in the club?'

'Carole?'

'Well, she is the head barmaid there. Can you imagine? Probably dresses like some twenty-euro tart.'

Sizemore smiled when he heard this.

'Twenty euros? Sadie doesn't get out much, does she?'

Ignoring this, I was now showing him Gerry's favourite tape recorder.

'Brilliant!' He handled it carefully. 'It looks exactly like a cigarette lighter. Oh, it is.' He flicked it on.

'Hence its popularity,' I said. 'But would we be

asking for trouble, using it now the smoking ban is in force?'

'I'll just play with it,' he said with a grin.

'We are meeting her in a hotel bar,' I reminded him. 'If you suddenly whip out a cigarette lighter, the anti-smoking police might pounce.'

'Let them. There's no law against *fiddling* with a cigarette lighter, is there? They'll just assume I'm a frustrated smoker.'

My God, was he turning into Gerry?

Hurrying through reception I was shocked to see Declan squashed behind the desk with the willowy Sasha. They were flicking through a leather wallet, their heads touching, and so engrossed in whatever they were looking at that they didn't hear my approach.

'Checking your money, Declan?' I teased.

He jumped guiltily. 'Sssasha is showing me her family photos.' He indicated the wallet.

Sasha looked at me, then at Sizemore, her huge sea-green eyes giving nothing away.

'Does she ever smile?' Sizemore asked as we left.

'Maybe she has no reason to. Naomi said she's had a terrible time of it. A nightmare journey from Russia to Germany, and an even filthier trip before she got to Ireland.'

'She *can* speak English?'

'She has an honours degree in languages. She speaks four. Including English. That's why Naomi employs her.'

'As a receptionist?'

'Trust me, that girl will work her way up to the top.'

'How do you know?' He turned.

'Because Declan likes her. He's only turned on by high achievers. He's a bit like those wild boars they have in Italy. The ones who can sniff out a precious truffle from a mile off?'

'I'm almost sorry I asked.' Sizemore pulled a face.

18

'Feckin' smoking ban.' The heavily made-up girl sitting opposite us was not happy. Even the soft hotel lighting couldn't disguise her scowl.

'Terrible,' Sizemore nodded in agreement.

'Feckin' facists.' Her eyes looked hungrily at the little lighter by his hand. Did she guess it was taping every word? Picking up every nuance of her inner city accent?

'Your club closes at . . . four? Five a.m.?' Sizemore's voice was almost too friendly. 'Eleven a.m. must be an ungodly hour for someone in your business.'

'I wasn't working last night.' She picked up her brandy, her gold bracelets glinting under the lights. 'I only do part time.'

'Ah.'

'Pay must be pretty good.' I stared at her bracelets.

'Two of these were presents from the boss. He's from the Ukraine. He goes back and forward a lot. Brings back stuff. You know.' She winked.

My chest tightened. I didn't want to be told about illegal trafficking between Ireland and Russia, or step on anyone's toes in the murky world of clubland. All I wanted was to get a result on the Bolger case, then sort out my own life, and live happily ever after.

I was thinking about this when Carole picked up the little lighter/recorder and began twirling it under the light.

'This is pretty cool. Real gold, is it?' she asked cheekily, as she fiddled with it, flicking it on and off, examining it extra closely, as if to authenticate it.

'Leitz?' She read out the name. 'It's not Gucci then?'

'I wish.' I laughed uneasily, wishing she'd put it down. It wasn't that good a recorder, although the man Gerry bought it from said it once belonged to a top KGB agent. If he thought that would make Gerry lust after it, he was right.

'It's a killer, isn't it?' Carole dropped the lighter carelessly and turned to Sizemore. 'Having a drink without a smoke? Like eating your dinner without salt. Bloody government will be banning this next.' She swished her brandy around the big glass, before downing it in a single thirsty gulp.

'Another drink, Carole?' Sizemore asked, as a waiter hovered nearby, eyeing the cigarette lighter with unease.

'Make it a double, handsome,' she said cheekily.

'And two more coffees please,' Sizemore directed the waiter.

'And some biscuits.' I wasn't being the outsider.

'So you worked with Seanie when he was involved in the Roxy club?' Sizemore played with the lighter/recorder, moving it just beyond Carole's reach.

'Oh, we knew each other long before that.'

'You did?' I didn't hide my surprise.

'Him and my Tom went to school together,' she addressed Sizemore. 'Been mates ever since.'

'Tom must be pretty upset so,' I said.

'Upset?' She clearly didn't like me. Maybe because I wasn't *handsome*.

'About the fire. And Kathy.'

'Oh yeah . . . But that was months ago.'

My shock at such blatant callousness had her explaining. 'I mean, Seanie is going to be OK isn't he? The papers said he'll recover.'

I glanced at Sizemore.

'He's strong,' she insisted. 'People think he's a big softy but he did Kung Fu or something after giving up the football! Has a black belt or something.' She turned to intercept her drink, snatching it from the waiter before he could put it on the table.

'Pretty shocking about Kathy, though,' Sizemore said.

'Well yeah, but . . . she wasn't a friend of mine . . . or Tom's . . . and she . . . well you're not supposed to speak ill of the dead, are you?' She stared at me, her black eyeliner making her eyes look enormous.

'You and Seanie were close?' I kept my tone light.

'We weren't shagging each other, if that's what you mean,' she snapped. 'But yeah we were . . . we are mates. Sometimes, when him and Kathy had a row he'd sleep on our sofa. She could be a right bitch. Dunno how he lived with her.'

'So they rowed a lot?' Sizemore encouraged.

'Christ, I'd kill for a ciggie.' She reached for the lighter, and began flicking it on and off again.

'Don't do that,' I said quickly. 'It has sentimental value,' I bluffed. 'A gift from my . . . mum.'

Actually, Gerry bought the little tape recorder in Prague. Third hand. He was in the Czech Republic chasing an absconding father when a man in a bar offered him the lighter/tape recorder for ninety dollars, clearly under the misapprehension that Gerry was a wealthy American. Gerry offered him twenty. The man settled for thirty, and a double Scotch.

Chin on hand, Carole leaned towards me. 'Kathy was weird.'

'How do you mean . . . weird?' I mirrored her pose like all the books say you should. Well, the ones I read.

'You know . . . weird. She had that abortion for no reason.'

I blinked. 'You mean miscarriage?'

'Well, if you want to call it that!' She gave a tight little laugh and swung around to face the bar. 'Where's that feckin' waiter? I need another drink, the measures here are piss poor.'

'I'll get it.' Sizemore disappeared over to the bar. Carole watched him go, her eyes taking in every inch of him.

I wanted to shake her. Tell her to concentrate. Force her to tell me everything she knew about Seanie and Kathy. 'Are you saying Kathy didn't have a miscarriage?'

She gave a little snort of laughter. 'You think she went into that fancy clinic to have a miscarriage? Booked it in advance? A miscarriage?' She gave another snort of laughter. 'Give me a break!'

'So you know for definite that she had an *abortion*?' I enunciated clearly for the tape.

'Well, Seanie didn't say it straight out. But he went through a full bottle of Scotch that night. I said he could sleep on our sofa, but he didn't do much sleeping. He was in and out of the bathroom all night, puking his ring up. I got worried, but Tom said to leave him be, that Seanie always puked when he was upset. Anyway, next morning he was gone. Left our bathroom like a right pigsty too. The stink was unmerciful! After that he sort of avoided me. Even in the club he kept his distance. Maybe he thinks I'm one of them pro-lifers.' She chuckled.

I doubted it. Five minutes in Carole's company was enough to convince anyone that the only thing she was *pro* was Carole.

'He did meet up with Tom a couple of times though.'

'Did he talk to him about the abortion?'

'Tom? Are you nuts? All they ever talked about was Man United, and that feckin' Champions League. Except for the week before the fire. Seanie went on a real bender that week. Told Tom he was having money problems. That the people who were giving him the loan for the new club were hassling him. Pressing him for quicker repayments, or something.'

'Who gave him the loan?'

'I dunno. Not a bank, that's for sure.' She turned to the bar again.

'How much was it for?'

'I dunno. People were quoting telephone numbers. A million? Two million? Jayyyysus!' she laughed.

'What kind of eejit would give Seanie Bolger two million euros?'

'Maybe he re-mortgaged the shop?'

'Couldn't have. That was already mortgaged to the hilt. Why do you think Kathy worked all them double shifts? One night he lost it with her, said they never saw each other. He ordered her to jack it in or he'd . . . but her job paid the mortgage and—'

'Seanie lost it with her? Did he hit her?'

'Don't be stupid,' she laughed. 'More like she'd give him a box in the snot.'

'She'd . . . ?'

'You know what I mean. She had him by the balls. He couldn't believe it when she first said she'd go out with him. He thought she was Princess Di. Dying to show her off he was, said she blew out a doctor for him. Jaysus. I thought she'd be wearing a bleedin' tiara,' she giggled. 'Turned out she was only a nurse! A feckin' nurse? I make more money working the bar.'

'Did he tell you she went to medical school?'

'To be a nurse?'

'A doctor.'

'Ah would you ever feck off. How could she be a doctor? She was popping pills like they were Smarties.' She scratched her arm as if the heavy bracelets were irritating her.'

'Kathy took drugs?' I inched the little recorder towards her, my eyes searching the bar for Sizemore, who was nowhere to be seen.

'*Kathy took drugs?*' I repeated clearly.

'Not that kind of drugs.' She made a face. 'She

was on all sorts of prescription shite. Prozac, and some other kind of feckin' anti-depressant. She had this mad little alarm on her watch so she wouldn't forget to take them. Bloody thing went *bing* every five minutes.'

'Every five minutes?' I echoed dumbly.

'That's what it seemed like. Tom said she only used it to get attention, so people would notice her. She was plain and gawky so maybe she did use the alarm for attention. But I think she *was* depressed. Sometimes you'd be afraid to look at her in case she burst into tears.'

'Did Seanie worry about her being depressed?'

'Well, yeah, but she could convince him black was white. She told him all women get depressed with their monthlies. Like it was normal or something. Anyway, he had other things on his mind, by then. Like how he was going to pay back all that dosh he was borrowing. And there was all that delay with opening the new club. Mad. We're packed out every night now, since the Russians took over and brought in them pole dancers.'

'Was your club going down the tubes when the shop burned down?'

'What?' She was admiring the lighter again.

'When Seanie's shop went up in flames.'

She nodded. 'Oh yeah. Shitty, isn't it? It never rains but it pours.'

'Did Seanie smoke?'

'Everyone smokes. Some nights you can hardly breathe in the Jacks behind our bar.'

'Doesn't the club enforce the smoking ban?'

'What do you think?' She was checking the lighter again.

'How do they get away with breaking the law?'

Her eyes flashed. 'Listen, I just do me job. I serve drinks and keep the punters happy. I'm not a bloody cop. Once I get paid and make enough dropsy I don't give a shite who does what. Where's that bloody drink? I can't hang around here all day.'

Sizemore was back at the bar now, watching us. I signalled and he was beside me in seconds. Carole snatched her brandy, draining the glass like there was a drought. Her third brandy, and it wasn't even midday.

She tucked her long chiffon scarf into her bag, popped a pair of imitation Gucci shades on her nose, and with barely a wave in our direction she disappeared out the door, rock steady on her mountainously high heels.

The ruddy-faced doorman gave her a scathing look as she passed.

'That was a sudden exit,' Sizemore said. 'What did she tell you?'

'Hear for yourself.' I reached for the tape recorder. It wasn't there. I lifted the plate of biscuits. Moved a glass. No sign of it. 'The tape recorder?' I quizzed Sizemore. 'Did you pick it up?'

'No.'

'It's gone.'

He was already halfway to the door, leaving me double-checking the curved banquette seat, and then the thickly carpeted floor. No joy. The recorder was gone.

The doorman held open the door for me, and pointed to the right.

'They went towards the green,' he said, his eyes alive with curiosity.

I ran, squinting into the bright sunlight after the cool darkness of the hotel bar. Bumping into people right and left. Crashing into strolling lovers, and groups of shoppers, forcing them to one side. Apologising as I ran.

'Hey!' a skinny little man shouted, when we collided so hard that his bouquet of carnations tumbled to the ground.

'Sorry,' I called over my shoulder.

I spotted Sizemore's tall figure up ahead. Standing at a travel agency window he was holding Carole by both arms, as if he was threatening her.

I was almost on them when a double buggy with two plump infants on board came speeding around a corner and sent me flying.

The girl with the double buggy was mortified. Apologising repeatedly she helped me to my feet as the two screaming babies attracted more attention than an armed smash and grab.

'You sure you're all right?' she repeated, as a crowd gathered.

'I'm fine,' I was insisting, when the skinny man with the damaged carnations appeared, and began calling me a rude bitch.

'Shurrup and leave the poor girl alone,' someone said. 'She fell, God love her.'

Then Sizemore was there, asking what happened. 'You OK, Annie?' he worried, his eyes darting from my white face to the incandescent bouquet man.

'She deliberately knocked me down. Hit me like a bleedin' rocket.'

'I didn't even see you.'

''Course you did. Now look at me bleedin' flowers!' The battered blooms were held up for inspection.

'We were chasing a thief.' Sizemore loomed over him.

'Oh, bleedin' Gards are yis? Well, I want her badge number. I'm going to sue for pain and distress. I have a plastic hip. *And* I want the price of me missus's anniversary bouquet.'

'Ah fuck off ye auld chancer,' someone said.

Sizemore blocked my view of the old chancer, but I knew he was pressing notes into his hand. 'OK?'

'What about me hip? That could be damaged?'

Sizemore gave him another couple of notes.

'You're a bleedin' gentleman.' He disappeared into the crowd.

'Show's over folks,' Sizemore said, and led me back to the hotel, his fingers practically making indentations in my upper arm.

'What's the rush?' I protested as he hurried me to a table.

He signalled to a waiter.

'Did you get the lighter?'

'Yes.' He dropped it on the table.

'So she did steal it?'

'She claims it got entangled in her scarf.'

'And you believed her?'

'Would you?'

'No.'

'Me neither. She has track marks on her arms.'

'She's a junkie?' I was horrified.

His mobile beeped, but he ignored it.

'Aren't you . . . ?' I pointed.

'No. Two malt whiskies please,' he ordered the hovering waiter.

'It's not even lunch time,' I protested. 'I can't drink whisky at this hour.'

'OK, coffee then? You look pale, Annie. Just sit there and take it easy for a minute. We're in no hurry.' He hunked down low to look into my face.

I turned away so he wouldn't see the effect his kindness was having on me. Couldn't have him thinking I was all weak and girly. And pliable.

'Annie?' He tried to turn my head around, but I held it rock still.

'Sorry.' He stood up. 'You're right. We should go.'

'Is your wife all right sir?' The waiter hesitated.

'Oh *Annie's* fine.' Sizemore didn't even blink. 'She's tough as old boots. Aren't you, Annie?' He shot me a look, then headed for the door, without even checking to see if I was following.

Sasha was taking a call as I walked in. Despite her heavily accented English she was handling it so well, I shot her a look of approval as I passed.

'Anniiie?' She put the caller on hold, and passed me a little wad of message slips. All of them beautifully typed.

I was in the lift before I realised Sizemore wasn't with me. Preferred to dawdle in reception with the beautiful Sasha did he? Not that I'd blame him. In his shoes I might have chosen to spend time with a girl who had a smile like an angel, rather than a grumpy PI whose mood seemed to change with the wind.

Anyway, I didn't mind being left alone with the tape recorder. There were a few things Carole said that I wanted to hear again.

In my office, I threw down my bag, tore the wrapper off a large slab of white chocolate, and hit the play button on the little recorder.

I had to decide if Carole was telling us the truth, but the more I listened the more I realised another pair of ears would be helpful. What the hell was Sizemore up to in reception all this time? We didn't need another letch. We already had Barney.

I'd have to put up a notice in reception.

THOSE WISHING TO OGLE PRETTY GIRLS MUST DO SO ON THEIR OWN TIME. AND NOT ON THESE PREMISES.

I reached out to buzz reception, then changed my mind. Sizemore's ego had been massaged enough this morning. First by me. Then by Carole. Calling him *handsome*. And then by Sasha giving him a killer smile as we came back in? Ruinous for any man.

Two minutes passed. Three. I crossed to the window to look down into the street. The tabloids were gleefully predicting that this heatwave would bring murder and mayhem to the streets of Dublin. There wasn't much sign of either. Just the usual traffic cock-ups. And kamikaze cyclists darting in and out between dangerously overloaded trucks.

Sizemore came in behind me. 'Feeling better are you? Thought I'd give you some space. Some quiet time.'

Quiet time? How old did he think I was? Three? He'd be putting me in the bold corner next.

We listened to the tape in silence.

'Need to hear it again?' I asked as it ended.

'No.'

'You sure?' I was surprised.

He nodded. 'What do you make of Carole's story of Kathy's dependence on antidepressants?'

'Hard to tell.' I rewound the tape. 'But if she was on heavy medication it could explain her decision to have an abortion.'

'Fear of side effects? Foetal damage?' He seemed unsure.

'Well, what other reason would she have?' I heard myself snap.

'But wouldn't her parents have known? They seemed close. Wouldn't she have told them?'

'About the abortion?' My voice rose in disbelief.

'Yeah.'

'You think she would have discussed having an abortion with her parents? Are you nuts?' I couldn't believe what I was hearing.

'They were clearly very close.' He was taken aback by my tone. 'They adored her. Surely if it came to a medical necessity, they would have . . .'

'Supported her?'

'I was about to say understood.'

183

'Maybe in some parallel universe. You still don't get it, do you? They would have feckin' disowned her!'

'So they wouldn't have known about the abortion? *If* she had one. Which is still open to question.'

'I think she had,' I said snottily.

'Did I do something to annoy you, Annie?'

'What makes you ask that?'

'Well, I . . . I know we got off to a bad start, but I thought we were doing fine, and now you seem to be antagonistic all over again.'

'Doing fine?' I laughed. 'You make it sound like we were dating!'

He actually flushed. But only slightly. Not the sort of big reddener I get for the least thing. He did blink though. And squirmed about a bit.

'Sorry if I crossed the line, Annie. I honestly didn't mean to.'

I got the tiniest twinge of guilt. Truth was he hadn't done anything wrong. He hadn't stepped over any line. He just . . . for some reason he irritated me. Made me mad. But that wasn't his fault. He wasn't to blame. I marched to the window so he wouldn't see my growing embarrassment. Down in the street the kamikaze courier cyclists were still darting about, taking ridiculous chances. Stupid arses.

Behind me I heard the door open. 'I'll talk to you later,' Sizemore said, and left.

19

The phones rang unheeded while Sandra carefully rearranged her nail varnish collection into its normal position on the reception desk. 'I hate it when people mess with my stuff.'

I put down my post, hit a button, and grabbed the receiver in time to hear a caller hang up. 'Sandra!' I frowned. 'They hung up.'

'Just my luck,' she grumbled.

I sighed in defeat. 'Not to worry. If it's important they'll ring back.'

'I didn't mean that! I'm fed up because I take two stingy days off and I miss all the excitement. First Declan gets arrested and you have to drive up the mountains to rescue him, letting Naomi take over in reception? Naomi?' She was awestruck.

'But only . . .'

'Then this glamorous Russian invites Declan to share her flat. I didn't even get to see her.'

'You and Jimmy were making a baby! What's more exciting than that?'

'You think lying around with your bum in the air is exciting? Even Jimmy got fed up after the first ten minutes. Not during the actual . . . you know, but afterwards. He legged it downstairs to re-pot his autumn bedding. I ripped into him when he came back, I can tell you. All very well for you, I said, you don't have to lie here, with your arse in the air, reading *Cosmo*. And what does he do then?'

'Please don't make me guess.'

'He grabs me and tries to start riding again? His hands are covered in John Innes compost and he starts . . . Get off me, I said, the book says not to have intercourse *too* frequently . . . something to do with weakening the sperm . . . but he takes this as a personal insult, gets all narky and we end up having a massive row.'

'You had a row? While you were ovulating?'

'Yeah. So he legs it to the pub, where he probably wanted to be in the first place because there was some stupid Interleague game on Sky. Now does that sound exciting to you?'

'Er . . . maybe not.' I checked that I had everything I needed in my bag. The most important item being a bottle of Southern Comfort. Sizemore and I were meeting an ex-neighbour of Seanie Bolger's family, and were hoping to get some good information from him, because he sounded as bitter and twisted as they come, therefore bound to enjoy telling tales against Seanie. And hopefully he wouldn't steal our tape recorder the minute our backs were turned.

Taping Carole's voice had been a waste of time. It took Lily in Mutual Irish three seconds to discount her as the anonymous caller.

'That's not the woman who rang in.' She was adamant. 'The anonymous caller had a . . . a sort of lilting voice . . . almost . . . musical. Have you ever heard Maria Callas sing?'

Sizemore had come back swearing like a trooper. 'Maria feckin' Callas?' he hissed. 'Now all we have to do is find someone who sounds like Maria feckin' Callas.'

'I think that's a positive description.' I didn't let him see how shocked I was by his attitude. His manners were definitely going down hill. Was it the agency, or was he just losing patience with the case?

'Very few people sound like Maria Callas,' I said.

'Jesus H Christ! I'm not sure I can take much more of this.' He scratched at a still fresh shaving cut, making it bleed again.

Looking at him I had to smother my laughter. He'd only been here a couple of weeks and already he was turning into one of the lads, cursing and scratching with impunity. He'd be lighting farts next.

'So Declan is shacking up with the Russian?' Her nail varnish collection safely in situ again, Sandra was hungry for fresh gossip.

'Nobody said he's shacking up with her,' I remonstrated.

'He's staying in her bed-sit! Of course he's shacking up with her.'

'Not necessarily.'

'Where's he sleeping then? In the bath? Barney said he's like a man in a trance when she's around.' She giggled with delight. 'Remember the time he got that crush on Naomi and we used to wet ourselves laughing? And I set my alarm early, so I could watch him drool when she came in?'

'And there was I thinking you'd turned into a workaholic.'

'Me? A workaholic? Are you mental?' She finally picked up the phone that had been ringing, ignored, for almost five minutes.

Listening to her charm the irate caller, I realised how dull the place would be without her. OK, with someone like Sasha in reception the phones might get answered promptly, but Sandra was the lynchpin of the agency. Everyone told her their problems. She didn't exactly listen, of course, but that wasn't the point. You could still tell her. She was always there. And she made great coffee. Even when you didn't want any. But her Jimmy was an old-fashioned husband. What would happen if he insisted that she gave up working to become a stay-at-home mum? Sasha was efficient and personable, and she gave Declan a place to stay, but she wasn't Sandra.

Caller sorted, Sandra reached for her nail file.

'I think I might try being a stay-at-home mum.'

I froze for a second, then, 'You mean this isn't your home?' I forced a laugh. 'I thought home was the place where you did your nails, gossiped with your mates and only answered the phone when you felt like it?'

'Give over, Annie.' She laughed. 'Or I'll bring me new foot spa in.'

What would we do without her? What would she do without us? Gerry gave her her first job at sixteen. Sent her to typing and computer courses. He even paid for her twenty-first-birthday party. He might even pay for her to have her hair straightened when he saw her latest style, which could best be described as a blonde Afro. She had seen it on two catwalk models and had to have it, regardless of whether or not she could now fit into Jimmy's van without opening the sunroof.

'Here's Sizemore.' She suddenly lit up.

He looked grim, his face as long as a wet weekend.

'Bad news?' I called after him.

'It's not good.' He glanced at Sandra. 'Let's go up to your office.'

We walked over to the lift, leaving Sandra burning with curiosity.

'Bolger's ex-neighbour changed his mind. He won't talk to us.'

'Shit!' I slumped with disappointment.

Sizemore hit the button, and we waited for the lift. Nothing happened. He stepped back to check which floor it was on. As there were only four floors in our building it wasn't exactly spoiled for choice. Although the lift sometimes behaved as if it was.

'How long has it been sitting up there, Sandra?' I shouted, when I saw the light flashing on the first floor.

'Er . . . I'm not sure.'

'The truth!'

'Twenty minutes?' Always in awe of glamorous Naomi, the last thing Sandra wanted was to squeal on her. She lived in hope that someday she might be invited to one of Naomi's fabled parties. The ones top fashion models were rumoured to attend with aging rock stars, and hip American writers who lived in Ireland to avoid paying tax. Naomi's parties sometimes got a mention in a Sunday gossip column, the pinnacle of success according to Sandra.

'Jesus,' Sizemore said. 'Bloody Naomi has wedged open the feckin' door again. Do you have to sub-let those two floors to Dreamland Interiors?'

Listening to him I thought how magical it must be not to have to worry about money. Never to have to count the pennies? Or battle with banks whose favourite word seems to be foreclosure?

'Let's use the stairs,' I said. 'Better for our health. Good for your heart.'

He shot me one of his unfathomable looks. Then to my utter surprise he reached out to caress my face.

In truth it wasn't really a caress. More a fleeting touch, because it was over so fast. Still, it froze me with shock. I stood staring up at him, until I realised that less than ten feet away Sandra was only short of standing on the desk to get a better view of us.

'Let's wait for the lift,' Sizemore said.

'Yes,' I whispered. My heart beating like a snare drum.

The lift appeared like magic, the doors flew open and three stylishly-dressed women stepped out, all three of them giggling like over-stimulated three-year-olds.

'I'm in love with the distressed shaker,' the first one squealed.

'Not me. I'll opt for country cottage flagstones, stripped units and exposed stone walls.'

'A Belfast sink! Pure white ceramic or—'

'No! I really fancy that distressed shaker.' The first voice drowned out the other two as she led them to the door in a cloud of expensive perfume.

'What's a distressed shaker?' Sizemore asked.

'Declan, after a night on the tiles?' I said, and immediately wanted to bite my tongue off in case he thought I was a caustic mare.

He mustn't have because he laughed so hard he started me off. We were practically clutching each other when Sandra yelled at us.

'Hold it! Hold the lift!' She threw down the phone. 'I've a news flash for you, Annie.'

Sizemore blocked the lift door with his foot.

'This had better be important, Sandra,' I said.

She raced over, panting like a wide-eyed puppy. 'It's mega! Seanie Bolger is conscious! He opened his eyes and spoke to his mother.'

The sister in charge of intensive care was adamant. 'Like I told all the other reporters, it's family only. Now go away, please.'

'We're not reporters,' I said.

'Seanie *asked* to see us.' Sizemore was learning to lie like the rest of us.

The sister shot him a withering look, then picked up the phone. 'This is Sister Horan. Will you send a porter up to intensive care? No, not Jack. Send me that new chap. The ex-heavyweight. The one who killed his last opponent.'

'She's bluffing,' I whispered to Sizemore. 'Stand your ground.'

I had almost convinced him, when this shaven-headed man-mountain appeared, his biceps straining the sleeves of his porter's uniform to bursting.

'Hi.' Sizemore gave him a friendly salute, and we legged it past him, and down the stairs.

The jeep was parked across from the hospital entrance. Sizemore slid behind the wheel, practically shaking with frustration.

'Nobody could have got past that . . . chap,' I consoled him. 'You did your best.'

'Not good enough was it?'

We sat there watching a stream of people going in and out of the busy hospital doors. Doors that seemed to be in perpetual motion, with the tireless ex-heavyweight standing just inside them, his beady little eyes scanning every arrival.

'We're never going to get near Seanie. We may as well leave.'

'There's Sadie!' Sizemore yelled, as a plump little figure in white strode past.

He legged it after her, greeting her like a long-lost friend. She seemed equally pleased to see him. They spoke animatedly for a few minutes, heads nodding in agreement. Then came another hand-shaking session, before Sadie disappeared in through the big swing doors. Sizemore got back in the jeep, rubbing his hands with glee.

'What did you say to her?' I asked as we sped away.

'I told her I have the release forms for Seanie's insurance payout, but I need his signature on them now that he's compos mentis.' He shot me a sly grin. 'I told her I have to witness the signing.'

'And she believed you?'

'She said she'll see what she can do.'

'Did you ask her about Kathy taking Prozac?'

He shot me a look of disbelief. 'I only had two minutes.'

'So what now?'

'Now we talk to the Newmans again.'

'When?'

'Now!' He swung the jeep off the busy roundabout and headed towards the more salubrious housing developments of Upper Sandeford and Dundrum, leaving behind the more basic two- and three-bedroom terraces of Tallaght. But even in the more rarefied tree-lined cul-de-sac where the Newmans lived, their three-storied house with its large dormer windows and highly-visible security lights, stood out, reminding me again, if I needed it, that Kathy and Seanie hadn't had a thing in common.

We rang the Newmans' doorbell three times, to no avail.

'Try again?' I asked Sizemore. He was just about to when a head popped up over next door's laurel hedge.

'They're away.' A heavily-wrinkled little woman, her grey hair pulled into a scalp-wrenching bun, peered suspiciously at us.

'Any idea when they're due back?' Sizemore laid on the charm like syrup.

'No.'

We stood dejected.

'Mrs Newman did ask if I would water their plants

until further notice. She wouldn't do that if they were planning a short break now, would she?'

'So *you're* the good neighbour they told us about,' Sizemore lied.

It worked. She invited us in. Even volunteered her name. Mrs Brent.

We perched on two plastic-covered Queen-Anne-style chairs in her stuffy living room, trying not to appear too edgy. But it's hard to relax when a cat the size of a small cougar stares unblinkingly at you, its yellow eyes full of evil intent.

'That's Bates. Don't touch him,' Mrs Brent warned unnecessarily. 'Cats like to make up their own minds.'

'True,' Sizemore agreed. He had already unnerved me by whispering that a vet buddy of his declared all cats to be domesticated psychopaths. But lovable ones.

'So you're friends of the Newmans?' Mrs Brent peered suspiciously at us.

'Actually we're more . . . er . . .' I floundered.

'Friends of Kathy's,' Sizemore said quickly.

'Poor Kathy. You look nearer her age all right. Did you work at the hospital with her?' She waited.

Sizemore sidestepped this beautifully. 'You probably knew her a lot longer than we did.' This time he was going for the old homespun charm.

'How could I? They only moved here four years ago. But a nicer family you couldn't meet. We attend prayer meetings together. They joined our prayer group almost immediately after coming here.'

'Very good.' I tried not to look at the cat.

'We hold them in our own houses when there are no other premises available.'

'How often?' Sizemore asked.

'I thought you were close friends? Don't you know how often they attend meeting?' She turned cranky again.

''Course we know,' I leaned towards her. 'But life is so fast paced these days . . . we get caught up . . . we forget the things that truly matter . . . forget about . . .'

'Faith,' she finished for me.

'Exactly. And of course we tried to give Kathy space . . .' I got a flash of inspiration, '. . . because of her depression.'

'The Newmans don't like to talk about that!' she snapped.

'But depression is an illness,' I said gently. 'Nothing to be ashamed of.'

'They weren't ashamed!' Eyes narrowing into slits, she stroked the cat until its purrs turned deafening.

''Course not,' I said quickly.

'Are you a nurse?' She peered at me. 'I don't remember seeing you at the funeral.'

'We've been away,' Sizemore jumped in.

'Where?' she snapped.

I looked around for inspiration and spotted a child of Prague statue. 'Prague,' I said.

'Prague?' She threw down the cat in disgust. 'That's in the Communist block.'

'No!' I corrected her. 'That was way back in . . . when, when . . . it's now . . .'

'Well, it used to be, and people don't change. Last week I had two Jehovah's Witnesses at my door. I told the previous two never to come back again, and what did they do? They sent their well-dressed friends knocking on my door. Now you two come here asking about the Newmans? Are you Jehovah's Witnesses?'

'No!' I laughed.

'He looks like one.' She pointed to Sizemore. 'He has the look.'

'I'm an agnostic!' Sizemore said.

'What?' Her lip quivered. 'And you have the nerve to come here asking about the Newmans? How dare you.' She got to her feet, forgetting about the cat, which had climbed back onto her lap. It landed on its back on the floor, and decided Sizemore was to blame. Before I could warn him the cat was inching towards him. It arched its back and hissed. He reached down to push it away and, with a lightning flash of a black paw, it slashed him hard across the back of his hand.

'Jesus.' He jumped up, a thin red crescent of blood appearing on his hand.

'How dare you take the holy name in vain in my house!' Mrs Brent was scandalised.

'He's American,' I tried to defend him.

Mrs Brent was having none of it. She ushered us out without a word of apology, or any acknowledgement of Sizemore's bleeding hand. As the door slammed behind us we looked at each other in disbelief, when we heard the sound of a dead bolt sliding into place.

20

Barney peered over my shoulder as I smoothed a flesh-coloured Elastoplast onto Sizemore's badly-scratched hand.

'You should have given her a kick up the arse,' he said.

'For God's sake, Barney, she's an old woman,' I protested.

'He meant the cat,' Sizemore said quietly.

I felt myself shrink with embarrassment. Bloody Barney. Whenever things were going smoothly . . . well, OK, semi-smoothly, he had to cause a ruckus. He shouldn't even be here. He was supposed to be over at Dirty McGill's. But being an adrenalin junkie he couldn't bear to keep away from where he thought the action was. He had burst in, insisting that there was *nothing* happening at McGill's. No hot cars being dismantled, no Class A drugs being distributed, not a single hint of any of the filth the cops said McGill was involved in.

He paused to look Sizemore right in the eye. 'Cats carry a disease that turns you blind.'

I wanted to let rip at him, tell him to feck off back to McGill's. The only reason I didn't was because I was concerned about Sizemore. Maybe that cat did carry something nasty.

'God's truth about the blindness!' Barney noticed my hesitation. 'One morning I caught the optometrist next door booting a feral cat off his doorstep, and he said he had no choice. He said cats carry toxic plas . . . yokey . . . something or other, said it can be deadly to humans. Turns us blind.'

'In their faeces.' Sizemore sighed.

'Ye what?'

'Cats carry toxic plasmosis in their faeces. To become infected you'd have to have direct contact with their faeces.'

'See?' I challenged Barney. 'Where did you think Sizemore had his hand? Up the cat's ar— bottom?'

'Bottom?' Barney chuckled at this lame attempt at refinement.

I wanted to clock him one. Sizemore and I were just beginning to jell again. Getting along nicely because we were both making such a huge effort. It was hard, but way better than banging heads every two seconds, so the last thing we needed now was Barney winding us up again.

I checked my watch. 'Shouldn't you be at McGill's, Barney? Won't they miss you?'

'No! It's like night of the living dead over there. Zombies R Us! All they do is sit around messin' with paperwork, totting up repair bills.'

'It is an accounts office.'

Barney scowled. 'DI Bailey said I'd be living on the edge. In physical danger every minute of the day. Ha. Biggest danger over there is bloody terminal boredom. There isn't a whisper of hot cars or . . . I haven't met a single thief or blagger yet. Even the repair shop is full of pansies. McGill is off sunning himself on the Costa del Sol, and his staff may as well be with him, because nobody is doing a feckin' thing in that garage, illegal or otherwise. This yoke is a waste of time.' He tore off his body mike.

'Don't do that! Gerry will have a fit.' I was horrified.

He gave me a look. 'Who's going to tell him?'

'I am! You're to stay on that case!'

'Aw, Annie.'

'You stay on that case, until I say otherwise.'

'But there is no case,' he whined. 'Bailey was blowing smoke up our arses . . . sorry, bottoms. Anyway, I'm on me tea break. I'm entitled to a tea break, aren't I?' He checked his watch, took a Kit Kat from my in basket, and began munching. 'Please, Annie?' He whined like a two-year-old.

'Ten minutes,' I said.

Satisfied, he sat back to enjoy the Kit Kat.

Sizemore went to the window to answer his mobile, which had been beeping politely for at least five minutes.

Barney gave a sly chuckle. 'He's wasting his time, hugging that window. Reception here is always shite.'

'His hand looks swollen,' I worried.

'Told you it needed medical attention. Let Doc Meehan have a look at it. He'll sort it.' Another chuckle.

'You can be very nasty, Barney.'

'I'm just showing concern for a colleague.'

'Liar. You just like to see people suffer. If Doctor Meehan gives him a shot he won't be able to sit down for a week.'

'Better that than losing his eyesight. Anyway, if you ask me there's a hex on the Bolger case.'

'Nobody *is* asking you!' I tried not to sound jittery. I'm as superstitious as the next person, and Sizemore *was* scratching his hand a lot. And grimacing.

'Think about it, Annie,' Barney's voice was a conspiratorial whisper. 'First someone robs Gerry's tape recorder, then an old biddy sets a vicious animal on Sizemore.'

'A vicious animal?' I laughed with relief. 'It was a tabby cat!'

'Well, OK, maybe not vicious, but one that could well be carrying a serious disease. If you ask me—'

'Shut up!'

'No listen, Annie—'

Sizemore came back, still scratching at his hand.

'Does it hurt?' I asked.

'A bit.'

'That'll be the hex.' Barney was thrilled. 'I've been telling Annie about it. People think a hex is all in the mind, but it ain't. I have experience of one. A guy who lived near me broke his ankle playing football when we were kids. Big muscular guy. Really strong. Arms like tree trunks. Thighs that could crack walnuts, then someone put a hex on him.'

My phone interrupted him and I grabbed it, gratefully.

'Hello. Annie McHugh speaking.'

'Are your knickers feeling tight, Annie? Is your beaver moist and juic—'

'You filthy pig!' I dropped the receiver like it was red hot.

Sizemore and Barney both moved like lightning, Sizemore got to me first.

'Dammit. He's gone.' He jiggled the phone furiously. 'Sandra? Did you just put a call through to this office? You sure? OK. OK.'

'Dirty bastard!' Barney spat. 'I'll cut his balls off.'

I slumped down in my chair. 'Don't start making a fuss. Please. And we're not wasting agency time trying to trace the call. The number is always withheld, or—'

'Right. Time we put the Gards on it.' Barney opened his mobile.

'No,' I said. 'I'm handling it.'

'Not very well by the look of you.'

'You did seem terrified, Annie,' Sizemore supported him.

'It's still *my* business! And it's ages since he last . . . his calls have almost dwindled to nothing. I'm not running to the Gards for help, I'm a feckin' PI for God's sake!'

'Annie, if—'

'Shut up, Barney. You and your bloody hexes anyway! Get back to McGill's. That's what you're being paid for. Sorry if you find it boring.'

I caught them exchanging glances, which really riled me. 'Butt out, both of you. He just . . . He just caught me on the hop! I'm not having the Gards tapping my phone. It's too invasive.'

'A tap would be invasive?' Barney growled. 'You looked like someone was assaulting you. Your face went grey.'

Trying to gather my wits, I stared at the floor. Sizemore hunked down to meet my eyeline. 'I can put a voice recorder on this phone. You'll be in charge of it. No one else will have access . . . no cops . . . nobody.' He waited.

I looked at him and made up my mind. 'OK.'

'When I offered to do that, you gave me a bollocking,' Barney grumbled.

'That was then. This is now.'

'Yeah but—'

'Enough.' I closed the lid on the first-aid box. 'We all need to get back to work. Sadie said we could talk to her again.' I looked at Sizemore. 'Let's see if she *can* get us in to see Seanie.'

He didn't seem convinced.

'We can try,' I pushed. 'Maybe go to the hospital late at night when things are quiet. A couple of words with Seanie, and we might get to the truth. I've never heard so many opposing stories in my life.'

'I'll come.' Barney became excited.

'You're working the McGill case.'

'Only during office hours,' he persisted. 'I could . . . hang around the hospital . . . keep watch while you sneak in to see him? Always handy to have someone keeping watch? Eh, Sizemore?'

Sizemore seemed to consider this, while absently scratching his hand.

'Get that hand sorted first,' Barney pointed. 'All messin' aside, it looks like it needs medical attention.'

'Is that your desk phone, Barney?' I turned to listen. He dashed out.

'I didn't hear a phone.' Sizemore frowned.

'Me neither. But I thought Barney might be getting to you with his stories of toxic plasmosis, and hexes that make people shrink.'

'Shrink?' He looked puzzled.

'His story about the footballer? Oh, you didn't hear the ending. Some poor kid had TB or something. He was wasting away. But TB sounded too simple for Barney, he had to make out that someone put a hex on his mate and turned him into a walking skeleton.'

'A walking—'

'Let's go, before he gets back.'

We tiptoed past Barney's door, which as usual he left swinging open.

'It *was* ringing!' He was yelling into the phone. 'Because you cut them off! I did not imagine it! What? Well if your flaky mates would stop hogging our phone lines I might get a few calls through. What? Well I'm more popular than *you*! You ditzy . . .'

'Just one big happy family.' I smiled at Sizemore.

He hit the button for the lift. 'Just like the Corleones.'

21

Sadie held her breath, as she awaited our verdict on her wholewheat raisin scones.

'Scrumptious,' I said truthfully.

'You really like them? Not too doughy?'

'They're perfect.'

'Very good.' Sizemore was less enthusiastic.

Hardly surprising. It was less than twenty minutes since our sadistic GP stuck him in the bum with a needle the size of a telegraph pole. To be fair, Sizemore hadn't complained. Much. But the tiniest bump in the road had him wincing, and he had refused Sadie's invitation to sit, even on her best chair.

'Glad you like them.' Sadie couldn't have been more chuffed if her scones had won an Egon Ronay award. She might be a skilled A & E nurse, but praising her baking was definitely the way to her heart. 'I wish I had some good news for you.' She tore her eyes off the golden scones. 'But I'm afraid those reports of Seanie Bolger's recovery were a bit premature.'

'Is he dead?' Sizemore sat without thinking, then shot back up again as if he'd been fired from a cannon.

'No! And he did open his eyes, but only for a second. And he moved his fingers – a fraction – but that's not unusual in that type of coma patient. I'm afraid those movements were involuntary.'

'But he spoke to his mum?' I swallowed my disappointment.

'*She* said he did. They were alone in the room at the time.'

'You think she lied?'

'Not necessarily. I . . . maybe he . . . made a sound . . . a noise? But I would be very surprised if he spoke with any lucidity.'

'The newspaper article said he spoke to her. Said "Hello Mum".'

'Newspapers report what people tell them,' Sizemore said, his expression miserable. I guessed this wasn't just because his injection site was throbbing; he was pissed because we had been taken in by the rumour mill. 'Are you saying that the whole momentary consciousness thing was wishful thinking on his mum's part?' he asked Sadie.

'She is his mum.' Sadie spoke gently. 'I've seen it before.'

'Shit,' he muttered under his breath.

'Sorry to dampen your hopes.' She cut the last scone in half, spread half an inch of butter on one half and bit blissfully into it. 'I shouldn't be eating these.' She patted her plump middle. 'But they are delicious, even if I say so myself.'

'Is there any hope of him regaining consciousness?' Sizemore sounded impatient.

'Half the country *is* praying for him.'

'What does that mean?' Sizemore frowned.

'I . . . I suppose it means there's always hope.'

He rolled his eyes in disbelief.

'What are his doctors saying?' I asked.

'I think you can guess what *they're* saying.' Sadie took a massive bite of the still-warm scone, sending a trickle of melted butter shooting down her chin.

'They think there's little likelihood of him recovering?' I prompted.

She wiped her chin carefully with a paper napkin. ''Fraid so.'

I turned to Sizemore with a gesture of defeat. 'Let's face it, we knew we were never going to get to speak to him. That was just wishful thinking. It was never going to happen. We were just . . .'

'Oh, you can speak to him.' Sadie cleaned her buttery hands. 'But I doubt he'll be speaking to you. Want that last piece of scone?'

I shook my head, and she looked wounded. 'I thought you liked them? Is it because they're re-heated? I didn't have the energy to bake this morning. We had two bad road accidents last night. The whole shift was a nightmare. People coming in in droves. Sleeping on trolleys. Chaos.' A shadow crossed her normally happy face, and I felt guilty for making her life even more difficult, by coming here and annoying her with questions. Always asking her about sad things.

'I actually prefer re-heated scones, Sadie.' I tried to smile. 'And yours are always delicious. I wouldn't care if they were a week old, ha ha.'

She made a grateful gesture.

'How was Kathy's health?' Sizemore interrupted us.

Sadie turned. 'Kathy's health?'

'Yes. Was she . . . did she jog? Watch her diet? Ever get depressed? You knew her well. You'd have know her habits.' His eyes drilled into her.

Flustered, she brushed an invisible crumb from her hands, her eyes darting to a nearby photo of her and Kathy posing proudly in their nurses' uniforms. For one awful second I thought she was going to cry, and I pictured myself having to comfort her. Having to apologise for Sizemore's sharpness. I was useless at comforting people I didn't know. Never understood the easy familiarity Sandra could adopt with perfect strangers. The way she, and her crowd, could hug indiscriminately. I need to at least know a person's background before I allow them any body contact with me.

But Sadie was brave. She didn't need comforting. She straightened her back and said, in brisk hospital tones, 'Kathy was as interested in keeping fit as any of us.'

'Was she depressed after her . . . miscarriage?' Sizemore pushed.

'Do you . . . do we really need to go into all this?' Sadie turned to me, but I immediately feigned interest in the remaining half-scone, forcing her to deal with Sizemore. 'What has Kathy's health, or even her emotional state got to do with a fire insurance claim?' she asked him.

Sizemore gave her an earnest look. I had seen Gerry use this particular look countless times. He had it down to a fine art. It was a look that might well be number one in the PI's secret manual of things

207

to do when you're completely fucked for an answer. It said – *You can trust me, I'm a professional.*

It was a look I could never quite master, but it worked for Gerry. And Sizemore.

Sadie hesitated for a second before giving in. 'Yes, she was depressed after the miscarriage. What woman wouldn't be?'

'A woman who wasn't happy to be pregnant in the first place?'

'Who told you that?'

'A friend of hers.'

'What friend?'

'A friend who is convinced that Kathy had an abortion.'

Sadie's mouth gaped, and the atmosphere became tangibly hostile.

Sizemore paused for a full second, then, 'Sadie?'

'You'd better go, I've given you enough time.'

'Sadie, he didn't mean to sound—' I touched her arm.

She brushed me away. 'I thought you were on Kathy's side. Instead you've been listening to salacious gossip about her. Just go!' She stood up, her chin quivering.

'I didn't mean to upset you,' Sizemore said. 'I just repeated what I was told.'

'Did you now? Well here's something you can repeat to anyone you like, Mr Sizemore. Hospitals can be hotbeds of gossip. And nowhere more so than in the busiest A & E departments.'

Sizemore's eyes widened in surprise.

'You look shocked? What did you think? That

hospitals are staffed by saints? Angels in white? Did you think that busy, overworked professionals never indulge in tittle tattle? Well, you're wrong. But a little harmless gossip isn't always bad. It can sometimes be beneficial in a fraught workplace! Help relieve tension . . . except when it's malicious and vindictive!'

Her voice was so full of fury, I wanted to duck behind the sofa, or at least make a run for the door.

Sizemore was made of sterner stuff. For the first time I saw why Mutual Irish wanted him on the case. It wasn't just because he was charming and handsome, and didn't suck his teeth. He was a highly skilled investigator. Even more importantly a no-holds-barred one. So like Gerry, it was freaky. They were born investigators. A breed apart. The faintest whiff of a clue, and these men were like hungry dogs with a bone. Wouldn't let it go 'til they picked it dry.

'So you're saying Kathy didn't have an abortion?' he said. 'You're telling me she wanted a baby?'

The fire left Sadie's eyes, and she suddenly looked tired. 'Kathy wanted a baby so badly, you couldn't even imagine her pain when she lost it.'

'Then why would a close friend of Seanie's tell me she had an abortion? Why would she tell me that when Kathy was in the clinic, having her . . . operation, Seanie was so upset, so angry with her decision to terminate the pregnancy, he spent the night throwing up?'

'I don't know why people say such things. And I'm not sure that I care. Now, if you'll excuse me, I've been on my feet for twelve hours straight. I'm exhausted. If I don't get to my bed soon, I won't make it into A & E tonight, and we're already dangerously understaffed. As anyone who *checks* their facts would know.' She held his gaze, her blue eyes icy.

Sizemore didn't flinch. It was Sadie who looked away first.

She handed me my bag, and hustled us out without a word. This time she didn't walk us to the gate.

At first I thought this was because Sizemore had offended her with his questions, but sitting outside in the jeep rehashing our conversation with her, I realised there was something else going on. Sadie said repeatedly that she was dead on her feet. Aching to get to bed. Yet for the ten minutes plus that we sat outside her house in the jeep, she stood at her window watching, her mobile pressed to her ear. And I didn't have to use field glasses to see that she was deeply upset over something. It was close on fifteen minutes before we drove off, and she was still at the window. Not looking out any more, but clearly having a heated argument with her caller.

'She's hiding something,' Sizemore said, as we pulled out into the traffic.

22

We arrived back at the agency in time to see the big front window getting the cleaning of its life. Already spotless, it was now in serious danger of being worn thin by Dick's flying shammy. Seeing us, he threw another bucket of water over it, and started attacking it enthusiastically all over again. Impressed, I stopped to have a word with him.

'Good work, Dick,' I shouted up the ladder. 'But no need to kill yourself. I only asked you to make a bit more of an effort, not wear out the glass.'

'*You* asked me to do a better job, Miss.' He worked frantically at the strip of clear glass that ran along the top of the tinted window.

I shrugged and followed Sizemore inside. 'Amazing the way a simple reprimand can galvanise people.'

'Amazing.' He laughed, and pointed to where Sandra and her two mini-skirted friends were leaning across the reception desk practically showing their knickers.

Before I could yell at them Milly, the prettiest, had unbuttoned the top of her blouse and was pressing a black lace bra against her generous chest.

'What do you think, girls? Will this push him over the edge?'

'It's definitely pushing your boobs over the edge.' Sandra hooted. 'I'd have to wear four chicken fillets to get that much cleavage.'

Dick's shammy practically broke through the glass. When I hissed in fury, Sizemore darted into the lift. 'Sandra!' I yelled.

'Oh hiya, Annie.' She swivelled on her skyscraper heels. 'We're helping Milly pick an outfit for her big date on Saturday. She wants to knock Liam dead,' she laughed, then frowned at my thunderous look. 'It's OK, I'm on my lunch break.'

'But did you know you had an audience?' I pointed.

Milly spotted him first.

'It's that effin sleaze-bag of a window cleaner!' she yelled.

'The dirty filthy git is . . .' Sandra was lost for words, an event in itself.

'He's been cleaning that same window for . . .'

They didn't wait for me to finish, just raced each other to the door. Outside there was a sudden scream, and Dick's face disappeared from the window. But judging by the ongoing howls he hadn't moved fast enough.

My mobile buzzed. Sizemore. 'Annie, I can see Sandra and her friends from here. Looks like they're killing that poor man. Shouldn't you . . . do something? Intervene? They are three big strapping girls and he's only a bag of bones . . . and . . . oh God, I think he's crying.'

'Sorry,' I yelled. 'Can't hear you. Bad reception.' I threw the mobile in my bag.

*   *   *

Sandra and the two girls came back, congratulating each other. Doing a little victory line dance. Milly, in particular, was almost scarily hyper. 'He won't be spying on anyone again in a hurry,' she said, and began whistling happily.

I hoped things hadn't got out of hand. I mean, he had no right to spy on the girls, but what had they done to him? Nothing too serious?

'You didn't . . . er . . . physically hurt him did you?' I wimped. 'I mean he's . . . a bit harmless.'

'Harmless? He's the one who spied on the women in the café lavvy!' Milly strutted like an amazon. 'He used to peep in through the skylight, when he was supposed to be cleaning it. That's why Mr Fusco sacked him.'

'I didn't know that.'

''Course you didn't. Fusco's had to keep it quiet, didn't they? Didn't want all them women taking a case against the café.'

'We could have him up for spying on us!' Sandra became excited. ''Course we'll have to wait 'til they discharge him from the hospital first.'

There was another explosion of laughter from the happy trio.

'Sandra! What did you do to him?' I was worried now.

She bit back a giggle. 'We made him drink his *own* water.'

'His own water?' My stomach churned. 'Oh please tell me you don't mean . . . ?'

'Yeah. The soapy water from the bucket.'

'Oh.' I laughed with relief.

'Not our fault he puts bleach in it. And vinegar.'

'Jesus, Sandra, tell me you're joking.'

'That's for me to know, and you to find out.' She nudged me cheekily. 'He's lucky we didn't drown him in it, the dirty little squirt.'

The lift doors shot open, and Sizemore appeared. 'OK, what did you do to the man? I heard him crying.'

'They just poured a bit of water over him,' I defended them.

'Sounded to me like they were torturing him.'

'We were going to. Then the squad car arrived and spoiled everything,' Milly pouted, and the three of them were convulsed again.

Milly checked the time. 'Shit. I was due back at the cosmetics counter ten minutes ago. Let's go, Noleen. Sandra, better luck next time love. Anyway, you're in no rush. You have tons of time.' She gave her a massive hug. 'And don't forget, my aunt wants her natal chart done before the end of the month, so get going on it.'

'See ya.' Sandra waved them out.

Watching them leave I noticed that Milly's glowing tan made the other girl look almost insipid. 'That's some tan Milly's got,' I said, 'I didn't know she was a sun worshipper?'

'She's not. It's St Trop. Magic, isn't it?'

It certainly was. The bottle tan looked so real, and was such a deep golden colour, it made Milly appear startlingly pretty. Well, prettier than she normally did. It also made her look half a stone lighter.

'Maybe I should get a St Trop tan,' I mused, thinking about the latest photo Sandra had persuaded

Gerry to email her from Arizona. Mad curious to see what the much-discussed swimming pool looked like, she had convinced him to send her a picture. And OK it wasn't quite of the Olympian proportions we had been led to believe, but it was amazing. Tiled in deep blue and with a backdrop of red mountains, it was completely eye-catching. Although not as eye-catching as the woman lying beside it. Sally was tanned shoe polish mahogany, and wearing a bikini that left nothing to the imagination. Her dark hair was so heavily highlighted she may as well have gone all blonde, and her smile was dazzling. Not at all like the smile of a woman in need of therapy.

'I'll make a booking for you,' Sandra volunteered.

This seemed to irritate Sizemore. But no matter how hard he glared at her, Sandra continued to search through her style magazine for the beauty salon number.

Sizemore drew me aside. 'You're not going to disappear off to France right now, are you? What about the case?'

'Ah that's at a bit of a dead end, isn't it?' I couldn't resist.

'No! I have two new numbers to call. One of them sounds promising. I'll try it again now.' He was gone. Taking the stairs two at a time.

'What's eating him?' Sandra asked as she hung up.

'He thinks I'm off on holiday. To St Tropez?'

'Jesus. Men are so feckin' thick. Even the smart ones. Anyway, the girl who does the tans wanted to know if you're up for an all-over job? I said yes.'

'Ah I'm not sure . . .' Already I was having second thoughts.

'No backtracking! You've been looking like shite since Gerry went off. You need to buck yourself up. An all-over tan will do it. Milly gets a bikini wax with hers. Do you fancy . . . ? OK, OK your appointment is for seven tonight.'

'It had better be just for a St Trop. *And* it better make my legs look like Milly's.'

'It will.' She was fully confident, which was good. So not only was St Trop going to turn me an enviable golden brown, it was going to extend my legs by at least three inches, *and* banish my cellulite. I couldn't wait.

'I wish Milly could meet a really genuine guy.' Sandra lashed on another layer of lipstick. 'She gave up her lunch break to come here and cheer me up. She's my best mate ever.' She brushed on lip-gloss, then peered critically at her reflection in her little mirror. 'I got my period this morning, so naturally I was feeling like cack.'

I wondered why having her period would make Sandra feel bad. She was always sparky, never let periods get her down.

Oh my God. The penny suddenly dropped. 'So you're . . . not pregnant?'

'No.'

'I'm so sorry, Sandra,' I commiserated.

'Ah, it's OK.' She propped up her little circular mirror again and brushed warm blusher on her cheeks, and then, as an afterthought, on her chin. 'If I *had* conceived this month the baby might have been an Aries.'

'An Aries?' I searched my mind for the right reaction to this. 'And you'd have er . . . hated that?'

'No, I wouldn't!' She swivelled. 'Aries kids can be brilliant. It's only adult Arians who think the world revolves around them!'

'Right.'

'But . . .' She pointed a finger threateningly. 'Suppose it was born on April the first?'

'That's er . . . what I meant!' I said, and wondered if I should say I had urgent business with Sizemore. Astrology was crap. Star signs were rubbish. They didn't make sense. How could you lump the population of the world into twelve simple categories?

'To be honest, I'd prefer a Taurian baby.' Sandra checked her teeth.

'You would?'

'Yeah. Easier to handle for a start. Like I told Jimmy this morning when he saw me getting the Tampax – If we strike lucky during my next cycle the baby will be a mid-month Taurian. Wouldn't that be brilliant?'

'Brilliant!' I echoed, thinking that if Sandra put half as much energy into her paid employment as she did into mapping out star signs, she'd be a millionaire before she was thirty. Instead she chose to spend chunks of her time drawing up natal charts for her wide circle of nutty friends. I had interrupted enough of her phone calls to know how much *they* valued this hobby of hers. Totally insane. As if a natal chart could give you a detailed insight into someone's personality. Or even tell you what road they're likely to take in their life. If things were that simple I'd pay a year's salary to have one drawn up on Gerry. That way I might know what was really going on in Arizona, not just whatever bits of information he was prepared to email me. Wouldn't it just . . . ?

I watched Sandra tidy away her make-up.

'Sandra, if I gave you someone's date, and exact place of birth, would you draw up a natal chart for me?'

' 'Course,' she beamed. 'Whose chart is it?'

'I'd rather not say.'

'It's Gerry, isn't it?'

'No!'

' 'Course it is. You've gone all red,' she giggled. 'I did a natal chart on him ages ago. I know things about him that *would* make you blush. Ha, ha.'

I bristled. How dare she know things about Gerry that I didn't. How . . . I pulled myself together. What was I doing, encouraging Sandra to babble about something as daft as star signs? Natal charts, my arse, Gerry would have said.

'OK. Get back to work, Sandra.' I headed for the lift.

'Gerry is a classic Aquarian,' she called after me. 'He loves people in general, but can be surprisingly impersonal in his close relationships,' she quoted.

'Hello? I'm an Aquarian,' I reminded her.

'Yeah. But your moon is in Sagittarius!'

This was ridiculous. Who could believe this rubbish? 'Er what does that mean?'

'It means you're funny.'

'Funny?'

'Well, we always have a good laugh, when you're around, don't we?'

I hit the button for the lift. Great. The stars said I was the agency clown. What a confidence builder that was. No need for the all-over tan, then.

'Annie?' she shouted. 'Want to know about Sizemore?'

I took my finger off the button.

'His moon is in Scorpio!'

'Well, that gives me a deep insight into his character.' I laughed, and put my finger back on the button.

'It means he's highly sexed,' she giggled. '*Very* highly sexed.'

My mouth suddenly went dry, and I eased my finger off the button.

'Er . . . anything else?' I didn't turn.

'You mean about Sizemore?' She sounded coy.

I said nothing. I wasn't falling into that trap. Plus I knew Sandra couldn't resist continuing. I was right.

'*His* chart says he's incapable of deceit in personal relationships, and he's very big . . .'

I waited.

'. . . on loyalty. He has extremely high standards. In all his relationships.'

I had no idea why this should make me feel slightly breathless. Even if I believed in astrology, which I didn't, Sizemore was just my working partner, and a temporary one at that. And here I was with my breath catching in my chest because Sandra said the stars decreed him to be highly sexed? And loyal? I definitely needed a reality check. Where was Barney when you needed him?

Then again, tons of successful people believe in

astrology. My Sunday paper had an in-depth interview with an award-winning composer who claimed he wouldn't put a pen to paper, or a finger on the piano keys, if his star sign wasn't aligned with Jupiter, or something, on that particular day. Was he joking? He rounded off the interview by giving the name of a major American corporation he said employed a professional astrologer to draw up astral charts for their aspiring directors.

Sandra wasn't finished. 'Be warned,' she shouted after me. 'Sizemore's chart says he can be duplicitous in his professional life.'

Duplicitous?

'What's wrong, Annie? All I said was . . .'

'You have too much to say!' I ripped into her. 'Are you paid to *work* here, or waffle on about stupid star signs? And how many times do I have to tell you that astrology is a load of shite! Now answer that bloody phone, or you'll be out of here, and reading tea leaves in a tent!'

I marched into my office to see Sizemore looking completely at home in my chair, my phone pressed to his ear as if it belonged there.

My sudden arrival didn't disturb him. He barely acknowledged my presence. Just put a finger to his lips.

Sod that for a game of soldiers! This was *my* office. *My* chair. And he signalled for me to be quiet?

Could be duplicitous in his professional life?

'Don't tell me to be quiet!' I bristled. 'We're going round in circles on this case, mainly because you refuse to acknowledge my lead. You seem to think you're a smarter investigator. I hate to disillusion you, but if that were true we'd now be talking to someone who knew Kathy in medical school, instead of coming up against a wall of silence about her time there. Knowing *why* she suddenly dropped out of medical school could help our case no end. So please get out of my chair, and let me figure some way to find an in.'

His eyes never leaving mine, Sizemore spoke to his caller. 'Thank you Professor Green, I'm very grateful. I've had some difficulty getting anyone from the college to speak to me. Yes, I appreciate that. But it had to be someone who was there when Kathy Newman was a student. Yes. I'll see you in the Fitzwilliam Hotel, then? The restaurant? Two thirty it is.' He hung up and went back to his own seat.

There was a low rumble of traffic from the street below. The odd impatient toot of a car horn. I managed to avoid Sizemore's gaze, by rearranging my phone cord which was stretched untidily across my desk. I straightened a pile of papers that the cord had knocked over. Then straightened them again. Making sure they were neatly aligned.

Sizemore coughed. Then to his utter and lasting credit he gave up waiting for me to apologise. Stuffing papers into his briefcase, he spoke as if my unseemly little outburst hadn't happened.

'That was Professor William Green,' he said. 'He'll be happy to meet us in the restaurant in the Fitzwilliam Hotel.' He checked the time. 'When he finishes his lunch. We have time to grab something ourselves first. My treat. What do you fancy, Annie?' He stood up.

I looked at the warm brown eyes, at the sculpted mouth that could be lambasting me for my rude outburst, then at the long slim hands that were closing the briefcase, moving against the soft leather as if they were born to caress.

'I'll have a burger.' I swallowed, and tore my eyes off his mouth.

'With onions?' His face broke into a slow smile.

'Yes,' I snapped. Then had to use every ounce of willpower I possessed, not to jump the desk. And then him.

23

The obsequious head waiter pointed to a table at the far side of the well-appointed restaurant. 'That's Professor Green over there. Sitting at the centre table? He has just finished his lunch.'

Even from fifty feet away you could tell that Richard Green was a gynaecologist. Maybe it was the way he held the silver sugar tongs. Or maybe it was because he was the only male under ninety unwilling to risk eye-strain to get a better look at the rear end of two model types, who were making for the exit wearing outfits more suited to a beach than a four-star restaurant.

'Professor Green?' Sizemore touched the neatly tailored sleeve.

The doctor turned, his faded blue eyes widening in welcome. 'Detective Sizemore?'

Sizemore smiled. 'This is my colleague, Annie McHugh.'

We shook hands.

The professor's handclasp was warm. 'Will you take tea? Coffee?'

'No thank you. We've just finished lunch,' I said untruthfully, because I was still digesting the fried onions I'd had with my burger, and all the signs were that I'd be tasting them for some time yet.

Sizemore asked Professor Green if he had any objections to our tape recorder.

'None whatsoever,' the professor said jovially.

The recorder in place, Sizemore asked, 'Can you repeat the story you told me earlier? Maybe enlarge on it a little?'

The Professor looked disappointed. God knows what he'd been expecting. More riveting conversation, maybe? Our ordinariness clearly disappointed him. He possibly expected PIs to speak from the corner of their mouths, like in the movies, or maybe flash guns, or something. But being a well-mannered doctor he pulled himself together, and began to repeat the story he clearly found boring.

'I lectured in Obs and Gynae and Kathy Newman was a student of mine. But not for long. She was dating my star pupil, a young genius from Malaysia.' He smiled briefly at the memory, before continuing. 'I believe they were seeing each other for the best part of two years. Then one night, after a private end of term party, there was a . . . a ruckus one might call it. It involved three of our students, Kathy, Mr Nigh, and another girl. A highly intelligent lass from Belfast. They were all roughly the same age, twenty two / twenty three. An age when passions are running high?' He gave Sizemore a look before continuing.

'An argument between the three apparently became heated. I wasn't there, of course, but I was told it was one of the girls who first became physical. Actually threw a punch.' He smiled. 'Oh yes, Detective Sizemore, girls have been known to throw punches.'

224

'Which girl?' I asked.

'Not for me to say.' He shook his head. 'But things became nasty, and Kathy picked up an ornamental dagger that was on display above the fireplace in the bedroom and . . .'

'The bedroom?' I said.

'Oh, didn't I say? The contretemps occurred in a bedroom.' He all but winked. 'And Kathy stabbed Nigh with the ornamental dagger.'

'She stabbed him?' I gasped.

'Yes. Wounded him quite seriously. Several ligaments in his arm were so badly damaged the surgeon on call feared he might lose all use of the arm. Fortunately he didn't. Although I'm sure he'll never regain full use of it. Nigh flew home within days of the incident, against medical advice, I might add, and all attempts to contact him or his family were rebuffed.' He looked off into the middle distance, his faded blue eyes becoming sad for the first time. 'He didn't return to his studies. Or to Ireland. Two months after the incident Tanya, the other girl involved, took a ferry to Scotland, booked into a B & B in a small seaside town, and took her own life. An overdose of prescription drugs, I believe. Kathy Newman was . . . shall we say . . . *encouraged* to leave the college? And that's about all I can tell you, Detective Sizemore. That's all the information I have.' He dabbed his mouth with a linen napkin, and signalled to the waiter.

'But what was the ruckus about?' Sizemore asked.

'Oh, what are such things ever about? Youth. Passion. Jealousy. Must I spell it out for you? A . . . a storm in a youthful teacup!'

'But Kathy stabbed a man? And the other girl took her own life? Did the Gards . . . ?'

'Nobody was charged, if that's what you're asking. And rightly so. Nigh's wound was . . . accidental. Kathy would not have intended to do him serious harm. Wipe out his future as a surgeon?' He tut tutted. 'Of course not.'

'And the other girl? Did the college investigate her death?' I waited.

'It's not the duty of a college to investigate a death that happened in another country.' He was unmoved.

'But surely . . . ?'

'Besides, nobody was totally surprised by her actions. She had always been rather difficult. Problematic. Bright, but too highly strung. One hesitates to use the word neurotic,' he said, without hesitating. 'Even the way she chose . . . taking herself off to a little Scottish village like that? Quite in character, really. Probably bore no relation whatsoever to the incident at the party. I've now told you everything I know, Detective Sizemore. It's more than anyone else will, I can assure you. Take my advice.' He patted Sizemore's hand. 'Let sleeping dogs lie. It's in nobody's interest to start resurrecting such unpleasant incidents.'

He signed the bill with a flourish, slipped the waiter a sizeable tip and got to his feet. 'Good afternoon Detective Sizemore. Ms . . . er . . . Annie.' He was gone.

The waiter reappeared. 'Would you care for coffee, madam? Sir?'

'Bring a large pot,' Sizemore said.

We sat looking at each other.

226

'Can you believe that man?' I said finally.

Sizemore shook his head.

'At least we now know why Kathy was on anti-depressants,' I added. 'If I was being lectured by men like him, I'd be shovelling tranqs down my throat. Did he actually say Tanya killed herself because she was highly strung?'

He nodded. 'Not big on sensitivity, is he?'

'Jesus, if everyone highly strung killed themselves the world would be depopulated in a month.'

Sizemore agreed glumly. 'His star pupil's surgical career was ruined? Another student was thrown out of college, and a third killed herself. And he calls it an *incident*?'

'Unbelievable.'

The waiter was at Sizemore's elbow again. This time offering to pour coffee from a tall shiny pot.

'No. I'll do that, thanks.' Sizemore took the pot, and waited until we were alone. 'I believe Green when he says no one else will talk about it. I've spent hours trying to contact people who were in medical school with Kathy. I started with a list of fifty. Got two replies. Both emails. Both of them polite PFO's. In desperation I moved on to a list of lecturers. You've just met the only one who would even discuss *the incident*.'

We sipped our coffee in disappointment.

'But it's not hard to guess what happened at the student party,' I said. 'Kathy caught Tanya and Nigh at it – her best friend, in bed with her lover? Are you surprised she went ballistic?'

'But it hardly corresponds with what we've been told about Kathy.'

'Jealousy makes people do weird things.'

'Em. Or maybe the picture we've been painting of Kathy isn't a true one.'

'Oh my God, you don't think *she* started the fire?' I perked up. 'If she had a wicked temper, it's always possible that in a moment of blind *rage* she torched the shop.'

'Let's not lose all sense of reality here.' Sizemore actually laughed.

'What's unreal about thinking she torched the shop? We've just been told that in a jealous rage she stabbed a man. Who's to say that in another fit of jealous rage she wouldn't torch a shop?'

'And then go back to bed? That's where they found her body, remember? In bed.'

'OK. OK.' I pushed my wild curls back behind the black velvet band I had worn in a vain effort to appear sophisticated. I had known instinctively that wild hair and jeans would get me nowhere in the dining room of the upmarket Fitzwilliam. OK, navel-bearing minis and straggily hair might be acceptable when you're six feet tall and stunningly beautiful. When you're average you need to toe the line.

'What are you doing?' Sizemore stared.

'Nothing!' I gave my unruly mop another backward tug, almost breaking it off at the roots. 'We've got to find whoever made that anonymous call.'

He gave me one of his long, slow smiles. 'You think pulling your hair out will help us there?'

'I'm smoothing it,' I snapped as it sprang back disobediently. 'Otherwise I'd take the scissors to the whole bloody thing. Or shave it all off. That would save me an hour every morning.'

'An hour? I don't understand.'

'After my shower? It takes me an hour to blow-dry it straight.' I had a sudden flash of Gerry standing at the bedroom door, tapping his foot impatiently, looking at his watch.

'Why not just leave it wet?' Sizemore asked.

My God, was he turning into Gerry? Well, maybe not. But neither of them had a bloody clue about women's fashions. They both thought I could go to work looking like Shaft.

'Annie?' He touched my hand.

'In answer to your question, are you completely insane? Or merely tasteless?'

He laughed. 'My father once accused me of just that. Being insane!'

'Your father?' I couldn't disguise my interest.

'Don't worry, I was only sixteen at the time.'

'You never talk about your family. About your parents? Your career?' I dared.

'Let's focus on the case for now, OK?' he side-stepped adroitly. 'If we could trace Nigh we may find out what really made Kathy tick. With no forensic evidence to prove the fire was deliberate, our only hope is proving that Seanie was capable of such an act. If he was provoked beyond endurance?'

'By Kathy?'

He nodded.

'What if she was provoked beyond endurance?' I snapped.

He shrugged. 'Less likely, but possible. Nigh might

give us the answer to that. They dated for two years. He should know how she would react if, for instance, a close relationship came under threat.'

'But we already know that.'

'Do we?'

'Professor Green just told us.'

'I wonder.' He became edgy.

'So you think he lied?'

'No. I just think there's a lot more to it. And the deeper we dig the murkier it gets.' Again that pensive frown.

'Are you saying Mutual Irish should just pay up, and be done with it?'

'What do you think?'

'No way! This case is my chance to prove I can . . .' I bit my lip.

'It's OK, Annie. I'll be judged by my results on this one too. Seriously judged.' His face darkened.

'Ow.' A sudden dart of discomfort had me clutching my chest.

'You OK?' He caught my hand again.

And the thing was, I liked it. Not the dart of discomfort, but his hand catching mine. I liked it a lot – the feel of his warm hand pressed against my skin. The unexpected roughness of his skin, nothing at all like as soft as I would have expected, given his perfect grooming. And, if I'm to be totally honest, I was beginning to like any physical contact with him. When he came close I forgot all about Gerry and Sally, and the swimming pool, and Sally and her wasp-sized waist, in the itsy-bitsy bikini that probably wouldn't cover my big toe.

'OK, Annie?' Sizemore was asking again.

Maybe I imagined the concern in his eyes. Maybe it was just wishful thinking. But I didn't imagine the way his hand tightened on mine, for whatever reason. I decided not to spoil the moment by telling him my discomfort was caused by the fried onions playing havoc with my digestive system. Repeating on me like bullets.

His fingers dwarfed my hand, their warm olive tones making my pale skin look lifeless by comparison. But that would be sorted shortly. Thanks to Sandra, I would soon have an all-over tan. I would be a deep, even gold. And glowing.

I couldn't wait. Even twiglet Sally, for all her perfection, had strap marks. For the first time ever, I would be one up on her. Only problem was, who would get to see my glowing all-over tan?

Sizemore stood up and moved aside to let me walk out of the restaurant ahead of him. I moved with a spring in my step, and swinging my hips as well as I could, given that the onions were still giving me gyp.

24

Forty-eight hours later the Gards raided Dirty McGill's Garage and came away with their biggest drug haul in ten years. Tons of pure, unadulterated cocaine. With a street value of five million euros. And our Barney was the hero of the hour.

McGill had flown back from Spain unannounced; and drove straight to the garage to look at a huge camper van that was in for a service.

'Clear off the lot of yis.' He had chased out mechanics and apprentices alike. Even kicking one young apprentice in the arse for daring to finish an oil change before leaving.

Barney didn't have a single word of incriminating evidence on his wire, but hearing about the hullabaloo in the garage workshop, he tore down to it on some pretext, saw McGill standing in the grease-pit alone, rubbing his hands with glee, and sweating profusely in the air-conditioned garage. Barney hid behind a Volvo estate and watched as the red-faced and sweating McGill, still wearing his Costa-del-Sol white linen suit, slid under the newly-arrived camper van waving a crowbar. And Barney knew.

'Pure greed. That's what did for him,' he said as we toasted his success. 'If he had just let the camper sit there until dark, no one would have been any the wiser. The false bottom was a work of art. But he couldn't resist. He had to have a look at his haul. DI Bailey says his fingerprints are all over it. All his smart planning, all the trouble he took hiring that stupid young couple to drive the camper back from Southern Spain, and he couldn't wait another few hours? He just had to have a look at all that coke. The minute I saw him standing there, sweating like a pig, his eyeballs like golf balls, I knew. I blew the whistle, and the Gards were on him like flies on shite!'

The drugs bust made the TV news. Every station, that's how big it was. No mention of Barney, of course. But the people who mattered knew the part he had played in the bust. He was delirious with joy. Watching the news on the small TV in our reception, he was torn between relief and disappointment that his name wasn't mentioned.

Milly and two of her friends had arrived to collect Sandra for a drink in a newly opened wine bar, but decided the craic was better in our reception. Barney poured everyone drinks like there was no tomorrow, then rang Gerry and put him on speaker.

'Well done, Barney! Very proud of you,' Gerry said. 'Have a drink on me.'

'Annie's case will be next to make the news.' Barney laughed, putting the fear of God into me. Sandra put on another layer of make-up, enough perfume to pollute the Western hemisphere, and helped pass around enough alcohol to paralyse anyone left standing. Barney whipped out his iPod to blast our eardrums with UB40, loud enough to be heard in Montego Bay.

The evening wore on and DI Bailey rang to congratulate Barney for the third time.

Unsteady on his feet now, Barney finally admitted to the part chance played in his big success. 'Jaysus, if I didn't go down to the garage lavvy for a slash, I would have missed it.'

'That's what good detection is all about, Barney,' DI Bailey said. 'Being in the right place, at the right time.'

Hungry now for more praise, Barney said, 'Let's ring Gerry again.'

'Gerry?' he yelled drunkenly. 'Thanks for giving me the case. I knew it would be big, but not this massive. Still, I knew I had to stick it out. Had to be in the right place, at the right time. Aw, thanks, Gerry. I was great, wasn't I? Born for it, DI Bailey says. What? It's UB40! OK, get back to your barbecue then. OK, for your swim then. Hey, when will you be back? Another bleedin' week? Or two? Jaysus. Yeah, we're managing. Doing better than when you were here. Ha ha. Yeah, she's on top of everything. A great boss. Wanna speak to her? OK, I can hear the kids calling you. I can even smell the steaks burning. Bye.'

Barney turned to give me a hug. Over his shoulder I saw Sizemore watching us.

When Naomi and two of her salesgirls swelled our ranks, Barney rang the off-licence for more drink. 'It's my birthday,' he lied. 'You have to deliver.'

An hour later someone suggested we all move on to a club.

'I'll ring Jimmy,' Sandra was totally blitzed. 'He'll bring the big gardening van. He can fit twelve in that, fourteen if he takes out all the moss peat.'

I caught Naomi's look of horror.

'We'll get taxis,' I intervened quickly. 'It's simpler.'

The phone rang again. 'Barney?' Someone yelled. 'It's the cops. I think you're being nicked.'

Barney came back from the call looking totally chuffed.

'Some of DI Bailey's crew want to join us to celebrate. Man, this is going to turn into a *real* party,' he said.

The Reggae music continued to blare. Sandra and her friends gave an almost professional-looking dance exhibition, while everyone else continued to drink as if we were on the brink of a drought.

'Drink up everyone,' Barney commanded. 'Then it's on to the Randy Goat to meet up with the others, and then we'll all move on to a club.'

The Randy Goat was bedlam. Everyone there had heard about the drugs bust, and Barney's part in it was the worst kept secret in Dublin. Total strangers were queing up to buy him drinks.

'But keep it quiet,' I heard him tell two young Gards who were pumping his hand in admiration. 'I was deep undercover.' He touched his nose. Well, he tried.

Even Naomi got drunk. A sight to behold. Especially when she took a fancy to a Gard at least twenty years her junior. Not that he was complaining.

Although I thought she might later, the way she was pouring Jack Daniels into him.

Early on she had trapped Sizemore in a corner. Whenever I glanced in their direction she was waving her hands about as she spoke, flashing her sparklers to let him see she was a cut above the rest of us. He watched me over her head, until I found my own quiet corner to sit down in and relax.

Three minutes later he was beside me, putting a glass in my hand.

'What's in it?' I asked, already semi-blitzed.

'White wine spritzer.'

'After drinking vodka? I'll be sick.'

He whipped the glass from my hand. 'Can't have you feeling sick.'

Some half-drunken eejit fell against him, almost pushing him on top of me. Our faces were so close I could feel his breath on my mouth, see the tiny flecks of gold in his eyes. As he straightened up, I willed the drunken eejit to fall against him again, maybe a little harder this time. Instead the selfish pig staggered off to fall against someone else who didn't even benefit from it.

Sizemore drained his glass, and again offered me the wine spritzer. 'No?' He seemed disappointed. 'How about if we share it. I'll take the first sip. Then you take your turn. Then I'll . . .'

His eyes were on my mouth, and I was moving closer when someone grabbed me from behind. Barney.

'Come and meet some of DI Bailey's team,' he slurred. 'And the man of the moment himself. Oh,

236

that's me, isn't it?' He laughed so hard he nearly fell over.

The next thirty minutes were a blur. I drank too much. Shook too many hands. Returned too many smiles. All the while trying to find my way back to Sizemore. Or at least to keep track of him. See what he was doing. The place was full of cop groupies as usual. All floating about, all on the lookout. Some of them had even better tans than the one I took so much trouble to acquire. Three times the girl had to spray me. And then I asked her to give my legs another go, just in case. The cop groupies probably didn't even have cellulite.

I spotted Sizemore across the crowd and was about to make my way towards him when Declan and Sasha arrived. Sasha was a godsend. She didn't talk much, but God she could keep Declan off the drink, and this was essential because his new case involved two small children. Well, actually, their nanny. She was suspected of meeting her boyfriend every day in the park and paying him more attention than her two tiny charges. If Declan got photo evidence of this, the kids' parents were going to take the nanny's agency to court.

'We can't stay,' Declan came back after congratulating Barney. 'I have an early start in the morning. I'm going to rig up a couple of secret cameras in the clients' house. If the nanny is messing in the park, God knows what she's up to in the house.'

'Good move, Declan,' I said, and I didn't just mean with the case.

He left, with the silent Sasha on his arm.

Every time I turned someone was putting a glass in my hand. The celebrations were getting too much for me. On my way to the exit I was hijacked by Sandra, Milly and co, and pulled into a drunken twirl.

I finally used the *I need the bathroom* trick and escaped. Outside, I leaned my forehead against a cooling stone wall, while waiting for the world to stop spinning. I suddenly felt a hand on my neck.

'Jesus!' I nearly jumped out of my skin.

'It's OK!' Sizemore was beside me.

'What a stupid thing to do in an alleyway!' I yelled. 'Sneaking up on me like that.'

'This isn't an alleyway, it's a main street.'

'Well, you still scared the wits out of me.'

He frowned. 'Are you drunk?'

'Certainly not!'

'Are you going on to the nightclub?'

'No.'

'Me neither. I'll drop you home. That's my cab,' he pointed.

We climbed in and sat without speaking, leaving a full three feet of mock leather between us.

'Is that Annie?' the cabby suddenly said.

'Who are you?' I grumbled.

'The night of the storm? Remember how frightened you were? I took you to the pub on the canal?'

Christ. The man must think I'm a complete alcoholic.

'I . . . we're celebrating tonight. It's a special night.' I found myself explaining.

'You the boyfriend?' He tipped the mirror to get a look at Sizemore.

Sizemore shot me a sideways look, but didn't speak.

'Your own business,' the cabby said, as I turned to look out the window.

'Here we are, folks. Number twenty-two. All the twos!' The cabby unleashed his rapid-fire cabby wit as he pulled up outside my house.

'Thanks.' I yanked at the doorhandle, then shocked myself, and probably him, by saying to Sizemore, 'I'd offer you a nightcap, but I'm sure you'd refuse.'

He leaned across me to hold the door closed. 'Try me.'

And for the second time in one night, our breaths almost meshed.

I swallowed nervously. Did he think I was . . . desperate? That I was going to beg him to . . . what? Have a coffee? Tea? Another drink? What exactly did a nightcap mean to someone like Sizemore? It was some time since I'd last been in this type of situation. He probably experienced it every night of the week. He probably . . .

'OK, folks! None of us is getting any younger.' The cabby eyed me in his driving mirror.

'I'd love a coffee,' Sizemore said.

'A man after me own heart.' The cabby held out his hand for the fare.

At my door it seemed almost natural to give Sizemore my key. He opened it easily, and then we were in the hall and suddenly all awkward and stilted again.

'Maybe you should go,' I said stupidly. 'It's a bit late for a nightcap.' I had absolutely no idea what time it was.

'True,' he said. 'But the cab's gone.' And he stood there looking at me. And I looked at him, and I was instantly sober, and never wanted someone so badly in my whole life.

'You want me to go?' He was breathing hard.

'I want . . .' I began, and then we were kissing. Kissing as if we had been born for just this moment. As if our mouths and bodies were made for each other. No more awkwardness. No hesitation. Just two pairs of hands eagerly opening zips and buttons, and touching and caressing every available piece of warm and willing flesh. His mouth found my nipples, and seconds later my hungry mouth was sliding lower and lower along his hard stomach, making him gasp. Then I was being lifted and he was saying *wait*. But I was beyond waiting. I wanted to shout I can't, but sanity somehow prevailed, and I found myself being carried upstairs, instead of being mashed against the knobbly hall table.

It was a wise move, because a bed was less likely to leave indentations in my back. Plus it may have added to the pleasure, because I had never before experienced such physical ecstasy in coitus. When I came my yells were deafening. Or maybe they weren't all mine, it was hard to tell, because by then we were so tightly enmeshed that it was difficult to know where my body ended and his began. I do recall a voice, considerably deeper than mine saying, 'Oh Jeeeesuus. Oh

Jeeeesuuuus,' over and over again. Then I exploded with pleasure.

Ecstasy was definitely the only word for it.

Euphoric describes how I was feeling when I woke. My whole body was still tingling, the sun was washing the room pale gold, and I only had to reach out to touch the body of the man who had given me such sublime pleasure.

I let my fingers trip playfully across the sheet. No? A little further. Still nothing. I jerked upright.

I was alone in the big bed. Sizemore was gone.

I should have known it was all too good to be true. After being callously abandoned by Gerry I thought I'd found heaven last night. But for Sizemore it was obviously just a good shag. Well, three. Even so. I'd been convinced I'd found something special. Worth keeping. Nurturing. Someone who would put me first. He clearly thought I was a good ride, but went home to sleep. Oh my God, I'd have to go into the office and face him. Act hip and cool. Brazen. Act as if I did this sort of thing on a regular basis.

How was it for you, big boy? Wink, wink. Fun, huh? Can't beat a drunken shag with a work colleague? Ha, ha. I do it all the time. Relieves tension. Hand me that file, will you?

I buried my face in the pillow, and screamed.

'Annie?' A warm hand touched my shoulder.

I turned, and there he was. Wearing nothing but navy boxer shorts. Holding a breakfast tray in his hands, and smelling of coffee, and mint toothpaste.

Mint toothpaste? My mouth tasted like I'd eaten a dead mammal.

'Coffee? Tea? Orange juice?' he smiled. 'Name your poison. I'm new at this.'

I couldn't speak. Just grabbed him by the boxers.

He all but abandoned the tray to jump into bed. 'Be gentle with me,' he laughed. 'I've got a murderously hard day ahead of me. I'm working with a real ball-breaker.'

Twenty minutes later he rolled onto his back to catch his breath.

'What are you on, Annie?'

I leaned across him to select a large piece of toast. 'Carbs.' I lay back, munching happily. 'I love them. Hot or cold. They totally energise me.'

'Give me some of that, then!' He made a mock grab at my toast.

I held it to his mouth, and fed him. Then kissed the butter off his lips, and together we worked our way through the plateful of cold toast, taking turns at feeding, kissing, and laughing at nothing in particular. And if the cold toast tasted like nothing on earth, his mouth tasted like heaven. Every time.

But we still had a case to solve.

'Right!' One last hungry kiss, and I sat up. 'Duty calls.'

'I didn't hear it.' He pulled me back down, and pinned me to the bed, raining mock bites on my neck, and running his tongue lower and lower until it became obvious that he was up for business again.

The phone pealed, forcing me back to reality.

'Leave it,' he mumbled, his tongue circumnavigating my navel.

'Can't. It's almost eight thirty.' I reached for the receiver.

'Hell . . . ooooo?' I stifled a groan, as Sizemore's tongue slid further southwards.

'Did I wake you, Annie?' The familiar muffle said. 'Are you naked? Are your legs . . . ?'

I screamed, and jerked upright. Sizemore's reaction was even speedier. He grabbed the phone, and gave an ear-shattering whistle into the receiver as I ran to the bathroom, dry retching.

'Annie?' He hammered on the bathroom door. 'Are you . . . ? Let me in.'

Inside, he rocked me against his chest. 'Has he called this number before?'

I shook my head. He stroked my hair, holding me so tight I could practically hear his blood boiling.

'I'll sort this, Annie. I give you my word. First you need to change your phone number.'

'He just . . . I'm not afraid of him . . . but he makes me feel . . . icky . . . dirty. And . . . hearing him this morning after . . . it was vile.'

'I know.'

'I'm not letting him get to me!' I determined. 'I'm not being his victim! I'm not!'

'I'll make fresh coffee.' He smoothed my hair gently. 'You go ahead and shower. Leave the door open if it makes you feel better. I'll be downstairs.' He turned to go.

'It's a big shower. Plenty of room,' I said, and pulled him in behind me.

25

Sandra looked like an animated corpse. 'Where did you disappear to last night?'

'Me?' I kept my eyes on my post. 'I . . . was wrecked. I went home around . . . midnight?'

She peered at me through pain-fogged eyes. 'Smart! And you look great. Even with your hair still wet.'

'It's the tan!' I blushed. 'Makes a huge difference.'

'Did you see Sizemore this morning?' She giggled, winced and clutched her forehead. 'He looks like he was in a train wreck.'

'What?'

'He's in bits. Wonder what he got up to?'

'God knows.' I turned to my post again.

'Are you blushing?' She tilted her head to check my face.

'I told you it's the . . . the tan,' I stammered. 'The St Trop.'

'You should keep using it, then. You'd never guess you were drinking last night. Naomi is so hungover she had to take the morning off. She got off with that young blond cop. I saw them leaving together. Maybe he's helping her nurse her hangover. 'Course she had her eye on Sizemore, but he disappeared. Probably with some slapper. There _were_ a few of them about.

Cop groupies!' She was dismissive. 'And you know what they say about posh blokes like Sizemore.'

'No. What do they say?'

'They like a bit of rough?' She winked. 'Everyone knows that.'

'Any calls for me?' I snapped.

'Yeah. Fiona was on. Said for you to switch on your phone, please. She said she couldn't get through to your house either. And Gerry was on, of course. Sounded a bit cagey. Maybe he couldn't get you at home either. All I could hear was Sally yakking in the background. *Gerry is this dress OK? What do you think of my hair? Will I take a sweater? Does my bum look big in this?*'

'Did she actually say that?' I chuckled, my jealousy a thing of the past.

'Well, no, but she might as well have.'

'But Gerry sounds crabby, does he?'

'Not exactly crabby, in fact he seemed relaxed. As if he's happy to be there, but trying not to let on. I told him he missed a great party but . . . he didn't seem bothered.'

'Talk to you later, Sandra.' I dived for the lift.

'No. Wait. Sizemore took my aspirin up to your office. As if it's aspirin he needs. But I'm curious to see how he's doing.'

And what could I say? Please don't come up to my office right now, in case Sizemore wants to surprise me. In case his idea of a joke might be to strip off and stand just inside the door yelling 'Ready when you are!' After last night, and this morning, anything was possible.

245

Outside my door I coughed, then rattled the handle loudly. When I scraped my heel along the floor Sandra looked worried. But I wasn't taking any chances.

I opened the door slowly. 'Good morning,' I bellowed. 'Sandra's here to collect her aspirin.'

Sizemore was inputting on his laptop. I couldn't say how he looked when Sandra saw him earlier on, but right now he would have won the good business award for personal grooming in the workplace.

'Morning,' he said, and continued working.

I was torn between relief and disappointment. Of course I hadn't wanted him to leap naked across the office at the sight of me, but did he have to be so . . . restrained? So businesslike?

Sandra collected her painkillers and departed.

'You OK?' Sizemore asked as I sat down.

'Perfect.'

'Thought we had better keep it cool and businesslike in the office.' He stole my plan. 'Anything else makes people uncomfortable.'

I couldn't have put it better.

'OK with you?'

'Perfect.' Feck you. I was supposed to say all that. I had pictured myself having to beat him off, with my desk lamp. And here he was all cool, calm and collected.

'Good.' His fingers flew across his keyboard.

'And of course we need to keep it businesslike while we're working the case. *Anywhere* we're working the case.' I kept my eyes on the desk. 'OK with you?'

A slight pause. 'Makes sense.' He held out his hand as if to seal a business deal.

I kept my hands by my side. 'Also, no touching.'

'That will be difficult.'

'Well, I'm afraid that's the deal,' I said, pleased to have struck a chord.

'I meant in the Honda. It's not exactly roomy.' He turned away.

'Are you?' I looked at him realising that his shoulders were shaking. 'Oh, you bastard.'

'It's not going to work, is it?' he groaned and came towards me.

'No, no, no. You were right first time. We have to get this case sorted. You said yourself we may both be judged on the result of the Bolger case.'

He pulled back. 'You're right, Annie. I know someone who would love to see me fail on this case.'

I waited, but his silence made it obvious that he wasn't going to tell me who it was.

'So it's business, business, business,' I said.

'Right.'

'Definitely no . . . you know.'

'Maybe during lunch breaks?' A little grin.

'We . . .'

My phone shrilled. I stiffened, and let it ring. Sizemore was on it in a blink. 'Annie McHugh's office. Yes, she's here. Who's calling?' *Fiona* he mouthed silently and gave me the receiver, taking exaggerated care not to brush against my hand.

'Hi Fiona.' I swung my chair so he could only see my back.

'Was that Sexy Sizemore?' she asked.

'Em.'

'Sounds as delicious as he looks. I don't know how you can keep your hands off him. Listen, I know you're mega busy but I thought I'd keep you up to scratch. Guess who's asleep upstairs?'

'Brad Pitt?'

'Nonna Molino.'

'Oh my God. How are things?'

'Hard to tell. All she's done so far is sleep, and Calum is absolutely transfixed by her. He just stands by her bed staring. I swear that's how he spent most of yesterday afternoon. Just staring at her. I might keep her here 'til he's twelve. Anyway, back to business, I really rang you about the dinner party. You haven't forgotten?'

'Nooo.' Of course I'd forgotten. Dinner parties were not high on my list of priorities right now.

'Dare I ask if Gerry will be back? Are you two even speaking? I hate to sound selfish but this party is very important to me. I can't have odd numbers at the table.'

Fiona could always put things in perspective. Family feuds, divorces, long-term couples splitting up, world hunger . . . getting the seating right at dinner parties was right up there with them.

'Er . . . *that* business is all a bit up in the air right now,' I glanced over at Sizemore. So handsome. So utterly sexy. So within earshot. 'They're all seeing a family therapist!' I whispered into the receiver.

'Who is?' Fiona was puzzled.

'You know,' I muttered. 'Gerry and Sally and . . .

I told you she thinks her two divorces may have psychologically damaged the kids.'

'Oh for feck's sake! She's a self-absorbed pain in the arse. Now, about the seating arrangements for my dinner party. Don't blow your top, but . . . if Gerry's not back would you consider bringing Sizemore? I know you hate him, but I'm not asking you to date him, just bring him to a dinner party. Go on! I'll be the envy of every wannabee top Dublin hostess. A single, deadly handsome, intelligent and well-heeled man in his thirties? They're scarce as hen's teeth this year. Well, every year. Please, Annie? Will you bring him? I know it's asking a lot of you, but do me this *one* favour. You won't even have to speak to him. I'll put him at the far end of the table, next to Lucy Moore and her new double-D breasts, which incidentally look like lead balloons.'

'What's the date again?' I didn't want to hear about Lucy Moore and her new breasts.

'Saturday, the thirteenth.'

'Oh. Not Friday then?'

She giggled. 'Pulease.'

'OK. Talk to you before then.'

'You will, but I don't want you saying I didn't give you enough notice. I'll remind you again nearer the date. Dress will be formal! *Very* formal!' She yelled, and hung up before I could tell her that not only was I now beautifully tanned, I had used a home rinse on my hair that made *it* glint like gold. Well, when I took the time to dry it properly it did.

Sizemore watched me, his expression curious. 'Everything all right?'

'I'm not sure. I think I've just agreed to go on a date.' I could be cool when I tried. 'Well, Fiona says it isn't really a date. But it sounds suspiciously like one to me.' I checked him out for jealousy from beneath my lashes.

He looked a bit disgruntled, if not quite suicidal. But a second later he all but threw a tabloid newspaper at me. 'Check out Ireland's favourite read.'

'Full of the drug bust, is it?'

'Yeah. But look at page five. You'll see something relevant to our case,' he said, his tone businesslike.

The picture on page five was of Seanie Bolger's mum. Whenever this particular redtop was short of a headline, they printed a photo of her going into the hospital, head bent, as she wept into a plastic-wrapped bouquet of flowers.

Seanie's mum still keeping a daily vigil at his bedside – said the caption.

But the choice of this particular photo was shameless. When you looked close you could see that Seanie's mum was dressed for cold weather. May, when the fire happened, had been bitterly cold, but this month's temperatures hadn't once dropped below twenty-five degrees.

Sneaky buggers were using the same old photo. Still, the actual story might be true. It would be worth going to the hospital to try and meet her. See if she would speak to me, face to face.

Sizemore had tried ringing her three days on the trot, without success.

Her response was always the same. 'Bugger off.'

And then a loud click as she lashed down the phone.

'I might try to speak to her.' I looked questioningly at Sizemore. 'Want to come with me?'

'I've got a list of calls to make today,' he said, without looking up. 'And I'm hoping to tape some more voices for Lily in Mutual Irish. Do you want me to come?'

'No,' I said. 'She might find it less stressful to talk to a woman.'

'Huh.'

I took the newspaper and left.

26

It was gone one o'clock, and the lunchtime traffic was gaining momentum when I spotted the stocky little woman hurrying out of the hospital gates. I checked her against the newspaper photo in my hand. It was Seanie's mum all right. Leaving after her morning visit. The tabloid got something right.

I watched her crossing to the tram stop, leaning into the wind that was promising another summer storm, already spattering the street with big wet drops. I gave her time to put down her bulging shopping bag, check her watch, and peer short-sightedly along the tracks.

I suddenly spotted a tram in the distance and immediately made a quick U-turn. Pulling up alongside the tram stop, I swung the door open.

'Mrs Bolger? Do you need a lift?'

She looked up at me, her little grey eyes squinting short-sightedly.

'May not be a tram for ages,' I smiled, hoping she was as short-sighted as she appeared.

'Which direction are you going?'

I took a chance. 'Er . . . Crumlin?'

'Perfect.'

For someone her age, and build, she was agile.

And fast. She was in the jeep, settling her shopping bag at her feet and clicking her seatbelt before I could change gear.

'Do I know you?' she asked.

'I'm Annie. I . . . I'm working for Seanie's insurance company. Mutual Irish?'

'Oh.' She swivelled. 'Have you got the cheque for me?'

'Er . . .'

'What's the delay? All I got so far were phone calls from someone who said he was investigating the fire. What's to investigate? The shop burned down, didn't it? Youse were quick enough to collect the premiums.'

'If it were down to me, Mrs Bolger, it would have been paid out weeks ago.' I hoped the words wouldn't choke me. 'But you know insurance companies. "Never pay out today what you can hold on to 'til tomorrow".'

She looked vexed. 'Bloody robbers.'

'I'll try to speed things up. How is Seanie doing? Any improvement?'

'Oh yes.' She lightened up instantly. 'He opened his eyes the other day. And when I squeeze his hand now, he squeezes back. He knows my voice, too. That means his brain is working OK. 'Course them doctors won't promise anything. They stroll in with their fancy white coats, and long, gloomy faces, thinking they know everything. Well, I'm his mother! I know my Seanie. He's getting better.'

I concentrated on my driving. This wasn't going to be easy.

'Traffic,' Mrs Bolger sighed, when we got stuck in

253

a bottleneck. 'I don't know why anyone drives, these days.'

'I find it . . . challenging.'

'Have you papers for me to sign?' she suddenly asked.

'Er . . . not yet.'

'Right. Then you can drop me off here. I'll walk the rest.'

'Ah sure I'll drive you to your door.'

'It's up to you.' She wasn't impressed.

We were approaching the end of Crumlin Road before she spoke again.

'Turn left here. Quick, before the lights. Now left again. That little road there.'

She pointed to a small run-down house, in a terrace of small run-down houses, all of them practically identical. 'That's it there. The last one. The one with the dog at the gate!' she ordered as if you'd be able to see a dog behind a solid five-and-a-half-foot gate.

I pulled over.

'That's Seanie's dog, King,' she said as a massive head appeared over the gate. 'Called him after Elvis, he did. We can't let him out. People are afraid of him.'

Hardly surprising. King was the biggest Alsatian I had ever seen. Definitely the possessor of the biggest canine teeth, which he was now baring threateningly.

I was apprehensively opening the passenger door for Mrs Bolger when the dog suddenly cleared the high gate and made straight for us. Before I could scream, he had his black nose stuck halfway down into Mrs Bolger's shopping bag.

'Good boy, King.' She patted his wolf-like coat.

'Good boy, King,' I echoed, my voice high-pitched with terror.

His massive head shot up, and the wolf-like eyes met mine. When a rumble like a developing earthquake began somewhere deep in his throat I closed my eyes, and waited for death.

Two massive paws rocked me backwards, and a tongue rasped against my chin like fine sandpaper.

'Ah Jaysus, King! Will you get off the girl. She's gone white as a sheet. Come into the house, love. I'll make you a nice cup of tea, with plenty of sugar.'

Mrs Bolger was a little dynamo. She ordered me to sit, filled the kettle, threw teabags into two matching mugs, opened a packet of Chocolate Goldgrain and forced one into my hand, while unwrapping a large greasy marrowbone for King. All this without once stopping for breath, as she outlined her future plans for Seanie.

'See that?' She pointed to a narrow hole in the kitchen wall through which you could see a small sitting room, complete with a floral chesterfield suite. 'I'm going to put a bed in there for him. He's bound to be bedridden for a while, and I want to be able to keep an eye on him.'

'Through the hole,' I humoured her.

She laughed. 'No! I'll be getting the whole wall knocked through! When we get the insurance money.'

I felt like slime. Drinking her tea and eating her Chocolate Goldgrain, while trying to collect enough evidence to prevent her son getting the insurance payout.

She dragged an ironing board from a press, and

reached into the hole to pull out what looked like a bag of crumpled rags.

'The man next door, Peter, said he'd knock the wall through for me but, God help him, didn't he do his back in digging the garden. I'm waiting for the money so I can pay someone to do it.'

The bag of rags turned out to be a bag of expensive-looking shirts. Well, they looked expensive when she finished spraying the collars and cuffs with liquid starch, and then ironed them to perfection. She slipped them one by one onto waiting hangers.

'I do a bit of ironing, love. You couldn't live on the pension.'

I tried to swallow my tea.

'Not enough sugar, love?' She got the sugar bowl and tried to spoon extra sugar into my already syrupy-sweet tea.'

'No thanks. It's sweet enough.' I covered the cup with my hand, which was the signal for King to pad over and lick off any remaining traces of Chocolate Goldgrain from my fingers.

'He likes you.' Mrs Bolger put another perfectly ironed shirt on a hanger. 'It's not everyone he'll lick. He's an army dog. Retired. Seanie paid good money for him, but he's worth it. Aren't you, dote?' She started on another shirt.

I wiped dog slime off my knuckles, and tried to shoo King away.

Again she began telling me about her plans for Seanie. I listened, knowing I should be pushing her for information about Seanie's state of mind before the fire. I needed to prove my case. Plus it would be serving justice if I could *prove* who started the fire. No one should gain from another person's death. So why was I finding it so hard to push Mrs Bolger into ratting on her son?

'Rasher sandwich?' she suddenly said.

'I beg your pardon?'

'Would you like a rasher sandwich?' She stood over me, wiping her hands. 'I usually have a bit to eat at this time. Only take me a minute to fry another couple of rashers. Maybe a bit of white pudding? An egg?'

'No thanks.' I smiled.

'Seanie loves a rasher sandwich,' she said. 'I used to say, "You won't be getting rasher sandwiches in that fancy new kitchen of yours. It'll be all quiches and vol-au-vents, and fancy things like that." That always made him laugh. Seanie loves a good laugh.' She went quiet.

'What about Kathy?' I asked quickly.

'What?' She frowned.

'Did they laugh a lot together?'

Her plump face scrunched up in recall. 'Kathy was *very* serious.'

'Not all the time, surely?'

'No. But . . . mostly. She was the one who wanted a shop. Seanie only agreed to it to please her. He was already head, neck and ears in debt, he didn't need any more trouble. But trouble seemed to follow him. Still, whatever Kathy wanted . . .' She sighed. 'He'd have pulled the moon out of the sky to make her happy. For all the good it would have done.'

'You think . . . she didn't love him?'

'I know he loved her. It was all about Kathy. Kathy

257

this, and Kathy that. Don't get me wrong, I'm not
saying she was bad . . . but there was no . . . no
warmth to her . . . if you know what I mean. He
thought if the shop did well that would make her
happy. I knew it would end in tears.' She sniffed and
blew her nose.

'Was she greedy for money?'

She came to sit beside me, suddenly looking old
and tired. 'If she was, she married the wrong man.
He went through all his football money before he
even met her. And trying to please her pushed him
further into debt.'

'What do *you* think she was after?'

'I don't know, love. But I never saw her laugh.
Isn't that peculiar? Seanie said it's because intelligent people take life more seriously. But there's a
difference between being serious and being bloody
miserable, isn't there?'

'Didn't her pregnancy make her happy?'

'Oh yes. For five minutes. Then she had the
miscarriage.'

'Sad.'

'Peculiar. One minute Seanie was over the moon.
Everything was great. Then I heard she'd had the
miscarriage. He didn't tell me, mind. I wouldn't have
known a thing about it if one of the club bouncers
didn't live down the road here. I met *his* mother in
the butcher's, and she told me. I'm in a butcher's,
buying a bit of stewing steak, when I hear me son's
wife had a miscarriage. I hadn't seen them for weeks.
I left message after message on their phone. Nothing.
I got the bus over to the shop and it was closed.

Kathy was back at work. Two days after a miscarriage? Seanie was up in the flat. Rotten with drink. Walking around in his jocks. That was two weeks before the fire. People say things happen in threes.'

'How do you mean?'

'He told me they were going to separate.'

'What?' I froze.

'He said not to tell anyone. Said they had to decide what to do about the shop. They could sell it, but it was mortgaged to the hilt. He was wondering if they should split the property into two flats. That way they could have one each. I told him that was the stupidest idea. You'll end up killing each other, I said. Little did I think that two weeks later she . . . terrible . . . terrible.' She blinked back tears.

King scratched eagerly at the back door.

'Cats!' Mrs Bolger let him out. 'Are you sure you wouldn't like a rasher sandwich, love?'

'No thanks. I'm . . . weight watching.' I got to my feet.

'You? You haven't a pick on you. You're a worrier, I can tell. That's not good.' She began pulling open drawers. 'Wait a minute, love, I'll see if I can find the letter from the insurance company. I can't make head nor tail of it. Maybe you'll be able to tell me when the money's coming. I don't want to have to go on me knees to the social, to get the down payment for Seanie's new bed.'

With time running out, and the Bolger case no nearer to being wrapped up, I was thrown right back into panic mode. It didn't help that Mutual Irish were now pressing us for a speedier result.

Sizemore remained confident. I think. Hard to tell, given that he came from a background of cold showers and stiff upper lips. A world where people masked their feelings with a polite veneer. My adoptive parents used to jump three feet in the air if the doorbell rang unexpectedly. And if a brown envelope arrived in the post they were only just short of legging it to a fallout shelter. But I suppose faking a child's adoption papers would make anyone nervous. They brought me up with oodles of warmth and love, but that didn't prevent me imbibing fear with my breakfast cornflakes.

After a long, restless night I rang Sizemore and insisted that we print out a full report on the Bolger case. Now.

'What time is it?' he muttered sleepily.

'It's five forty-five!' I said. 'If we leg it to the office straight away, we could get an early start, *and* get one of the lads to run a critical eye over our preliminary report before they get dug into their own case. A fresh eye might work wonders.'

'Where will we get a fresh eye at five forty-five in the morning?' he mumbled.

'Just get to my office,' I ordered. 'By the time we get the damn thing written and printed out, Barney and Declan are bound to be in.'

'OK, OK. Can I have five minutes to shower?'

'Noooo!' I didn't want to be distracted by visions of him in the shower. Didn't want to start picturing the way the water cascaded down that long firm body and dripped off the end of his . . .

'What?'

'Of course you can shower!' I hung up and rang Declan, the perfect antidote for impure thoughts.

'You're absolutely right, Declan, it is the middle of the night,' I cut through his drowsy whine. 'And you owe me a favour.'

A long pause while he considered this. 'OK. I'll be there.'

I was out the door and revving the Honda in record-breaking time. And thanks to my early morning dash I found a free parking space. Possibly the only one in the whole of the Greater Dublin area.

Sizemore eventually appeared in, looking surprisingly bright eyed and bushy tailed for someone who'd had to be bullied out of bed. But then he had attended an all-male boarding school, and I knew from Fiona, who heard it from Heather Flanagan whose brothers attended such an establishment, that in those places the prettier boys learned to vacate their beds early to avoid being roggered senseless by their prefects.

'Morning boss.' He smiled as he came in.

I handed him a giant mug of black coffee. He raised an eyebrow at the bucket-sized mug, but didn't comment further.

We drank our coffee in a companionable silence, while keeping a businesslike distance between us. We got down to work on the report, and somehow managed to compile an impressive-looking file on the case. Well, impressive if you weren't expecting actual closure on the last page.

What we needed now was a critical pair of eyes to read through it and give us a hard-hitting, no-holds-barred opinion.

An hour later Declan crept in, looking like Julian Clary.

'Jesus!' Sizemore stared.

'Not quite,' I gulped in horror.

Declan was wearing pink. From head to toe. Even his combat trousers had a pinky hue to them, while his socks and un-ironed shirt, which I recognised as once being white, were a deep, salmon pink.

'Don't ask,' he growled, and made straight for the coffee.

'Sasha?' I winced.

'She can be ruthless.'

'Were you drinking?'

'No. Well, I found a drop of wine in the press. A thimbleful.'

'*All* your clothes?'

He nodded.

'I don't get it?' Sizemore was puzzled. Obviously

he had never seen what a red jumper can do to a whole washing machine full of clothes, when the water temperature reaches eighty degrees.

'He's led a sheltered life,' I explained to Declan, and refilled his empty mug.

He stared jealously at Sizemore, while refusing all offers of milk or sugar.

'It's only a rough prelim, Declan,' I pleaded, when he groaned at the mountain of A4 pages awaiting his perusal. 'And you did speed reading at law school, didn't you?'

He mumbled something unintelligible, before stamping off to his own office, carrying the Bolger report as if it was a nail bomb.

Declan arrived back with the report, his clothes looking pinker than ever, although we were becoming accustomed to the look; even if he wasn't. He slammed the bulky file on my desk. 'There's nothing there to prove Bolger torched the shop. It's all supposition,' he said, looking like he wanted to bolt.

Sitting in his spot by the wall, Sizemore chewed the end of his gold-topped pen, and tried not to stare at Declan's screaming pink shirt. 'Mutual Irish can only give us another two weeks. After that it's . . .' He ran a finger across his throat.

Declan brushed at his cuff as if he was hoping the pink would wipe off. He looked miserable. But then Declan doesn't do happy. Ever. I leaned over to squeeze his pink sleeve consolingly.

'Did you hear me?' Sizemore sounded impatient.

'We have fourteen days to come up with some hard evidence against Bolger. If we fail Mutual Irish will be forced to pay out the three million. Treat the anonymous call as a hoax.'

'But you don't think it was?' Declan tore his eyes off his pink cuff.

'No. The whole thing stinks. I don't believe it's a coincidence that on the night of the fire Seanie just happened to park his flashy MG a safe distance from the shop, when he always left it out front. Then there's the . . . tell him about the dog, Annie.'

'Seanie left his dog at his mum's house,' I obliged.

'Seanie adores his dog,' Sizemore clarified. 'He let it sleep by his bed. Yet the night of the fire he suddenly decides to leave it at his mum's house? Why? The Gards say it was because he was planning to take Kathy away for the weekend.'

'Seanie's mum told me they were separating!' I said.

Sizemore was now pacing the floor. 'Even if they were planning a weekend away, surely he'd leave the dog to guard the shop? That whole area is a cat burglar's dream. So what does Seanie do? He drops his big Alsatian at his mum's house, throws her a few bob, and leaves? Next time she sees him he's in a coma.'

Despite himself Declan became interested. 'But if Seanie needed money so desperately why didn't he sell the shop? Why risk torching it while his wife was sleeping upstairs? Did he want her dead?'

'No. He thought he was being clever. Selling a business can be expensive. Estate agent's fees, solicitor's fees, capital gains, if there are any. Torching the place he figures he can pocket a clear three million, *and* come out of it like a hero. I think he missed being in the headlines. Missed being the golden boy of soccer. Saving his wife's life would have guaranteed him a place in the headlines again.'

'Well, he made headlines all right.'

'Yeah. Not the way he planned. His mother claimed what he wanted most was to impress Kathy. Saving her life would have been pretty impressive.'

'So . . . what's eating Annie? You scared he'll get away with it?' Declan's narrow eyes were sharp as razors.

'I . . . I . . .'

'Annie's conflicted,' Sizemore interrupted. 'She met Seanie's mum.'

'I see.' Declan nodded.

'Don't look at me like that, you two! It's not just some *female* thing. Nobody could fail to notice that while we're trying to save Mutual Irish millions that poor woman can't even afford to have a hole knocked in her kitchen wall!'

'Can't let personal feelings interfere with the job,' Declan said.

I shot him a look that had him squirming in his pink shirt. He's telling me that it's unprofessional of me to feel sorry for some poor old woman, but he felt entitled to do a GBH over some pampered dogs? Serve him right that Sasha put a red jumper in with his washing. I wished I had her guts.

'Declan's right,' Sizemore said.

I shot him a drop-dead look for good measure.

'I don't envy you this one.' Declan slapped the file dismissively.

'We still have the anonymous caller.' Sizemore tried giving me a conciliatory smile. 'Lily, who took the call, said she never forgets a voice. She's been registered blind since she was ten, so her hearing is honed to perfection. If we find that caller we could still be home free.'

'Brilliant!' I forced a smile. 'So all we have to do is record the voice of every woman in Ireland? That's how many? Say two million, give or take? Then we'll sit Lily down and have her listen to them. And we have two whole weeks to do it.'

There was an awkward silence.

'Cheer up, guys!' I swung around. 'Our other macho PI may yet come to our rescue. Barney's been looking at second-hand lie detectors, to help with his dating agency case. He's hoping to get one online.' This time I couldn't even force a laugh.

'One that works?' Declan frowned.

I shot him a look.

'Stupid question,' he agreed.

The phone shrilled. I grabbed it, hoping for good news. OK, a small miracle. Maybe Barney's second-hand lie detector *would* work on a comatose patient? Or maybe Mutual Irish's anonymous caller had just walked into the agency to tell all? Maybe Seanie's mum won the Lotto? Maybe . . .

Sandra's voice trembled, 'Annie, it's Alicia Stowe, she . . .'

'Oh for God's sake, tell her to push off!'

'No, hold on. She's in hospital. Her stalker attacked her last night.'

'Oh my God. Is she all right?'

'No. And she won't talk to anyone except Gerry, so DI Bailey said maybe . . .'

'Bailey? He knows Gerry is in America.'

'Yes. He wants to talk to Sizemore.'

'You mean Barney?'

'No. He definitely said Sizemore.'

I handed the phone to Sizemore, who looked as mystified as I was.

'Hello?' He frowned into the receiver. 'Oh yeah, it was a great night.' He avoided my eyes. 'Sure. But . . . I'm not actually a McHugh Dunning employee. OK, if you think it would help. How bad was the assault? Oh, nasty. And it *was* her stalker? OK, I'll be there in ten.' He was on his feet, pulling on his jacket.

'He thinks she might talk to me,' he answered my questioning look.

'Her stalker is real?' A little chill started somewhere in my toes.

'Yeah.'

'And he definitely attacked her?'

He nodded. 'It sounds bad. They're studying the X-rays now.' He threw Declan a quick wave, and disappeared.

'Got to go, Annie. I've got to trail my horny nanny,' Declan said.

'Your . . . ? Oh right, go ahead, Declan.'

It was five thirty p.m. and still no word from

Sizemore. I packed up the Bolger report and took it home with me, planning to read through it again while I soaked in a long hot bath. But by the time I struggled through the rush-hour traffic I was too worn out to even run a bath. I settled for a quick shower instead. Then made a pot of bowel-scouring coffee, piled a mountain of cushions onto the big sofa and settled down to study the report. Was there anything we had missed? Some tiny clue that could help us out?

After reading it for the trillionth time I gave up. It didn't help that Alicia Stowe's face kept coming between me and the page.

I turned on the TV. Settled for watching a TV programme where a middle-aged American actress (her face looking like it had been trapped in a wind tunnel) was trying to convince viewers that her new exercise video would not only take years off them, it would guarantee them multiple orgasms. Or their money back.

I watched it anyway, although I was firmly convinced that if Alicia Stowe had suffered life-threatening injuries my guilty conscience would prevent me from ever again enjoying a single orgasm, let alone multiples.

The actress completed her vaginal tightening exercises, and was moving upwards to jowl firming ones, when my phone shrilled. My caffeine overload working like rocket fuel, I shot to my feet.

'She's going to be fine, Annie.' Sizemore sounded relieved. 'They've controlled the bleeding. It was all coming from one bad tear on her scalp. She was covered in blood. Like a scene from a horror movie, the cops said.'

'Oh God,' I shivered.

'Horrendous, but not life threatening, so relax. Her X-rays are clear. Apart from having a dozen stitches in her scalp, and possibly a nasty scar, she'll be OK.'

'But I kept dismissing her,' I accused myself.

'Everyone dismissed her, Annie. I probably would have too.'

'You spoke to her?'

'No. She was too heavily sedated by the time I got here. I hung around thinking she might come to but she was too groggy to make sense. Sadie was still on duty, and she filled me in. She seems to have dropped the notion that I'm Satan personified. She says their only concern now is Ms Stowe's emotional state.'

My breath caught. 'Was she . . . sexually assaulted?'

'No! She'll be discharged tomorrow, after the psyche department have a word with her.'

I lay back against the scatter cushions in relief. 'And her stalker? What about him?'

'They have a guy in custody. Don't seem to know what to charge him with.'

'For God's sake, he attacked her! He's been stalking her for months!' I yelled, then forced myself to speak calmly. 'And I didn't believe her.'

'You're not to blame! Even the cops thought she was fantasising.'

I sniffled.

'He was hiding in her attic!'

'Jesus.'

'When he heard her coming he smashed the lights so the place was in complete darkness. It must have been terrifying.'

'I'm doubly ashamed now. I should have done something to help her.'

'Sadie said they'll look after her. Their psyche department is supposed to be tops. You get some rest, Annie, it's been a long day. You've been running around since dawn. I want to spend time going through our interview notes again. See you in the morning.' He was gone.

See you in the morning? Disappointment hit me like a tidal wave. I'd been convinced that, given the delay, he had been planning to call in on me. Why else would I be sitting here in my best nightie? OK it wasn't one of those erotically charged beauties that were all over the glossy magazines this year, but it was still better than being caught out in my Homer Simpson PJs with the back flap.

See you in the morning? What did that mean? We had shared an incredible night after Barney's party. It was magical. Well, maybe not as magical for him as it had been for me? But still. Sod him anyway. I thought we made each other so happy that night. Three times. Four, if you count the standy-up one in the shower the next morning; although that one could be classed as a sympathy shag, because I was still upset over my dirty phone call. That call definitely got to Sizemore because he pulled strings to have my home number changed within the hour, then later that morning he got me *and* Sandra a couple of noisy tin whistles, which worked a treat because dirty caller didn't like noisy whistles being blown in his ear.

So was that it with Sizemore? His kind deed for the day? Or night? Oh my God, had that whole night with me just been one long sympathy shag? Did I look so lonely and forlorn after the party that he was moved to . . . ? Oh my God, was I that obvious? That pathetic? Getting an all-over fake tan that he probably didn't even notice because he was so used to the sun-kissed beauties in the US? And using that stupid rinse on my hair because Andie MacDowell, or some other lying movie star said it changed their lives.

I went to the kitchen and rummaged through the cupboards until I found a half-empty / half-full bottle of Southern Comfort. Legging it upstairs, I told myself I didn't need a glass. It wasn't like I'd be raising a toast to someone. I was alone. Except for the half-empty / half-full bottle of Southern Comfort, which I intended to drain to the very last drop.

I hugged the bottle and tried to figure out why men left me? What did I do that frightened them off? Did I say the wrong thing? Was I sometimes a bit too bolshy as Barney once claimed? Sod him too. And Gerry. And Sizemore. Mostly Sizemore for leaving me sitting hopefully in my best nightie.

I tilted the bottle and drank the Southern Comfort from the neck.

*   *   *

I was woken at seven fifty by a loud ringing, which turned out to be the dreaded bedside phone. 'Hello,' I rasped.

'Ms Stowe's stalker isn't a stalker.'

'Who is this?' I mumbled, opening both eyes.

'Sizemore. Who were you expecting? George Bush?' His laugh bounced off my skull.

'Could you lower your voice a little?'

'Oh, like that is it?' Another knowing laugh.

'Tell me about the stalker.' I was slowly coming to, livened by curiosity, and the realisation that I wasn't hungover. There must have been less Southern Comfort in the bottle than I thought.

'There is no stalker,' Sizemore said. 'The man they have in custody is Ms Stowe's next-door neighbour.'

I sat up. 'The one she accused of playing Led Zeppelin to annoy her?'

'That's the one. The Gards have finished interviewing him. When they brought him in he had a black eye and a split lip. He says he was up in their shared attic, minding his own business, when Ms Stowe attacked him. You still there?'

'Yes. But there's no such thing as a *shared* attic, is there?'

'I'm not sure. I do know that the neighbour had taken over part of hers to facilitate his expanding plant collection. Been doing it for some time, apparently. When he heard her coming up the ladder he smashed the overhead light. Said he thought his life was in danger because all he could make out in the darkness was some lunatic coming at him with a cricket bat. He claims he merely defended himself, by hitting her on the head with an organic plant feeder. Bailey says the guy is a skinny five foot three, and that he definitely lost the fight. Ms Stowe *is* a bit of a tigress, isn't she? How tall is she? Five nine? Ten? Not lacking in the chin-hair department, according to Bailey.'

'But why was her neighbour growing plants in his attic? Plants need daylight.'

'Or special ultraviolet lamps?'

'But why not just plant them in the garden? What the hell was he growing anyway?'

'Marijuana.'

Wide-awake now, I laughed until my head began to hurt. This whole hullabaloo was over a few stupid grass plants? A skinny pot head defending himself with an organic plant feeder? Sizemore and DI Bailey had carried on as if they were hot on the trail of Al Capone, while I waited hopefully in my semi-seductive nightie?

'Are you listening, Annie?' Sizemore asked as I continued to giggle.

'Will they charge him?'

'Will you stop laughing?'

'No.'

'Then I'm not giving you any further information.'

'Good. Because I have no interest in hearing about a nutter who grows grass in an attic, and given that Ms Stowe is OK, I'll bid you good morning.' I hung up, and went to have my shower.

I was fully refreshed, scrubbed a deeply satisfying

pink, and about to get dressed when the doorbell rang. My huge white bath towel covering me from neck to knees I plodded down to open the door a crack.

'Good morning.' Sizemore stepped in, carrying an enormous McDonald's breakfast.

'Want to hear my new take on the Bolger case?'

'Maybe.' I eyed him warily.

He looked me up and down, his eyes smiling. 'Drop the towel and I'll tell you.'

My stupid heart pounding, I stepped back.

'No bloody way!' I darted up the stairs. The cheek! Did he really think I could be bought for a McDonald's breakfast? That I'd be up for another pity shag? He'd been living in America for too long.

I was in my bedroom, struggling to pull on my knickers under the towel, when I was grabbed from behind, and the musky scent of Issey Miyake teased my nostrils.

I tried to remember the rules of a self-defence course I once took.

'Let your whooooole body relax.' The Scottish martial arts teacher used to croon. 'Then grab the bugger between the legs, and twist *harrrd*.'

I went for it. Did exactly what she said. Well, except for the twist part, because she never said how to react when the body part in question springs to life in your hand. Forced to improvise I came up with a better idea to immobilise him. I dropped my towel and leaned back, giving him a clear view of my breasts. Why not? I was still inordinately proud of my all-over tan, and moderately excited by our impromptu little wrestling match.

'Oh God,' he said, and reached out for me. With his mouth.

Bliss.

Some mornings should never end.

28

Sizemore was parking the jeep outside the Newmans' when I spotted the wizened little face peering out from behind next door's rose bower. Mrs Brent was on the prowl again.

'Ignore her,' I warned as she viciously dead-headed a climbing rose then threw us a challenging look.

It was too beautiful a day for a confrontation. Mediterranean warm again, and with barely a breeze to nudge the leaves of the lime trees that lined the quiet cul-de-sac, this was a day for pleasantries. Plus half the elderly residents of the cul-de-sac seemed to be outdoors, tending their already perfect grass verges. I kept my head down, intent on not giving Mrs Brent any excuse to call me a filthy Communist within earshot of this genteel blue-rinse brigade.

Sizemore gave her a friendly wave. 'Nice day for gardening,' he said, and leaned on the Newmans' doorbell, as if we were invited guests.

Chutzpah is the only word for it. It's almost a requirement for any upwardly mobile PI. I'm still working on mine.

Mrs Newman opened the door, her eyes heavy

276

with sleep. Or was it medication? And yet she looked surprisingly fit, wearing a bright summer dress, and a smattering of freckles across her nose. And as if she had lost at least five pounds. She didn't seem at all surprised to see us, greeting us as if it was the most natural thing in the world to have two private investigators land on your doorstep the very morning you arrive back from holiday.

'You look very well,' I said politely, as she invited us in.

'I'm feeling lots better,' she said. 'Richard was right.'

I waited.

'He said we needed a holiday.' And that was that.

Her husband came downstairs as we crossed the hall. He was deeply tanned; his thinning hair bleached pale gold by the sun, only the unrelieved black of his business suit and dark tie appearing slightly incongruous against the bright blue of his wife's cotton dress. He gave us a brief nod of recognition, before turning to her.

'I'm off, Janet. Need to see what they've been up to at the radio station. Three weeks is a long time to leave that lot unsupervised.' He sounded boastful. 'Did you pack my new tapes? Put them in the side pocket of my briefcase?'

'Yes. All numbered. Exactly as you requested.'

I half expected her to salute.

'Could we have a word with you, Mr Newman?' Sizemore asked.

'Sorry. No time. Duty calls. And don't tire out my wife. She needs her rest.'

He brushed cheeks with his wife, and he was gone.

'Is your husband broadcasting full time now?' Sizemore asked as if he hadn't already made it his business to double-check this. 'I thought he was in the bank.'

Mrs Newman flushed with pride. 'He took early retirement. To focus more on his broadcasting talks. He's very committed. Do you listen to Christian broadcasting?'

'Er . . . every chance I get.' Sizemore's smile was disarming.

Mrs Newman relaxed. 'Then you'll know why we were in France. Such a joy to hear the Mass in Latin again. And to meet so many like-minded people. We feel renewed. Didn't expect to come back to this heat, though.' She fanned herself with a small pamphlet with a sad Jesus on the cover.

I was about to ask her if we could open a window, but Sizemore beat me to it. 'Should I open a window, Mrs Newman?'

'Oh no. Richard left them closed. Don't open them.'

We sat there sweltering, afraid to look at each other.

'We were, er, wondering if we could talk about Kathy?'

'They have extreme heat in France, you know.'

'Interesting,' Sizemore nodded. 'Your husband was very generous to Seanie and Kathy, wasn't he? He helped them raise the finance for the shop.'

'Kathy hated that shop.' She straightened a wayward antimacassar.

'But your husband helped them buy it?' I said.

'A florist's dear.' She gave me a look.

'A florist's?' I was puzzled. The Lingere Lounge?

'It was a florist's when Richard first saw it. A sweet little shop. Are you fond of flowers?'

'Mad about them.' This time Sizemore and I felt free to exchange looks.

'Red roses are my special favourites,' she offered.

'So the shop was . . .'

'Richard has green fingers. He has so many talents. God-given talents.' She looked around as if she was checking to see that everything was as Richard left it.

'Did, er . . . did Seanie ask Richard to help him borrow money to buy into a nightclub, Mrs Newman?'

'A *night*club?' She made it sound like a brothel. 'Oh no, dear, Richard wouldn't be involved with anything like *that*!'

Searching for an opening, I picked up a photo of a broadly-smiling Kathy. 'Kathy looks so happy here.'

'Happy?' Her head jerked back, as if I had said something odd.

'Don't you think she looks happy?' Sizemore took the photo. 'This was obviously taken when she was living here with you. She looks . . . carefree.'

He was trying to provoke a reaction. It was a classic PI move, but I worried that if he pushed it Mrs Newman might do a Sadie – clam up and show us the door.

She didn't. She leaned closer to him as if it was a relief to have someone to confide in. Her voice little more than a whisper she said, 'Richard did become concerned for her after the marriage. He worried that she was . . . losing her faith.'

I could practically see Sizemore holding his breath.

'She wasn't, of course. Pastor Dewmore assured us that she was merely going through a transition. He came to France with us. He's a living saint.'

'But . . . Kathy's marriage, was it happy?' I frowned.

'She wasn't losing her faith. It was just a transition,' she said dreamily.

'Mrs Newman?'

'Richard said special prayers for her. Then he made the plans.'

'What plans were they, Mrs Newman?'

'He wanted her to work with him at the radio station. Build up a real following.'

'He wanted her to give up nursing?'

'She wasn't happy. She had tried medical school . . . that didn't suit her. Richard has endless patience . . . endless . . .' She was away with the fairies.

'Mrs Newman?' Sizemore took her hand.

'Em?'

'About Kathy,' he reminded her.

'Oh yes. Richard says she had a voice made for broadcasting. It's not something that can be manufactured, you know. It's a gift, Richard says. Something you're born with. Kathy had that gift, Richard says. He was right as usual. Radio is a very powerful medium. People underestimate its power . . . Richard . . .'

Sizemore tried to steer her back to the subject of

Kathy. 'About Kathy . . . was she . . . leaving Seanie?' he asked.

'Richard says we don't pray enough. We must stop questioning the ways of the Lord. Show faith, without question. But it's hard to lose your only child.' Her lip quivered and she started to cry. 'I miss my daughter.'

We left her to her grief.

'Richard says, Richard says.' Sizemore started the jeep. 'Wonder what Richard said when his darling daughter said she was marrying a club bouncer? An ex—'

'He couldn't have been too horrified. He helped him finance the shop.'

'He thought he was financing a florist's! Seanie probably told him they'd be selling floral crosses. He certainly didn't think they would be selling open crotch panties and rubber sex aids. I don't know which of them is the worst.'

'Open crotch panties or . . . ?'

'Seanie or Richard! One of them is a sneaky sleaze-bag! The other is a tight-arsed fundamentalist.'

'Maybe the Newmans . . . ?' I paused.

'Maybe they what? Aren't nuts? Come on, we came here to discuss Kathy and Seanie's relationship, and all we got was religious hokum.'

'Faith can be a consolation.'

'Let's drop the subject OK?' He hit the acceler-ator hard, sending the jeep speeding through an amber light, which turned red before we made it halfway across the junction.

'Sizemore?'

'Let's not talk about it, Annie!'

'Fine. I just thought I'd warn you that there's an unmarked cop car behind us. They're definitely watching us, I think they're about to flag us down.'

'Fuck.'

The Garda driver waved us over. Sizemore hit the brakes, and reached behind the mirror for his licence.

A familiar figure stepped out of the cop car. DI Bailey. He fastened his jacket and, taking his time, sauntered back to us to squint up at the jeep window.

'Hiya, Annie. Sizemore. How's she cuttin'?'

'Morning, Paddy,' Sizemore said. 'What are you doing in this neck of the woods?'

'Serving the people of Dublin,' Bailey grinned. 'I thought you might like to know that that guy we busted for growing weed in his attic – the suspected stalker? The Brit police say they have a rap sheet as long as your arm on him. They want to interview him about an armed robbery. If our lads weren't keeping an eye on Ms Stowe's house, he might have done more than hit her. We owe you one.'

'Don't mention it,' Sizemore said quickly.

'Oh, by the way, you do know there's a speed limit on this road?'

'Sorry. I was distracted . . . worried about a case.'

'We all have worries. Breaking the law won't help.' Bailey saluted him and sauntered back to the unmarked Garda car, something about his slow walk making every passing motorist observe the speed limit.

'Why do they owe you one?' I asked Sizemore frostily.

'I, er . . . I may have asked them to keep an eye out for Ms Stowe. But only in passing. It was the night of Barney's party and the conversation turned to protecting the public. Don't look at me like that, Annie. OK, I may also have said that if they were in the area they er . . . I said she *might* be in some danger. You're the one who told me about her!' he accused.

'Yes. And you agreed that she was a nutter!'

'Even nutters can have stalkers.' He started the jeep.

'Jesus, Sizemore what is it with you? You meet Bailey twice and suddenly you become bosom buddies? Exchanging all sorts of ideas. I've been working with you every single day, and I hardly know a thing about you.'

He shook his head dismissively.

'It's true! I have no idea what you like, what you think . . .'

He laughed. 'You've got to be kidding!'

'Well, except for . . . *that* sort of stuff! Bailey seems to know more about you than I do, and I'm assuming he didn't sleep with you. Did he?' I gave a mock frown.

He shook his head solemnly. 'Naaa. He's not my type. I like them witty, clever, curly haired, sometimes bordering on the irrational, and with a fake tan that makes their nipples stand out like door-knobs.' Laughing now, he raised an arm to protect himself against my barrage of slaps.

Even so, I got one quick one in.

'OK, OK.' He fended me off with a laugh. 'What is it you want to know about me?'

'Are you married?'

'What?' He nearly ran another red light.

'Just answer the question. Are you married?'

'No!'

'Ever been?'

'No.'

'Ever been engaged?'

'No.'

'Why are you back in Ireland?'

'I was fired. Drummed out of my chosen profession.'

'Which was?'

He paused, and a little chill slid along my spine. Oh God. Oh God. Don't let him be a defrocked priest. Anything but that. No, he said drummed – that's military lingo. Was he a spy? One of those people who poison other spies with umbrellas?

'You wouldn't have heard of it . . . Special Protection Force,' he finally said.

I relaxed. They were just fancy US cops. Nothing untoward there.

'Why were you fired?'

'I . . . almost killed a man.'

I stiffened. 'Accidentally?'

'Deliberately.'

'Who was he?' I squeaked.

'A man I was sent to protect.'

We were now passing a sun-drenched park, the high jeep giving us a clear view across the parched grass. I could see children playing on swings, mums chasing wayward toddlers, teenagers entwined on the grass, all those normal everyday things that people do on a sunny day. Sizemore had tried to kill someone! I sat frozen in my seat.

'Annie?'

'What?' Even to my ears my voice was a high squeak.

'He was a bad man, Annie.'

'So if . . . if you think someone is bad, it's OK to kill them?'

He stopped the jeep. Pulled over against the grass verge, and leaned on the steering wheel to look at me.

'He was a very powerful man. A respected politician. Deeply religious. Ambitious. There was even talk of the White House. He worked hard. Made enemies, which is why he needed protecting. Whenever he had a particularly frustrating day, he went home to his charming wife, and . . . beat her senseless.'

I pressed a hand to my mouth.

'I worked on that protection rota for four months. During those four months he had a lot of frustrating days. My last day there, he . . .' He cleared his throat. 'He always locked their bedroom door before he . . . started on her. Even took off his expensive watch, I learned later. That last day he . . . forgot to lock the

285

door. She ran out screaming, her nose bleeding, her top lip smashed open. He followed her, and resumed the beating. She fell and he kicked her over and over while their two small children watched. I got him back into his room and locked the door. On the inside.'

He started the jeep, and we drove back to the agency in silence. Walking into the agency there was such a distance between us that we might have been strangers.

'Just one more question?' I asked without looking at him.

'Yes?'

'Does DI Bailey know what happened in America?'

'Bailey knows everything about me.' He sounded relieved.

If he thought that made things better between us he was a lot dummer than he looked.

29

Fiona and I strolled across her manicured lawn; carrying glasses brimming with the heavenly white wine the Molino family produced by the truckload.

Nonna Molino was already in the garden. Snoozing. Sleeping off her lunch on a well-shaded sun lounger, as if her neck-to-ankle black dress didn't offer her enough protection from the sun.

'Mad, isn't it?' Fiona chuckled. 'She says she loves the sun, yet she never lets it near her?'

I had only popped in for five minutes, in the hope of getting Fiona's opinion on Sizemore, well actually on a supposedly hypothetical situation regarding a man who had possibly beaten another man to within an inch of his life. Even if the beaten man deserved it, was I comfortable with this? With a man who was capable of doing this? But as Fiona had already polished off three glasses of the potent Molino wine before I got there, I felt it might be more circumspect to avoid any mention of men.

Fiona had other ideas.

'So, how goes it with Sizemore?' she asked. 'Are you two even civil to each other yet, or will I still have to seat you at opposite ends of the dinner table?'

Damn. The famous dinner. I had almost forgotten about it.

'I thought the *fancy* dinner party would be cancelled, on account of your visitor.' I nodded towards Nonna Molino.

'Actually, having her here is no pressure at all. On the contrary, she's turned out to be a great help around the house.'

I eyed the frail old Nonna sceptically. She looked as if the slightest puff of wind would blow her over the nearby beech trees, and on up into the cloudless sky. 'You're kidding!'

'I swear. She's taken over all the cooking. And she's spotless. I don't have to lift a finger after her. Especially not in the kitchen. And Calum adores her. He'll eat anything she cooks. Remember the battles I had trying to get a sliver of veggie into him? She shovels them into his mouth now, while babbling in Italian. The woman is amazing. Feckin' Mary Poppins with a bun. Life is so good, I'm seriously thinking of letting Mrs O'Kelly go. *And* there's another plus to having Nonna here. She is so great with Calum that Pino and me are actually getting to spend some time together, undisturbed, if you know what I mean?' She did a happy little twirl.

I glanced at the sleeping Nonna and wondered if she'd be up for a bit of private investigating. I could do with a miracle worker right now, even if they did only speak Italian.

'I'm assuming Gerry won't make it back for the party?' Fiona asked. When I paused she continued, 'So when *is* he due back?' She flopped lazily onto a thickly padded sun lounger without spilling a drop of her precious wine.

'God knows.' Avoiding her eyes, I sat down. 'He seems to think everything is running smoothly without him. His only concern now is for the children's well-being.' I didn't say Gerry was beginning to feel like a stranger to me. That when I closed my eyes now it was another face I pictured closing in on mine. Another fit body giving me such joy that it was hard to recall being intimate with anyone before him. Days passed now without me giving a single thought to Gerry. *Or* Sally. I couldn't care less now about their ongoing sessions with the family therapist. Or any other sessions they might be having. That all seemed so far away now. So removed from my everyday life.

'And is it?' Fiona asked.

'What?' I turned, startled.

'Is everything running smoothly without him?'

I closed my eyes and saw Sizemore's face. His worried expression when he told me how he lost it with the wife-beater. His shame. He didn't have to confess that to me. He could have kept it to himself. But Sizemore was an honourable man. Honest. A trait I find endearing. I have always despised liars.

'Actually, it is.' I held my face up to the sun, and smiled.

Fiona leaned on her elbow, to stare at me. 'You don't look like a woman who's missing her . . . oh my God, Annie . . . you're not . . . Jesus, Annie, who is it?'

'Wwwhat?'

'It's Barney, isn't it? You're having a fling with Barney!'

'Feck off,' I laughed.

'I knew it. I knew you were doing it. You're feckin' glowing.'

'It's the fake tan!'

'Fake tan my arse! Although that should have given me a clue. Your man is away, and next thing you're rushing off to get yourself an all-over tan? Then you start putting rinses in your hair? What's next? French underwear? Silk knickers?' She chortled.

I tried, but there was no stopping her. She was in full flow, and loving it.

'Anyway, the writing has been on the wall for ages about you and Barney. I always knew you two would get it on someday. Nothing permanent, mind. Just a fling. I used to actually worry about it. I swear. But shag it, Annie, life is short. Except if you're Nonna Molino.' She glanced over at her. 'Every neglected woman should get herself a temporary toy boy. Is he any good?' She paused, her eyes dancing with curiosity.

'For the last time Fiona, I am not *doing it* with Barney!'

'Are too!' she insisted. 'Last time I phoned you I got the funniest vibe. I knew you were hiding something. And Barney always fancied you.'

'Barney fancies *everyone*.'

'Huh? Why didn't you tell me that before you jumped him? I'd have been in there myself.'

I was scandalised. 'Shhh Nonna Molino will hear you!'

'She's deaf as a post, thank God. Plus she doesn't understand English.' Still chuckling, she reached out to hug Calum who, attracted by our laughter, had come over to sip at her wine glass.

'See, now this is the only thing that worries me about having Nonna Molino here.' She smoothed Calum's blond hair adoringly. 'Is this little angel developing a taste for wine because Nonna Molino lashes it into everything she cooks?'

'Silly. He's just thirsty.' I pointed out the obvious. 'See?'

Calum was now drinking ravenously from his plastic cup.

'Oh thanks be to Jesus,' Fiona relaxed again. 'I was afraid it was in the genes. Remember my uncle Ned? He'd drink whiskey off a sore leg. They said it started with my gran putting Guinness in his bottle, because he was a sickly baby. He had to be institutionalised in the end. He started having visions of Pope Pious the tenth. Or was it the twelfth? Anyway, tell me the truth, and shame the devil, Annie. Are you or aren't you having it off with Barney?' She squinted at me.

Tell her . . . tell her . . . she'll understand . . . she knows Gerry left you high and dry . . . well vulnerable . . . what are you afraid of . . . that she'll let it slip at a mothers and toddlers meeting and then it will spread and someone in the agency will hear and I'll be fucked . . . and not in the pleasurable sense . . . and . . . maybe when the case is sorted and Sizemore goes back to Mutual Irish . . . maybe then I'll tell her . . .

'Owww!' I yelped as a plastic shovel came flying through the air and landed on my head.

'Jesus Christ! That little sod!' Fiona was on her feet. 'I'll kill him. Are you OK, Annie?' She was torn between ministering to me and running to the woven fence on the eastern side of her garden. The plastic shovel culprit was peeping over, clinging to the fence by his fingertips.

'It's nothing, Fiona.' I got up.

'Nothing my arse. That kid Ralph is a demon seed.' She shook her head in disgust. 'Or maybe he behaves like that because they leave him with that nanny all day, and she just sits around texting. God knows who to, because she doesn't speak a word of English. Ralph entertains himself by throwing things over the fence at Calum.'

'Hatcalum,' Calum echoed, wide-eyed.

'Why don't you let him come in here and play? They're about the same age aren't they?'

'I'm not babysitting their kid! Anyway, me and Nonna Molino were planning to take Calum to the park to feed the ducks later.'

'Lucky you. Wish I could go to the park.' I picked up my bag.

'What's stopping you? You can take a break.'

''Fraid I've had my break.' I checked the time. 'I've got to go, Fiona. This case I'm on is a . . . it's difficult.'

'You take that job too seriously.'

'It's a serious job.'

'Maybe, but you could lighten up a bit, it's not all life and death, is it?'

'Sometimes it is.' I thought of Kathy Bolger.

'See, there you go again! Looking as if it's the end

of the world. It's just a job, Annie. At the end of the working day you should be able to close the door behind you.'

'You can't do that when there are ethical questions involved in a case.'

'Ah, your problem is you're too honest. Too many fuckin' scruples. Oops.'

Fortunately Calum was well out of earshot. Shouting up at Ralph.

'I'm a professional investigator!' I laughed. 'I'm supposed to have scruples.'

'One or two, maybe.' She took a refreshing sip of wine. 'You don't have to be swimming in them.'

I turned to go. 'I really wish I could hang around. It's such a glorious day.'

'We'll be having tea soon,' she tried to tempt me. 'Nonna Molina made tiramisu. And her almond cake is to die for.'

'Stop it, Fiona.' I tried not to drool. 'I can't stay. I'm already in trouble with this case. Got to get things moving again.' I checked my watch for the second time. 'I'm so far behind I'll get—'

'What? Fired? You're the feckin' boss. What are you going to do? Fire yourself?'

'Ralph is climbing over the fence,' I warned.

'Jaysus.'

I gave her a quick hug and left.

I was midway along the quays when my mobile buzzed. I hit speaker.

It was Sandra, excitable as ever. 'You better get back here, Annie. There's war. Sizemore is like a demon, and I don't blame him. Barney is a shit. Guess what he did now?'

'No idea.' I waited to hear that Barney had insulted her in front of a client. Or maybe one of her mates, by telling her she was getting too fat to wear belly-tops.

'Remember he volunteered to try tracing some of the people on your case list? On the net? Before he started the dating agency case? Remember he said he wanted to help you out? Although Sizemore was already working on . . .'

'Fast forward, Sandra. Please,' I said impatiently.

'OK. Barney got a reply about your case! But he never opened it. Too excited with his new dating agency case. See, that's why *Gerry* always insisted on weekly meetings. When everyone has to give a weekly report it . . .'

'Sandra!'

'I know. Fast forward. Luckily I decided to have a quick look at Barney's emails and . . .'

'Sandra!'

'He got an email from a doctor—' She broke off to speak to someone at her desk, leaving me hanging on.

A click, then Sizemore came on. 'Annie? Where are you?'

'Annie?' Sandra shouted over him. 'Wait 'til you hear.'

Hear what? All I could hear were voices shouting each other down. Everyone trying to be heard above everyone else.

'Where are you, Annie?' Sizemore repeated.

'I'm just passing the Four Courts,' I said calmly. 'Coming up to the Halfpenny Bridge now. Oops . . . getting a rude hand signal from a truck driver. Oh sorry, he's actually waving me on . . .'

'This is serious, Annie!' Sizemore cut across me. And it was serious.

Nosing through neglected emails Sandra found one from a doctor of psychology, with a practice in Singapore. This doctor said he'd be happy to talk to the McHugh Dunning investigators. He was extra busy right now as he was travelling extensively, publicising a book he had written on childhood traumas, but he would be in Heathrow Airport on the evening of the fifteenth, and have two full hours to spare between flights. His name was Doctor Peter Nigh.

'He's the guy Kathy caught in bed with her best friend!' Sizemore could barely contain himself.

'But this *is* the fifteenth.' I went icy cold. 'And it's already four thirty!'

'I know. But Sandra is pulling out all the stops,' Sizemore said. 'Right now she's on hold, waiting to speak to some pilot neighbour of yours who may be able to get us a couple of standby seats. Put the boot down, Annie. Get here as fast as you can.'

30

Heathrow airport was teeming with people. All of them in a hurry to get to someplace else. Sizemore led the way through the throngs, taking the flak for me, as we battled our way past baggage trolleys laden with enough luggage to last three lifetimes, and lethal pushchairs carrying exhausted babies. We even crashed into a scout troop led by a Hitler clone in drip-dry shorts.

I knew it would be hell trying to get from arrivals to departures in the time allotted to us, but we had to try, if we were to meet Dr Nigh. This was a one-off opportunity for us. Check-in time for his Boston flight was exactly forty minutes after we arrived in from Dublin. I ran like never before. Swearing with every breath to kill Barney if we didn't make it in time.

Breathless and sweating, we arrived at the bar where Dr Nigh had promised to wait until nine thirty. It was now nine ten, and the softly-lit bar was a sea of people.

'Damn! We should have had him paged.' Sizemore took out his mobile.

'No time.' I cupped my hands around my mouth, and yelled, 'Doctor Nigh? Is there a Doctor Peter Nigh in the bar?'

Sizemore cringed. He denied it later, but I saw him. Nothing wrong with my eyesight, or my voice, which probably shattered windows in approaching aircraft. Ignoring the curious stares, and approaching security guards, I was cupping my hands in preparation for another bellowing session, when a slim Asian man appeared in front of me, his expression bemused.

I didn't want to imagine what he was thinking. But faced with a wild-haired woman, her fake-tanned face running with sweat as she called out his name, he was remarkably contained. If this *was* our doctor, he had travelled to Heathrow on a five-hour flight and still managed to look as if he had been dry-cleaned from head to toe. His black hair was neatly gelled into place, and his smooth mahogany skin was enviably stress free.

'Doctor Nigh?' Sizemore asked.

The immaculate black head nodded.

'I'm Niall Sizemore, and this is Annie McHugh of McHugh Dunning.'

I pressed my arms against my sides, terrified to move in case a whiff of sweat escaped my armpits, and offended this squeaky-clean man.

He greeted me as if sweaty, bedraggled people were everyday fare to him. But then he was a psychologist.

'You made it.' He flashed a charming smile, offering me his right hand, only a slight stiffness in the wrist joint giving any hint of the trauma it had suffered in the medical school melee twelve years before.

*   *   *

Doctor Nigh was a dote. He ordered drinks as if we had all the time in the world. As if he wouldn't shortly be boarding another flight, to face another round of gruelling interviews about his book – a study of the long-term psychological damage caused by childhood traumas. He didn't even object when Sizemore slapped a tape recorder in front of him.

Listening to his tranquil voice I made a mental note to buy his book the minute I got home. I found it hard to imagine this man playing frenzied rumpy-pumpy behind his girlfriend's back. On the way here I had formed a clear mental picture of him. Given that he was a proven letch, I naturally assumed he'd be a repulsive git. A loud, egocentric bombaster who spoke with a forked tongue. And was careless about his trouser snake.

And here we were, faced with this gentle, charming man.

'I was saddened to hear of Kathy's death,' he said.

'You're aware that we're investigating the possibility that it wasn't an accident?' Sizemore said.

'I gathered that.' A nod.

'Would you mind telling us what happened between you two? Why you broke up?' Sizemore glanced anxiously at his watch. 'We're especially interested in the college *incident*. The reason you gave up your surgical studies?'

'Of course.' The doctor's hands lay quiet in his lap, the white scar running down from his wrist clearly visible.

'Kathy and I met in our first year at medical school,'

he began. 'We were both rather innocent. Naïve. Both felt like outsiders. Possibly we bonded because of our shared backgrounds.'

He saw my surprise. 'My parents are staunch, unyielding Catholics.'

I felt myself blush. I had assumed he'd be a . . . a what . . . a Buddhist?

'For me, meeting Kathy was love at first sight. That wonderful, terrifying, magical thing we call first love.' He smiled. 'She was very modest. I was a priggish young man, so that meant a lot to me.' He wrinkled his nose in distaste at his former self. 'Our fellow students were almost frighteningly promiscuous.' A smile took the sting out of this remark. 'Kathy and I were close but we never consummated our relationship.'

For the first time he looked sad.

'Kathy's friend Tanya made a good chaperone. She was always there. It became the college joke. Having two girlfriends? We were a familiar trio around the campus. Then there was a jolly end of term party, in a private house. It belonged to a classmate's parents, so most of us stayed over, sleeping wherever we could. I was flying home the next day, and was feeling particularly sad to be leaving Kathy for the long holidays. When I woke in the small hours, I decided to go down to her room. I wanted to say my goodbyes in private.' He paused. 'Or, who knows, perhaps I was . . . hoping . . .' He coughed. 'I found her in bed with Tanya.'

'Because all the girls were sharing?' I nodded.

'No. They were alone together. Making love.'

I felt like I had when my ears popped on the plane coming over. The way all sound had faded into the distance, until I swallowed and it all started up again. In the bar suddenly there were glasses rattling at a terrible rate, bottles clinking, and the endless buzz of conversation.

While I sat like a zombie, Sizemore cleared his throat noisely. 'Could you . . . could you be mistaken, could they have been . . . ?'

'They were making love, Mr Sizemore.' Dr Nigh was calm as ever. 'I *was* a second-year medical student. My knowledge of physiology was way beyond rudimentary.'

'So you walked in on them.' Sizemore used his cop voice. 'What happened then?'

'I'm afraid I behaved very badly. Said nasty things. Accused both girls of nefarious . . . But you don't need to hear what I said.'

'The . . . the girls . . . what did they . . . ?' I recovered my voice.

Doctor Nigh spoke calmly. 'Kathy confessed that she was in love with Tanya. Had been since the day they met. Tanya said she loved Kathy. That I had been little more than a cover for their relationship. I'm afraid I also reacted very badly to that. I smacked Tanya repeatedly. Might have continued to do so if Kathy hadn't sprung to her defence. There was a ceremonial dagger on the wall above the bed, and . . .' He paused. 'You know the rest, of course. No need for repetition. I'm sure the whole college was more than happy to tell you what occurred then. Except that they all got the coupling wrong, and for Kathy's sake I made no attempt to clarify things.' He looked at his watch. 'I'm overdue at check-in. My flight will be called soon. You understand that I have only told you this in order to help your investigation. I can rely on your discretion?'

'That goes without saying,' Sizemore said.

I watched as the doctor stood up. 'Just one more thing, Dr Nigh? Kathy did eventually marry. So she *was* attracted to men, as well as women?'

He studied me, his eyes patient. 'As friends, yes. Not sexually.' He picked up his weighty brief-case.

'Are you positive about that?' Even while I was saying it I knew I was being idiotic, standing there in my worn jeans and scuffed trainers, questioning the expertise of a famed psychologist.

He nodded calmly. 'I'm sorry if that wasn't what you wanted to hear.'

Sizemore shook his hand. 'Thank you for meeting us, Doctor Nigh. Have a safe journey.'

'A pleasure.' He was gone.

We sat staring after him.

'God, I need a drink.' Sizemore's head almost dropped between his knees.

'Me too. A large one. Are you buying?' I looked over at the packed bar.

Sizemore didn't move.

'Well, that's one for the books, huh?' I said grimly.

'Yeah . . . but where the hell does *that* leave us?' He sounded weary.

'Gobsmacked?' I nudged him.

He sat up and forced a smile. 'The case Annie! Where does that leave our case?'

'Don't ask me. Right now I'm wondering what *that* would feel like.' I indicated a huge travel poster across the way. Blown up to ridiculous proportions it showed a curved white beach, fringed with swaying palm trees, and underneath the palms sat a carefree, bronzed couple drinking a well-known beer, and looking indescribably happy, the lucky sods.

Sizemore looked at it, and sighed. 'They're just happy they didn't have to queue up for the beer.'

'What a romantic devil you are.'

'I'm just thinking about poor old Nigh.'

'He's done very well for himself.'

'A lot better than Seanie.'

'Oh my God, you think that's what happened that night? Kathy told him that she batted for the other team?'

'No idea.'

'Me neither. Will we have that drink now? My brain is still seized up with shock.'

'Yes, but let's try another bar. This place is making me . . . claustrophobic.'

Two drinks and several long silences later, the shock of Nigh's revelation was finally wearing off. Plus we realised there was nothing we could do about the case while we were trapped in Heathrow.

'What to do. What to do.' Sizemore drummed his fingers on the low bar-table.

'You could slip up to the bar and get us another drink,' I suggested.

He laughed. 'Oh, don't hold back, Annie. Speak your mind.'

'Oh just get the feckin' drinks! My head is done in. The last thing I expected to hear was that Kathy and what's her name were at it like knives.'

He'd been about to get up, but sat down again. 'How the hell could Seanie not have known? How long were they together, for Chrissake? I mean, what sort of idiot can't even tell that his wife prefers women in the sack?'

'Nigh thought she was in love with him, and he was halfway to being a doctor!'

'No wonder he took up psychology.'

'Yeah. Whatever happened to boy meets girl, they fall in love, and live happily ever after, with their two-point-five kids, in a nice suburban house. Oh, hang on, that must have been in a fairytale I once read. When I was four.'

Sizemore waved a finger in reprimand. But he obviously agreed with me because I saw him smiling to himself as he hurried to the bar. Then he was back, and drowning my vodka with lemonade. Starting on his before he even sat down.

We finished our drinks in silence. Both of us lost in our own thoughts. After several minutes of this I chanced a look at Sizemore. He was watching me.

'What?'

His eyes smiled into mine. 'Guess what I'd like to do right now?'

I tried not to blush. Didn't want him to see how much the drinks had already relaxed me. Plus I didn't want to appear too eager. Or let him know the same idea had already crossed my mind. Twice. After all, our return flight wasn't until early morning. What else was there to do here? We couldn't work on the case. That would have to wait until we got back. And there were loads of hotels around Heathrow.

I fluttered my lashes playfully.

'I'd like to get hammered.' Sizemore punched the table so hard the our glasses rattled. 'There isn't a damn thing we can do about the case here, and I don't fancy sitting around twiddling my thumbs for the next six hours. Getting hammered strikes me as the only realistic option.'

I stared at him in disbelief.

'Sorry, Annie. Have I shocked you?' He pulled back.

'Well, yes. With your lack of imagination!'

'What do you mean? Do you want to go into the city?' He was puzzled.

'Only if we can't get a room around here.' I nudged his knee with mine.

He stared. 'You mean . . . ?'

I gave him a look.

'I thought you . . . since I told you what happened in the States you've barely been civil to me.'

'Ah, that's just my way! When I'm busy, I'm busy. Preoccupied.'

'But when I tried to speak to you about anything except the case you . . . ?'

'My mind was elsewhere!'

'You said your friend was fixing you up with a date.'

'Oh lighten up, Sizemore. We don't have all night.'

'But how did I get it so wrong? I honestly thought you were finished with me.'

Two feet away from us, three bearded men were idly strumming guitars. A travelling folk group? They suddenly burst into song, singing in harmony, in Estonian, or Latvian, or something equally painful.

Sizemore continued to tell me what he thought I thought about what he did in America. Happily I couldn't hear a word he was saying. I merely sipped my third vodka and watched the way his hands and his mouth moved as he spoke. And while he was telling me what he thought I thought, I was actually thinking that there should be a law against one man being so physically perfect, when there were so many unattractive men . . . close by. Still . . . if Sizemore had suddenly gained two stone and grown a raggedy beard I would still have wanted to go to bed with him. He was so . . .

The singing stopped as suddenly as it began.

'. . . that you wanted you to know,' Sizemore finished.

'Well, happily that's all cleared up!' I said. 'Are we going to find a hotel?'

'I can't figure you, Annie?' he laughed. 'Sometimes you take my breath away.'

Oh joy.

The bearded trio drained their pints and started singing again.

I got to my feet. 'Now, don't get the wrong idea,

305

Sizemore.' I had to yell to be heard over the singing. 'I might just want your company in a hotel. Don't assume I'm always on for a quick shag!' I bellowed. Then froze, when I realised the song had ended just as I said – assume . . .

It felt like the whole airport was staring at me.

'Strewth!' A deep Aussie voice drawled from somewhere behind me. 'Who said that? I've been lookin' for that woman all my life.'

A mortified Sizemore led me away. There is no word to explain how I felt.

We arrived back in Dublin to be greeted by torrential rain, and morning gridlock. It was still July but it looked like our glorious summer was a thing of the past. We got to the agency at ten fifteen, both with killer hangovers and eyes reddened from lack of sleep.

Sandra welcomed us like a couple of prodigals. 'You're back!' She beamed happily. 'We missed you. Was London nice? Were your flights OK?'

'Yeah. Thanks for booking us business class.'

She shot me a nervous look. 'They were the only seats I could get, at such short notice. Your neighbour turned out to be a big spoofer. He's . . .'

'Who?'

'The Danish pilot! Fat lot of good it did, saying you were a friend of his. Aer Lingus fired him ages ago. I felt a right twat asking to speak to someone who got fired.'

'Fired?' I was shocked.

'Well, OK, he probably got redundancy, but he's

been out of work for weeks. The girl I spoke to said he's going to live in Cork or some little town in the west, or maybe in . . .'

'Not now, Sandra! I'm wrecked.'

'OK, OK. No need to snap my head off.'

'Well, look who's here.' I pointed as Barney appeared, looking more nervous than I'd ever seen him.

'I . . . hear you got to speak to Dr Nigh?' He kept a safe distance from me. 'Bet you got some top information there.'

'No thanks to you,' Sizemore said.

Barney's Adam's apple bobbed up and down like a mouse in a sack. 'Sorry. What can I say? The women in the dating agency were driving me demented.'

'I bet they were,' I said.

'No, listen, Annie, some of the ones who weren't getting dirty mail were practically asking me why not. They didn't want to get it, but they didn't want to be left out of the loop either. Sounds crazy, but it's true. I . . . I couldn't think straight. Honest to God, Annie.'

'So you didn't have five minutes to check your emails?'

'I . . . I forgot the old ones.'

'No excuse.'

'You're right. You're dead right. Lucky Sandra opened the email, huh?' He shifted uneasily from one foot to the other.

'Lucky for you.'

'Sorry.'

'Sorry won't butter the parsnips!' Sizemore said as he headed for the stairs.

Sandra watched him go, her forehead wrinkled in confusion. 'Sorry won't butter the parsnips? What does that mean?'

I had no idea. 'I'll let Barney explain,' I smiled.

I knew he wouldn't have a clue either, and I wanted to embarrass him. We had come within a hair's breadth of missing Dr Nigh, thanks to him, and the information Nigh gave us was invaluable. We now knew that Seanie Bolger had a strong motive for killing his wife. Sexual rejection was up there with material greed as one of the major causes of spousal murder, according to statistics.

'It means it won't get the job done?' Barney suddenly said.

'I still don't get it,' Sandra said.

Neither did I, but I wasn't about to lose face by admitting it.

'It means Barney is a slacker,' I said, with a flash of inspiration. Then I caught Barney's expression and wanted to bite my tongue off. Barney is a good investigator. OK, he sometimes gets a bit overly enthusiastic about the wrong things. And sometimes forgets to check his emails. So what? It had all turned out all right in the end. If we hadn't gone to Heathrow Sizemore and I might have continued our stand-off for weeks. That would have been such a shame, given the great time we had in the hotel.

I got a sudden rush of emotion. I loved the whole world and everyone in it.

'Come on, Barney,' I said. 'I'll treat you to a large

cappuccino in the café. I hear they have two new waitresses?'

'No thanks. I wouldn't want you to think I'm slacking.' Ignoring the waiting lift he slumped upstairs, his hair falling into his eyes.

31

'Oh, not again!' For a second I thought Sadie was going to close the door in our faces.

'Oh, come on, Sadie,' Sizemore pleaded. 'You said I did a good job sitting by Ms Stowe when all the A & E staff were too busy? Please?'

'Ten minutes then! Jen will time us. You won't get around her.'

Jen turned out to be her housemate. It was the first time we had met because every other time we were here she was at work. I suppose hospital lab technicians do work nine to five. But today she was sitting by the window, her spiked red hair gleaming in the sun as she watched the goings on in the street outside. But only a complete eejit would buy her apparent fascination with a gang of noisy refuse collectors.

'What difference does it make if Kathy was gay?' Sadie's smile was nowhere in evidence today. 'Do you want to pillory her, for her sexual orientation?'

''Course not!' I was indignant. 'But she *was* married. Surely you can see the difference this new information makes to our investigation?'

'And the tabloids,' Jen said curtly, without turning. 'Don't forget the tabloids.'

'We don't talk to reporters,' I said.

'Maybe not, but can you guarantee that some little toe rag won't get hold of your *new information* and plaster it across a front page?'

'We're only interested in finding out if the fire was malicious,' Sizemore said.

'Will that bring Kathy back?' Sadie said coldly.

'It could tell us if someone wanted to harm her.'

Jen dropped her bin-watching act. 'You think Seanie . . . ?'

'I'm an investigator,' Sizemore shrugged. 'I just collect facts. I don't make . . .'

'Bollocks. And you can drop the macho charm. It's wasted on me. You wouldn't be here drilling Sadie if you didn't think there was something suspicious about that fire.'

'Jen, please. It has nothing to do with us,' Sadie pleaded.

'Of course it bloody has. He's here to dig the dirt. Him and miss *butter wouldn't melt*, there.'

It took me a second to realise she meant me.

'I'm not . . .' I began.

Jen elbowed her way past me. 'I need a drink.'

Right then I would have killed for a drink. Tea. Coffee. Alka-Seltzer. But I had a feeling we weren't going to be offered any kind of refreshment here today. For some reason we were now the enemy.

'You never said Kathy was gay.' Sizemore did his best not to sound accusing.

'So?' Sadie's quick laugh was more of a dismissive snort.

'So you knew?'

'Yes.'

He frowned. 'How long have you known?'

'Always.'

'But you didn't think to mention it to us?'

'I didn't know it was compulsory to mention sexual orientation to fire investigators?' Sadie's face hardened.

'It . . . it would have helped.' Sizemore smiled. 'And we are discreet.'

'Bully for you.' Jen came back carrying what looked like half a pint of whiskey.

'Was Kathy leaving Seanie?' I asked Sadie.

'Yes.'

My breath caught, but Sizemore didn't even blink. Jen practically slapped the glass tumbler into Sadie's hand, and stood waiting as Sadie took a nervous sip, and then another.

'She was tired of playing a role. Going to come out. God knows, maybe it was time to give Seanie a break too. Not that he had a clue. He thought her coldness in bed was caused by her religious upbringing. '

'Take a proper drink, Sadie,' Jen ordered. 'It's your day off, for fuck's sake.'

Sadie took a miniscule sip. Jen watched impatiently, then grabbed the glass and took a mouthful, before handing it back to Sadie. They handed the glass backwards and forwards, as they shared the whiskey without asking me, or Sizemore, if we had a mouth on us.

'Seanie!' Jen suddenly hissed. 'Pity about him! Kathy was the one forced to live a lie. First by her parents, and then him.'

'Her parents knew she was gay?'

'Are you for real?' Jen dismissed me. 'They're a couple of religious nuts. Have you met them? Kathy lived in terror that they might find out. She said it would kill them. Their little princess a lezzie?' She gave a mirthless laugh.

This time Sadie took a proper slug of whiskey.

'So now you know,' Jen said. 'Kathy lived a life of pure hell, swallowing handfuls of antidepressants so other people could live happily. Hey! Maybe she started the fire?'

'She's joking,' Sadie said.

'You reckon she finally told Seanie?' Sizemore asked.

'You mean the night of the fire?'

He nodded. 'How do you think he would have reacted?'

'Are you asking if he burned the shop in retaliation?' Jen gave another mirthless laugh.

'I'm asking you how you think he would have reacted to his wife confessing that she was gay.'

'Confessing? It's not a crime to be gay.'

'He didn't mean it like that,' I said quickly. 'He only meant . . .'

'What are you, his fuckin' interpreter?' she spat. 'Why don't you go and harass Kathy's weird parents. They ruined her life. She lived every day ashamed of what she was. Trying to be the daughter they wanted. She even got married, for fuck's sake! No wonder she worked nights. Golden Balls? Give me a break.'

Sadie turned to me. 'Did Seanie start that fire?'

313

'I honestly don't know,' I said, as Sizemore checked his watch.

'We'll see ourselves out,' he said, as Jen was about to attack him again.

'Where are we going?' I asked, once we were back in the jeep.

He made a swift U-turn.

'Mutual Irish.' His mouth was tight. 'I want Lily to hear this tape.' He took the little recorder from his pocket.

'Sadie didn't make that call.'

'What about Jen. Her *house* partner. That Jen is one very angry girl.'

'Angry enough to make a call blaming Seanie for the fire?'

'Let's find out.'

Thirty minutes later we left Mutual Irish in a deep gloom. It had taken Lily less than four minutes to discount both voices.

'It was a long shot,' I tried to cheer Sizemore up as we drove off. 'But worth a try.'

His mobile rang. 'What is it, Barney? It better be important,' he barked, then listened intently for a couple of minutes. 'OK I'll have a look at it.' He threw the mobile on the dashboard.

'Everything all right?' I asked.

'Barney wants a favour.'

I waited for him to explain. A mile later I was still waiting. We were crossing O'Connell Bridge when my patience ran out.

'And the favour is . . . ?' I prompted, as if I were speaking to a reluctant two-year-old.

He shot me a sideways grin. 'Barney wants me to view a wedding video with him.'

'Of course he does. He's trying to trap a filthy sex pervert. Possibly a dangerous misogynist. So what does he do? He invites you to watch a wedding video with him. That makes perfect sense to me.'

Barney was slotting the video in the player when Sandra came in with a pot of coffee, and a giant pack of Mikado biscuits. She poured coffees all round, and slipped into a chair next to me.

'It's like the multiplex.' She giggled and reached for a Mikado.

'Who is watching reception?' I asked.

She left without a word, but managed to slam the door so hard the lights blinked.

Barney hit the remote control. 'The dating agency pervert may be in this video, so watch closely,' he said. Then hit fast forward so all we saw was a blur.

'No need to view it all,' he explained. 'Most of it is rubbish.'

He continued to fast forward all the *rubbish*. The bride's arrival at the church, the actual wedding ceremony, even the wedding breakfast. The emotion-filled speeches whizzed past our startled eyes. Only when the guests began to leap around like demented grasshoppers, to the music of a terrible four-piece band, did he slow the video to a normal viewing speed.

'OK, watch the curly haired guy dancing next to the little fat bridesmaid,' he ordered.

We watched.

'See the way he keeps managing to brush up against her? Watch that groin movement? See how she keeps trying to avoid him? She reckons he's the perv who is sending the doctored photos. When he wasn't trying to brush up against her, she said he was clicking away with his digital. And only at women, mind. She joined the dating agency a month ago, and within a week she received three doctored photos of herself. In all three her hair was curly and brown. Like in the wedding video? Her hair is now blonde. She's been having it bleached for nearly a year now.' Barney sounded triumphant.

'Who is the guy?'

'A cousin of the bridegroom. But nobody likes him. I've checked. He kept asking the band to play "The Birdie Song". Interestingly enough another guest at this wedding also joined the Emerald Hearts Introduction Agency. And *she* got filthy emails, with doctored photos attached.'

'So all three know each other?'

'Not really. They only exchanged brief hellos at the wedding. You know what weddings are like. Friends and relatives from both sides get together for the big day then, if they're lucky, they never see each other again.'

'Ships that pass in the night,' I said.

Sizemore got to his feet.

'Where are you going?' I turned.

'I have to pick something up. Let's go, Annie.'

I grabbed my bag, and two Mikado biscuits. I hadn't had lunch, and seeing all the fancy wedding nosh, even at warp speed, reminded me that I was starving.

'But what about the video?' Barney said. 'I was just about to rewind it for a second viewing. I thought you'd help me decide if that is my perv dancing to "The Birdie Song".'

'Get Sandra,' I said. 'If there's one thing she likes more than a wedding, it's a wedding video.'

'And he is your perv, Barney,' Sizemore assured him. 'Even if he isn't, he deserves to be busted for getting them to play "The Birdie Song".'

This time I didn't have to ask Sizemore what was on his mind. He was so excited by his new theory he couldn't wait to tell me.

'I want to talk to Mrs Newman again. Ask her a favour. Something Barney said set me thinking. Remember his remark about weddings bringing disparate groups of people together.'

'And that's very true.'

'Yes. But what's the one thing they all have in common?'

'They all hate "The Birdie Song"?'

He shot me a look.

'OK, they all know either the bride or the groom?'

'Exactly. It's the one time friends, relatives and acquaintances, maybe even enemies, of both bride and groom gather together.'

'Oh my God. You think the anonymous caller could be on Kathy's wedding video?'

He nodded. 'Remember the first day we spoke to

Mrs Newman? There were photos of Kathy everywhere. And yet she said she couldn't bear to watch the video.

I bet that's partly because of all the well-wishers. All the voices. You know how everyone tries to shout out their best wishes? Others wanting to yell funny comments. It may be a long shot, but what if our anonymous caller was . . .'

'Speaking to the camera?' My breath caught.

'Well, if she doesn't speak, we're fucked.'

I crossed my fingers. 'Please God. Pleeeeease.'

'That's it, Annie. You pray. I'll get the video, then ask Lily in Mutual Irish to listen to it.' He took the corner into the Newmans' quiet cul-de-sac on two wheels.

'Mr Sizemore?' Mrs Newman looked surprised to see us.

She was even more surprised when Sizemore asked to borrow her daughter's wedding video.

'Absolutely not.' She stepped back in shock. 'Out of the question. It's our only copy. Richard would be furious with me if I allowed it to leave the house. He watches it all the time. Says, it's his greatest treasure. A living album of precious memories. Kathy looked like a fairy princess that day. Richard would . . .'

'I only need it for an hour, Mrs Newman. An hour. Please?'

'Out of the question. Richard wouldn't allow it.' She began closing the door.

I was walking away, when Sizemore came up with the compromise.

'Mrs Newman, would you allow me to bring

someone here to . . . er . . . listen to the video? It would be in your interests.'

Mrs Newman was a gracious, if still slightly spacey, hostess. Whatever she was on, she clearly had a repeat prescription, there was no doubting that. Still, she had good manners, inviting Lily into her stuffy living room, and offering her the most comfortable chair, with little or no fuss, which pleased Lily enormously. On the way over Lily had remarked that one of the penalties she paid for being registered blind was the way most people treated her as if she was also stupid.

Mrs Newman made us coffee. A first. She then left us to view the precious video unsupervised. Although I suspected she may have been saving herself the heartbreak of watching it with strangers.

I never met Kathy, but seeing her in the video, walking down the aisle, reed-slender and almost ethereal in white, I got a massive lump in *my* throat. Even Sizemore was moved. But not for long, because he was soon fast-forwarding the video to the segment he was interested in – where the wedding guests spoke to the camera.

He scratched impatiently at his growing chin stubble while the best man made an excruciatingly long speech. He didn't dare fast-forward this for fear of missing out on comments made by several of the guests, some of them women. And each time we turned hopefully to Lily.

She sat there, shaking her head whenever Sizemore asked if he should rewind. Seanie came on screen, to make a brief, but witty, speech. A puffed-up

Richard Newman spoke endlessly about God's gifts, somehow managing to bring the words Christ and Saviour into every sentence.

I had a feeling we were out of luck, but Sizemore continued to watch Lily, his eyes full of hope.

She listened intently to voice after voice, her only response a quick shake of the head. We were coming to the end of the long video. All that was left now was the throwing of the bridal bouquet. And given what I now knew about Kathy, I guessed that the throwing of the bouquet was unlikely to cause a flurry of excitement among her close women friends.

Resigned, I watched as Kathy held the rose-packed bouquet head high.

'Ready to catch, girls?' She thrilled amid shouts of delight, and laughter.

Lily was electrified. 'That's it! That's the voice!'

'Which one?' Sizemore puzzled. 'Hang on a sec, I'll rewind a bit, give you a chance to clarify.'

He rewound the tape at speed. Ran it again, watching closely for Lily's reaction. Waiting for her to identify the voice from among the noisy squeals and drunken laughter.

'There's the bit!' He smiled.

'I didn't need to hear it again.' Lily spoke with assurance. 'I recognised the voice instantly. *"Ready to catch girls?"* That's the woman who made the call!'

Sizemore went green.

'But that's Kathy Bolger's voice,' he said. 'Kathy was dead when you got that call.'

Lily's round cheeks flamed bright red. 'That's the

voice that made the call. I never mistake a voice.' She raised her chin defiantly.

Sizemore nudged me. *Tell her she's got it wrong*, he mouthed.

I shook my head. He grabbed my arm, and we argued back and forth, soundlessly, but obviously not soundlessly enough because Lily suddenly said, 'Sizemore? Annie? What's going on?'

'Sorry, Lily.' He let go of my arm. 'But this time you have made a mistake. Dead people don't make phone calls.'

'That's the voice. I recognise it. *She* spoke to me on the phone.'

'Maybe if you had another listen,' I said gently. 'Maybe if you . . .'

'Don't patronise me, I don't need to have *another listen*. That's the voice that made the call.' She was feeling behind her for her bag, getting to her feet. 'Now, if you don't mind, I'd like you to drive me back to work.'

'Kathy Bolger couldn't have made that call,' Sizemore said firmly. 'She was already dead by then. Burned to a crisp.'

There was a gasp from the doorway.

Mrs Newman was leaning against the doorjamb, the colour draining from her face. Clinging to the dark wood for support, she began to shake, her eyes rolled, her knees gave way, and she hit the floor with a dull thud.

'What happened, Sizemore? What happened?' Lily reached out to him.

32

We made a miserable little group, as we huddled in a quiet corner of The Randy Goat. Faces grim, we drained our glasses with an unprecedented lack of enthusiasm, everyone afraid to mention the un-mentionable. Everyone hoping someone else would.

Naturally it was Barney who broke the silence. 'Is there *any* chance that Kathy Bolger is still alive?'

I thought Sizemore would garrotte him. Choke him to death with the fancy silk scarf the grateful owner of the Emerald Hearts Introduction Agency had presented him with. But Sizemore wasn't given to physical violence; well, not since he left America. He sat now like an ice carving and spoke through gritted, albeit perfectly even, teeth. 'I am not . . . repeat, not . . . ever going to say this again, so listen closely. Kathy Bolger *died* in that fire.'

'But Mutual Irish said Lily never mistakes a voice?' Barney said.

'I don't give a flying fuck what Mutual Irish say!' Sizemore finally lost it. 'I saw the autopsy report. It didn't make for pleasant reading, but the DNA tests are infallible. Kathy Bolger is dead.' He got up and stamped off to the bog for the second time in ten minutes.

'Never seen him like that before.' Declan watched him go.

Barney turned to me. 'Is Newman definitely going to sue us?'

'He might calm down.' I tried to be positive.

'I dunno.' Barney wasn't convinced. 'The way he burst in this afternoon, I thought he was going to box Sandra.'

'He is livid,' I agreed.

'Well, his wife *did* have to be sedated, after you and Sizemore . . . And their solicitor said she has a heart condition.'

'Whose side are you on?' I snapped.

'I'm just saying that hearing someone accuse your dead daughter of making anonymous phone calls would be a bit hard to take. Not surprised Newman lost his head?'

'I think Newman's real problem is with us watching his daughter's wedding video, without asking his permission. He's a control freak. Thinks he rules the world. Him and Jesus.'

Richard Newman had hand delivered a letter from his solicitor. Apart from Newman's fury, the tone of the solicitor's letter implied there was worse to come than the enclosed court order barring Sizemore from coming within three hundred yards of the Newmans. They had also sent a copy of the letter to Mutual Irish, and hinted that they had evidence that this wasn't the first time someone brought a case against Sizemore. As for me, they behaved as if I had bombed Iraq, so chances were I'd be next on the barring order list.

Sizemore came out of the Jacks looking so constipated he'd have been better off staying in there. My chest tightened when I saw him putting his mobile back in his pocket. Terrified that he might be considering going back to the States, I warned the others to shut up about the Bolger case.

'And not a word to anyone about this Newman business either,' I was saying, when I realised it was already too late. One of the detectives from Bailey's squad had stopped Sizemore, and was patting him on the back in that daft way men have of offering each other sympathy. We were doomed. Gossip was endemic in Dublin, and bad news spread like a bushfire.

Spider the barman limped over to us.

'Toss Nolan wants to buy you a round.'

'Why?' Barney snapped. Everyone hates Toss Nolan. Known as a sly go-by-the-wall, he fancied himself as our competition in the inquiry business.

'Dunno.' Spider picked at a spot on his chin. 'He just said. What'll I tell him?'

'Tell him to up his medication,' Barney said.

'Tell him no thank you.' I kicked Barney under the table. Last thing we needed right now was to make more enemies.

Spider limped back to the bar.

Barney watched him go. 'That little bollix Nolan! He can smell trouble. Look at the smirky gob on him.'

We all looked. Toss Nolan thought he was smiling, but we all knew he was smirking, something he only did when he knew the competition was in trouble. He was probably already hoping to gazump us with

Mutual Irish. Planning to offer to work for them for five euro an hour.

Barney sneaked another look at him.

'Evil little shite! Where does he get off, offering to buy us a drink?'

'I have an idea,' I whispered. 'Let's send him one. Really freak him out.'

'Nice one, Annie,' Barney encouraged.

'What does he drink? Scotch?' I asked. 'Let's send him a double Scotch. With a twist of lemon!'

Declan tried not to laugh.

'Ah, feck it,' Barney said. 'Lets send him a fuckin' bottle.'

Declan laughed out loud.

'Right,' I said to Spider, who was back ear-wigging. 'Give Mr Nolan a bottle of Scotch. With our compliments.'

Spider gaped. 'A bottle? We don't usually . . .'

'Just do it, Spider, or I'll have your bollix,' Barney hissed.

'Awright!' He was gone.

Barney and I high-fived each other gleefully, then drummed our feet on the floor when we saw Nolan's expression. We raised our glasses in salute and waved.

'That'll teach him to offer us a drink,' Barney laughed. 'He's lucky we don't march over there en masse, and beat the living shite out of him.'

'You're my hero, Barney,' I said.

'Remember that when you see me selling *The Big Issue*.'

We were still chuckling as Nolan left the bar, tucking the bottle of Scotch into his windcheater.

'Top that you little bollix!' Barney said.

'Here's to McHugh Dunning!' I raised my glass.

'Has anyone told Gerry we're being sued?' Declan asked quietly.

There was a sudden silence. Declan sighed and got up to leave. 'See you tomorrow.'

'Where are you going?' Barney asked.

'Home.' Declan pulled on his leather jacket. 'Sasha has dinner ready.'

'Ah! Has Declan got a little wifey waiting for him?' Barney chuckled.

Declan marched to the door, paused, and came back.

'Good for you, Dec!' Barney pulled out a chair for him. 'Let her put it under the grill like all the other little wifeys. Now, what are you having? A double lemonade?'

Declan cleared his throat. 'I . . . er . . . I meant to tell you earlier. We're getting married,' he said.

For the second time in five minutes you could have heard a pin drop at our table. I honestly thought Barney might burst into tears. He didn't. But it took him several seconds to pull himself together. And when he did speak it was typical Barney.

'Who to?' he laughed.

'See you tomorrow.' Declan turned to go.

'Congratulations, Declan.' I grabbed his hand, and kicked Barney's ankle.

Barney's face was a picture. 'I mean, what the fuck, Declan? You barely know her? Yeah she's a fine thing an' all, but Jaysus, Declan. And your timing is a bit off. The agency is falling apart and you . . .

Is it the citizenship thing she's after? If it is, that could be messy. Owww!' he yelled, as I kicked him again.

I smiled at Declan. 'Tell Sizemore,' I said. 'He could do with some *happy* news.'

Declan touched my cheek briefly, and left without speaking to Sizemore, who was now in a huddle with three cops, all of them gesticulating wildly, all of them clearly offering him ways out of the mess he was in. Er, *we* were in.

Sizemore eventually came back to the table looking a lot less depressed than he had earlier. 'Two of Bailey's people tell me they worked a case where they were threatened with legal proceedings, and it all came to nothing.'

'Brilliant,' I said, knowing in my heart that Newman wasn't a man to let things go. He was a man who held grudges. I saw it in his face when he stormed into the agency. He was used to getting his own way. Underneath the smart suit and civilised veneer there was someone you wouldn't want to cross.

'Are you meeting with the Mutual Irish legal team tomorrow?' Barney asked Sizemore.

'Yes.'

'Good.' Barney was sloshed. 'Ask them what's the legal position on an Irish guy marrying a possible illegal immigrant. Could he be busted?'

Sizemore looked questioningly at me.

'Don't ask me,' I said. 'I have enough to worry about right now.'

'Here's a few saltines for you, Annie.' Spider put

a little plate of saltines in front of me as carefully as if he was presenting me with a bowl of beluga caviar.

'I'll take some of them,' Barney grabbed a handful. 'Annie has more on her plate than she can handle right now.'

I gave him what I hoped was a withering look.

It was ten a.m., the clouds were practically touching the pavement and the agency felt like a morgue. Declan and Barney were out working cases, and Sizemore was closeted with the heavy-duty lawyers in Mutual Irish. The Mutual Irish people were only concerned with protecting their own arses. They didn't give a damn about McHugh Dunning. Why else would they want to see Sizemore on his own, when there were two of us working the case. Lesson learned. McHugh Dunning were expendable. They'd throw us to the wolves if it suited them. The publicity alone could destroy us. We were the bad guys who had harassed a grieving mother, causing her to have a near stroke. And I would have to explain it all to Gerry. This could be a very, very bad day for me.

Sandra came in, bringing me coffee, two Nurofen, and an offer that in normal circumstances should gladden the heart of any employer.

'Don't worry, Annie, if push comes to shove, you don't have to pay me this week.'

'What do you mean?'

'Barney says we may be in financial trouble. So you can hold onto my wages for a couple of weeks, if that'll help.'

My throat closed, but I remained deadpan. 'But what if you conceive this month? I thought you were planning to spend money on your flat? Turn your second bedroom into a nursery? In preparation for your little . . . will it still be a . . . Taurean?'

'Oh, didn't I tell you? There's been a change of plan there. We're going scuba diving instead. You know Milly's new boyfriend? Well you don't, but anyway, he's a photographer, well not a real professional one, but his camera club arranged a group trip to Jamaica, and two people dropped out so me and Jimmy are going instead! I can't wait! It's for the last two weeks in September, so if I got pregnant now, I'd be puking my ring up in September, so we're . . .'

'Back on the Featherlite?' I sighed, and swallowed the Nurofen.

She laughed. 'I'm totally excited. *Hello!* had a five-page layout on scuba diving this month. It's so cool. All the top models go scuba diving. Some of them topless!' She giggled. 'Maybe that's why the camera club want to go? *Heat* magazine says it's the hottest new trend. They had big colour pictures of totally famous people diving off these gigantic yachts. I definitely recognised Claudia Schiffer. And Naomi Campbell. And I think two of them foreign princesses whose names I can never remember, and a whole gang of other skinny people. All wearing scuba diving gear. We're going to take lessons. Are you jealous?'

'Madly,' I said, wishing I could lie down. 'Smart move choosing scuba diving over pregnancy, though. Scuba diving won't give you stretch marks.'

She giggled with delight. 'I've tons of time to have

kids. I mean look at you, you're not afraid to wait, and you must be nearly . . .'

'Thirty-four, Sandra! Not quite menopausal!'

'I dunno. My mum had hot flushes at thirty.'

I was still reeling at this when the phone shrilled. Sandra got there first.

'Annie McHugh's office. May I help you? Aw, hi Fiona!' She chuckled. 'Yeah, she's here. We're discussing her menopause. No, I know she isn't! I didn't mean it like that.' She handed me the phone, rolling her eyes heavenward. 'Some people are very touchy.'

I took the phone. 'How are you? No hot flushes I hope?'

'Jesus, that Sandra is off the wall. All ready for Friday, are you?'

'Friday?' What was she on about? God, my head was killing me. Stress exacerbates the mildest hangover. I dreaded to think how Barney and Sizemore were feeling. I had grabbed a cab at eleven and left them drinking with a gang of cops.

'You've forgotten, haven't you?' Fiona wailed.

'No.' What was she on about?

'You've forgotten about my dinner party!'

Jesus. 'No, I . . .'

'Don't lie, Annie. Well, you've got forty-eight hours to get ready. I want you and Sizemore on my doorstep at eight thirty sharp.'

'Sorry, Fiona, I'm afraid that's . . .'

'Eight thirty sharp!' She hung up.

I waited 'til my head eased, then told Sandra to get Fiona back on the line.

'You're not cancelling!' Fiona said. 'You're not!'

'Fiona, I absolutely respect you and I wouldn't do this if I had any choice but . . .'

'Noooo Annie!' She wailed.

'Sorry, Fiona. I'll take a raincheck. I'll babysit Calum for a month. A year. I'll . . . my big case has just gone belly up. We may be taken to court!'

'I gave you tons of notice. You can't let me down. I've told everyone you're coming.'

'Who is everyone?'

'All the other guests. I told them I was having two detectives to dinner. They're all dying to talk to you. Crime is *the* hot dinner party topic right now. Everyone who is anyone has been burgled, at least once. And of course Heather Flanagan had to have a Garda inspector to dinner last month. She's been lording it over everyone since. She only came to my coffee morning so she could boast about how entertaining he was. You'd think he was bloody Morse. As I said to Pino, he's just a bloody Garda inspector, wait 'til they meet Annie and Gerry . . . well, it'll be Sizemore now. Then Monica Maycock said . . . you remember Monica from the cake auction?'

'No.' I nursed my head.

'Of course you do! Tall, skinny redhead? Always breastfeeding her baby?'

'Oh yes.'

'See. I knew you'd remember. Her husband runs that little art gallery off Grafton Street. Well, she's planning on having a Garda *superintendent* at her next party. So you *have* to come to mine. I'm not letting

331

her get one over on me as well. She's already green with envy because I said I have a friend who is an actual private investigator! I'm always telling people about you. You could hear a pin drop the last time I spoke at my Mums and Toddlers group about the time you broke up a porn ring.'

'I never broke up a porn . . .'

'Yes, but *they* don't know that. And you have to jizz up your talks at the Mum and Toddler group, or nobody would shush the kids. You can barely be heard anyway, with the racket some of those kids make, grabbing and biting each other, and . . . ha, ha, . . . sounds like me and Pino on our first date.'

'Fiona, I can't possibly go to a party the day after tomorrow.'

'Yes you can!'

'Can't!'

'Let me speak to Sizemore.'

'He's not taking calls this morning.'

'Don't tell me he's in trouble as well? I can't wait 'til Heather Flanagan gets an eyeful of him. She'll be green with envy. That's another reason why I want him here, I don't care if he has to be stretchered to the table.'

'We're being threatened with a lawsuit, Fiona. If it goes ahead, and they win, we could be out on the street by Christmas.'

'Don't be melodramatic. Anyway, if you are having business problems a jolly dinner party is exactly what you need.'

'A *jolly* dinner . . . Jesus Christ, Fiona!'

'Yes! A jolly dinner party with four sensational

courses. Antipasti, tagliatelle, boeuf en croute and your favourite tiramisu for dessert. How does that sound?'

'Fiona, if you mention food again I'm going to throw up.'

'What is the matter with you, Annie?'

'I've just told you! I have a hangover.' Actually, my hangover had dissipated. The Nurofen had worked. It was my gut-wrenching fear over a possible lawsuit that had me quivering in my shoes.

'Please, Annie. You have to come. I promise you I'll keep the conversation light. If anyone even mentions their property portfolio I'll . . .'

'What about Heather Flanagan's Tuscan castle restoration?' I slumped.

'I'll gag her.'

'Fiona, you hate those people almost as much as I do. Why do you socialise with them?'

'Everyone needs a social life. This time next week we could all be dead.'

She'd been watching CNN again. You could always tell.

'Sorry, Fiona, I'm being paged. Enjoy your party.'

'You're mean!' she yelled. 'If you don't turn up our friendship is over. You're the only one I really *want* at my party! And don't forget to bring Sizemore.' She hung up.

Passing through reception I knew by Sandra's expression that she had listened in to the call.

'Annie?' Her eyes were big as saucers. 'Why don't you want to go to Fiona's party? You're always saying the food at their house is to die for. And you really like Fiona. And Pino. So why not go?'

Totally exasperated, I set my face inches from hers. 'Have you any idea how serious this lawsuit could be? Do you know how worried I am about it? And Sizemore isn't allowed within five hundred feet of the Newmans. He's being treated like some sort of common criminal for simply doing his job. How do you think that makes me feel?'

'I dunno.' Her eyes narrowed suspiciously.

Shit. Had I had given myself away? Sandra adored Gerry. Thought he was God. Nobody would be allowed to usurp Gerry, even though he was over in Arizona possibly doing very ungodly things with his ex. I was now resigned to this, but Sandra might see things very differently.

'When is Gerry due back?' She frowned.

'No idea. You know he always plays his cards close to his chest. So your guess is as good as mine. Meantime, I'm not letting someone treat one of our investigators – even a temporary one – like dirt.'

'You're right, Annie!'

''Course I am! Now if anyone asks where I am, Sandra, tell them I'm out doing my job.' I turned to go. 'Give me another couple of those Nurofen, just in case.'

She was dishing out the tablets when Declan bounced in.

Tablets forgotten, Sandra nudged me.

'Good morning, Declan,' we chorused.

'Good morning, ladies.' He sprinted up the stairs.

'Bloody hell!' Sandra stared after him. 'Is he on drugs? Do they give them drugs at them AA meetings?'

'Don't be stupid.'

'Well, he's on something. Did you hear him? And he bounced up the stairs.'

I didn't want to pass on Declan's good news yet. Mindless talk about scuba diving models had already tested my patience. Endless chatter about a wedding might totally do my head in. All I wanted now was to get the damn Bolger case sorted.

'I'm going to the café for a breather, Sandra. Ten minutes tops.'

'Okey dokey!'

I'd almost made my escape when the phone buzzed. 'McHugh Dunning Detective Agency! May I help you?'

Her eyes widening in surprise, Sandra signalled to me, and put the caller on hold. 'Jesus, Annie, it's Toss Nolan? He wants to talk to you.'

'No way.'

'I'll tell him you're not here.'

'Hang on, let me think.' I chewed my lip, wondering what Nolan was up to. Had he come up with some fiendish plan to punish us for sending him the bottle of whiskey? Or had he heard . . . ? 'Give me the phone, Sandra.'

'You sure?' She was nervous.

'What can he do? Blow a whistle in my ear?'

I took the phone and holding it a safe distance away said nervously, 'Hello?'

'Annie?'

'Yes.'

'Thanks for the whiskey.'

'I . . . you're welcome.'

'Heard about your bit of bother with Newman.'

'I have no idea what you're talking about.' I bristled. 'We're not having bother with anyone.'

'Sure. Just the same, check out his radio producer.'

'His radio producer? What about him?'

'*Her!* She's a tasty little piece.'

I caught my breath. 'Wwwhat are you saying?'

'I'm not saying anything. You're a PI. Check her out. Maybe put a tail on Newman. You might find something to your advantage. Put a stop to his gallop. Him and his lawsuit!' There was a click.

'Toss? Mr Nolan?'

He was gone.

'What did he want?' Sandra was agog with curiosity.

'Nothing. Get me Sizemore. No, wait, he's with Mutual Irish all day. And then he's meeting that sound engineer. He won't give up on that anonymous call. Get me Decl . . . no, get me Barney. And hurry up for God's sake, this is important.'

'What did he want, Annie?'

'I said get me Barney. I want him back here ASAP.'

33

Barney gave a long sigh, and peered out into the rain. Squinting through the jeep windscreen, he nodded towards the brightly lit mews house. 'It's been three hours since he went in there, Annie. I hope the bugger hasn't slipped out the other door.'

I grabbed the field glasses to double-check the registration plate of a silver-grey Merc that was sitting under a tree at the far end of the rain-swept mews.

'No. His car is still there,' I said. 'See it? Almost hidden under that weeping willow.'

Barney hissed impatiently. I didn't blame him. He wasn't the only one bored stiff by all this hanging about. Staking out Richard Newman's producer's home had lost its appeal for me ten minutes after Newman disappeared in the back door.

'Lucky dog, Sizemore. Escaping this crap.' Barney put his feet up on the dash.

'Lucky? The guy is worrying himself to death. He's now convinced that it *was* Kathy Bolger's voice on that anonymous call, and . . .'

'Yeah, yeah. And he knows in his water that it *was* Jesus-freak Newman who cut and spliced her voice tapes to make the call.'

'You don't believe it?' I was surprised.

'That Newman wanted to drop Seanie in it? Sure I do. But why does Sizemore want to prove it? That'll be the death knell of Mutual Irish's malicious fire theory,' he warned.

I wanted to say that Sizemore had something called ethics. But I didn't. I kept that comforting thought to myself.

'This is now bigger than a single case, Barney,' I said instead. 'Newman is hell bent on ruining McHugh Dunning, and you know it.'

'And why? Because we caused his darling wife to have an attack? So why is Sizemore farting about in that recording studio, when he could be here getting evidence that Newman is screwing around behind his darling wife's back?'

I glared at him. 'Did you want to be somewhere else tonight?'

He squirmed. 'Well . . . I was on a bit of a promise.'

'Jesus. Do you ever think of anything else?'

'I've been working flat out, Annie. And my last two cases *were* heavy duty.'

'So now you're too big for boring stakeouts?'

'Nooo. And fair enough, that rotten barring order prevents Sizemore being here, it's just that . . .'

'You're permanently horny!'

He laughed. 'Couldn't have put it better myself.'

'You *and* Newman.' I nodded towards the house.

He sat up in disgust. 'Aw here, Annie, he's a dirty old letch.'

I gave him a look.

'Can I have some coffee? Please Annieeee?' he pouted.

'No. We have to save it. We could be here all night.'

An hour later the rain eased slightly, giving me a clearer view of the mews house. It had probably started out as a one-bed cottage, with an outdoor privy, and a scullery the size of a postage stamp, but was now a stylish pied-à-terre. Split-level, and with a wall of glass along one side, to enhance its south-facing timber deck. Its market value was possibly two million. Barney guessed nearer three.

We agreed on one thing – radio producing must pay pretty well. Then again, Nolan had hinted that this woman did more for Richard Newman than produce radio programmes. Which was why we were here, long lens at the ready.

'That sly little bugger, Toss Nolan! Wonder where he gets his information?' There was a trace of envy in Barney's voice.

'Maybe he hangs out with the right people.'

He shot me a dirty look. We had tailed Newman and his producer all day. Separately. But time after time we almost came face to face as they met up. At one o'clock they lunched together in a little French restaurant on the green. At four thirty they spent twenty minutes arguing in a private park, to which Newman had a key. When the producer left the radio station at nine p.m., Barney followed her on foot. Trailing Newman an hour later in the jeep, I ended up in the very mews where Barney was standing, drenched to the skin, and cursing everyone connected to the case.

'More coffee?' I held up the thermos.

'Thanks.' He drank thirstily.

'You think he's there for the night?'

'Only if he's on Viagra. How old is he, anyway?'

'Sixty? Ish?'

When he didn't respond I drained the last of the coffee into my Simpsons mug, and turned to slide the empty thermos behind my seat.

Barney became alert. 'Oh oh. The lights have gone off in the house.'

I straightened up. 'Maybe they like to pray in the dark?'

'Pray? That's a new name for it. Got any chocolate? I'm starving.'

'Check the glove compartment. Might be some in there.'

He opened it eagerly then slammed it closed before I could look inside.

'What?' I turned.

'Nothing.'

I sighed. 'I know Gerry keeps cigarettes in there. It's hardly a secret.'

He shot me a curious look. 'How do you reckon he's doing with the family shrink?'

'I'm sure he's doing fine,' I snapped. 'Gerry takes parenting very seriously. He'd give his life for those two boys.'

'What about you?'

'What do you mean?'

'How do you feel about . . . ?'

'They're not my children.' I deliberately misunderstood.

Barney took the hint and shut up. He was smart enough to know that some things were not up for discussion. Well, except if you wanted a row. My personal relationship with Gerry, or what was left of it, was my private business. We sat in silence, listening to the rain, until sheer boredom forced him to make conversation again. 'Fiona's being a bit weird these days. I met her in Café en Seine and she kept giving me these funny, sort of knowing, looks.'

'She's just wound up over her big party.'

'Party?' His eyes lit up.

'A dinner party! You'd hate it. She's been planning it forever. Gerry and me were to be her star guests. Sort of like a grown-up show and tell. Apparently detectives are all the rage at today's fashionable dinner parties. Something to do with the growing crime wave,' I smiled. 'Then Gerry had the audacity to feck off to the States, leaving Fiona high and dry,' I said wryly.

'Fiona won't be short of dinner guests. Not if Pino is doing the cooking.' He was watching the house again.

'Maybe. But she's fixated on this detective thing. Thinks she'll lose face with her new social set if her dinner party doesn't outshine theirs. Even worse, her Mum and Toddlers group might drum her off their teething committee.'

He looked mystified. 'Why would she give a formal dinner party for Mums and *Toddlers*?'

'Oh for feck's sake, Barney, are you even listening? You're as bad as . . . Jesus . . . duck . . . duck! Newman's coming out the gate!'

'Fuck! He's coming over!'

Before I could stir, Barney had grabbed me, and was kissing me energetically. I had no choice but to cooperate because Newman was now standing right next to the window behind me.

There was an unmerciful bang on the glass, accompanied by an angry shout. I sat rigid, as Barney pushed my face into his jumper, and threw his head back to groan loud enough for Newman to hear.

'Aw Jaysus, Mary, you're the best ride in Dublin.' Barney groaned again.

I thought Newman's fist would come through the glass.

'You in there,' he bellowed. 'Open this door.'

Barney opened the steamy window a crack.

'What are you doing here?' Newman boomed.

'What the fuck does it look like?' Barney growled in his best hard-man accent as I kept my face in the shadows.

'This is a private mews,' Newman said. 'If you're not out of here in two minutes, I'm ringing the Guards.'

'Fuck off, yeh crabby auld bollix.'

Newman's producer came running out of the house, her long brown hair flying in the wind. Despite the rain she was clad only in a flimsy dressing gown and slippers. She tugged anxiously at Newman's sleeve. 'Leave it, darling! They're just scum.'

'Who are you callin' scum, yeh auld hure!' Barney shouted.

Terrified that Newman might recognise me I slid lower and lower until my face was mashed against

Barney's middle. From this ignominious position I reached for the ignition.

'Hold on. I've seen this jeep before,' Newman spluttered. 'You're . . .'

I released the handbrake, and the jeep began to roll forward.

'You're from that private . . . !' Newman ran alongside us.

Barney moved like lightning. Grabbing his camera, he hit the window button, and leaned across me to hang out the open window, taking shot after shot of Newman and his rain-drenched girlfriend, as the rain continued to plaster her flimsy dressing gown against her well-toned body.

'Got enough?' I asked from between Barney's legs.

'Go!' He fell back in through the window.

I drove, spewing back loose gravel. Tyres squealing, I turned into the main road, flooring the accelerator, until Barney yelled in terror, 'What the hell are you doing? Are you trying to kill us?'

'They might be following. And we're already in enough trouble. That barring order could well extend to all of us. What if we end up in jail? What'll we tell Gerry then?'

Barney dismissed my fears with a wave of his digital camera. 'Newman will be licking our arses when he sees these shots. We'll have *him* over a barrel. We now have prime evidence of his extra-curricular rumpy-pumpy!' He chuckled. 'Mr holier than thou, lay preacher, and bosom buddy of Jesus, adulterously screwing his nubile young producer? Did you see the baps on her?'

'Barney!'

'Well, I couldn't help noticing. Wonder what the tabloids would pay for these beauties?' He gave the camera a lingering kiss.

'Behave yourself, Barney. We're professional investigators, not some kind of sleazy paparazzi!' I turned to look at him, raising an eyebrow. 'Fifty grand maybe?'

This time his noisy kiss landed on my face.

Barney lined up our pictures on the computer screen. Mine weren't up to much, just a collection of shots of Newman leaving the radio station, walking in the private park with Gooding, the two of them waving their arms about like windmills, before going their separate ways as rain began sheeting down. I did have one good shot of a tight-faced Newman parking his car under the willow tree a long distance from Gooding's house. And a couple of him slipping in through the very distinctive gateway of her mews cottage.

Barney's pictures blew mine out of the water. Close-ups of Gooding standing in the rain clutching Newman's arm, her dressing gown blowing open to reveal what she was wearing underneath. Nothing. Then shot after shot of Newman raising his fist at the jeep, wearing a totally different shirt from the one he'd been wearing when he arrived at the house.

Barney and I hugged each other with delight.

'Gotcha!' Barney yelled.

'Busted!' We danced around the office.

I paused for a second. ''Course he could just have gone to her house to change his clothes?'

'Sure. Isn't that what everyone's boss does at the stroke of midnight?'

'OK. Do we email or courier the photos?'

'Email. It's quicker. But just send three, and hold off on the really incriminating ones. He knows what we have, but I don't want his poor wife seeing them and having another attack.'

'Why not? Let Newman try explaining those enormous baps away. The randy old bugger!'

'Barney!'

Resigned, Barney sent the least offensive pictures. But even they were pretty damning.

It was now one thirty a.m. I suddenly realised that apart from our laughter, the place was so silent you could almost hear our hearts beating.

'Let's ring Sizemore!'

'It's half one in the morning!' he protested.

But I was already dialling. 'He'll be anxious. And Mutual Irish will be giving him hell over that barring order. Gerry said they can turn into storm troopers at the first hint of bad publicity. One slip and it's a bullet in the head. And Sizemore is the new boy over there, remember? They've probably been waiting for him to slip.' I didn't add that I was missing him. That the barring order was hurting me too, by keeping us apart.

'His mobile is off.' I slumped in disappointment.

'Ring Gerry!' Barney enthused.

'No. It's . . . late.' I replaced the receiver.

'Not in Arizona.' He inched me aside, and began dialling.

'No signal there either.' He grimaced, then tried again. 'Nothing. What's Sally's home number?'

Sally's phone was picked up on the third ring.

'Hey kiddo!' Barney yelled. 'Is your Dad there? Oh. The Desert Inn hotel?' A pause. 'What time will they be back? Not 'til tomorrow? OK. No, it's OK. I'll talk to him then. Tell him Barney rang.'

He hung up. 'Not there.' He gave me a funny look. 'Sally?'

'No, she's . . . they're er . . . out somewhere.'

'Without the boys?'

'Yeah.' Another embarrassed look. 'I suppose they wanted a bit of time to . . . to discuss stuff without the kids ear-wigging. You know . . . stuff the therapist said.'

I nodded, swallowing hard. 'No one left to ring then?' I forced a laugh.

'We could always try waking old Toss?' His smile was equally forced. 'See if he has any more hot tips for us?'

'Dream on.' I picked up my bag. 'I'm for home. Will you lock up?'

'Sure. You OK?'

'Why wouldn't I be?'

'True. We did some good work tonight, you and me.'

'Night, Barney. Do you need a lift?'

'Na . . . the bike is just around the corner.'

'See you in the morning.'

'See ya, Annie.' His eyes looked sad.

I was almost home when I remembered that Barney's motorbike wasn't anywhere near the agency. It was parked over the other side of town, near the radio

346

station. I considered turning back, but decided against it. If Barney wanted a lift he would have said. He possibly needed time to think. I certainly did. And most of my thoughts were taken up with Sizemore. Given his experience in the States that barring order had to be especially galling for him.

I was putting my key in the door when I heard my hall phone ringing. Dropping my bag, I raced to answer it. 'Sizemore?' Too late. The caller had rung off. And no messages.

Frustrated, I tried Sizemore's number again. No joy.

I ran a bath, ducking under the hot bubbles as if this would compel the phone to ring again. It always had before. Soaking in a hot bath was practically a guarantee that the phone would ring. Not this time. Although I gave it every chance, waiting until the water was borderline icy, and my skin almost prune-like, before I gave in and grabbed a towel.

I was tempted to have a hot whiskey, but resisted. I needed to be razor sharp tomorrow. To have a firm plan for when Newman appeared. I knew he'd storm into the agency first thing. Those pictures would guarantee it. As for the Bolger case falling around my ears, I'd deal with that afterwards. Keeping the agency going was my primary concern now.

I changed the sheets before falling into bed. No reason. Well, OK, maybe the tiniest little hope that I'd have a surprise visitor.

I slept undisturbed until the alarm rang at seven fifty. Eyes heavy with sleep I padded into the bathroom, and on into the shower. Holding my breath I hit the cold tap. After the first two agonising seconds, it felt strangely invigorating.

I put on make-up, with an extra steady hand. I was drying my hair, trying to force it into a semblance of a style, when the phone shrilled. Throwing myself across the bed, I all but strangled myself with the cord.

'Sizemore?'

There was a soft click, then nothing. Crushed with disappointment, I forced myself to focus on the day ahead. After all, I had an important job to do this morning. Two important jobs. Both of them could decide how I spent the rest of my life.

I gave up on my hair and slipped into my best business suit, and left for the agency.

34

'Gerry's been ringing and ringing.' Sandra greeted me with a handful of messages. 'I gave him your new home number again, but he said will you *please* switch on your mobile.'

I scrunched up the little papers and dropped them in the bin. 'Anything from Sizemore?'

'Nope.'

'Get Fiona for me, will you?' I asked. 'I'll be at my desk.'

She was curious, but for once didn't moider me with questions. 'Sure, Annie.'

Fiona came on all defensive. 'I didn't really mean to . . .'

'You don't have to say anything, Fiona! Just listen. The way things are piling up here, I'm not sure that Sizemore will make it to your party. No. Listen! I'm definitely coming. And I promise to bring a PI with me. And no it won't be someone who'll pick his nose in between the petits fours and the coffee, so relax! I'll even let you choose a dress for me, if you have an hour to spare at lunch time. I don't have anything remotely suitable for a posh dinner party. No! Forget this morning, I'm busy.' I arranged the line of photos at my elbow. 'But I'll take a long lunch break.'

'Oh, Annie.' She was practically tearful. 'I knew you wouldn't let me down. I'm sorry I said all those horrible things to you.'

'That's OK. Got to go. Talk later.'

'Annie?'

'What?'

'I'd never serve petis fours! They're so passé.'

I hung up with a sigh.

The phone rang instantly. Gerry's voice was so clear he might have been calling from next door. 'Annie? What the hell is going on over there? I've been trying to reach you all—'

You have in your arse. I put him on hold and buzzed reception. 'Sandra, Gerry is on the line. He's probably calling from the Desert Inn hotel. I want you to tell him I have severe laryngitis, and my GP says I won't get my voice back for days. Tell him to just email the office. He should be good at that by now, after all, it's been his favourite form of communication over the past few weeks.'

She hesitated, but only for the briefest second. 'I'll tell him, Annie. I . . . are you all right?'

'I'm OK.'

'I'll talk to Gerry.'

'Thanks, Sandra.'

I rearranged the photos of Richard Newman on my desk. Changed my mind and put them back in the drawer. Took them out again and chewed my lip. What if I played it wrong? What if he grabbed them, and legged it off with them? My whole plan could go up in smoke. I should have let Barney make extra copies.

Ethics my arse, had been his frustrated comment when I refused.

I looked at the photos again. Moved them closer to my elbow. This time facing me. The sight of them lined up on the desk should be enough to unnerve Newman. I took a calming breath, and waited.

Ten minutes later Sandra buzzed me. I had barely put the phone down when Newman strode into my office.

Ignoring the chair I had placed a good eighteen inches from my desk, he stood looking down at me. 'I can have you charged with invasion of privacy Ms McHugh.'

I kept my eyes on my blotter, and waited for him to sit.

'And trespass,' he bluffed.

I glanced at the photos.

'Did you hear me, Ms McHugh?' His colour rose. 'Or is it Mrs . . . Where is Mr Dunning? Let me speak to your boss.'

'You're speaking to her, Mr Newman.' I looked directly at him for the first time. 'Please lower your voice, there are other people working on this floor.'

'What . . . ?' He lost his train of thought.

'Right.' I jumped into the breech. 'You're here because we have some interesting pictures of you, Mr Newman. Yes . . .' I peered closely at them, blinking back as if I found them offensive. 'The three you have already received were comparatively innocuous compared with . . .' I gave an involuntary shiver.

He sat down hard, the colour draining from his face.

Shit. Did he think we had *dirty* pictures of him? What the hell did he get up to in that fancy mews house anyway? Make him the offer, Annie, before this gets out of hand.

I cleared my throat busily. 'I have no interest in your *extra-curricular* activities, Mr Newman,' I began, hoping Barney wouldn't burst in and blow my carefully staged scene. 'My sole interest is in the welfare of this agency and its operatives. If you are willing to have that offensive barring order nullified, *and* guarantee to forgo any further legal proceedings against McHugh Dunning, I'll hand over every single photo we have of you and your . . . er . . . your . . .' I waved my fingers.

His relief was almost tangible. But he couldn't resist a face down.

'You find the barring order offensive? My wife could have died.'

'I regret that your wife was distressed by a careless remark made by one of our . . . operatives, but given . . .' I frowned hard at the photos, 'given these images, I find your husbandly concern a little overdone.'

'My wife has a serious heart condition.' His mouth was a tight, angry line.

'I have received assurances that your wife is in robust physical health, Mr Newman.' I outstared him. 'And given the remark she overheard, I have to inform you that we have a voice expert who would be happy to give evidence in any court that the voice heard on the anonymous call to Mutual Irish did belong to your late daughter.' I hoped the lie wouldn't choke me. 'He demonstrated how it was done. If you want we can give another demonstration for your wife.'

My eyes challenged his, until he looked away.

Heart racing, I continued. 'What shocked me is that someone with your religious convictions would . . . stoop to such subterfuge. Altering tapes of your late daughter's voice? Using them to make an anonymous call?' I shook my head, dropping my face into my hands as if such wickedness was beyond my comprehension.

Checking his reaction through my splayed fingers I could almost see his brain ticking over, searching for a way out without losing face.

'And then . . . then these . . . ?' I gestured to the photos.

'I'll have a word with my solicitor,' he said.

Without raising my eyes, I handed him the phone.

He dialled. Barked orders at someone called Mason, Mason and Brewers, telling him, or her, that he wanted the barring order rescinded. 'I don't care what it takes, just do it!'

I took a sip of water, while carefully nudging the little cigarette lighter/tape recorder closer to the phone.

But he wasn't getting off that easily. I needed to know everything he did about the fire; if I was to solve this case. Increasingly nervous that one of the other PIs might burst in on us, I needed to speed things up. With another man here, I knew Newman would clam up. Never allow himself to lose face. He thought he was an alpha male, with a direct line to

God. Happily I had no place in that equation. I was just a woman. A woman who couldn't even control her own hair, which was now curling to the point of frizz.

He finished his call, hanging up with a confident flick of the wrist, satisfied that he had just sorted what could have been a very sticky situation for him.

Keeping my voice even, I asked, 'Did you have to use your daughter's voice to besmirch Seanie? Was there no other way you . . . ?'

'Besmirch? What was there to besmirch? He's a nothing. A fool who threw away what little God-given talent he had on drink and drugs. Then used his facile charm to convince my daughter to marry him. He made her miserable from the day they married. Was I to stand by and allow him to gain from my daughter's death? Let him get away with it?'

'Get away with it?' My chest tightened. 'You . . . you have evidence that he . . .'

'Evidence? I had evidence that he made her miserable.'

'But the fire?'

'The fire was an accident.' He was dismissive. Then, seeing my stunned reaction, added, 'But one he could have prevented. On two previous occasions those overhead lights triggered small fires in the shop, causing minor smoke damage. Kathy confided in my wife, but swore her to secrecy. Said Seanie told her their premiums would skyrocket if the insurance company considered the shop a fire risk.'

I froze. So the fire *was* an accident. A feckin' accident. Seanie hadn't . . . the Gards were spot on with their reports. It was all a stupid, preventable accident. And Newman knew it. So why make that phone call to Mutual Irish? Did he genuinely believe he was avenging Kathy by blaming Seanie? By preventing him getting the insurance payout? Why not make the call to Mutual Irish in his own voice? Tell them what he'd learned about the earlier fires? Why the subterfuge?

My head spinning now, I was still trying to figure out Newman's reasoning when he stood up, his eyes icy cold again. 'He killed my daughter. He knew that wiring was an accident waiting to happen.'

'But . . . so did your wife?' I dared. 'And she didn't tell anyone. Not even you.'

'Of course she told me . . .' He reddened.

'She told you?' I gaped.

'*After* the event,' he snapped. 'Long after.'

He was lying. I just knew it. But why? 'Your wife didn't mention the earlier fires when I interviewed her.'

'My wife has been on antidepressants since the tragedy. Her concentration is poor. She . . . she forgets things, and . . . I encourage her to forget . . . to put it behind her. It makes our loss less painful.'

Oh my God she *had* told him. *Before* the fatal fire. It was written all over him. She told him, but he wasn't listening. Too busy rushing off to meet his young producer? And later when the guilt became unbearable he had to lay it at someone's door. Seanie's. Then warned his wife not to mention the earlier fires, in case . . .

There was a long silence as we eyeballed each other.

'It was Seanie's responsibility! His shop!' he hissed.

'But you knew those lights were dangerous.'

'I . . . I assumed . . . anyone would assume he'd had them made safe!'

I couldn't hide my revulsion.

'Don't you look at me like that! I loved my daughter. He made her life hell. I wasn't even aware that she was on Prozac. Prozac!' He spat, his face a map of misery. 'That's why she didn't waken that night. He's responsible.'

'Her friends wanted her to leave him,' I challenged. 'They said you told her that was out of the question. Why?'

'Why?' The question shocked him. 'Because marriage is a sacrament! An indissoluble Sacrament between two people . . . *until death us do part*.'

I wanted to jump over the desk and punch him. But I'm a professional investigator. Professional investigators never allow their personal feelings to interfere with the job. Instead I unlocked the top drawer of the desk, took out every photo we had of him and his lover and slid them towards him.

He stuffed them into his briefcase. 'What about those?' He pointed to the little selection at my elbow.

'These? Oh they're just holiday snaps.' I threw one across the desk. In it Sandra's deeply bronzed friends were laughing like drains, clinging to each other as they sped across the Mediterranean surf, on a giant inflatable banana.

His reaction to that photo gave me the only satisfaction I was to get all that morning.

'Goodbye, Mr Newman. And . . . have a nice day,' I said.

I waited until the door closed behind him before switching off the little tape recorder. Then I began to write my report. I was anxious to get a copy to Sizemore ASAP. Give him the good news before Mutual Irish made him disassociate himself entirely from us.

35

Determined to cheer me up, Fiona led me along a jam-packed Grafton Street. 'No more talk about work, Annie. We're going to find you the dress of your dreams.'

I shot her a look of disbelief.

'OK then, the dress of my dreams.' She laughed, and pulled me into a softly-lit fashion emporium, where the air reeked of expensive perfume and money.

She let go of me, and flicked through a small rack of designer dresses, like a madwoman on speed. Refusing all offers of help from a rake-thin salesgirl with breast implants that would poke your eye out, she dismissed dress after dress despite my protestations that at least three of them seemed perfectly suitable to me. We were, after all, looking for a dress for a small dinner party, not a presidential ball.

'Can I help?' The salesgirl tried again.

Fiona snorted derisively. 'If this is all you have to offer, I doubt it. I need a dress with real pizzazz. A dress that says *hi everybody – here I am*! But not in a vulgar way. I want one that says I'm vibrant and sexy . . . yet classy.'

As this particular shop spent a fortune marketing

itself as the leading exponent of this exact style, I felt the busty salesgirl was entitled to bristle. 'Have you looked at this rail, madam?'

'What do you think I've been doing? Swinging on it?' Fiona asked.

Then came two seconds of girly hair tossing while they tried to out-pout each other.

'Fiona, if you're not happy . . . we can try elsewhere.' I tugged at her elbow.

'You're right!' Fiona flicked back her long glossy hair again, out tossing the salesgirl by at least two inches. 'Lets go where my platinum cards are appreciated.'

This comment galvanised a whole flock of bored salesgirls. We were suddenly surrounded by a whole tribe of size eight people, all of them with bony wrists and necks like giraffes. All of them determined to outdo each other.

'Have you seen the new line by Stella McCartney?'

'This is the latest Paul Costelloe.'

The race was on.

Previously unseen dresses were suddenly swished along racks, and placed right under our noses. A couple of stunning creations appeared out of nowhere, superb designs that needed little or no promoting.

One of them was strapless, and in-your-face sexy. 'This is sooo this year. Bias cut, and calf length to show the ankles to best advantage. The shot silk pattern on the bodice is so cleverly woven; it would showcase your décolletage beautifully.'

'My bust?' Fiona gave a loud snort. 'We're shopping for Annie, not me!'

Three pairs of expertly made-up eyes turned to look at my now flaming face. All three instantly slotted me into the simpleton fashion category. Or someone on day release. And given my earlier encounter with Newman and his skewed morals this was pretty much how I was feeling anyway. To make things worse it was now only six and a half hours to Fiona's dinner party, and I was still dateless.

I decided to do something about that.

I was sneaking into a changing room to text Sizemore when the salesgirl with breast implants found me. 'This is a very special little strapless . . .'

I turned away to continue texting. CAN YOU MEET ME FOR DINNER TONITE? 8.30?

'Excuse . . . me . . . dear?' The salesgirl spoke slowly.

I looked at her well-meaning face and felt a serious headache coming on.

The rest of the shopping trip passed in an analgesic-induced blur.

There were odd lucid moments. Like when I heard Fiona explaining, 'Yes she has a good figure. Problem is, she slumps when she's worried, and she worries a lot.'

'It shows.' Even the breast implant girl was becoming depressed, and she had so little reason to be.

'Terribly pale,' another voice said, as if being pale was a major fashion faux pas. And to think I'd spent all that money on a St Trop.

With all the talk about my fashion failings, and the non-stop chatter about strapless versus halter neck, bias cut versus straight lines, Fiona never once let slip that this shopping trip had only one real purpose. We were here to find a dress that would outshine anything worn by her arch-rival, and founder of the breakaway Dublin four branch of Mums and Toddlers – Heather Flanagan. Plus I would also have to outshine Heather's most recent star guest – Harry Deegan. Deegan was a detective seargent famous for being wounded in the Dublin drug wars of the nineteen eighties when he took a direct hit from a Jack Russell which was thrown from a first-floor balcony in Fatima Mansions. Short of being hit by a Retriever there was no way I could outshine Deegan, but Fiona lived in hope.

She eventually found a dress that even I liked.

'All we need now is some suitable underwear,' she shrilled joyfully.

That was it for me. Her use of the royal *we* was definitive proof that Fiona had finally gone over to the dark side. She was clearly infected with the girly shopping madness that we had spent most of our teens despising, as we strutted around in baggy denims, our Oxfam shop jackets covered in anti-everything badges. And I was her prisoner.

We finally staggered out of the overheated shop, our progress handicapped by three massive carrier bags. Only one belonged to me, because despite having a wardrobe bursting with suitable dresses, Fiona fell in love with a full-length evening skirt in raw silk. And of course she needed a very special top to go with it, and what use was that without a very special pair of evening shoes. A very special necklace completed the outfit, and all but maxed out her two remaining credit cards.

And we hadn't yet found *suitable* underwear.

'What exactly constitutes suitable?' I hissed.

'Relax, Annie. It's not like I'm going to force you to buy crotchless panties or something equally tasteless,' she said, as if she hadn't been guilty of that in the past. 'When will you learn to trust me?'

She pushed me into Brown Thomas, and began drooling over displays of Agent Provocateur underwear. 'Look at them, Annie. This is what you need under that gorgeous dress.'

'I have tons of underwear.'

She rolled her eyes heavenwards. 'You can't wear tatty old underwear with *that* dress.'

'My underwear isn't tatty. It's . . . functional.'

'Trust me, Annie, nothing spoils the line of a well-cut dress like cheap underwear.'

I was still defending my underwear when my mobile beeped.

A brief text from Sizemore. TONITE NOT POSS. RAINCHECK?

'Annie?' Fiona nudged me as I stood there, my heart freezing over.

'Give me a sec. I need to send a text.' I sent a hurried message to Barney.

His reply was instantaneous. DINNER? YUM, YUM. TIME AND PLACE PLEASE. At least someone wanted my company tonight, I consoled myself, smothering the unworthy thought that Barney would accept a free dinner invitation from Hannibal

Lecter if it came near the end of the month. Sizemore hadn't even bothered to come up with an excuse! Feck him then.

'What do you think of this, Annie?' Fiona was holding up a scarlet-ribboned basque with matching panties that were little more than a promise.

'Not much,' I sulked. 'Couldn't you find anything a little *more* risqué?'

She looked so shocked I couldn't resist pushing the envelope. I stood there like a sulky child shaking my head as she held up piece after piece of beautiful underwear, only nodding when she teasingly produced something the size of a corn plaster. In black silk.

'Are you serious?' Her mouth gaped.

'Why not?' I grabbed it, and darted into a changing room. *Oh my God, what was I doing? A man turns me down, and I start dressing like a hooker?*

'Do you know how much that is?' Fiona watched me struggling into the corn plaster.

'Don't care.' I shrugged defiantly. 'All bets are off now. From now on I'm going to let it all hang out.'

'Jesus, it certainly will.' Fiona watched as I strutted about in the practically pornographic black silk.

'Think Barney will like it?' I posed.

'Like it? It will probably give him a coronary.'

'You think?'

She laughed. 'Well, given that he fancies you in your Homer Simpson PJs and St Bernard vest, there's no knowing what heights he might rise to if you wear that.' She ran a nervous finger along the smooth black silk. 'You'll probably have to call in the paramedics.'

Admittedly I was shocked when I realised what the price of giving a man a coronary came to. Not that my mind was on shopping any more. Bloody Sizemore! Bloody cheek. A raincheck? Where the hell was he anyway? And who did he think he was? I gave him my unconditional support over that barring order, and he throws a dinner invitation back in my face. Practically told me to stick it. After the nights we had shared? The frenzied passion? We had even showered together! That's practically like being married. A raincheck? Stupid bloody Americanism.

When I slapped my credit card on the counter Fiona misread my sulky expression.

'Ah sod it, Annie! It's only money. And well worth it. Trust me, I know,' she laughed. 'I'm on husband number two, remember? I know whereof I speak. I know what makes men tick.'

'Wish you'd tell me then,' I grumbled.

'Oh give over, you've always been popular with men. But would it be fair to say that *both* my husbands still worship me?' Again she tossed back her long shining hair.

'Well . . . yes,' I agreed glumly.

It was true. Pino absolutely adored her. And Sam, her first husband, probably wouldn't have divorced her, if his girlfriend hadn't become pregnant.

It was six thirty and I was kneeing open my gate, while struggling to hold on to my case papers and fancy shopping bags, when a large hand appeared out of nowhere.

'Let me take those, Ms Dunning.' The voice made me jump.

The Great Dane from next door was standing directly behind me. Resplendent in his pilot's uniform, all white shirt, shiny wings and bits of dazzling gold braid.

'Ms McHugh,' I corrected him.

'Ms McHugh *Dunning*.' His smile became flirtatious.

I muttered under my breath.

'How is Mr McHugh Dunning?' He took my bags, flashing a smile that probably broke a thousand air stewardesses' hearts. 'Still in America, is he?'

This took me by surprise, until I remembered seeing him talking to Gerry the morning he left for the States. The morning my dirty phone calls started again. I looked into his open, friendly face, into his clear blue eyes, and was struck by a very ugly thought. The problem with my pervy calls was that they had always been unaccountably intermittent. No real pattern to them, which was why they always managed to take me by surprise. I realised now that there had been a pattern to them. They came in clusters. And only when Gerry was away.

'Do you miss him?' The Great Dane asked, his accent telling me how ludicrous I was being. Even mumbling through the thickest woolly sock couldn't hide that accent, could it?

Plus this man had been my close neighbour for three years. He was a pilot, for God's sake! Above reproach. No, hold on, he wasn't a pilot! Not any more. Sandra said he'd been fired by Aer Lingus.

She had tried to tell me something else about him, but I cut her short, too excited after my night of passion with Sizemore to want to hear about anything as mundane as people losing their jobs. But if the Great Dane was jobless, like she said, why was he still wearing an Aer Lingus uniform?

We were at my door now, and he was so close behind me I could feel his breath on my neck. My hand trembling like a leaf, I rammed the key in the lock, pushed open the door and turned to relieve him of my bags. His smile now rictus firm, he refused to surrender them, and tried to edge past me and into the hall. I blocked him by sheer force of will, and a leg placed across the doorway.

'Thank you.' I made another attempt to wrench the bags from his now vice-like grip.

Still refusing to let go, he bared his teeth in what he obviously considered a charming smile. Too late. I was already hearing the theme music from jaws in my head.

'I'll take them inside for you.' His accent disappeared.

Jesus, was I being paranoid? Fiona used to accuse me of that. She said it was a family trait, that my Dad practically dug a moat around our house to prevent strangers gaining access. Whatever it was, some deep-seated instinct told me to remain cautious. This man was becoming aggressive, his attitude unpleasant.

He made another attempt to step into the hall. This time I threw my full weight against the door. Oh God, it wouldn't close, his big shiny shoe was in the way.

My mobile suddenly rang, making us both jump. Taking advantage of this lucky break, I slammed the door shut, and leaned against it trying not to dissolve in tears.

My shopping! He had my shopping. The bastard! He even had the risqué underwear I'd paid a fortune for.

Barney's number flashed up on my mobile.

I put it to my ear. 'Barney?'

'Hi! Is it half eight at your house? Or half eight at Fiona's?'

I laughed with relief at the sheer normality of his call.

'What's so feckin' funny?'

'Nothing.' I heard a car start up. 'Hold on a sec.' I opened the door to see the Great Dane driving away from his house as if he was being chased by demons. If only.

My bags were on my doorstep, totally intact.

'You can come here whatever time you like Barney. You'll be sooo welcome whatever time you appear.'

'Have you been drinking?'

'No. I just got in from work! I'm just happy to hear from you.'

'Jaysus!'

36

Barney looked magnificent in his navy pin-striped suit. Or maybe nervously magnificent would be a more apt description, because he persisted in tugging anxiously at the Italian silk tie I had borrowed from Fiona.

'Are you sure Pino won't recognise it?' I had asked her. 'It'll be hard enough getting Barney to wear a suit. He'd go ballistic if he thought I was making him wear one of Pino's ties.'

'Pino has a trillion Italian ties,' Fiona said. 'He doesn't remember half of them.'

Pino threw open the door to greet us with a beaming smile. 'How are you two? Oh my God, is that my tie?'

Fiona appeared out of nowhere, and kicked his ankle viciously.

'Annie, darling, you look like a million dollars.' She was in full hostess mode. Far too jubilant to acknowledge Pino's yelp of pain. 'And you've got your hair in a French chignon? La-de-dah. You could have worn a tiara with that.'

'Jaysus.' Barney choked back a laugh.

'Shut up, you,' I said.

Fiona chuckled happily. 'Oh just listen to you two. You could almost be an old married couple.'

'Don't start, Fiona!' I said, my nerves jangling like bracelets.

'Hello Zoe, darling!' She turned to greet another new arrival with a flying air kiss. But couldn't resist making a face behind her back as she led us into her ballroom-sized living room, then onwards towards a massively stocked bar, firing names left and right, and in such terrifyingly high-pitched tones that only a dog could hear them.

'Who?' Barney kept asking, as we ran the gauntlet of her Mums and Toddlers group, and on past their neatly-tailored husbands who all, without exception, looked as if they'd rather be on the golf links. But seeing the size of the drinks Pino was handing out, I guessed nobody would be unhappy for long. Blitzed out of their heads maybe; but definitely not unhappy.

Fiona parked us with a mixed group whose names we also didn't get, and darted away to impress more people.

'I thought you said a small dinner party?' Barney tugged nervously at his borrowed tie as we watched more people arrive. 'The place is already milled out of it,' he exaggerated.

'That's Fiona for you. She never does things by halves.' I smiled in the general direction of everybody.

We were knocking back our drinks when an elderly man appeared and made straight for us. Bordering on the obese, and with a startling haycock of white hair, he frowned into Barney's face.

369

'So you're the private detective?' He pumped Barney's hand, eyes narrowing with interest. 'You're a lot younger than I expected.'

'I am?' Barney fidgeted.

'Indeed. You don't look old enough to own an investigative agency.'

'He doesn't.' I forced a laugh.

I was about to explain when I was practically knocked over by a group of people all anxious to congratulate the elderly man, who turned out to be a high court judge who had recently won an award for putting the most people in prison, or something.

Barney and I exchanged glances, wondering what the hell Fiona was playing at. She had practically forced me to come here, insisting that I'd be the only representative of law and order. Well, me and Barney. And here we were, two lowly PIs. Totally outclassed by a judge.

'Fiona?' I tried to pull her to one side.

'I know what you're going to say,' she muttered. 'But I swear I didn't know if he'd make it tonight or not. Pino has been asking him for weeks. He dines regularly at the restaurant. Pino had to promise him beef olives with artichokes to entice him here.' She turned to the white-haired judge. 'Judge Dennis, this is Annie. *She* owns the McHugh Dunning Detective Agency.'

'With my partner.' I clutched my empty glass.

'Ah. So you're the *junior* partner?' Judge Dennis growled at Barney.

'Actually, he's my toy boy,' I babbled nervously.

Everyone laughed, except the judge, who looked like he might give me six to twelve months. Please God, I thought, don't let me be seated next to him. Please.

'My . . . my business partner is in the States,' I said, adding quickly. 'On business.'

'On business?' The judge's shrewed eyes smiled.

He was actually quite sweet, for someone who sent people to prison. But as his only interest, apart from food, appeared to be the law, I knew we were in for a hellish night. Listening to him answer a long question about the Criminal Law Act of 1997, even Barney's eyes were glazing over. Then Barney stiffened and his mouth dropped open. An attractive girl had just arrived in, and threw off her coat to reveal a chest like the upper balcony in the Gaiety Theatre.

'Sorry I'm late, darling.' She brushed past Barney to kiss the judge on both his chins. He responded by patting her shiny blonde hair.

'His daughter?' Barney gawked.

'His wife.' Fiona passed around a plate of Florentine tartlets.

Ignoring our astonished reactions, Fiona didn't miss a beat. 'Florentine tart, judge? Leah?'

'Thank you, Fiona.' Leah took a mini bite from a scrumptious tartlet, giggled and proceeded to feed the judge the teeth-marked remainder. She dabbed his podgy mouth after every bite.

'She his taster?' Barney stared.

'She used to be a legal secretary,' Fiona explained.

'Good at handling briefs, was she?' Barney

chuckled, then gasped hard when Fiona's elbow collided with his lower ribcage.

I left Barney ogling the judge's wife, and followed Fiona into the kitchen to enquire about Nonna Molino.

'Where is she? Locked her in the garden shed did you? Is the honeymoon over?'

'Certainly not. She's upstairs reading Calum a bedtime story.'

'I thought she was helping with the cooking?'

'Helping? The woman is a miracle worker. Look around you. Starters are all ready, the main course and two alternative desserts are in the oven. She even made bread rolls. They're still steaming hot, look.'

Pino came in to fret over the double oven. 'Nearly there,' he muttered, checking enough beef slices to feed a multitude. He lashed more wine-laden stock over them, before timing the desserts carefully. 'Twelve minutes tops, then we—'

'Pino?' Fiona clutched at his arm. 'Annie wants to say hello to Nonna Molino.'

Distracted, he gave the beef slices another wary poke.

'Go on, take her up,' Fiona pleaded. 'I'm busy with the guests.'

'Let's go, Annie.' Pino could refuse her nothing.

'Where are you going?' Barney called, as we hurried through the living room.

'To say a quick hello to Nonna Molino.'

'I'm coming too.' Barney tore his eyes off the judge's wife.

Upstairs Calum was sleeping like an angel. But

Nonna Molino continued to rock contentedly in the big curved chair, reading happily from a book of Italian fairy tales, as if she still had an apperceive audience.

She broke off to greet us, kissed me warmly, and called me bella Annieee. Then, clipping back her few ribs of white hair, she stared suspiciously at Barney. Or it may have been at the familiar borrowed tie.

'Barney.' He introduced himself with a bow.

She pumped his hand fiercely, scrutinising him with her piercing brown eyes, before rattling off something to Pino, in rapid-fire Italian.

Pino laughed.

'What did she say?' Barney asked eagerly.

'She said you're too young for Annie.'

'Oh no, tell her we're just friends . . .' I began. But Nonna Molino was busy laying down the law, waving a warning finger at me, then back at Barney, as she continued to lecture us in jet-propelled Italian.

We waited for Pino to translate.

I suspect he gave us the shortened version. 'Mamma says you have babies in your eyes, Annie.' He laughed. 'For that you need a strong man. Not a boy. Strong men make good babies.'

Pino and I were laughing our way downstairs, debating how many babies you could actually fit in an eye, when we realised Barney wasn't following us.

I ran back up. Found him sitting dejected on the top step.

'I'd make lovely babies,' he sulked.

*　　*　　*

The dinner went like a dream. Nothing at all like the nightmare I'd been expecting. With his adoring wife by his side, and a generous supply of Irish whiskey inside him, the judge proved to be highly entertaining. Best of all I didn't have to come up with a single answer to Dublin's growing lawlessness. The judge had all the answers and served them up with such verve and wit he even had Barney laughing. And did he love his food? When the dreaded Heather Flanagan tried to get him to slate young repeat offenders he shot her down politely.

'Let's not insult this glorious food by giving it anything but our fullest attention,' he said, as Pino served him extra beef olives with artichokes.

Fiona was in seventh heaven. Nonna Molino's food was a hit. And between them Fiona and Pino were playing a blinder.

Even bitter Heather Flanagan couldn't poison the happy atmosphere. But there was no mistaking her desire to. She sat watching Fiona's triumph, waiting for an opportunity to pounce. She listened, her lip curled nastily, as Barney and I answered one or two questions about our work. Barney had the guests howling with laughter as he repeated the story of how he lost half his chest-hair when a misinformed club bouncer ripped off his body mike, thinking he was the one carrying drugs.

The judge laughed so hard he had to dry his eyes.

Fiona threw a triumphant glance at Heather Flanagan, who was sitting opposite me looking like she had swallowed a wasp. Heather waited 'til there was a lull in the conversation before asking.

'I hear you've been working with Niall Sizemore, Annie?'

Sensing a trap, Fiona froze, her fork halfway to her mouth.

But I answered with easy confidence. 'Yes.'

'I hear he's being sued.'

'No he isn't.' I felt myself flush.

'I heard he's being taken to court? He harassed some poor grieving woman to the extent that she had a serious heart attack? Or was it a stroke?' Heather waited, her eyes glistening with malice.

The whole table went silent. Everyone stopped eating to look at me.

'I can tell you for a fact that's a completely unfounded piece of gossip!' I said, my heart pounding like a kettledrum. 'Sizemore is a highly-trained investigator. He has far too much respect for the rule of law to harass anyone.'

Twenty pairs of eyes turned to Heather, who sneered dismissively, 'Respect for the law? My cousin George was in Blackrock College with him. He said he was wild. He said he was smoking marijuana when he was sixteen.'

'Oh, who wasn't?' her husband said. 'Eat your stuffing, Heather.'

There was a low ripple of laughter. Fiona shot me a pleased look.

'Sizemore?' The judge's voice boomed from the top of the table. 'Isn't he Hugh Bateman's son.'

'That's right.' Sensing another golden opportunity

to humiliate Fiona, Heather perked up again. 'Sizemore is his mother's maiden name. He adopted it after his parents' messy divorce. She was a bit of a radical, in her day. Defending the scum of the earth in court. That's why Bateman divorced her. That's probably why he shipped Niall off to America. The shame must have—'

'Nice chap, Niall,' the judge boomed. 'I met him once or twice. Hugh must be pleased to have him back in Ireland again.'

'He is nice.' I smiled at the judge, my heart bursting with gratitude. 'I would trust Niall Sizemore with my life.'

'Good. Hugh still on the board of Mutual Irish, is he?' The judge sliced into his beef olives.

'Think so,' someone said.

'He is,' another voice verified. 'Best MD they ever had. I didn't know he had a son.'

Barney's eyes met mine over the flickering white candles.

But the conversation had moved on to the rising cost of child care.

'Stay for another brandy, Annie.' Fiona was floating on air. 'Do! You helped make tonight a success, you and Barney. You certainly had Heather Flanagan on the run.'

'It's late, Fiona, and my head is splitting. Great party, though.'

'Wasn't it? I never thought I'd see Heather Flanagan leave with her tail between her legs. She's always such a bitch.'

'Why do you invite her?'

'Because she always invites me to her parties, silly! She'll be hosting that big September bash for the homeless, and she's already refurbishing her whole kitchen to make the rest of us feel bad. Putting marble tiles everywhere. Walls, floors, everywhere you look. She's ordered an Aga the length of Wicklow Street!'

I gave her a look.

'Oh for God's sake, Annie, it's her own money. Anyway, Calum loves playing with her kids, so there.'

'Cabby's getting impatient, Annie,' Barney called.

I hugged Fiona and darted out to the cab. The cabby chewed gum non-stop, played an old AC/DC tape at full volume, and drove as if he was practising for the Monte Carlo rally.

'Drop you first, Annie?' Barney shouted as we were thrown around the back of the cab like human dice.

'Please,' I yelled back.

'Bloody Sizemore, huh?' he yelled. 'And there we were, feeling dead sorry for him. Thinking he'd be out on the street if he didn't kowtow to Mutual Irish? Turns out his old man is on the feckin' board? Probably keeping a director's chair warm for him. Jaysus.'

Even if I had thought of a suitable reply, AC/DC would have drowned it out.

'That's Sizemore's car,' Barney yelled in my ear as we approached my house.

'Where?'

'There! Outside your house. What the fuck's he doing here at half one in the morning?'

'You go on, I'll deal with it.' I grabbed my bag, as the cab screeched to a halt.

'No way. I'm coming with you.' Barney was hot on my heels.

'Go home, Barney.'

'No. I want to see what he's up to.'

'Go home.'

The cabby stuck his head out the window. 'Could yiz make up yer bleedin' minds? I have a wife and a six pack waiting for me.'

'Go home, Barney. I'll deal with Sizemore.'

'Sure?'

'Positive.'

The taxi drove off and I hurried over to peer into Sizemore's car. He was sprawled along the back seat, fast asleep, his long legs dangling across the back of the front passenger seat.

I banged on the window. He sat up, blinked sleepily, and climbed out rubbing his eyes. He looked like he'd been in a train wreck. Covered in dust and grime, and with a purple bruise marking one perfect cheekbone.

'What are you doing here at this hour?'

'I've been here since eleven.' He checked his watch. 'Have a nice dinner did you?'

Was he trying to wrong foot *me*? I hadn't heard from him in thirty-six hours, except for that snotty refusal to my dinner invitation, and now he . . .

He was walking towards my house.

'Where are you going?' I got between him and the gate.

'I need coffee.' He fought to keep his eyes open.

'Well I hope you have some in your flat.

Goodnight!' I was closing the little gate behind me, when I spotted the shadowy figure in the garden next door. Peering hard I caught the glow of a cigarette in the moonlight, then a glimpse of shiny gold wings.

Sizemore saw me start. 'Who is that nutter? He's been there for hours watching me. Who is he? Neighbourhood watch?'

'In that uniform?' I muttered. 'I don't think so. You'd better come in.'

37

'You look amazing,' Sizemore slumped into a chair as I busied myself making coffee.

'You look like you've been rolling in filth,' I snapped.

It was true. In the harsh florescent light he looked even worse than he had in the moonlight. I had never seen him like this before. He was wearing filthy jeans, what appeared to be old Dr Martens, and a T-shirt that even I wouldn't give house room. Was this a nouveau homeless look? A ploy to gain sympathy? If it was, he was out of luck. I only invited him in because seeing the other nutter freaked me so much. Spoiled for choice, I was. Invite Sizemore in, or risk a nocturnal visit from the psycho next door?

I slid a steaming mug across the table. 'Coffee. Milk. No sugar.'

'Thanks.' He caught it, and drank gratefully.

'Mutual Irish beat you up, did they? Before they fired you?'

He looked puzzled. 'I . . . they didn't fire me.'

'Course not. How could they? With your father on the board. The MD, is he?'

'Oh shit.' He put the mug aside, and dropped his

head into his hands, which were as filthy as the rest of him. I counted three broken nails amongst the grime. Not that I was interested. He could have three broken teeth for all I cared. 'I wanted to tell you myself.'

'When?' I kept my chin high. Let him see I didn't give a damn anyway.

He shot me a pleading look. 'Sometime? Maybe when . . . Christ I'm wrecked, Annie.'

'Yes. Too tired to go out to dinner. Too tired to lift a phone. Too tired to . . .'

'My phone is broken.'

I raised a disbelieving eyebrow.

'A brick fell on it.'

I nearly laughed. That had to be the lamest, if the most original, excuse in the universe, for not calling someone.

'So you didn't get my text about Newman?'

'Oh I got that before . . . before it smashed.'

Nice one. This guy could think on his feet. Well . . .

He slumped on the table. 'The legal eagles will sort out whether Seanie gets any insurance payout or not. Those earlier fires . . . a major factor . . . should have been reported. Well done on getting that information, Annie. And taping it was crucial.'

'Is that why you came *rushing* back to the agency?' I asked sarcastically. 'To congratulate me on saving Mutual Irish from having to pay out a few million?'

'Sorry about that. There was something I had to do first.'

'Like what?'

'Please, Annie, I'm truly exhausted. Could you drop the attitude?'

'The attitude?' Hot anger was now welling up inside me. More anger than I even felt with Newman. 'I supported you unconditionally over the Mrs Newman fiasco. I talked Barney into giving up his first free night for weeks to stand in for you on the mews stakeout. You didn't even ring me to say thanks. You never once mentioned your family connections with Mutual Irish. And you accuse *me* of having an attitude?'

'Please, Annie, I'm sooo tired.'

'Finished your coffee?'

He nodded.

'Good. You can feck off then. Get as far away from me and my attitude as you can, because I'm going to bed, and I'm taking my attitude with me, and I'd advise you to get out of my house before I brain you with something.'

He didn't budge.

'Did you hear me?' I yelled.

He nodded. 'What about that weirdo next door?'

'He can feck off as well.'

'Be serious, Annie. He's been hanging around out there for hours. And were my eyes playing tricks, or was he wearing a *pilot's* uniform?' He waved a filthy hand. 'How weird is that?'

'Nearly as weird as your behaviour over the last twenty-four hours. I wind up our case, send you a full report and you don't even bother to text me?'

'I told you, my phone got smashed.'

'Yes, of course. A brick fell on it? And before that happened, what? You mislaid my phone number?'

'No. Before that I was having the mother of all battles with my father.'

I stared at his filthy face. 'I heard he's proud of you. I can't imagine why.'

He hooted with laughter. 'Proud of me? He's so ashamed of me he can't stand to look at me.'

'But . . . he gave you a job?'

'On condition that I didn't use his name. Bad enough that his only son became a flatfoot cop. But to have a barring order against him? While working as a PI?'

'A PI is pretty low.' I nearly laughed. 'But you lied to me.'

'I didn't actually lie! I omitted to tell you something. Give me a break, Annie. I'm wrecked.'

'When *did* your phone get smashed?' I asked quickly.

'When I was knocking down Mrs Bolger's kitchen wall,' he said wearily. 'I went to see her after getting your email about Newman. I felt sorry for her. She's still convinced Seanie will be going home. She invited me in, gave me a rasher sandwich and explained her plans for knocking her two rooms into one. Then she got upset, told me she can't get anyone to finish the job. Well, not for free. I couldn't walk away. That's why I couldn't meet you tonight. Didn't want to leave it half finished. Now every muscle in my body is aching. And a bloody brick landed on my phone.' His eyes started to close.

The strength of my feelings for him suddenly hijacked me. Took me by surprise. A sudden warmth welling up inside me making me want to hold him.

Protect him. Kiss his filthy mouth. Squeeze the living breath out of him. Jump his bones until he begged for mercy. But he was utterly filthy, and sweaty. And I was wearing my brand-new dress, and underwear, and I might have further use for both.

'Do you want to have a shower?' I leaned towards him.

He groaned, obviously thinking this was a euphuism for something more energetic. 'I'm wrecked, Annie.' He slumped even lower, his eyes closing fully, so his thick lashes swept his cheeks.

'Of course you are.' He might be filthy, and wrecked, but he was so hot. 'I'm just offering you a shower,' I said. 'What sort of woman do you take me for?'

'Sorry, Annie.' So polite. So polite, I loved it.

'That's OK. I'll run the shower for you.'

Upstairs I ran the shower and watched him pull off his T-shirt, then the filthy boots.

'I'll help you with your jeans.'

'Aw, Annie,' he protested.

'I'm just helping.'

'Forget it,' he muttered. 'I'd need a shot of adrenalin before I could even . . .'

'Funny you should say that. I'm wearing something under this dress that . . .' I let my precious dress fall to the floor.

The phone woke me. But Sizemore had already picked it up.

'Hello?' he mumbled sleepily. 'No, you don't have the wrong number. This is Annie's . . .' He handed it over. 'It's Fiona.'

Fiona could barely speak. 'Jesus. How many men are you . . . ? Last night it was Barney, and now . . . is Sizemore in your bed?'

'It's a long story, Fiona, and I'm tired.'

'I'm not surprised! What are you using . . . some kind of man bait?'

'It's not how it seems. I asked Sizemore if he wanted a shower and—'

'And he ended up in bed with you?'

'No. Well, yes. But you see I think the Great Dane next door has been making sex calls to me and . . .'

'Jesus, Mary and Joseph, is no man safe?'

'Stop that!'

'What?'

'Not you, Fiona. It's Sizemore, he keeps nudging me in the back with his . . .'

'Annie!'

'With his hand. He's shocked to hear that I suspect my neighbour of making those nuisance calls to me.'

There was a sudden loud ruckus in the street outside. Sizemore was out of bed in a flash, peering out the window. 'Come here, Annie,' he ordered. 'Come and see this.'

I put my hand over the receiver, and giggled. 'I've seen it remember. Pretty impressive all right, but right now I'm busy talking to Fiona.'

He shot me an amused look. 'Annie!' he pleaded.

'He wants me, Fiona. Got to go.'

'He wants you? Jesus, Mary and Joseph, I . . .' For the first time since ever Fiona was speechless.

'I'll ring you later.' I hung up.

I ran to the window to check out the street below.

Sizemore pulled me close. 'It's a removal van,' he pointed. 'The weirdo is leaving.'

'That's what Sandra kept trying to tell me,' I hugged him in relief. 'He's going to live in Cork.'

'You sure he was your caller?'

'As sure as I can be.'

'Right, we're not letting him go like that. Have you some jeans I can borrow? I'm going down to have a word with him.'

'No, please. He's leaving. Let it be, for now. I'll ring DI Bailey, he'll sort it. Don't spoil our day. Anyway, you're still officially working for me and I'm telling you to leave well enough alone.'

'I can't just let him . . .'

'Leave it, Sizemore! You're not a cop any more!'

Our eyes duelled for a second, then my mobile shrilled and I tore around looking for it. Trying to recall where I had dropped it last night. I finally found it on the bathroom floor under my new Agent Provocateur underwear.

Barney's number flashed up.

'Annie, I just got a call from Gerry.'

'And?' I closed the bathroom door. No need for Sizemore to hear this.

'I think I should warn you he may be staying on in the States for . . . for a time. The family counsellor says they need a lot more sessions than she originally thought. You OK with that, Annie?'

'Oh, I think I'll manage.' I couldn't hide my relief. I needed time to sort out a few things . . . including how deeply I felt about Sizemore. OK, my heart went ballistic whenever he came close and every other part of me went wet with desire . . . but was that enough? Was I ready to commit to another relationship?'

'The counsellor says the kids are coming on in leaps and bounds since Gerry arrived,' Barney continued. 'Young *what's his name* has stopped farting in class, and David hasn't run away since.'

'Maybe Gerry should consider staying in Arizona permanently.' There. I'd said it.

'What?' Barney sounded shocked.

Well, given that Gerry hadn't got the guts to say it, someone had to. We both knew our relationship was dead as the dodo, so he might as well stay in America.

Barney waffled on for a bit, embarrassed as hell.

'Talk to you tomorrow, Barney,' I finally cut across him.

'Yeah. Yeah.' It was his turn to sound relieved.

I was happier than I'd been in a long time. Delighted to be free to make plans for the agency I loved. I reckoned I'd made a good job of being in charge for the past weeks. I had saved Mutual Irish having to pay out a lot of dosh, which meant McHugh Dunning's reputation would be sky high. Plus we would get a nice fat percentage of the savings. And we already had our retainer fee. *And* we had a long list of new enquiries. Including one from a high court judge. If things continued like this it wasn't beyond the realms of possibility that I would buy out my now distant partner. And, of course, there was Sizemore.

'Annie?' he was calling now. 'He's gone. The van's gone. Come back to bed.'

The agency definitely needed four full-time PIs.

Possibly five. I could do a lot with five full-time PIs. Especially if one of them had connections.

'Annie?' Sizemore was becoming impatient. I liked that about him. I also liked that all it took last night was one look at my corn plaster underwear to make him forget about his aching back.

'Annie?'

I slipped into the soft underwear and hurried into the bedroom to stand by the bed.

'What's up?'

'You're kidding.' He laughed, and pulled me under the sheet.

Outside, a powerful motorbike tore past with a deafening roar. And a gang of noisy kids were playing an uproarious game of football practically under the window. It didn't disturb Sizemore. Amazing the recuperative powers of some men. One minute they're exhausted from one too many sessions the night before, and then the sight of a teeny little piece of underwear has them firing on all cylinders again.

I had to free up my mouth to ask him a question. 'How would you react if I offered you a permanent job?'

'What?' he panted.

'You heard me. Could you work for me, full time?'

'I'd do anything for you.' He trailed his mouth across my breast.

'I'm serious. Would you . . . ?'

'Anything you want. Anything,' he breathed, his mouth working it's way southwards.

That was good enough for me. And no sense in putting him off his stroke now by telling him that the next urgent case on our books involved a builder who was suspected of breaking every safety regulation in the book. To get the necessary evidence on him one of us would have to work as a builder's labourer, hard hat and all for a couple of weeks. Barney was already booked for the next month, and Declan was getting married, and there's no way I could pass for a builder's labourer. Besides, I'm the boss. I call the shots now.

With a deep groan of satisfaction, I slid further under the sheet. Bliss.

Annie's New Life

Maureen Martella

Annie's discovered a case of mistaken identity . . . her own.

After thirty years of being Annie McHugh, Annie discovers that she is, in fact, someone else. Her beloved and hugely respectable parents forged her birth certificate.

She hires Gerry, a private detective with a strong look of George Clooney, to track down her real mother. But how is it that when Annie goes to confront her mother in her large mansion in the smart end of Dublin, she ends up working for her instead?

Will Annie reveal the truth to her frosty new employer? Is this the beginning of Annie's new life? And has Annie completely finished with Gerry's services?

Annie has decisions to make . . .

'Quirkily and humorously told'
The Times

'A hilarious romantic comedy'
Best

arrow books

A Perfect Partnership

Maureen Martella

In a world that isn't made to measure, has Annie found the perfect fit?

Annie McHugh should be happy. She's 5'6", seriously pretty, and despite a ravenous appetite for cream cakes, is a perfect size 10. Well, 12 . . . ish. She also runs a detective agency with her delectable partner Gerry.

But Annie has a secret. She longs to handle an investigation, to escape from her desk and get down and dirty with the agency detectives. OK, she already gets down and dirty with Gerry . . . but that's personal. Her dream is to become an investigator.

All that's standing in her way are three macho detectives, and an increasingly surly bank manager who calls with irritating regularity, demanding that she get the agency account out of the red, or else . . .

'Delightful . . . private detective Annie McHugh, and her wild exploits and mistakes will have people laughing out loud'
Irish Examiner

'Fans of private detective agency boss Annie McHugh will be thrilled that her new adventure is out'
Bella

arrow books

Maddy Goes to Hollywood

Maureen Martella

A gloriously escapist romantic comedy starring an unforgettable heroine

At thirty-three years of age Maddy O'Toole is stranded on Cold Comfort Farm, deep in rural Ireland, with a monosyllabic husband, two children, and her mother. The only bright spot in her week is the American television soap she's addicted to.

Then she discovers that her long-lost sister Gloria is living in Hollywood. No sooner has Gloria invited Maddy – and sent the ticket – than Maddy's on the plane. But what she envisages as a short break ends up changing her life.

For when she arrives at Gloria's hopelessly luxurious Bel Air home she falls helplessly in lust with her sister's gorgeous and gentle actor boyfriend, Carlos, none other than the star of her favourite soap.

It's not going to endear her to her sister, but Mandy can't bring herself to contemplate going home . . .

'For anyone who dreams of escape – read and aspire'
Irish News

'Destined to be a blockbuster'
U Magazine

arrow books